I0654448

Ravens

Return

By

Catherine Gruben Smith

Illustrated by

Emilie Gruben

Sola Deo Gloria

Scan here for a curated playlist!

Cover created by Casey Webb.

All scriptures are taken from the King James Version of the Bible.
Copyright © 2022 Catherine Gruben Smith – Sola Deo Gloria
ISBN: 978-1-955639-93-4
3rd edition. All rights reserved. If you try to steal it, you may find yourself
disintegrated by laser fire. Or worse.

"And not only so, but we glory in tribulations also: knowing that tribulation worketh patience."
- Romans 5:3

To Charity:
Your enthusiasm for these books, comprehensive world-building skills, and friendship have helped to form the So-journers. Keep the vision, m'dear.

Note to Readers:

Sign language is another language, not just a form of English. A signer thinks in pictures, they sign what they see, not full sentences. I have tried to portray some of the differences in the instances where Joe uses his gloves or is teaching the twins. But throughout most of the book, I translate Joe's dialogue as I would any language; making it smooth and sensible in English, just as someone would do in their mind when watching a signer.

Contents

Introduction

A fleck of ash from the charred body stuck to the statuette. Freddy Masterson frowned and gently brushed off the statuette of a woman in a toga. As he positioned it on his shelf, another fleck showed gray against the marble. Freddy's annoyance at the art dealer flooded him again. First the man had been fool enough to insist on a fee, even knowing Freddy's reputation. Then he had the effrontery to cover this priceless art with the ash from his incinerated body!

Light from the hidden floodlights in the garden glowed through his patio doors and glittered on the black marble of the statuette. The fountain in the koi pond bubbled in the quiet night wrapping around his headquarters. Freddy felt delight touch him as he fingered the statuette again. It wasn't often things felt perfect. But there were moments like these…

A glowing ball materialized in Freddy Masterson's garden, white light sizzling over it in lightning bolts. The ball pulsated, undulating and changing shape, its dazzling white light filling the garden. A sharp hissing killed the quiet, the sound of a freezing wind whirling and battering the sculpted bushes. Leaves and branches, dirt and grass, they rushed toward the glowing ball, pulled into twisting tornadoes by the freezing wind. Water sucked out of the fishpond and whirled toward the ball. Freddy watched one of his two-foot koi sucked up with it.

For an instant the pulsating wildness filled his garden. Then it disappeared, leaving five agents standing in the center of the mess. Laser rifles hung from their shoulders. Utility belts around their waists bulged with tools designed to mangle and destroy humanity. The tallest, a powerful man with a twist to his thick lips, stood a little in front of the rest. As if the others hung back, unwilling to come too close. A head dangled from his left hand.

Simmons stepped forward, his grisly prize swinging at his side like a priest's censer. His boot landed on the flailing koi. The fish stopped struggling. Freddy's lips pursed, his little eyes hardening in his fat face. He had raised that koi from a fry. Simmons stalked onto the porch, leaving a thick trail of mud. He dropped his prize on the patio table. It landed with a heavy thunk.

"Tell your boss, Freddy, mission accomplished," Simmons grinned. His voice came rich and triumphant, a lilt to it that said he had enjoyed every moment of the work.

"You could tell my partner that yourself," Freddy answered, contempt dripping from the words, "if you hadn't dropped your useless souvenir on top of the projector." Simmons lost his grin. He pulled the head from the patio table, letting it swing by his side again.

A blue light sprung into the night from the center of the table. A three-dimensional form stared out at the gathering. Simmons blinked, his fingers nervously fiddling with the thing in his hand as he stared at the lifeless eyes of a wolf head.

"So you decided to bring me proof of Zero's elimination." The voice drifted from the hologram projector, cold, an evil humor riding it. A shudder ran down Simmons' spine. When the Wolf was amused, someone had a very bad day. "Took you long enough to track him down."

"It didn't take us long to find him. He dove into the Faeryland swamp, but we ran into a band of their confounded knights before we could dig him out again," Simmons reported. He pulled a disc from his hand and held it up. "Most of the time we spent after we recovered Zero. We recorded his end, as you requested."

"Freddy, see that gets sent down the channels," Wolf ordered, the voice almost bored. "In case anyone else thinks it's a good idea to take something and run, that should at least be

Wolf

a warning."

"Did he tell you before...well, that," Freddy asked, flicking a finger at Simmons' burden, "was he trying to get information to someone, or just wanting the cash?"

"Oh he said many things," Simmons answered, with a sick amusement. "But he would have said anything at that point."

"Whatever, he's dead," Wolf butted in. "I don't care if he was acting for the greater good or his own skin, others know not to cross us and that's all that matters. I'm not here to talk about one measly death. It's time to go over the plan for the Prophet's Peace heist."

"One thing first, if I may," Freddy said, a fat hand rising in an apologetic gesture.

"What?" Wolf barked.

"Simmons brought me your instructions, and I duly contacted the person you named. She arrived today and brought me an envelope. She reports you left it in her country estate sixteen months ago," Freddy said. He pulled a simple white file folder from the shelf beside him. Knick-knacks rested in sheltered alcoves in that shelf; each knick could have fed a family of eight for a year, while each knack cost considerably more than that. The black marble woman rested among them, life-like enough she seemed to be watching the scene with her black eyes. "I received it only an hour ago, actually. I expected the documents and the Sojourner's book. It has been months, nearing a year, and you know I have a proper place to keep ancient documents! If they are left out too long the natural brittleness of the papers–"

"The book's been secure," Wolf broke in. "I just dug it out and it's on its slow way to the Trio in Story Land."

"Um, I know I presume on your patience," Freddy blinked, "but I thought you were essentially buried at the moment."

"I've only stayed because I've been cultivating contacts, reminding a few people who the Wolf really is. Recall, Freddy my boy, there's always ways to do what you need to," the Wolf answered, amusement riding the tone. Even Freddy felt chills run down his spine. The thought of additions to the contacts was terrifying in itself, the Wolf already had a network stretching into every corner of the known world; when the Wolf showed bared teeth people died hundreds of miles away. They all knew Wolf was capable of anything, of taking over any operation, of overrunning any life and turning it to their own desires. Some of the "ways" the Wolf had used in the past paraded through Freddy's mind and he remembered again why this creature sat at the top of the FFs. Some called the Wolf ruthless. To Freddy, that word barely even touched the surface of the seething mass of high intelligence, malicious humor, and narcissistic Wolf.

"I saw the note dropped to trap me here, I know who or-chestrated it." The humor left Wolf's voice, swallowed by a thick, hot hatred that dripped and burned, growing with each word. "It was that creature calling themselves the Black Raid-er, the one that foiled us in Atlantia a few months ago. I want information on them. Whoever they are, I get to take them out personally." On the patio, agents dropped their eyes, feet shuf-fled, and several reconsidered their life choices in that mo-ment; the Wolf's anger and hatred played through every soul, chilling their hearts. A breath sucked in through Wolf's nose, as the speaker forced themselves under control. When the voice came again, it was cold and quick, as lifeless as the head turning slowly on the hologram's platform. "My agents have orders to deliver the book to you. Pick it up in the People's Kingdom when you head there for the next SALDT prototype, whenever the old man finally gets it done. And Freddy, you worry too much. So what if the book disintegrates?" Several chins dropped, eyes bugging in the agents scattered around the porch. Books were too precious to speak of like that. "If we can't exchange it for the treasure the Hillsons have, the book is useless to us. And while we're on the subject, I am not pleased the Hillson twins are still at large."

"Yes, well, we last saw them with the little beast musician and his doggy companion," Freddy spoke up, his voice a little too quick. "It is easy enough to find that caravan again and raid it. We will have them soon. But I'm afraid I allowed myself to be sidetracked by what the messenger didn't bring, I needed to ask you about the item she did deliver," Freddy interjected, quickly changing the uncomfortable subject. "The folder came without instructions except for the order on the front to await your orders about opening it. May I inquire...?"

"Insurance, Freddy," Wolf drawled. "Or revenge. Maybe both. If there ever comes a stretch of time longer than two months when you don't hear from me, open the envelope. It has detailed instructions for how to start the world on a hunt for the book thieves."

"What?!" several voices on the patio burst out, shocked out of their scared silence by the implications.

"And one assumes those labeled the book thieves are, in fact, not us?" Freddy said, his voice calm and his face amused as he glanced at his agents.

"Correct. Freddy, who in this wide old world does everyone already hate and want to hunt down?" Wolf asked.

"The Christians– Oh, I say, that is brilliant," Freddy commented, interrupting himself as he understood.

"Right. Inside that envelope are names and places and notes, ready to deliver, things people will believe. 'Proof' of the Christians involvement in the book thieving that's been driving the world crazy these past few years. Once we have these next heists done–"

"'Heists,' I thought it was just Prophet's Peace?" Simmons broke in. His eyes widened as he realized he had said it out loud, and his lips worked, trying to think of the best way to rectify his interruption.

"Wrong, sweetheart, there's more," Wolf drawled. "While we're enacting the heist in the Prophet's Peace, we're distracting their soldiers by letting them utilize our SOLDT to attack the little kingdom just north of their borders. That's your job, Simmons. About a week before we move in on the *Koran*, another team moves in on Heist 1, the Geatland's vault, and snags their book and the cream of their hoard. Freddy, I see your greedy little fingers twitching." Freddy's hands whipped behind his back, and Simmons didn't bother to hide a smirk. "Forty-sixty split, you provide the manpower and I give you the brains."

"I don't suppose I have to inquire which number in that figure is mine?" Freddy said, a hint of annoyance underlying it.

"Hey, if you want more you can always try Zero's method. Maybe you would be better at hiding then he was," Wolf said, amusement back in the voice. No one answered. They all knew the Wolf was very capable of hunting without help; Zero's death wasn't the first recording to travel down their channels. "Heist 1 doesn't take much brains though, even you could probably do it, Freddy. That tiny little country doesn't have normal security. It's a boring but necessary job, and then we get to move on to the good stuff. Only one annoyance stands in the way of pulling these last few heists, opening that envelope, and retiring to watch the hunt for the rest of our lives. Hey sweetheart, you with the head, want to guess what it is? You're security after all." Simmons felt his throat constrict and his tongue suddenly seemed as thick and lifeless as a slab of ham. But he tried to make the answer competent.

"The Black Raider." It came out a growl, the fury of a wild animal underlying it as anger boiled in him, directed at the one drawing the Wolf's attention to him. "In my defense, when he first showed up it wasn't even an annoyance, just an anomaly. None of us guessed it would actually turn into a danger to our business."

"No one, really? Oh wait, one did. I did, idiot, I told you to take him out," Wolf snapped, the hot hatred dripping from the words again. "Never mind, I don't want your excuses about how slippery he is, and now I want him myself. Unlike you, I tend to use my head before I rush headlong at someone. What's the one thing we've noticed about this Raider?"

No one said anything. The silence dragged on for half a minute as the dead wolf's head spun in a slow, blue circle on the hologram projector.

"Oh for crying out loud, you're all helpless without me!" Wolf snorted. "He has a weakness for the vulnerable. If someone needs saved, the Raider will pause on his way out to try and do the saving. He has a special weakness for Christians, he turns up almost every time you snag members of the Way. Freddy, is she still here?"

"Your exceptionally pretty messenger was good enough to say my cook is the best she's found. She is still enjoying tea in my salon," Freddy answered.

"Of course she is," the Wolf said. "Give her the profile I've just given you, and any other details about the Raider you think of. She'll hand you back a plan even you people should be able to follow. Tell her I want the Raider in our hands within six months. Got it?"

"Yes," Freddy answered, succinct and competent. He could tell when the Wolf's patience for chit-chat ran out.

"Good. Finally." Wolf sounded exasperated. No one on the patio moved, terrified of becoming the object of that annoyance. A soft sound, the whisper of a siren, sounded in the background of the hologram feed. "I'm a little busy here, Freddy, get your notes from our last meeting and send them to your cronies. The Prophet's Peace security is good, but I just walked through our opportunity today and it will work if you actually stick to my plan. The opening only comes once every six months, we have to be ready the next time its ready for us. Get everyone briefed. I'll expect you to have the general scheme fixed in your people's minds the next time I check in."

The wolf head blinked off, and the soft glow of the garden's hidden floodlights took over.

Freddy reached back on his shelf for his personal pad, then turned and walked toward the patio table, leaving his precious knick-knacks for a time.

He never noticed the statuette's left eye sparkled a little brighter than her right one.

Countries away, the bug hiding in the statuette's shiny left eye relayed the words into Joe's earbud. The bug would be fried during the FF's weekly security sweep. But that statuette, planted where Freddy couldn't resist it, had already done its work. Joe heard every word as he crouched on a boulder strewn mountainside, watching the pass leading from the Tao.

His face was grim and strained, his eyes bright as he calculated. All of this was bad news, really bad news. Until he could deal with that folder, even the Wolf's life must be protected at all costs. And that really, really put a damper on the plans Joe had painstakingly laid down over months of hard work. He would have to personally stop his own schemes now, and start again from scratch. Wonderful.

But it had been the right call to leave the twins in KAM. Joe knew Freddy had pinpointed the Ravens as a threat, that was painfully obvious from the way the fat man set the Advancers on him last week. That meant the Ravens' wagon could not be a safe haven for the twins until Joe let Simmons raid and harry the wagon and convince himself the Hillsons were no longer there. Joe had only given himself two days to enjoy Anna and Nehi's company and recuperate from the Institute. Then he and Beau slipped off, headed here. To crouch on boulders in the cold wind, waiting and watching.

The pass leading from the Tao stood out like a jagged knife wound against white skin. Eight months out of the year even the pass filled with snow, and made the Tao unreachable to the rest of the world, but for today it remained clear. The reddish iron rocks of the pass stood in sharp contrast to the towering snowy mountains. Cold wind whistled through Joe's shaggy hair, whipping the blond strands against his face as he stood up. He saw Beau's goggles focus on him, the chimera's hand going up to zoom in. Joe signed, swift and steady, settling Beau's part in the chimera's mind. His signs stilled, and Joe dropped to his crouch again behind the boulder. He stayed silent and absolutely still, planning, reworking ideas, his thoughts dancing and pirouetting through his agile mind, never still, never at peace. Not with the whole flock of God to protect.

A storm was predicted tomorrow.

It had to be today.

Joe crouched among the boulders, still and silent, his mind whirling with all he had just heard, playing it over and over as the minutes ticked on, setting each word firmly in his memory. What were they planning for his alter ego, the Black Raider? How could he combat it? How could he fight against it when he didn't even know what it was?

A burst of blue light flashed into life for an instant at the curve of the pass. Joe's eyes fastened on it, focusing on the hole of melted rock the laser fire left behind. He forced the Wolf's plots into the back of his mind and focused on the now. Another burst of blue laser fire flashed into life for an instant. Joe pulled his goggles down and settled them over his eyes. He began to hop down the boulders, a tiny black dot amidst the gray monstrosities tumbling down into the valley. He didn't wave at Beau to get ready. He knew his friend had already seen him, and didn't need any other order; the chimera understood his job.

Joe's soft boots landed on the valley floor and he flipped his hoverboard off his back, switching it on.

A patched, grimed, tarnished oval shot over the pass and toward the valley, steam pouring from it in torrents. Some of the steam came off the sides, a sure sign of a hoverer in trouble. Joe watched the hoverer wobbling and could almost feel the driver straining for control. He mounted his board.

A sleek silver machine roared over the top of the pass. An elongated oval, steam barely showing as it concentrated every jet perfectly, wind bubble shining in the sunshine. A Toaster laser stood mounted on the nose, manned by a Tao warrior in full armor, his feet encased in metal boots attached to the prison ship. The laser fired again. It clipped the edge of the battered hoverer, and the machine jolted to the left. It rammed into the side of the pass, sparks flying from the red rocks.

Joe leaned forward, Dark Ray in one hand, his pockets filled with useful items. In a move that defied death, he suddenly spun sideways, the steam from his board spurting in a cloud as it pushed off nothing but empty air. He snatched a long stick-like gadget from the ground, and for an instant his gloved fingers touched the grass and pushed, rotating himself back up. His hoverboard flipped, the steam drove him forward, and the stick clipped to a holder on his back. His board shot off, darting toward the pass and the running battle. No, it wasn't a battle. There was no contest to this flight and chase, the Tao prison always reclaimed its inmates, or left corpses on the valley beyond the pass.

But today the Ravens stood waiting.

Out of the corner of one eye Joe saw Beau's hover board, and knew his big friend ran right on target to his left. The mute leaned right, giving themselves a little more room for their pincher maneuver and, hopefully, making it less obvious.

He prayed these Tao warriors were the same as most; proud, and convinced a lone figure could pose no real threat against the might of one of their ships.

Another shot came from the Toaster, and the tarnished hoverer jumped. It wavered and shook, and Joe could hear it rattling even over the noise of the cold wind cutting into his face. He counted in his head as he pushed his speed, rushing toward the battered machine.

Three.

Two.

One.

Joe leaned right, and his board shot straight for the hoverer. He darted into view of the driver's little window in the ancient machine, and caught a glimpse of the man inside. Dark curly hair, olive skin tight against a thin, strained face... Except for the habitual frown and added years, he might have been a double for Nehemiah. His dark eyes latched onto the blond-headed mute and his mouth dropped open. Joe's hands came together, his thumbs and first fingers forming a square. He winked and gave a sunny smile. The man laughed, nodding at the mute, perfectly willing to call things square between them if the Ravens could get this prison ship off his tail.

Joe only let the interaction last two seconds. Then he leaned again and his board darted off, out of sight of the escapee and his ancient, borrowed hoverer.

The prison ship whooshed out of the pass onto the smooth grass of the valley.

Two lone figures closed in on its sides.

A cone of blackness clamped over the Toaster, beaming from Joe's Dark Ray. A scream, furious and agonized, came from the warrior. The laser pulled apart, bent and broken, pieces sheering off. As the black cone disappeared, Beau's shot beamed through the ship's metal casing straight through to Joe's side. The hole was small, only a finger's width in diameter, but it cut straight through the ship. The Ravens zoomed in close, their boards' steam mixing with the prison ship's white cloud. Two long, thin sticks shoved into the hole on the ship. An open flame showed for an instant in the mute's hand. Joe and Beau shot off, hunched low over their boards, the wind tearing into them at their speed.

The flame shot through the sticks pushed into the hole.

A white flame rushed into the sky. A deep throbbing "boom" shook the ground, making even the hoverboards jump.

The prison ship sheered in two. The nose planted into the ground with a noise like thunder. It lifted into the sky, just in time for the broken steam jets of the second half to ram it. Metal shrieked, and diamond glass shattered, the two halves of the ship colliding with each other, rolling and rending and wrecking the valley.

Ten yards ahead of it, the earth-shaking tremors hit the ancient hoverer hard. The steering stick jammed. The man inside had an instant to glimpse gray boulder, then his copper oval smashed into it.

Steam and boiling water jetted into the sky, as copper twisted, and chips of boulder flew. Joe's face paled, his green eyes wide. He leaned in, sending his board straight through the mass of steam pouring from the wreckage. He kicked his board out, landing in a handspring as the hoverboard shot away unmanned. Joe catapulted himself toward the wreckage. His hand smashed onto the button and the top popped, hinges groaning and shrieking in protest. The mute planted his feet against the top, his back pressing against the lid of the ancient machine, every nerve keenly aware the engine could explode any second. The lid swung open with a sharp clang.

The man lay in a limp pile. Blood leaked down his neck from a head trauma, but the belts had held most of the damage off. Joe's knife flashed in the wet air as he sliced him free and wrapped an arm around his chest. A silent, gasping roar broke from the mute as he dragged the bigger man from the hoverer wreckage. He dropped from the vehicle, blowing hard, the man's head cradled on his shoulder. Smearing blood on his face. Joe's boots scrabbled, dragging him farther over the wet, steaming ground. A sharp hissing started from the engine. The mute gasped again, muscles straining, trying to move faster, his arms locked around the man's chest.

A huge, hairy arm slammed around their waists. Joe jerked into the air, his grip still locked around the driver, as Beau's board sputtered and fought with the sudden added weight. The jets skimmed the ground, and Beau kicked the board's steam off, leaning back to lift the nose into the air, riding it like a bucking horse as he held his little master close.

The hoverer wreckage exploded in a massive ball of yellow and white. A wave of heat and force rolled into the Ravens and they staggered. Beau spun so his back was toward the explosion, hunching over the two people dangling from his arms. A plume of water cascaded into the air, and the massive hiss of flames and water meeting filled the valley. Steam covered everything like a warm, wet fog.

Beau gently sank to his knees. Joe's feet touched the grass and he dropped, laying the man on the ground, steadying his injured head carefully. Blood covered the left half of his face. The mute's white hand fumbled at the driver's neck to search for a pulse, as Beau pressed a wad of bandages to the injury, applying pressure to try and stop the bleeding. The steam swirled and whispered around them, covering everything in an unnatural white cloud. Joe's tense shoulders eased a fraction.

"He's alive," Joe signed, sitting back on his heels. His eyes went to the dark mass of the prison ship's wreckage, an indistinct black hill in the midst of the swirling steam. "How many?"

"Two. Both dead," Beau rumbled. Joe's shoulders fell, his head drooping. Beau stared at him, and a large tear rolled down one hairy cheek. But as he sought for the words to speak to his little friend, Joe's back suddenly stiffened. One hand went to his ear as his expression sharpened.

"Freudian IDP in trouble," Joe signed, his movements quick and even. "Evil ordered a raid." His eyes darted to the man, the bandages quickly soaking. "Glue, get him to the cabin, find someone to bring along and take care of him."

"You–" Beau rumbled, alarm shooting over his face.

"I have to get to the IDP," Joe signed, and his hands ran over his pockets and jacket, checking on his supplies.

"Food? Sleep?" the chimera rumbled.

"You can in the wagon, big guy," Joe signed with a smile, and snatched his board from the ground. Annoyance hardened the chimera's face. The mute slapped his friend's shoulder, leapt on his board, and then darted away. The steam cloud swirled up at his passing, then closed slowly back into the white shifting cloud.

"Meant you," Cobeau growled. A sigh blew through the chimera's thick beard, and he turned toward the man lying still and bleeding on the ground.

Chapter One: Glue Needed

"Have mercy upon me, O LORD; for I am weak: O LORD, heal me; for my bones are vexed." -Psalm 6:2

The building covered the red clay like a black slug, cutting off the dry grass and little bushes from sunlight and starving it, killing it slowly. Atif couldn't help thinking the building enjoyed causing slow death. The clay-colored plastic bubbled over the steel framework, bloated and ugly and functional. He recognized many of the people tacking down the edges, erecting the framework for the last room, carrying in stores and weapons... They matched the building growing into their temporary camp. Each of them pieces of a monster, bloated, ugly, and horribly functional.

A sharp hissing came from higher up the dry country; a hoverer steaming down toward the building spreading over the grass. Atif shifted his glasses smoothly to the gold-colored hoverer, following it as it moved at high speed. Sleek, powerful, a machine of beautiful symmetry and perfect design. The gold oval swung to a stop by the building and rested on the grass in a cloud of steam, cooking the plants like spinach. A tall form stepped out of the white cloud. Muscles rippling, thick lips curved in a sneer, his small eyes running over his agents building the slug-like camp. Atif slowly lowered the glasses, his face a grim mask. His team watched him, eyes darting from their boss to the busyness in the canyon below them.

"Did it work?" Naqi burst out. "Is this what we were looking for?" Atif's eyes didn't leave the tall form below him. The man had found a shirker, an agent leaning on his tool, resting instead of riveting the steel framework together. The tall one's fist struck, then struck again, and again, hammering into the shirker with steady brutality. Even from here Atif could see the tall one's lips part in a grin as his fist rose and fell. He nodded slowly.

"Yes. We found the snake."

Joe rammed into the bricks cementing the massive wrought iron gate in place, and just leaned there. His arms shook, muscles jumping. He gulped air through the black fabric wound around his face, one hand straying to his aching head. As if holding it would help the pain go away. His mind moved sluggish and almost numb. Couldn't be this exhausted, too much to do tonight. But too long, too long with no break, no rest, no time to breathe, or eat, or even think. He counted in his mind as he sagged panting against the bricks. Months. Five months since the first raid, then the first note from Simmons, taunting and calling on him to save his brothers. Five months without one hour of peace, almost six months of leaving Nehi and Anna stranded in KAM. Nehi, Anna, what were they doing? Had they forgotten him by now? Joe heard Cobeau's soft strides behind him. The mute straightened quickly, forcing himself into an attitude of competence.

"I'll get the Greens, send them to you," he signed at the big chimera, forming the words with difficulty with his shaking hands. "Get them on the wagon and out, even if I don't make it."

"Joe, can you?" Beau whispered, and Joe winced. His whispers sounded like a gale blowing.

"Sign, Glue," Joe signed at him. "I can."

"But you've done so much this week," Beau signed, then paused and blinked. "Didn't it take a week to get the Markors and Tanners out?"

"One day for both, Glue, yesterday," Joe signed, a little smile breaking over his face under the mask at his big friend's inability to judge time. Cobeau shook his head in dismay and signed almost desperately.

"And no sleep last night, Master! You must stop, you can't–
" Joe gave him a warning punch in the arm.

"Joe, no master," he signed, his hands cutting vicious arcs
through the night air. "We are not leaving them here to die.
Can't. I can't. Wait in the shadows, be ready." Joe let the air out
of his lungs, wiggled his stick-thin body between two of the
poles of black iron, and was through the gate and into the
Kingdom of Gaia's Recycling Center. One waving train of ivy,
gently scraping the black dirt, was the only sign of his passing.

The heavy footsteps of a guard turning the corner to the
front of the fortress broke the stillness. The chimera slipped
into the deeper shadows, his short Brunhiem laser ready and
the rough bricks pressed into his thick hide. A sharp sigh
sobbed from the chimera as he watched his Joe swallowed by
the blackness through the gate. *Jesus, keep him safe,* he prayed
silently, his big hairy head lifting to the stars twinkling above
the Gaia forest. His eyes closed, and his immense shoulders
lost their tenseness as he nodded. A smile moved the bushy
black hair on his face. Jesus heard. Jesus always stayed near.
Joe would be all right.

On the other side of the gate, Joe froze in the deep blackness of the tower's shadow. A breeze teased through the soft
leather onto his skin, granting him an instant of relief from the
balmy night. He focused on a short guard, boots thudding into
the brick walkway as the man moved on his rounds into Joe's
sight.

The guard turned the corner around the large brick building rising on the left, blocking out the few stars that managed
to shine through the enclosing forest. Joe darted across the
courtyard and leapt for the tower. His fingers tightened on a
loose piece of brick four feet over his head. He reached up,
lodged his other hand into a crack in the mortar, and climbed.
The Black Raider moved swiftly and silently up the side of the

building, peeking in windows and listening at cracks. The shadows and thick ivy proved his allies as he moved through the still night.

A guard caught sight of the shifting black shadow and spun on his heel, raking the sky to see what had made it. He saw nothing between the moon and the tower and turned back again; the shadowy form had disappeared. A shudder ran through him, and he glanced at the dark forest, tightening the strap on his laser rifle. He reminded himself tree spirits were rarely called malevolent. A few good witches in the south of the kingdom came to mind, and knowing where to turn if anything weirder came up made him feel a little better. He spun back to his rounds, his boots thudding rhythmically into the brick pathway.

Joe had found an unwatched window. He crouched in a darkened corner on the fourth floor of the tower, his brown-dyed eyes on two technicians walking past. He caught a discussion of a patient's x-rays and hoped the girl made it despite their predictions. They turned a corner and Joe shot off, darting down halls and ducking through doors, crouching on floors and hanging on ceilings. The mute was as silent as the shadows. No one noticed him any more than a crack in the ceiling as he moved upward, delving deeper into the heart of the tower, looking for the young Christian couple marked for death by the Recyclers.

Simmons had turned them in. And again left a note for the Black Raider, calling on him to rescue. A part of Joe screamed that it was a trap. He knew it was part of a trap meant to wear him out and catch the Raider. But the rest of him couldn't walk away. Not when it was his fault. Not when they were slotted to die because of him. Most of him just moved, doing what he had to do, not thinking. Too exhausted to think anymore.

The door to a darkened office on the seventh floor swung open as a shadow stole silently inside. The door closed softly and Joe's penlight clicked on. He glided to the desk and his thin, gloved fingers shuffled through the papers scattered over the top, then moved smoothly to run over the drawers. Each item he touched returned meticulously to its original place, nothing shifted even a millimeter. His fingers stopped, hovering over the lower right drawer in the massive desk.

A piece of string lay pinched there, gyrating from the air blowing through the vent. Small, brown, uninteresting...except if it fell out, the owner would know someone had been tampering. This drawer held something interesting. Joe placed a finger on the string, holding it in place as he swiftly picked the lock and pulled the drawer open. It was too shallow. He ignored the papers and junk piled high as his hand slid inside, ran along the edge, and found the catch in half a second. The fake bottom popped up, and Joe stared at a large blue paper. He lifted it, one part of his brain registering the schematics and diagrams, as the rest of him ran an eye over the room, making certain everything was just as he had found it. Except the schematics resting in Joe's pocket.

The mute slid back out into the corridor, his head buzzing with exhaustion, and began his hunt again.

But Joe froze as he was about to run from one shadow to another, his gaze riveted on a too familiar figure. Simmons stepped out of the elevator. His knuckles cracked as he walked down the hall, and a wince cut across Joe's face. The man turned into a private office and Joe breathed again. The mute darted across the hall and into a small, dark room next to the office. He pulled a pair of headphones out of his pocket, attached them to a slim, rectangular box, and stuck that onto the connecting wall with the office. There was a bit of crackling, but when Joe adjusted his box he could hear the conversation in the next room just fine.

"–don't know why you're so sure he'll be here," a nervous, deep voice boomed. "This Black Raider is no fool and knows you'll be waiting for him."

"Of course he knows," Simmons sneered, and Joe shuddered, skin prickling and nausea gnawing at his stomach. That voice carried so many horrible memories with it. "But he'll be here anyway. He's ready to fall now, he'll make a mistake soon enough. That prig of a lady was right, even geniuses make mistakes if you wear them down enough and keep shoving them toward a cliff. If not tonight, he will fall the next time. Did you seal off the top floor like I said?"

"Yes, he can't get to them by any ordinary means," the deep voice answered.

"Good. I've got a message for you, Doc, from the Wolf." Joe could hear the chair creak as the man shifted uncomfortably. "We're starting our last set of heists next month. You're to get the sarin dosages ready for the Prophet's Peace. Make sure its strong enough to kill even the biggest and baddest, got it?"

"But what if–"

Joe pulled his box off the wall and shoved it into his pocket along with the earphones. He had heard enough, and it was time to get the Greens out. He slid out of the hall and across to a window, checked it for alarms, disabled them quickly, and slipped out. The small shadow shifted steadily up the side of the brick building again.

Fifteen minutes later Joe found what he was looking for. Set on the highest floor of the tower, a young couple curled on a loveseat, the only occupants of a comfortable pastel blue room. Joe pulled a round object from his pocket and attached it to the window. It was a half foot in diameter with a diamond cutter on one side and a handle on the other. As swiftly as he could without losing his hold on the wall, Joe gripped the handle and began to turn it.

His actions slowed as his eyes fell on the couple comforting each other. They looked very much in love. It looked...so warm, so happy, even as they waited to die. Would he ever find something like that? He shook his head viciously, ignoring the pain slicing through his brain, and told himself not to be a fool. *No dreaming, Joe, dreamers and GIs don't mix. Besides if you ever did find someone you could love, what would you do? You move more like a monkey than a person,* he told himself as he turned the handle slowly, careful to keep the diamond from squealing on the window pane as it cut through. *If you really loved her you would have to walk away. You don't even have a last name to give her! Still... Someone who would call you 'dear.' Who noticed, and even cared, if you were hurt. Who would pay attention when you had something to tell her, and understand it. Someone who would dare to love you back. Someone you could really open up to–*

The window cutter came away in his hands. Joe, too tired to even control his own thoughts, wasn't ready for it. His arms flailed in midair, a desperate gasp sucking into his lungs. The glass cutter sailed off, tumbling ten stories to land with a soft thump in the flowerbed. He arched, flinging himself forward and his fingers found the stones. Joe clung to the tower, knuckles white, heart hammering, eyes screwed shut to keep from staring at the ground. See?! he told himself fiercely. No more dreaming, Joe! How many near misses is it going to take for you to put it into practice? Always one more, his heart told him. Joe sighed in the darkness, forced his thoughts away, and reached for the hole in the window with his black swathed arm. A click of the lock sliding back came from the door. He pulled his arm away and squirmed to the left, curving his body around a protruding stone next to the window, keeping close enough to his hole to hear what went on in the room.

A young woman in a pastel lab coat came in and closed the door behind her. It locked automatically and Joe's brain whirred through the options and identified the make of lock. That kind should only take about eight seconds to open. The woman turned and smiled at the couple, then glanced at the chart in her hand.

"Is it time already?" asked Mrs. Vera Green, the young woman on the couch. Her voice carried a hint of fear, a gentle longing for life.

"No, no, not yet," the woman with the chart answered as she sat down in an armchair. "I'm just here to explain the procedure and see if there's anything we can get for you. It will only be a few minutes till you're in the next plane and someone else will be responsible for you."

"Why can't you just say, 'a few more minutes till we kill you'?" Charlie Green commented, his voice tired and quiet.

"But it's only a path to a different life–" the young woman started in surprise.

"Could you just finish what you came to say?" Charlie interrupted. The young woman went on to explain the procedure and what was expected of them to prepare for the injections. Joe prayed she would hurry, trying desperately not to shift his position; movement might be seen.

"Oh, and one more thing. My superior wanted me to give you this," the young woman wound up, reaching into the pocket of her lab coat. Joe forgot about his aching body and trembling muscles, forgot to fear someone would see him, the nagging terror of knowing Simmons waited just inside. He stared at the plain white envelope as the young woman passed it to Charlie Green.

"What is it?" he asked listlessly.

"I don't know. He said to give it to you and tell you it was for a person in black, in case you saw him," the young woman answered.

"Person in black, what's that supposed to mean?" Vera asked.

"I don't know. I thought you would," the young woman shrugged. "Well, that's it." She knocked on the door, it swung open, and then closed behind her as she stepped into the hall.

Joe stared at the envelope. Again? And what about the perfect timing, did they know he was out here? He stared blearily at the white envelope, trying to second guess the enemy. His brain fogged again. He stopped trying to think and just moved. Joe stuck his arm through his hole, ignoring the couple's quiet murmuring on the couch.

With two more tools, and several great feats of agility, he managed to pull the heavy window open enough to get himself through. It was a well-oiled window and Joe made it a habit to move silently. The first the couple knew of his presence was a black gloved hand appearing under their noses, a metal IDP cross resting on the palm. Vera yelled and clutched at her husband and even Charlie squeaked. A note appeared on the palm with the cross.

I'm a brother, here to get you out.

"What...who..." Charlie stuttered, but Joe didn't listen. He darted to the door, probing the lock with a round string of blue plastic. No alarm on the lock, good. Joe's hands shook and it interfered with his lock picking. It took him nearly twenty seconds to unlock the door that should have taken eight. Joe pulled out his dart pistol and motioned the Greens to him. Vera looked at Charlie. He hesitated an instant, then moved to where this small, black clothed person wanted him. Joe pulled open the door.

A wild beeping wail sliced through the three people standing in the blue room. The sudden volume vibrated in their bones and guts. Even the guard outside the door dropped his rifle to clutch at his ears. He fell to the ground unconscious, his hands still over his ears, a tiny dart from Joe's gun jutting from his neck. Joe grabbed Charlie's hand and ran. Speed was their only chance now that the alarms were off.

Fool! Why hadn't he thought of the door itself being wired?

Because he had stopped thinking.

Stopped thinking in a way that could be called useful, anyway, when the exhaustion took charge of him. Joe cursed himself liberally as he raced the Greens down the stairs. It had been an idiotic mistake, almost certainly a fatal one. He had to drop two security officers and a janitor on his way down. He spun around another landing and the bottom of the stairs appeared, dim and stark with its cold gray bricks and dirt. The mute jerked his two charges into the stairwell, shoved them into the little space underneath the metal stairs, and darted into the courtyard alone. He took care to be seen this time.

A shout rose in the courtyard, then another. The piercing alarm stopped; the quarry had been spotted. Charlie and Vera caught their breath, ears ringing, and throats tight as they listened to the shouting guards.

"Suspect headed east!" one yelled above the others. Priming lasers whined in the dark night outside the tower. Vera buried her face in her husband's shoulder and prayed desperately they wouldn't hit the little person in black. Feet pounded down the stairs over their heads, guards and security officers dashing outside. But no one looked underneath the stairs. Lasers whined, soldiers shouted, and the sounds drifted farther away. More whines joined it as more guards with lasers ran toward the hunt, but the sound came so distant it drifted faint and dull on the balmy air. Silence fell in the little anteroom. Charlie and Vera sat rigid, praying to the only One who had any power to help the situation out there, and agonizing over whether to make a break for the gates.

Another pair of feet rang on the metal stairs above them. The Greens hardly noticed the rhythmic noise as it steadily descended. But these footsteps stopped at the bottom of the stairs.

A chuckle sounded in the stillness.

A dark, malevolent, amusement danced on that sound. Real terror gripped Charlie and Vera. It clawed at their stomachs and clamped over their lungs. They thought they had been as terrified as a person could be that night. With that cold, cruel chuckle they learned clammy terror is different than fear. The footsteps cracked into the bricks and dirt that made up the floor, heavy and deep, and coming toward them. A rifle tip tapped on the metal stair just above their hiding place, an old-fashioned projectile weapon that could do debilitating damage and still leave its victim alive. The two knocks reverberated around the stairwell.

"Anyone home?" called a voice, teasing, cruel. Vera and Charlie clutched each other, staring at the rifle muzzle making escape impossible. Terror pounded in their chests.

Chapter Two: House Raid

"I am a stranger in the earth: hide not thy commandments from me." -Psalm 119:19

"Can't you stay for dinner, Anna?" Gail Jones prodded. Her lip pushed out in a playful pout, making her double chin a marked feature.

"You know I have to rush back to help Mrs. Sireton get things ready for prayer meeting," Anna grinned, "you're just being facetious and trying to tempt me."

"She's found you out, Mrs. Jones!" Mr. Jones cackled, slumped in his battered recliner, his habitual mug of coffee in his hand. "I hate to see you go though, Anna. You're like a breath of fresh air in this stuffy old place."

"That's what he thinks of my housekeeping skills," Gail said, rolling her eyes, and Anna laughed. Mrs. Jones lost her teasing manner and turned suddenly serious as she took Anna's hand. "You know you and your brother are always welcome here, don't you?"

"I know it, Mrs. Jones." Anna's smile lost the twinkling humor; it held warmth and thankfulness, but sorrow lurked in the crinkles beside her dark eyes. "Ever since Joe and Cobeau left us stranded, you and Mr. Jones have been like an uncle and aunt to us. Thank you."

"Just so long as you know you're welcome here at any time," Gail nodded, and added a motherly pat to Anna's hand. She let go and regained her quick, teasing manner, turning to pick up the laundry she had laid aside while visiting. "Though make sure Nehi changes his clothes after leaving the factory. The smell from sheep rendering stays, and stinks like nothing else I've come across." She draped a doily over her arm and made a shooing motion toward the white kitchen door, clucking like an enraged hen. "What are you standing there for, go get some soup and carry it back to Mary Sireton! She needs your help, child, after her difficult childbirth last month. You should know better than to stand here lollygagging about Elizabeth's engagement to Peter, really girl!"

"Oh, and I wonder who started that conversation?" Anna laughed. The humor came easily; it was so pleasant to talk about something happy and sweet. And her best friend, the pastor's daughter Elizabeth Bight, falling steadily deeper for her brother's best friend Peter, had been awfully sweet to watch. Anna considered herself entitled to a slice of their wedding cake, as she had been the one to set up the trellis outside the Bight's home, herd everyone away from the couple, and switch the violinist to their favorite song that night he finally proposed. Her lecture the afternoon before (when she had gotten in Peter's face and told him to stop wasting time he may not have) probably helped too.

Anna let the subject lapse, and trotted obediently toward the kitchen. As she pushed through the door the scent of the soup rolled around her, mixing with the coffee always kept warm on the hob, and the spicy delight of cinnamon. She had come to love the smells of this kitchen during the past six months.

Six months. And not a hologram call, or even a note by raven... Six months to the day she and Nehi had wandered back to the basement after a tour of town and found an infuriatingly short note. Anna glanced around, making sure she was still alone, and slid her fingers into the leather wallet Nehi had given her for her birthday. It belted comfortably around her waist, and was the perfect size for her pencils and the plastic pad she laid her drawing books on. But recently it held one more item. She pulled out the crumpled note, fragile with time and handling.

Nehi and Anna; Beau and I are leaving to get the FFs off your trail. We shouldn't be too long, I hope. See you soon!

Stay safe.

Nothing more. Twenty-seven words for a six-month absence. Was Joe even still alive?

Anna shoved the note back in her pouch, lifting her head and forcing her shoulders not to slump. No being melancholy! Joe would find them. Even when she and Nehi left to go hunt for the Bible again, he would track them down. They would have to leave soon to start the hunt, with or without the Ravens. The world needed the Sojourners.

But today, right now, Mrs. Sireton needed dinner. Anna sat the smaller pot Mrs. Jones kept for company on the counter and picked up the soup pot bubbling on the stove, dragging herself back to her life.

A sharp bang rang from the living room, as the front door flew open and smashed into the wall.

"Freeze!" a harsh female voice shouted, ringing through the little house. "UPC[1], we have you surrounded!" A sharp exclamation came from the Jones. Anna heard a mug clatter onto the floor and shatter. Heavy boots tromped into the living room, many boots, and Anna knew what she heard. Soldiers pouring in, sweeping the room and surrounding the Jones.

"Why, what have we done?" Mrs. Jones said, her voice high and scared. Anna slid up to the kitchen door, slowly, carefully peeking through the crack, her heartbeat steadily speeding.

"You are known Christians," the female voice barked. "Tanzid! Stand watch." A tall, black-skinned, incredibly handsome young man slid into view of Anna's crack. He wore a black jumpsuit, the material rubbery and a little shiny, zippers marking pockets in strange places. A huge rifle lay strapped across his back. It looked almost like a log. The black carbon of

---

[1] United Peoples Commission, a non-Christian group running under most kingdoms in the Book Base Age employing handpicked specially trained agents to help shape the world according to their ideas and protect those they deem need it. The UPC do not approve of Christians.

the stock overlaid a transparent dusky gray barrel. Anna could see the glow inside that barrel; the huge rifle was already primed and ready to fire. Anyone carrying that heavy and bulky of a weapon came prepared to sacrifice their comfort for efficiency. This agent was not someone to mess with. Anna shifted her gaze from his weapon to his face.

Her mind immediately flew to Joe's blank looks. The mute's expression when carefully hiding his thoughts and feelings.

Gail Jones reached for her husband, her face scared. Mr. Jones stepped forward, wrapping his arm around her shoulders. KAM soldiers fanned out around the room, standing silent and steady around the couple.

"Tanzid, is it?" Mr. Jones asked, studying the tall guard with the huge weapon. The agent's gold-flecked eyes flickered toward him, his face still blank. Mr. Jones swallowed. But his voice came steady as he spoke again. "What are you going to do with us?"

"You are Christians. You haven't even bothered to deny it. Deportation." Tanzid's voice was rich and deep, the intonations flat. Mrs. Jones' fingers tightened around her husband's arm, her eyes growing wider. She had never been farther than forty miles from Freedom, KAM's capitol.

"Where? When?" she asked.

"The People's Kingdom, tonight. Now shut up and sit down."

The Jones sat. Abruptly, as if their knees gave out, huddled together on their faded living room couch. Anna shifted back a step, slowly, silently. She had to get the news out to Nehi and the others.

Tanzid's gaze flew to the crack in the kitchen door, noticing the movement. Two gold-flecked eyes latched onto Anna's dark ones.

Anna darted backward, throwing the soup pot as she

moved. It clanged as it landed on its side, and a wide lake of boiling soup pooled over the tiled floor. She darted away from it to the cellar door. Anna jerked the small door open, and the dark mustiness hit her in the face. The memories of her four months as a slave in the cellars slammed into her like a physical blow. The smells, sounds, faces, soul-emptying emotions, it coursed through her in that second. But she didn't have time to stand and sob. She dashed through onto the creaky old stairs.

A sharp bang rang behind her as the agent shoved the kitchen door open. A "shwip" followed, melding with a crunching thud. The agent hit the floor with a boom that shook the house. Halfway down the cellar stairs, his crash landing spurted gray dust onto Anna's head. Her heart thundered as she darted into the musty darkness of the cellar. Had he seen her before she slipped downstairs? Or just the sliver of her face through the crack in the door? She couldn't be sure. Anna snatched a dusty piece of fabric from a pile of scraps and dropped it over her head as she leapt onto a table underneath the little rectangular window leading into the backyard. She unlatched it and rolled out onto the cool green lawn.

A shout came from behind her. A clump of grass next to her hand erupted in flames and a miniature volcano of black earth. Anna clutched the fabric draping her head and face and darted toward the fence leading to the next yard. The rough wood scraped her hand as she vaulted over it. Anna scowled as she took off across the neighbor's yard, ducked through their gate, and raced down the alley. Shouts rang behind her, and one fence post erupted into flames as a laser hit it. She spun into the main road, down another alley, and ducked into the busy shopping thoroughfare of downtown. Anna melded with the crowds, working her way swiftly toward the seedier end of town where Nehi's factory lay. She knew she could lose the pursuit in the busy city. But she kept glancing at her hand, the palm leaking crimson down a jagged scrape.

She had left blood on that fence. The UPC reportedly had the best equipment and the smartest agents alive. They could do DNA tests and get a mockup of her coloring, her age, probably even her general features. Added to whatever Tanzid had actually seen before she disappeared down the cellar steps... Anna grimaced as she slid into the little entryway between two buildings, waiting for the five o'clock bell for the factory to disgorge its workers. She was in trouble.

Of course some of her grimace came from the smell. Sheep rendering wasn't a pleasant-smelling activity. But it was one of the few jobs Nehi could get with his migrant card. And it paid much better than he had expected. The KAM citizens didn't think rendering sheep fat was an exalting enough position, and left the opening for non-citizens. They would rather take lower pay for better places, with job descriptions that elevated their sense of worth. Nehi found his worth in something besides his job; he was perfectly happy using God's creation and earning a good paycheck to provide for he and Anna. It helped that it was even a part time position, and left two work days a week for his "side missions" with Peter and Paul.

The whistle shrilled through the factory, announcing the end of the day, and Nehi joined the stream of workers headed toward the exit. But as he emerged gratefully into the evening sunshine, still wiping his hands on his pants to be sure they were clean, his mind wasn't on sheep fat. Nehi spotted his sister immediately. The willowy figure in the leather dress, leaning against the wall with her hood up, trying to look inconspicuous and failing miserably. Anna was as bad an actress as Joe said. Nehemiah's frown deepened as the thought of his little friend seared through him again.

Six months today. Where had Joe gotten to? Had he ever intended to come back for them, or was that just a lie to sweeten his desertion? No. Joe had promised not to lie to them, and Nehi was convinced of his sincerity in that. Which meant something had happened to keep the Ravens away. Anna looked at him as Nehi worked his way through the flow of exiting humanity towards her. His stomach tightened at her expression. It looked like she had news, and it wasn't good.

He took her arm and they silently threaded their way through the crowd, then broke away to trot over the cracked sidewalks and dirty shopfronts. Lounging transients eyed the two young people and Nehi picked up the pace. Most places in Freedom were clean and safe and even pretty. But back here on the edge of town, the slums were ruled by the bums. Those who chose not to work, and preferred to take their living from the government. Or from the wallets of those who wandered too close. Ten silent minutes sped under the twins' feet, until they emerged into the parkland.

The Forest lay at the south side of Freedom. Man-planted and carefully tended, it only felt like a forest in some parts of it, most of it seemed more like a public garden. But the twins had wandered the whole ninety acres by now, and knew the secluded spots that were actual woods. Nehi drew them deep inside one wild copse, until the lighting turned from bright sunshine to mottled shadows, shifting in the breeze, and they knew they were alone. He spun to his sister.

"What's happened to turn your hair gray?"

"What?" Anna blinked. She put her hand on her head and a puff of dust rose into the cool air. She sneezed and Nehi laughed at the expression on her face. Her hand shot out to ram into Nehemiah's chest pushing him back a step. "Don't tease, it's too terrible for that! The Jones have been tagged by the UPC. They're being deported tonight to the People's Kingdom, and they'll be murdered there!" She sniffed, ran a dust covered arm across her nose, and sneezed again.

"The UPC! Are you sure?" Nehi gaped. "Paul said they haven't been a problem for nearly two years."

"It was UPC, the lady said so when she burst in."

"Gosh. Wait, the lady said so? Ann, how close did you get? Did they see you?!"

"I...don't know. But they have my DNA."

"What!"

Anna sighed and started to explain as she moved off through the trees, heading back toward the Siretons and their basement lodgings.

"I guess I shouldn't have paused for the time it took to dump the soup," she concluded wryly. "I might have been able to get out by the gate instead of vaulting over the top, if I had moved a little faster."

"I doubt you'd have gotten out at all if you hadn't used the soup," Nehi muttered grimly. "Anna, I don't know what to do about this. If that agent decides to run a check, and he actually saw you clear enough for a description, they'll have you."

"They'll have us," Anna corrected. "Probably the Siretons too. Should we just leave now?"

"Not tonight. It will take a few days for even the UPC to track you down, if they decide to do it. And tonight will find me on the road out of town, doing what I can to rescue the Jones."

"I thought you would say that," Anna said. The words came out neutral; she couldn't decide whether to be scared over the possibility of losing her brother or proud of his bravery. She decided not to decide. "Mrs. Sireton and I will host the gathering tonight while you menfolk go partying with lasers and rescues, because as Paul always says, 'People notice when you change things.' For tonight at least we should keep doing what we've always done."

"Yes, people notice change. Especially when they've been conditioned to watch each other and report anything 'suspicious.'" Nehi grumbled. His steps slowed, his eyes moving around the trees, drinking in the scent of the woodlands around them. "Anna, I've had my moments of wondering if... Maybe we could just stop. We've almost settled here. This is a decent country if you keep your head down and..."

"We're not just here for ourselves," Anna said, her voice quiet. "Our real home will never be here. Keep the vision of our real home burning in front of you, Nehi. While we're here we need to be doing everything we can to further God's kingdom and please Him. For us, right now, that means–"

"–finding the Bible and getting the Sojourners back up and running." Nehi nodded. "We need that Bible back. Even here, in a kingdom that's almost free and prosperous, there are so many holes created by the absence of the Sojourners! No light from the Bible's steady truth, no army to help defend against threats, no bursting economy to offer loans, no diplomatic prods based on common sense and a knowledge of God's reality... Even KAM is tottering without the Sojourners."

"And as the Judges' children, we have a special responsibility to find our Bible and restart the kingdom," Anna put in, and Nehemiah nodded. Then a smile broke suddenly over his face as he moved off again.

"But the real problem with staying here is a lot simpler," he said. "You and I aren't great at keeping our heads down."

"We care too much," Anna nodded, but she didn't smile. "About the truth, and other people. We need our country back, Nehi, where we can live like we're supposed to!"

"It's time, we should be out there, hunting it down." He stopped as the trees began to thin. Anna saw his fists ball as he stared at the rolling parkland without seeing it.

"The Ravens?" she asked quietly.

"Yeah," Nehi sighed, a long, tired sound. "And especially Daniel. I always miss him, it's like another hole carved in my soul beside the yawning cavern Mom and Dad's deaths left. But at times like this, when I don't know what to do next, and I know we really should already be gone, out looking for our

Bible, and I don't even know where to start... Daniel would know everything! He would probably already have a plan laid out for the next year."

"And he would grump and gripe at us until we agreed to it," Anna chuckled, the sound a little wet. Her smile died. "And now we don't know what's happened to any of them." She spun to Nehi, her shoulders slumped, eyes begging. "Do you think we'll ever find Daniel? And Joe, will he and Beau come back?" A long, tired sigh drifted from Nehi. He started to walk again, his strides swift and purposeful.

"I don't know. All I know is what we have to do next. And that's a rescue and prayer meeting. We'll need all the prayers you can give us."

"Here they are, Mary. Hannah and Thomas, safe and sound," Paul told his wife as he ushered their oldest children into the bedroom. The two little ones tore forward and leapt on their mother's bed, with all the boisterous love and excitement of a five and three year old. Mary gave a cry of relief and enfolded them in her arms, relishing in the scent of sweat, finger-paint, and peanut butter.

"Mommy, Anna didn't come to pick us up and we got extra snacks and played on the playground till Daddy came!" Thomas said excitedly.

"Slide," Hannah said, making the motion with her chubby arm.

"Very fun, dear," Mary said, hugging her close again.

"Brother?" Hanna asked, looking around the room. Mary pointed to the bassinet, and the little girl bounced over and started cooing at the baby, as Thomas ran on about their day.

"Okay, time for you two to go get ready for bed," Paul interrupted authoritatively. Uttering pleas and complaints, the two children clambered off and made their way out to obey, their feet dragging.

"Paul, what do you think happened to Anna and Nehemiah?" asked Mary, searching her husband's face.

"I don't know, but I don't like it. I got a message from the IDP leader today. The UPC is at work again," Paul said grimly, sitting on his wife's bed and taking her hand. "Some of our people may have been tagged. You know how Anna and Nehi are! Their absence could be anything from a rescue attempt to an all-out assault on the Advancers' Institute."

"Oh, Paul, the UPC! Should we call off our meeting tonight?"

"No, I think that would just bring down suspicion. Best just keep doing exactly what we've been doing, and hope for the best."

"Anna! Your hair is gray. That's funny," Thomas' shrill voice rang from downstairs, and his delighted laugh spiraled up to the bedroom. Paul and Mary looked at each other with relief as Nehemiah's laughter melded with Thomas and they heard the twins chattering with their children. A moment later Anna and Nehemiah trundled into the room, with Thomas and Hannah hanging on them; instead of retiring to their personal quarters in the basement as the twins usually did at this point in the day. Paul quickly shooed the children out to get ready for bed again and looked at the twins. He raised an eyebrow.

"The Jones have been tagged," Nehemiah answered the look. "By the UPC. They're being transported out to the People's Kingdom tonight, and I'm going to stop it."

"Then my report was correct," Paul said, his lips a grim line. "Of course news from our IDP leader always is. Darn it! It's been two years since the UPC has been causing trouble, I assumed they were no longer a threat. Apparently, I was wrong." Paul ran a hand through his sandy hair and stood up. He crossed to the dresser, pushed a button on the side, and a click filled the still room. The wooden side sprung away, swinging on hinges bolted to the inside. Paul reached into the hidden compartment and took out his Brunhiem rifle.

"Mary, can you and Anna entertain tonight?" Paul asked, checking over the weapon. "I'm going to join our young friend, and I'm sure Peter will want in on it too."

"The Three Mighties strike again!" Anna said, but her smile didn't quite reach her eyes. She spun and faced Mrs. Sireton. "I nearly forgot! Hannah's teacher caught me walking before I went on the run from dark agents, and asked me to tell you the school isn't open tomorrow."

"I wish it would stay closed," Mary said wistfully, her eyes on the sleeping infant in the bassinet. Her gaze darted up to the twins. "Is it true the Sojourners were allowed to keep their children home with them, that the parents could actually be the teachers? Wait, you were running from whom?"

"Of course most of us were able to learn from our parents," Anna shrugged, ignoring the last question. "That's how the Bible says it should be, ideally."

"But KAM knows if they get to train the next generation they'll always have a following," Nehi added.

"You get to keep the children home tomorrow, at least. Their teacher said something about protesting for more funds," Anna finished.

"I don't know why they bother," Mary said. "It's well known there's no money to distribute, and besides it won't do those schools any good even if they did get more funding."

"Is the country really that bad off?" Nehemiah asked in surprise. "It looks fine."

"It looks fine, but it's been on the verge of collapse for fifty years," Paul answered. "I don't know how they've lasted this long, with their fluctuating laws, the people's apathy, and the government pouring money out from both hands. Money to support those who choose not to work, money to keep schools running that are always needing more, money to pay for the Institute, money for this and that bum. Before long we're going to earn just enough to become a prime target for their higher taxes, and then I don't know what we'll do."

"We'll worry about that later," Mary said, getting up slowly. "Right now let's get ready for company, and you boys had better check things over for tonight...if you're determined to try." Nehemiah and Paul both nodded. Mary looked away, forcing herself not to frown, knowing them too well to try and persuade them otherwise.

Hannah's enraged shriek rang from downstairs, screaming that Thomas had pulled her hair. Thomas tried to yell over his sister, then broke into a roar and shouted she had punched him. The twins hid a grin as the parents exchanged a weary look. Anna and Nehemiah moved discretely off to the basement, their quarters. Yellow lighting closed around the twins as they walked down the carpeted stairs, spilling from floor lamps and little reading nooks scattered around the area. It lit up the wood paneled walls and comfortable floofy furniture, and Nehemiah felt peace pouring into him as he walked through the living area toward his little bedroom.

Anna stepped into the white-tiled kitchenette and began to put the clean dishes away as Nehemiah disappeared into his room. The last clean mug clinked into the cupboard. There were no more to wash. Anna looked around the spotless little kitchenette and wished she had something else to do here. It was always a comfort to putter around a kitchen, and she needed comfort. Nehemiah strolled in, wearing black slacks and his black leather jacket, fastened down the side with dull lack-luster metal buttons. A pair of soft black gloves and a ski mask poked out of one pocket. Anna began to reorganize the cup cupboard. Nehi delved into the cookie jar and leaned against the counter as he munched. Time ticked on, as cookies disappeared and mugs clinked.

"Are you worried about the UPC?" Nehemiah broke the silence as he straightened and moved to the sink to wash out his milk cup.

"Not until tomorrow," Anna said firmly. "I'll let myself worry then, but not tonight. Be careful, Nehi." She took his cup and waved it at him before she put it in her newly organized cupboard. "But God will be with us both, and we can handle it!"

"Just what we need, a cup-le of jokes always help the mood," Nehi grinned.

"Be careful with my new cupboard, it might mug you," Anna said, with a playful poke at her brother's ribs.

"Don't worry, I wouldn't sneak any away, I don't want to be a s-mug-ler. Now come on, let's go put the pillows right before people get here." The two disappeared into the living room, chattering cheerily. But in the back of her mind, Anna's thoughts kept turning to their missing friends. She would have felt so much better if Joe had been here to go with Nehemiah tonight! Where was the little mute?

Chapter Three: Cliff's Edge

"Behold, I am the LORD, the God of all flesh: is there anything too hard for me?" -Jeremiah 32:27

A tiny pop sounded from the tower doorway. The rifle tip pitched forward and a powerful man crashed on top of it.

A shaking black gloved hand reached into the alcove under the stairs and motioned for the Greens. Charlie and Vera scrambled out, breathing in ragged gasps as they staggered over the fallen man. The little person in black grabbed Charlie's wrist and jerked him toward the door.

Outside air swirled over them like a damp blanket. The black hand tightened and the black form leaned into a run, soft boots digging into the path as he darted toward the gate, dragging his two charges behind him. The night seemed to mock the flying group with its oppressive stillness, as the towering gray buildings rose like monuments to a false peace, glowering over the runners. They made it to the gate without being seen, thanks to the guards still out hunting for the Raider on the other side of the tower. The wrought iron bent outward, creating an opening to fit a normal sized human. Good old Beau. The huge chimera stepped out of the shadows as the panting, reeling group thundered up to the gate. Joe shoved the Greens into Beau's strong arms and darted back toward the towers, ignoring how much he would have loved to crash in those arms himself.

He had to give them something to chase or Beau would never get to the wagon undetected and move it out. But Simmons was here! Why had he used his darts, darn it, why hadn't he just killed the man?! What if he woke up? What if he came– Joe forced the thought out of his mind and ran, shoving his dart gun back into his pocket and concentrating on breathing. It was very difficult. The world spun around him and the shooting pain in his head grew steadily worse. Two searing lights started up on the tops of the north and south towers and pierced the darkness in the courtyard.

"There he is!" a shout rang out. Joe veered to his right, into the north tower. He would have no chance out in the open, not with the floodlights on. He pelted up the metal stairs and wondered vaguely why no one tried to stop him. All the guards were outside chasing him, of course. And the other people here didn't want to get in the way of a masked madman. Joe thought it should be funny, but wasn't sure why. He caught his foot on the last step and fell heavily into the bare hallway at the top of the tower. His lungs felt like they were going to explode as he heaved and gasped, trying to drag air in past his stitched side. He wished he could just lay there and let them explode.

The sound of pounding footsteps ringing up the stairs invaded his consciousness as he sprawled on the floor. Joe's hands dug into the dirty wood and he forced himself up. The window outside, the only place to go now. He darted for it, clicking his titanium dirk into the custom built slot on his boot heel. One quick kick, and the heel of his boot hit the center of the pane, the dirk smashing it first with devastating force. Glass shattered into the courtyard. Joe swung himself outside through the flying shards, one hand slipping the dirk from his heel back into its hidden sheath on his calf. A cone of searing light played over him as the searchlight from the opposite building found him. Burning white lasers lit up the wall around his body, leaving holes dripping molten rock. Joe scampered the few feet to the top of the tower and heaved himself up, bricks chipping and melting with the impact of the beams. He slumped onto the roof below the little brick railing, wheezing and every muscle jumping and trembling with fatigue.

A trapdoor two feet to his right banged open. A Krackmen

laser muzzle shoved through and leveled at the mute, glowing red, primed and ready. Joe went into a roll automatically. The whining laser burst holes of melted brick just behind his flying form. He dashed toward the far edge of the tower, saw dark flowing water below him, gripped the edge, and vaulted over. He didn't pray, he didn't even think. The mute had just enough sense left to straighten out before he hit.

Water slammed into his legs with a force that felt like hitting concrete. Freezing, oxygen-sucking water swirled over his head, pulling at him, choking him, tugging him under. Self-preservation kicked in as his mind staggered, and Joe fought the water like the monster it was. His head broke the surface. Rushing water, whistling wind, shouting guards, it all flooded over him as he struggled and gasped, shaking from the cold. The current moved fast, swirling and battering his body. This must be a river, not a lake or...something. He had studied the map, why couldn't he remember? Joe gulped in air and tried to force himself to think. His mind numbed with his freezing fingers. He fought on, barely keeping his head above the water. The current pulled and tugged him, the banks on either side black smudges that seemed unreal and unreachable.

A darker something loomed up ahead of him. He clutched at it as a last hope. His fingers curled around it, and the thing bent, bowing under his weight. Joe's grip tightened and his shoulders jerked out of the water. He hung there, the current battering his bruised, heaving lungs. A tree branch. That's what he held, the very end of a great tree branch stretching over the river. Joe wished he could stop gasping and get enough air to satisfy his burning, aching lungs. Hand over frozen hand he began to haul himself to the bank. The branch suddenly lifted upward, growing into a bow shape. His fingertips brushed it, but his clutching hand gripped empty air. Joe tumbled into the river again. Survival instinct tightened his left hand, still numbly gripping the wood behind the bow, and the branch bent under his weight.

Water tumbled and roared over his head, and he fought against it, jerking himself out again. His own chokes and gasps echoed in his mind as the branch bobbed and he struggled, barely getting his second hand around the wood. The river's roar sounded like laughter, cruel, mocking laughter. He didn't have the strength left to reach the branch over his head. There was no way out of this cold, swirling river. Joe's grip began to loosen. No! Don't give up, just a little more strength and you'll have it... Just a little more strength... But I've already used so much. So much... His hands began to loosen again. Joe tried to tell them not to and found he couldn't. He lost his grip of his right hand and the water closed over his head. A desperate struggle, and Joe pulled himself out enough to breathe. The laughter rolled around him, and with it came the faces from his past, evil faces, watching him writhe and struggle. A silent scream, weak and gasping, ripped from him. He went down again, his mind whirling into nightmares.

A hand engulfed his left wrist, still stubbornly clutching the tree limb. A pinching, strong grip pulled, and the drowning, laughing river fell away. Night air whistled around Joe as someone dragged him up from the water to the bank. He struggled feebly, terror waking him up just enough to dread who had him now. Soft, damp earth banged into his side as he hit the bank. The hand let go of him, and he sprawled there, choking and vomiting river water. A warm, familiar, hairy pair of arms slid under his shoulders, turning him, lifting him, drawing him close against a massive, warm chest. Joe gasped in relief and thankfulness, as his body heaved, gagging and coughing water out of his lungs.

Beau! How the chimera found him there was no knowing. That lovely and wonderful instinct of his probably. But he was safe again in those lovely, wonderful arms. Joe sagged against Cobeau, his lungs still burning and heaving. His fingers automatically twisted in the chimera's soft leather shirt, like a scared child silently begging his father to keep holding on. He let himself drift off and the world dimmed and fuzzed around him. He didn't remember Beau's walk back to the wagon. Only the feeling of lying safe and still for the few minutes it took to get there.

Yellow light, heat, the sense of being indoors, it washed over him as colors swirled in fuzzy patterns in his vision. Joe closed his eyes, steadied his breathing, and forced himself to concentrate past the fog and the numbing pain in his head. He opened his eyes and focused. He saw feet; large hairy, smelly feet. The mute turned his head with a huge effort. Painted trees, flames burning in their gas stove, all the comforts and safety of his own wagon. Joe lay in the Day Room next to the stove. A blanket wrapped around him and delicious heat crept into his exhausted body. Beau's hairy, worried face filled Joe's vision, the chimera's soft brown eyes pleading. With an effort Joe disentangled his arm from the blanket.

"Thank you," Joe signed to the big chimera. A huge smile crinkled Beau's face and he brushed Joe's sopping, blond hair out of his eyes affectionately. "Did we get them?"

"Yes," Beau straightened and pointed at the night room door. "On the bunks."

"Asleep?" Joe asked in surprise, his signs slow and clumsy.

"Out," Beau nodded.

"Wait...you didn't knock them out?" Joe signed, starting to sit up. Pain shot through his head, his muscles jumped, and he slumped back again.

"You did the Markhors."

"They were so panicked they were dangerous! The Greens weren't." A horrid thought struck him. "Did you use the right doses in the needles?"

"Needles?" Beau said, his great face crinkling. Joe gaped at him.

"You didn't use the serum?"

"Serum?"

"Glue, you didn't–" Joe gave the air a vicious uppercut and Beau grinned and nodded. Joe started laughing. "Those poor people!"

"I shouldn't have knocked them out?" Beau asked, his hairy face wrinkling in confusion. Joe kept chuckling and thanked God again for his big friend. The laughter did him more good than anything else could have, and Joe felt strength flooding into him. He sat up and leaned against the stove, trying to explain to Cobeau why he shouldn't have punched the Greens unconscious as the big man began to move around the room gathering dinner things. Joe could tell he wasn't getting through and gave up. Instead, he climbed slowly, achingly to his feet, staggered into the night room, and used his serum to make sure the couple stayed asleep. It seemed easier than trying to explain why their rescuers had punched them. And definitely easier than dealing with people he didn't know. He teetered back in and slumped against the stove again with a gasp. He sat there, relishing in the heat seeping into him and listlessly watching Beau stirring something on the burner.

"I heard Evil talking about the Wolf's plans, Glue," he signed after a few minutes. He knew the big man wouldn't understand even half of the conversation, but it felt nice to sign it to someone. "Wolf is about to launch the next set of heists. That despicable person could have it all, but instead is tearing the world apart. We have to stop Wolf, before more countries go into disintegration." Beau picked Joe gently up and plopped him in one of the chairs at the little fold-out table. The chimera plunked a bowl of steaming stew in front of him, and sat down with one of his own huge bowls.

"I hoped to have Knee-High and Beauty with me before I went after Wolf," Joe signed. "I needed them when…but I guess we'll just have to do our best. They've probably forgotten us anyway and started a good new life. I hope it's a good life." Joe picked up his spoon and stirred the stew silently for a minute. The sight of that unappetizing mix in his bowl depressed him. The thought of Anna and Nehemiah depressed him much more. He stirred his dinner without tasting it as Cobeau noisily ate his. They had done all right for the first two months without the twins, Anna had put up a stash of food for them while she was here. But like every other good thing in his life, it eventually ran out. Joe and Co had to go back to scrounging what they could on their own. It was very hard to stomach their cooking after Anna's good stuff.

"Nehi and Miss Beauty?" Cobeau asked, having caught the two names in Joe's signs. Joe nodded and sat his spoon down.

"Do you think they're happy in KAM, Glue?" he signed, his motions small, shoulders slumped. The big chimera just shrugged. "It's been months, and we haven't even sent a message to them."

"How? Eat."

"I don't know how." Joe rubbed a hand over his brow irritably. He picked up his spoon again and lifted something gray, fuzzy, and dripping out of the stew. "I wondered what happened to those socks," he signed. Cobeau's spoon paused halfway to his mouth and he looked at his stew. Joe grinned, pushed his bowl away, and laid his aching head on the table.

"Aren't you going to eat?" Beau rumbled. Joe flung up his hands dramatically.

"Alas! Those gray socks will no more adorn my feet! I can't eat the stew that made them obsolete," Joe answered, a small twinkle coming into his bloodshot eyes.

"Joe...I'm sorry," the chimera rumbled, his face twisting in sympathy, his eyes dimming with tears at the thought of his little friend's loss. Joe smiled and patted his arm.

"I was joking, Glue. It's all right, I have other socks," he signed easily. But in his heart another weary stone fell and lodged with the others there; it felt so long since he had any-one to joke with. The soft light left his face, muscles hardening and falling into grim lines, melding with the scars. He sat up stiffly, his signs even and contained. "There was an envelope. Did you get it?" Beau pursed his lips and studied Joe silently. The mute gave him a smile that was very far from his green eyes and held out his hand. Beau handed over the white enve-lope and shoved his chair back to get at the icebox.

"We have other things, not stew," he rumbled. Joe pulled the single sheet of paper from the envelope and sat staring at it. He didn't answer. Cobeau shook his head, watching.

"The same?" he rumbled.

"It's King Hrothgar who's going to be harassed now," Joe signed, his expression remarkably blank.

"The same?" Beau insisted. Joe bit his lip, crushed the pa-per, flung it across the room, tucked his knees up to his chest, and buried his face in them, all in such quick succession it was almost one movement. He kept his head pressed into his knees as he signed.

"The same. It is my fault, Glue, just like Evil says. If I hadn't started digging into the FFs in the first place they wouldn't be going after all these innocent people to get at us. I had him down tonight, I should have killed him! But I couldn't think, I… It is my fault they're dying, and I won't let it happen. I can't let it happen. We go there now." Beau slammed the icebox shut and turned to face him.

"No." The chimera's rumble filled the little room. Joe's head lifted and he stared at his big friend. Beau stepped around the table and crouched next to his self-proclaimed master, his face at a level with Joe's, his hand engulfing the mute's thin shoul-der. "Not your fault. That evil, evil Simmons man is doing it so he can have you. Not going to him anymore."

"Glue…" Joe stared at him, stunned, his mind fumbling for an answer. But only one thing surfaced. "You've never told me no before."

"No," Beau said again.

"But...who's going to stop the FFs? They're going after that weird little kingdom's book, and making it bloodier because of my meddling, if we don't–" Beau pushed Joe's hands down gently.

"No."

"Glue, you've seen disintegration, we can't just–"

"No."

"We have to."

"Master–" Joe raised a hand in annoyance and Cobeau corrected himself quickly. He caressed Joe's wet, dirty hair lovingly and decided it was time he gave his friend a speech. "Joe, you have not slept. You do not eat. You could not pull yourself out of a river. What good would you do? You try to save every hurting person, but you can't. Tonight you did not kill because you are good, you have made yourself good. Not thinking, so inside you acted, and that meant chose life. He is not like you. He is evil. And he wants you. He will not have you. You call me your Glue. You're falling apart. Let me put you back together. You cannot save everyone, Joe. God can. Pray, think, send messages. Do what you can. Not all things."

"So many will die if we don't–" Joe broke in, a wail in the exaggerated motions. Beau's big, gnarled hands engulfed the mute's, pushing them down gently, his big head shaking.

"You forget who God is. He is big enough to do what we can't," the chimera rumbled. "You can't save everyone. God can. Stop, Joe. Miss Beauty and Nehi need you so they can live. The IDP needs you to stop Wolf to live. You must stop now to help them. That evil, evil man will not have you. If I have to tie you in a corner to make you stop running to him, I will. Trust. Relax. Eat. Sleep. Let me be in charge for a little. Please?" The words hung in the air as bloodshot green eyes stared into huge, begging, brown ones. A ghost of a smile played over

Joe's lips. He nodded.

"Okay, boss," he signed. Beau beamed. He patted Joe on the head and stood up, pointing at the mute.

"Eat. Sleep. Relax," Cobeau ordered. The large form squeezed out the peaked door to start Prissy towards the border to drop off Charlie and Vera with the IDP stationed in the little town at the edge of the Gaia.

Joe watched him go in amazement. Beau had never said that much at once, not since he had pulled the chimera out of the work station five years ago. Joe absently braced himself against the wall as the wagon began to jolt forward. He remembered his idiotic mistake with the door earlier that night and realized Cobeau was right. What good would he do in this state? He couldn't stop it, not now.

Wolf's trap had been bated and slowly closing for months now. It would have snapped shut on the Raider tonight if Beau hadn't intervened. Joe had waltzed into the trap and just kept running. Like a clockwork car headed toward a cliff. Tonight Beau leapt in front of him just before he ran over the edge. Joe stared at his friend's huge bowl, blinking at the seat the chimera had left behind. A little smile twitched over his face. Good old Beau. Everyone thought he was an idiot. And in some ways he couldn't think as well as other humans. But then there were moments like this...when the people around him lost it, mired down in existential "what ifs" and the chimera's common sense and unshakable faith rose like a wall to stop a suicidal leap.

Good old Beau.

Joe slid gently off the chair onto his bruised knees. His head bowed, his hands lifted, and he went to the only One he could talk to without his signs.

"My Jesus, You Who are the Almighty King of the world, the sovereign Creator of all things, I've slipped again. I've forgotten to rely on You. Jesus, You called me to this task. And You grant

me the strength to go through with it. I know You do, I've seen it again and again! You have gone before me in every job since I started, and yet I let myself forget to come to You. To trust that You are holding me fast, as I help Your people and fight against Your enemies. Forgive me for my unbelief. For not worshiping. For my selfish arrogance in looking to myself. Thank You for Beau, for the gift of a friend watching out for my body and soul. Please, Jesus, please, grant me more help, grant me Your wisdom, go before me again, and oh dear Savior, dear Master, grant me help! I need someone else in this situation to have a chance at winning out! But Lord, if it is just You and me and Beau..." A sigh rattled from the mute, his head bowing lower, almost touching the ground, dirty water dripping from his hair onto the floor. *"Master, I am your slave. And so grateful for it. Dear Jesus, if it be Your will that I alone fight this war, so be it. I will win it with You or die trying."*

Joe's eyes fluttered open with an effort and he climbed to his feet with a silent groan, reaching for a cubby filled with papers. At least the Raven would send a warning. The steady scratch of his pencil filled the quiet room as he began to write. He would rest, and let Simmons drop out of the picture at least for the two weeks it took to get to KAM by the shortcut. Under Beau's careful care, he should be recovered enough to step up in time to stop disintegration, if Hrothgar didn't manage to keep their book from the FFs. Joe paused in his busy scribbling and calculated for a minute. And seeing Anna and Nehemiah would help. That would help get him on his feet almost as much as resting for two weeks.

Joe smiled as he finished scribbling and suddenly found he was hungry. Soon, maybe Anna would be cooking again. And good old, thoughtful Nehi! What had he found to do these past months? Almost six months... His mind flew to the conversation he had overheard before this whirlwind had trapped him in its coils. Joe had that meeting between Freddy and the Wolf memorized, he had gone over it so much. He moved to the table. Now, because he was such an idiot as to run straight into Wolf's trap and keep going, the FFs had been given six months to plan. They were about to launch their next attacks. The beginning of their last before retirement, a bloodbath of a retirement. And as far as Joe knew, he alone stood in their way. It was time to stop planning and move. So many lives hung in the balance.

And more too, a treasure that could send ripples into future generations. Only he and Wolf knew of its existence. And the Wolf stood prepared to destroy it all. The Raven had to hobble the Wolf's movements and stay a step ahead of the FFs to have any chance at keeping that hope for the next generations. And he had to do that alone. He couldn't trust anyone else with the knowledge he held about that treasure. Not yet. The world wasn't prepared to accept it.

Part of it all meant getting Anna and Nehi up to the cabin. Things were moving, it was time, now. The Hillsons were both a shackle and a hinge in this situation, knowingly or not, everything pivoted around them. He needed to get the twins in place.

Joe reached for his papers again and pulled out a thick envelope. His hand moved under the table and he shifted a screw to the side. A hidden drawer popped open. Jewels sparkled as the wagon's yellow light hit their facets. Four large stones, beautiful and rare, laid amidst fourteen smaller stones, wrapped in shining silver filagree, delicately and beautifully twisted. The necklace was an exquisite thing. A work of art. And the jewels themselves nearly priceless.

Joe shifted another screw and a second drawer popped open. Jeweler's tools sparkled up from a black cloth laid in the bottom of the drawer. He picked up the tools, steadied his shaking hands, and carefully pried off a smaller jewel on the top of the necklace. Joe flipped it, drilled a tiny hole in the back, and reached for one of his miniature trackers. He carefully fastened the jewel back down again, wrapped the necklace in the black velvet cloth, slid it into the envelope, and scrawled instructions on the front.

The mute paused, his pencil going to his lips as he considered it again.

Yes, this was his best option. Another overthrow in Story Land hovered in the wings, just days from sweeping through the kingdom. Once the dust settled, the Hernons would be very firmly in power. Which meant now Joe had options for necklace-wearing targets. The Wolf had the Bible and documents with Story Land agents right now. Joe knew that meant the Ill Trio, and he knew how those nasty agents operated. This necklace tracker should give their location as soon as the Ill Trio stole it off the ornery gal Joe was sending it to... Yes, it ought to work. Provided the timing played out. The Ill Trio would be moving the Sojourner's book soon, transferring it to Freddy's annoyingly secure hands. This maneuver should give Joe about a week's extra time to locate them, find the Bible, and recover it, before the Trio moved out toward the People's Kingdom. And allow time before all that to pick up the twins, stop the disintegration of two more kingdoms, and possibly a third. He hoped. He really hoped that was the case. Joe finished scrawling his note and slid the envelope back in the drawer.

He froze mid movement, staring at a small red velvet cloth shoved into the back of the hidden drawer. Joe reached for it, slowly, gently, picked it up, and let it tumble onto his palm. The cloth fell away and a man's large silver ring glinted in the light. A golden cross lay etched across the silver, glittering up at Joe as he stood still, staring at it. His green eyes crinkled with an old, tired sorrow, his lips tight. The red cloth flew around the ring again, he pushed it into the back of the drawer, and shut it quickly.

With a silent groan he climbed on the table and shoved the skylight open. He braced himself with his hands on the skylight as he sent a whistle soaring into the sky. A black speck dropped from the blackness of the night. The soft sound of feathers reached him, and the noise of air stirred by swift flight. Meathead swung in through the skylight, perching on Joe's shoulder and pecking affectionately at the mute's dirty blond hair. Joe clucked to him, dumping raven snacks on the wagon top with one hand, and reaching for his note to Hrothgar as the raven leapt over happily and began to peck. A moment and the note was attached, and Meathead given his instructions. The raven gave a sharp caw, his wings lifting in his exuberance. A flurry of feathers and wind, and he lifted off, soared into the sky, and was lost to sight in the darkness.

Joe dropped to the ground, swayed and caught himself on the table, then crossed to the icebox. Time to find a dinner that didn't contain socks, as he didn't want quite that much fiber in his diet. Joe paused as he looked at the oak tree painted over the table. Anna and Nehemiah...an addition was needed, and now he had time to do it if Beau insisted on his relaxing. And he always planned best when his hands were busy. He grabbed a block of cheese, closed the icebox, and headed to find his paints. Happiness began to steal into him for the first time in months. He was headed back to his friends, real friends!

Joe leaned down to look for his paints and found himself lying on the floor, his head spinning and pulsating with pain. For a moment he felt like he was going to be sick, and he curled into himself, breathing shallowly, his eyes half closed. The migraine faded a fraction and he relaxed enough to take a bite of the cheese. Oh well, while he was down here he might as well take care of Beau's second command. Joe pillowed his sick head on his arm, and curled up in his dripping, filthy clothes. But a smile flitted over his face as sleep began to steal over him. Nehemiah and Anna waited at the end of this ride.

Chapter Four: Raids and Ravens

"This is my commandment, That ye love one another, as I have loved you." -John 15:12

"Three of us hijacking an Advancers' van to free the Jones, this is madness!" Paul murmured, his voice muffled by the knitted mask pulled over his head. He slumped against the brick wall, the building a dark mass looming over him in the black alleyway. His clammy hand ran up and down his rifle, rubbing the smooth carbon and metal.

"With the way you handle people, I handle explosives, and Nehemiah handles guns, we'll be fine, Paul. Besides, it's a transport wagon, not the Institute," Peter murmured back through his own mask. His brown eyes shone with excitement and his voice tingled with it as he knelt in the dark alley digging through a bag. He stood up beside Paul holding a fuse and a wad of something wrapped in wax paper. Both of them turned, tense in the darkness, looking to the youngest member of the company. Nehi stood at the entry of the alleyway, watching the road. Hope, his Compton laser pistol, dangled from his gloved hand. The other hand rested in his pocket as he leaned easily against the wall. If it weren't for his black mask and incredibly fancy laser, Paul would have sworn he was just an ordinary citizen of the KAM, out enjoying the balmy summer night. Paul fingered his rifle again and wished his hands would stop sweating. He had been on many of these raids since Nehemiah had joined their ranks, but he would never be able to be calm about it.

"This is madness," he murmured again. Nehemiah chuckled.

"Yes, Paul, it's madness. The same sort of madness that Jesus had when He climbed Calvary for us. You don't have to go repeating it like that every few minutes, it sounds as if you were sorry to be here."

Paul swiped his hand over his sweaty brow.

"That won't do any good with your mask on," Peter snapped.

"Will you two relax?" Nehi murmured. Paul started to answer, but Nehemiah held up a hand for silence and leaned out into the street.

"Here they come," he said. "Are you ready, Peter?" Peter took a deep breath, and nodded. "Off we go." Nehemiah slipped the safety off Hope, pulled his copper goggles down over his eyes, and stepped into the street. He fired two shots at the approaching van, his Compton silent, its gamma ray beams invisible to the human eye. Two sharp bangs split the quiet night, the front tires of the vehicle bursting open. The exposed rims of the tires screeched on the asphalt as it skidded and pitched, mixing with the screams of those aboard the white transport. Paul winced at the horrendous sound as the van lurched past their alleyway. Peter darted toward it, Paul at his heels. The noise cut through them as their feet pounded over the concrete sidewalk and onto the asphalt. The white wagon teetered on two wheels, and fell to its side with a rending crash. Another shot and a stream of dense black smoke rose from the engine. Coughs and yells spewed from the driver's seat, till Nehi's voice cut through the melee.

"Raise your hands and come slowly away from the van if you want to see tomorrow's sun!"

Paul leveled his Brunhiem at the muscled back of a handsome dark-skinned man in the black suit of a UPC agent. The huge barrel of a blaster lay by the man's feet, and Paul could see the agent's fingers twitching, longing to dive for it. He prayed the man just obeyed, as he moved with Peter to the square back of the van. Peter quickly began stuffing something white from the wax paper into the lock. It smelled foul. The driver and UPC guard raised their hands and approached the dark patch Paul knew was Nehemiah. Paul kept his rifle steady.

"Face the wagon," Nehemiah ordered, the sound drifting through the smoke and thick, humid air. Two dull thuds rose above the sound of the hissing engine and Paul's taut muscles relaxed a fraction as he dropped his rifle to his side. Nehemiah knew how to club with a pistol as well as he could shoot with it. Those two wouldn't stir for a long time now. But his heart always leapt into his mouth when Nehi used his Compton like that. If the laser broke, the ball of dark energy and the ball of dark matter could manage to combine, and form a black hole in the street to swallow them all.

Sizzling started up beside him. Paul stepped back quickly, his eyes snapping to Peter's short fuse burning in the lock. A dull bang, a puff of black smoke, and metal pieces from the van's lock spewed hissing into the street. Paul darted forward, his rifle ramming into his ribs as he slung it over his back. He gripped the doors and heaved them open, the hinges squeaking.

"Bert, Gail, are you in there?" he said into the darkness. Two shocked gasps came from somewhere inside. Paul took that to be a yes and reached his hand into the dark. "Come on out, your exportation has been postponed!" A portly hand took his and the short, plump forms of Mr. and Mrs. Jones slid out to huddle in the street; shocked and disheveled, but otherwise unhurt. Paul led them back to the alleyway at a run, glancing at his watch as he moved. Fifty seconds from start to finish! Not bad. Paul spun to point the triumph out to Peter. Then he caught sight of his young friend's face. Peter's lips pressed tight together, his face lined as his eyes swung from point to point, watching for something.

"What's wrong?" Paul asked sharply.

"Nehi isn't here," Peter growled.

Soft, thudding footsteps drifted to them from down the

street. Paul and Peter swung in front of the Jones, shuffling deeper into the alley as they pulled their lasers up. The soft whine of the weapons' priming surrounded them, melding with the glowing circles at the end of the rifles as the energy gathered inside. The footsteps turned toward them, then Nehemiah burst into the little group, his pistol still in his hand, his goggles pushed on top his head.

"Someone's reported us already, there's a patrol coming this way," Nehemiah said.

"Then the quicker we get back–" Paul began but Nehemiah interrupted him, a habit Paul found very annoying.

"They're too close already, if they search this area they'll find the tunnel. You take the Jones back home. Peter and I will lead the patrol away."

"But–" Paul began to protest but Nehemiah and Peter spun out of the alley and pelted down the street. The whine of a siren rang through the night as the two young men were spotted. The patrol roared past in pursuit. A shout lifted from someone, as the lights of the sirens swung off into another street. Paul shook his head, marveling again. If all Christians could react as quickly and bravely as those boys and Anna did, this world might not be in such a dreadful state. The Sojourners created remarkable people.

A flash of insight darted through him as he realized what that statement meant; following the codes laid out in the Bible created remarkable people. So why weren't there more like that in his own IDP group? Could there be more in the Bible they didn't know? Or had they allowed too much of KAM to seep into their lives?

Paul pushed the thoughts into a section of his mind to be pondered later, and pushed a hand into the Jones' backs, shepherding them to the tunnel leading to his basement.

Nehemiah and Peter raced out of the alley, their boots ringing on the street. A shout came from the patrol as they took the bait. The asphalt burst up in little hot explosions behind him as Nehi gripped the corner of the brick house and spun onto another street. For a moment, they were out of sight of the patrol. The young men leaned into their run, changing their weight so their steps were quiet. With a burst of speed, they gained enough distance that the two were spinning around the next corner when the patrol twisted into their street. But still a shout lifted, and Nehi glimpsed a soldier pointing at their reflection in a house's window.

Nehemiah tucked Hope back into the holster strapped to his leg as he followed Peter down the winding street through a neighborhood. A grimace cut over his face as he saw his own reflection staring back at him from the hundreds of windows facing the street. They would never lose themselves with those reflections screaming their position to every pursuer. A hot hunt began, twisting through the streets of Freedom, the patrols' slow motorcars belting out the whining siren of the KAM Patrol. Over and over Nehi and Peter lost them, only to be spotted again.

Peter ducked through yards and down alleys, spun onto street after street. Asphalt, trees, garbage, vagrants, the stench of a big city rose around Nehi as he ran. And always his own reflection chased him, flashing past in the windows. The patrol roared hot on their heels. They raced on, and soon found themselves in the heart of the city. Huge buildings towered over their heads, nearly blocking out the night sky. If only they would block out those confounded windows! Peter's breath spurted out of him in pained bursts, and Nehemiah noticed his friend's arm clinging around his side, as if he were getting a stitch. The patrol sirens wailed. The noise grew closer.

A man stepped out of a side street, straining to see what all the commotion was about. His muscular hands twitched in the hopes of a new plaything; even from a block away Nehe-miah could see it. Nehi gasped, his blood rushed from his head, and his nerves spasmed inside him. Terror eclipsed eve-rything. Well over a year had passed since he had been in the power of those hands, thrown to Simmons in his light-killing rooms. But Nehi's body and mind reacted like it was yester-day. Nehi's arm shot out, clutched Peter's shoulder, and jerked him into the only place they could disappear, a wedge of darkness yawning on their left.

Concrete walls met just in front of them, forming a V, as two skyscrapers met in a sharp angle about six yards from where the boys stood. A dead end.

The two stumbled to a halt, Peter's breath wheezing and panting with exertion, and Nehi's wheezing and panting in panic. The sirens ground to a halt outside their hiding place, and Peter and Nehemiah looked at each other. They were trapped. Nehemiah forced himself under control. He reached for Hope and began to carefully check to see that she was in order for her last fight. Though his wonderful laser wouldn't do much good, the lead shields were already popping up in the street. The KAM soldiers had no desire to expose themselves to enemy fire.

At least it would probably only be reeducation at the Cen-ter here. He preferred that to being recycled to a higher plane in the Kingdom of Gaia. Or executed by the Guardians in Kil-lipolis. Or Simmons...the memory of those strong hands and that cruel smile flooded Nehemiah's mind. He quickly pushed it away, rubbing Hope's cool metal and forcing his trembling to steady. It had been easier to leave Abid and Simmons be-hind here in KAM. He had a settled, steady life, and even got to attend church every Sunday and hear good preaching. Some-how it had helped to push the doubts and fears and phobias from his old master away.

But tonight, with that one sighting of his nemesis, it all

flooded back in. Nehemiah shivered and prayed and leaned against the wall beside his friend, trying not to think.

The thought of leaving Anna behind invaded and sent a stab of sharp sorrow through him. It would be very hard on her. But she was brave, and competent. And maybe Joe would decide to come back someday.

"You are trapped," a voice called from the street outside, ringing loud and metallic through a megaphone.

"No, I thought we were just resting," Nehemiah muttered, and Peter grinned at him through his panting.

"Come out now with your hands up, leave all your weapons behind you," the voice continued. Peter and Nehemiah leaned against the building and waited. They had no intention of coming out meekly. Miracles had happened before now, a chance for escape might still present itself. The voice repeated its earlier statements. And repeated them again.

"I don't suppose he's ever heard of variety?" Peter panted.

"I expect he's reading from his manual of patrol protocol," answered Nehemiah. A whine started up, and a red beam pulsed in the building between the two young men. A hole two inches wide smoked when the light died. Nehemiah spun, searching through the opening. He spotted the reflection of the patrolman leaning over the lead shields to sight his Krackmen again, and raised Hope. The patrolmen slumped, his body thudding into the lead shield, rolled over it, and splayed in the middle of the street.

Piercing whines filled the air, and lasers cut into their alleyway, burning holes in the buildings beside them. A sharp hiss broke from Peter and he grabbed his right arm. Nehemiah shoved him to a darker patch of blackness, Peter stumbling, his breath coming in sharp gasps. Nehi leaned him against the wall in the deepest shadow and stepped closer to the edge, till he could see patrolmen reflected in the windows of the building across from him. He dropped three quickly, grimaced as he saw the rest fling themselves behind the shields, and moved back to Peter. His friend sat slumped against the building, his knees pulled up near his head, his hand still clutching his arm.

"Is it bad?" Nehi asked kneeling beside him.

"I don't know," Peter hissed through clamped teeth. It wasn't good, judging from that voice. Nehi gripped his friend's arm and ripped off the smoldering sleeve. An inch-wide hole sizzled in Peter's arm. Nehemiah could see the graffiti on the wall through it. At least it had missed the bone. He sat back on his heels and began to rip the sleeve in strips. Images of Peter having to heal that in the Center flooded Nehi, and of Elizabeth waiting and crying over her lost fiancé. And Anna, her radiant smile faded and worn because of him. His shoulders slumped, his hands dropping to his lap.

"I'm sorry I pulled us in here," Nehi said. "I panicked. There's no other word for it, I just panicked."

"I noticed," Peter murmured through clenched teeth. Then he realized even through his pain what an answer like that must make his friend feel and forced his mind to focus on his words and not the burning hole in his arm. "But it doesn't really make a difference, I was done anyway. Couldn't have run much farther." Peter glanced up, curiosity showing on his strained face. "We've been in a lot of situations, but I've never seen you react like that. What was it?"

"You are trapped. Come out now with your hands up, leave all your weapons behind you," the voice called, sparing Nehemiah the answer. A metallic clinking drifted to them from the street. Nehemiah's slumped head rose slowly, and he met Peter's gaze; fear mirrored his own there. That sound was unmistakable. They were setting up a Toaster, a massive laser.

"That's going to take out the side of these buildings when it goes off," Nehemiah muttered as he did his best to stop the blood welling from Peter's wound. Come to think of it, why was he doing that with a Toaster facing them?

"Not to mention what it's going to do to us," Peter gasped, as Nehemiah drew a strip of shirt tight around his wound.

"This is your last warning," the voice called from the street.

"No, this is your first warning," a deep growl re-bounded into the street from somewhere over the heads of the patrol-men. Nehemiah fell back against the building, almost laughing in shock and relief. Joy flooded him nearly as strong as the ter-ror had a few minutes earlier. He knew that deep, menacing growl! A loud exchange began between the patrolmen and the deep voice, but Peter and Nehemiah weren't listening.

As soon as the growls started over the patrolmen's heads, a zipping sound started over Peter and Nehi. And then a patch of the black sky fell in their alley. At the second glance, they could see the small form crouched on his toes and the fingers of his left hand, coiled with energy, ready to strike in any di-rection, like a cat that had just tumbled off a roof in front of a growling dog. He was swathed all in black, only his bright green eyes showing. A black cord wound around his middle and reached out of sight above them, while he held a second cord clutched in his right hand. Nehemiah's emotions had been through the mill that night and as those familiar eyes, surrounded by elegant black leather, looked into his and laughed silently at his knitted mask, he couldn't decide whether he wanted to hug him or punch him. Joe didn't give Nehi the chance to do either.

The mute shot to Nehemiah's side, handed him the thick black cord, wound it around his waist and right leg with quick, expert movements, and gave it a sharp tug, all in about two seconds. Nehemiah gasped as he jerked upward, the rope cut-ting into him, his speed making the air bite and tear at his skin. He overshot the top of the building and twisted desper-ately in midair, scrabbling for the roof, as he tried to stop him-self from tumbling back down into the alley. His right side col-lided with the hard concrete, and he rolled onto the roof. The

The Black Raider

mute shot up over the building, holding a wriggling Peter, twisted elegantly, and landed easily on his toes beside Nehi. Nehemiah caught Peter as his patrol bating buddy staggered away from the mute, his eyes wide and scared.

"It's all right, Pete, they're friends, it's the Ravens finally back," he said quickly. Nehi felt Peter shaking and realized he was going into physical shock. He tore his coat off his back, wrapped the soft black leather around Peter, got him sitting on the roof, then spun to Joe. The mute crouched, swiftly winding the black cords into a compact metallic box. Nehi snorted. "Some friends, they disappear on you for half a year and don't even send a greeting back by raven!" Joe allowed himself the luxury of free hands to sign an answer.

"You're alive, aren't you?" Before Nehemiah could reply, a massive form materialized out of the blackness. Peter jerked back with a muttered exclamation but Nehi grinned, bouncing on his toes at seeing them both here.

"All's well, Master," Beau's deep voice growled. Joe slammed a small fist down on Cobeau's huge foot. White teeth shone in the dark as the chimera smiled and corrected himself. "All's well, Joe." The mute stood up, the zip lines wound carefully in their box. He leapt to Peter and knelt down beside him. A friendly smile crinkled his eyes behind his mask and one hand waved in a friendly, quick way. Peter's stiff shoulders relaxed a fraction and his lips twitched as he started to answer the smile. Joe jabbed a syringe into Peter's arm. The young man's eyes rolled back in his head and he tipped to the side. Cobeau swept him up, cradling him in his hairy arms, as Nehi stifled a shout.

"What was that for?" he demanded, gesturing to Peter. A snore came from the young man.

"Easier to carry, and easier on him," Joe shrugged. "Come on." The mute leapt over the edge of the building, disappearing from sight. Nehi darted forward, gaping over the edge. Joe trotted over the next skyscraper's roof, lightly leaping duct work and air conditioners, as if they were twigs in a field. Nehi stared at the three-foot gap between himself and the next building. The sidewalk gleamed eleven stories below him. A burly elbow prodded him in the back.

"Go on," Beau grunted. Nehi steeled himself and took a step back, readying to jump.

A sharp whine erupted behind him. A three-foot-wide laser melted through the top of the building as the Toaster laser came into play. Nehemiah yelped and half jumped, half fell over the gap. He landed in a hard, ungainly roll on the other building top and staggered to his feet. Joe stood watching him at the edge of the roof, the elegant tail of his mask fluttering in a teasing breeze. Nehi resisted the urge to be annoyed and jealous at how easily and epically Joe handled this whole situation, and just ran to catch up. He moved around the duct work.

As he gained Joe's side, the mute gripped his shoulder and leapt. Nehi followed the pull of that strong, thin hand, doing his best not to look down.

They shot over a four-foot gap, reaching ten stories straight down. But their boots thudded into solid building, and Joe landed running. He kept his hand on Nehi's shoulder. The bigger boy staggered into a run beside him, his feet stinging with the impact of the leap, his breath snatched by the impact of what they had just jumped. But Nehemiah recovered himself and started to move smoothly beside Joe. Beau came up on the mute's other side, his big feet as noiseless as Joe's soft bootfalls, his own Black Raider outfit a mirror of Joe's elegant epicness. Nehi felt like a heavy-footed amateur.

A red ball lit up the night to their right. The heat from the Toaster's massive beam washed over the runners. Glass and steel melted under its touch, concrete caving into the hole it left behind. Nehi's heart beat so hard he could feel the pounding in his chest as he followed Joe. The mute picked up the speed and aimed for the edge of the building.

Joe planted one foot on the railing and shoved off, arching through the night air in a beautiful dive, arms stretched out in front of him. Nehi had an instant to glimpse a four-foot gap leading to a roof nearly six feet below them. Then he leapt, two footed and ungainly. But he had Hope out as he moved, and he spun to look below him, staring down her barrel.

He had two seconds to see them. KAM soldiers in the street below, the Toaster mounted on a truck bed, following the runners as they leapt over the rooftops. Nehi tapped his goggles, zooming in on the scene. Then his finger pressed onto Hope's trigger. One of the Toaster's tripod legs melted, sheered through. The massive laser toppled, as the soldiers threw themselves out of its way. The bang of the Toaster hitting the street echoed up to the little group as they landed with three solid thumps on the rooftop. Nehi hit it hard on his left shoulder. He rolled immediately, taking some of the weight of the fall off. But his arm felt numb as he shot upright and moved into a run beside his little friend. Joe's green eyes met his. The mute nodded, respect in the movement. Nehi glowed.

Then came the next leap, the terrifying nothingness of empty space under them, then the bone-jarring thump as they landed again. Nehemiah ran on, and he felt like shouting out of sheer exuberance. He was bruised and hunted, but adrenaline sang in his veins and the Ravens ran beside him.

Joe aimed for the edge of the building, but this time Nehi saw him reaching for his ropes again. The mute tossed one to Nehi, and he wound it around his waist, watching Joe carefully and trying to mimic the mute's deft knots that created a harness. Joe tossed the box onto the edge of the roof. Nehi heard it fall with a clang, saw the metal of the box fizz and discolor as it reacted to the concrete, fusing onto it. Then the mute reached the edge. He gripped his rope with his leather gloves, leapt with his feet together, spun in midair, and disappeared into the darkness beside the building. Nehi clamped his teeth together and did the same maneuver as best as he could. Out of the corner of his eye he watched Beau following, Peter cradled in the crook of one arm. The small box pulled the ropes together, swinging the threesome into a line, one over the other.

Dark air whistled around Nehemiah as he fell. The rope cut into him, slowing his descent. But he still fell. The KAM window panes making up the building beside him spit his reflection back at him. The young man watched himself whistling down nine stories, and time seemed to slow. He glimpsed movement below him and shifted his gaze down a story.

Joe's reflection shone just below his. The mute's arm flung out, a new rope seeming to fire from his hand. The end of the rope clanged onto a manhole cover. The mute jerked, the rope retracted, and the round cover rattled out of the way. Joe disappeared into the hole below the street. Nehi just had time for his eyes to widen and his throat to constrict. Then the light died as he dropped through the darkness of the hole.

His feet landed with a force that felt like it broke his knees. He rolled forward immediately, head tucked behind his arms, spinning onto his back. For a moment he lay there and blinked at the moon shining through the hole. Then Beau's huge form blocked it out. The chimera landed beautifully, gripped the three ropes in one of his huge hands, and gave a sharp tug. The lines snapped off at the top and tumbled down onto the group. Joe jerked his second rope and the manhole cover slid back in place with a clang. The moonlight snuffed out.

Nehemiah closed his eyes slowly as he got to his tingling, bruised feet. His pulse sang in his ears. He could feel bile beginning to bubble in his stomach, trying to rise. He hated the dark. He hated closed spaces. He really, really hated dark closed spaces. Ever since Abid's black box and Simmons' regime, anyway. All his concentration flowed into forcing himself not to hyperventilate.

A penlight pierced the darkness, hitting his face. Nehi gasped and didn't care who heard it. The light flicked away, moving over Beau and Peter. A click came from the darkness behind the light, the mute telling them to move. The tiny beam began to shift down the drainage tunnel, picking out foul smelling puddles to avoid. Nehi scrambled to keep up with that light.

The sound of tires rumbled above them as the army rushed past the innocent manhole cover, looking for their quarry. Hot steam shot through vents as hover cars followed the truck. Nehi heard soldiers shouting orders and yelling back reports. But the sounds came muted from the thick street over their heads. The noises began to fade as the group moved farther along the tunnel.

Two eyes shone red in the reflection of the penlight, and Joe paused. Nehi and Beau froze beside him, staring at the three-foot rat caught in the light. They stood and stared, making no movement, nothing to startle it. The rodent bared yellowed teeth and hissed. It turned, tail whipping into a puddle as it moved, and splashed off into another tunnel. Joe started off again.

"Thanks. For rescuing us back there," Nehi said. His voice echoed off the walls, and he hated the way it shook. He swallowed, trying to force the clamminess from his skin as his phobia played through him. "So where have you been?" No clicks or gestures came from the dark blob of Joe. Nehi reached over the mute's head and prodded Beau in the shoulder. Not gently.

"Out," Beau rumbled. "But back now."

"Yeah, I did notice that," Nehemiah said, a little sharply. Joe clicked twice, an order to stop talking. Nehi knew the mute was right; their voices echoed down the tunnels, and it was liable to either spook the rats down here, or draw out something worse. He closed his mouth and kept walking.

Chapter Five: Notes and Goodbyes

"The LORD is nigh unto all them that call upon him, to all that call upon him in truth." -Psalm 145:18

Wulfgar gripped the pommel of his sword, kneading it in his hand. The sky remained blue. A bird sang off in the distance. Nothing disturbed the peace of the morning as he stared at the Barrow.

A simple mound of grass in a clearing set amidst the great northern woods, the Barrow didn't seem anything worth guarding. But Wulfgar stood tense and alert, his eyes scanning the forest. He knew Halbred watched from under the tall aspens across the clearing, and the knowledge brought a measure of comfort. Shield-Bearers for the king, they were two of the honored few who knew what truly lay beneath that Barrow. It didn't hold a dragon, sleeping on a hoard, just waiting to be disturbed to rise and devastate the countryside with fire; that tale served its purpose of keeping the locals from wandering in this area, but the truth contained something more dangerous and precious.

The Barrow hid the kingdom's book. The document that was their governing base, the charter granting the right for the kingdom of Geatland to exist. Without that history lying inside the Barrow, this small kingdom would be wiped off the face of the earth. No kingdom was allowed to exist without a book. His was an honored task indeed, one reserved for true heroes.

Wulfgar kneaded his pommel again, his knuckles white. He scanned the trees above him, searching for the source of his unease. A squirrel leapt from a twisted oak limb onto one of the whispering, waving aspens, chattering and crying as it moved. Wulfgar's gaze darted around the woods, searching for what had frightened it, his heartbeat steadily rising.

Something was out of place today. He could not name it, could not determine where it came from. But the birds did not sing. The squirrels ran and chattered in anger. He had stood guard here in all weather, at all seasons of the year, he knew this clearing. And something today felt...wrong. His eyes went to the aspen stand. He couldn't see Halbred in the midst of the white bark and whispering green leaves. But that, at least, was normal, Halbred was an expert at remaining unseen. Today Wulfgar wished he could see his fellow Shield-Bearer. He wanted to whisper to him to be on guard, to see if Halbred knew what made the birds silent, the woodlands feel tense and still.

The soft flutter of wings reached his hearing, and Wulfgar's gaze flicked upward. A black raven settled in a beech, three feet above the warrior. The bird cocked his head, bright eyes staring down at Wulfgar. The man watched it, strangely certain the bird watched him back. Sunshine glinted off the sleek black feathers. The bird's head shot to the side, staring behind Wulfgar.

The warrior dodged left. A white light burst into a ball of flame in the tree trunk beside his face. Heat struck out at him, catching the side of his cloak in flames. He flung himself to the side, unclasping his cloak and drawing it over the damp earth as he rolled, smothering the fire. He slid to a rest behind a great oak's trunk, his blade drawn in his hand, his eyes wide with his fear.

A demon! Or an actual dragon awakened? Nothing he knew could create such a fire as that! Wait, his brother had spoken of a fight on the border with Ravenswing Ashe-Maker... hadn't the little one used something akin to this magic? Wulfgar tightened his grip, shifting his shield up and lifting his sword into a high guard. One thing he knew. This was not Ravenswing. This was no ally to the Geats. He closed his eyes and strained his hearing, searching for anything out of place.

A strange humming whine drifted from his right. As he focused on it, Wulfgar heard the sound of footsteps mixing with the noise. Hard and steady. A man marching, unafraid of being noticed, unapologetic in his intrusion into this sacred place. The footsteps drew nearer to Wulfgar's tree. He could discern a second step behind the first, lighter, quicker. A woman?

White fire flashed amidst the aspen stand across the clearing. A high cry broke the stillness of the woods, long and agonized. The sound stopped, dissolving into the whispering of the leaves. Wulfgar felt sweat trickling down his spine. He had heard such cries in battles on the border with the wild beasts. The times were blessedly few, but he recognized the screams of the dying.

Halbred no longer guarded the Barrow.

Only Wulfgar Blade-Dancer stood in the gap, keeping the hope of the kingdom in safety.

The footsteps drew nearer to his tree. Wulfgar waited, still and silent, his hands clammy on the leather of his sword's handle. The naked blade sparkled in the sun's light, Honor-Keeper, sword of his house. Its steel had seen combat, driving back the beasts, defending the people of Geatland from invasion by hunger driven animals. But it had not drawn human blood. He forced his shoulders to untense and readied his mind. The footsteps reached the edge of his oak.

Wulfgar swung around the trunk, stepping into his swing with his sword-on foot. Honor-Keeper slashed down from the upper guard, moving at such a speed the blade blurred and flashed. It bit through sinews and bones, metal and cloth. Wulfgar jerked her back, his vision filled with red and black as a stranger in odd tight clothes collapsed on the ground. The thump of the body's fall filled Wulfgar's hearing, sending his head buzzing and his bile rising. But he didn't heed it, just closed the distance toward the next threat. A woman, slim, hard, brown hair cropped around her face, lips painted unnaturally bright red. Her upper form was obscured by a bulky vest with pockets bulging, her lower form accentuated by black pants. He took it all in at a glance as he moved, his weight shifting again, his sword in the middle guard behind his shield, darting out toward her throat.

White light filled his vision. A hole melted through his shield and through him. Pain pulsed in his chest. His strength drained from his limbs, sapped by the pain. Cold and weakness claimed him. He fell to his knees, then tumbled slowly forward. Unable to stop it. The earth met him, and Wulfgar Blade-Dancer lay still, his hand white as he clutched his sword's handle. He felt the footsteps vibrate in the damp earth as the woman stepped over him; silent, ruthless, striding unhindered to the Barrow.

A flutter of wings reached Wulfgar through the ringing quickly overtaking his ears. He forced the darkness hovering in his vision away and sucked a breath into his hemorrhaging lungs. He had precious few breaths left, he knew.

The bright raven danced on the ground beside him. The bird's head tipped, croaking as he hopped closer to the warrior. A black leather pouch dangled from the raven's leg. Wulfgar reached for the bag with his left hand. He recognized its make. With an effort that seemed more than he could achieve he reached past the drawstring and pulled a notepaper partially out. His finger dripped red on the white. Shaking, his vision darkening, Wulfgar scrawled five words onto the paper. His hand hit the ground, the effort more than he had left in him. The last sound he comprehended was the harsh caw of the raven, rising into the sky.

May it find Ravenswing!

The words of a conversation Wulfgar held once with the small warrior returned to his fading mind as he lay on the damp earth; the Shield-Bearer and his brother Wiglaf, leaning on one of the wreathed posts of Heorot Hall, the stranger perched on the ground in front of them, scrawling on his white notes. Ravenswing had told them of One over himself, over all things. One he termed, "Jesus." Wulfgar had not understood all of the words on those notes. At the time it seemed obscure and ethereal, nothing he needed while working on the solid ground. But as he lay now on the hard wet earth, his life quickly ebbing away, it was all that mattered. This Jesus held life for all eternity. And He held it out freely, one had only to believe. So be it...

Wulfgar's eyes dimmed. His last breath stirred the grass in front of him.

Beyond the dead warrior, the Barrow's hidden door closed softly behind the form of the woman. A bag swung at her side and a book rested in her arms as she strode across the clearing into the aspens to reach her extraction point.

High over her head, a raven winged his way over the treetops. The bird clutched a wallet in his strong talons, and a note rested in his pouch. Only a few words, dirty and grimed.

Book stolen. Aid us Ravenswing.

It took Nehi and the Ravens another forty minutes of quick walking to wind their way to the Sireton's basement. Joe's penlight picked out the lock and steadied there. Nehemiah slid his key out and shone it in the lock. The heat rays activated the pins, slamming them into place, and the door clicked open.

Anna sailed through the door, blocking most of the light trying to stream through. She rammed into Nehemiah, gripping him around the chest. He fell back a step, grunting at the pressure on his new bruises, his arms full of sister.

"Nehi, don't you ever go and scare me like that again!" Anna scolded, her voice muffled against him. "You've been gone for hours, and after Paul coming back and telling us you went patrol bating again and–" She stopped short and jerked back, staring.

"Joe!" Anna squealed. The little mute laughed and gave her a quick hug as he followed Cobeau into the room. The Ravens were dressed in ordinary black slacks and turtlenecks and Nehemiah wondered idly what they had done with the rest of their Raider outfits. Nehi just glimpsed an empty syringe as it disappeared inside the mute's pocket. He looked at Peter and saw him stirring, stiffening and blinking hard. Cobeau plopped Peter on the same couch he had laid Joe on months ago, as the young man blinked and looked around him groggily. Today the noise was considerably greater, as the Wednesday group had waited up, praying for the two missing young men.

Elizabeth and her father rushed to her betrothed, with Doctor Foster ambling behind. Nehi grabbed his little friend by the arm, determined not to let the mute disappear again if he could help it, and dragged him along toward the couch. Joe didn't seem to mind. The doctor leaned over Peter's injured arm, poking it with a practiced eye, as Mary ran for the household doctor's kit, and conversations buzzed through the comfortable basement.

"Will he be all right?" Nehi demanded over the babble of voices.

"It will be an impressive scar," Doctor Foster answered, his craggy face as mournful as a hound dog on a hot day; but that was the doctor's usual look, and Nehi found it encouraging that he seemed normal. The doctor turned and took a syringe and a bottle of pain killer from the kit Mary laid open beside him, his movements unhurried. "It seems to have missed anything of vital importance, it may not even need therapy for him to keep the use of his arm."

"So...he's all right?" Anna prodded, standing beside Elizabeth. Her friend clutched at Peter's good hand, trying not to panic.

"Oh yes," the doctor said mournfully. "Nothing a few days rest can't heal." His face brightened. "Unless it gets infected."

"Which is why you're giving him antibiotics now, of course," Anna said quickly, one hand going to her friend's arm as she turned to her. "Elizabeth, he's fine. Stop squeezing the life out of his fingers."

"What happened?" Paul demanded, stepping up beside Nehi. Nehemiah suddenly found himself in the center of a milling crowd, everyone begging to hear their story. He kept a hold on Joe as he began to lay out the facts, as if he was afraid the mute might suddenly dissolve if he let go of his arm.

Joe's eyes lit up as he saw the trays on the coffee table. He detached Nehi's fingers from his arm and plunked down on the soft carpet beside his friend's feet. Anna watched as seven mini quiches and four large brownies disappeared inside the little mute. She found a happy glow warming her at watching the food get inside that stick-thin frame. Then Cobeau and Nehi noticed the snacks too. The trays emptied quickly.

As Nehi gave their story, Joe's green eyes moved, darting around the room and resting with intense joy on the two Hillsons. Nehemiah didn't mention his sighting of Simmons, having no wish to go into that explanation with this many people, but otherwise told the story without deviation. When he got to the entry of Joe and Co, the mute crossed his arms, and used the motion to surreptitiously jab Nehi, hard. Nehemiah took the hint. He didn't mention the black garb, or the meticulous efficiency of the two traveling musicians. He just stated they rescued them out of it and got back again, by God's good grace. The group gaped, entranced. As Nehi finished, fourteen different voices burst into life, discussing the matter. But six stayed remarkably quiet.

Peter lay still, happy to have Elizabeth so caring, and Elizabeth cared in silence, happy to have Peter be still. Anna, Nehemiah, Cobeau, and Joe sat on the carpet near Peter's couch, silent. Usually the Hillson twins would be the most prominent voices in the room, their words like dance steps, whirling around each other, playing off the other's thoughts, soaring and dipping and leading the laughter and the thoughtful pauses. But now they sat silent. Paul noticed it, and his eyes darted from the twins' tight faces to the Ravens, sitting still and quiet. He began to politely push his guests up the stairs. The chorus of noise receded. Soon only the six remained, quiet enfolding them. Joe shifted so he faced the couch and his signs could be easily seen.

"It's good to see you again, Beauty," he signed.

"I'm not sure I'm speaking to you, not yet," Anna replied with a toss of her pretty head. Joe raised his eyebrows.

"That sounds like Knee-High's greeting," he signed.

"Disappearing for six months without a word is likely to get that sort of reaction," Anna said, annoyance dripping from her.

"We left word," Cobeau said, his big, simple face crinkled in concentration as he worked at following the conversation.

"Beau, Nehi and I came back from our first tour of Freedom and found a note from you two saying 'We're leaving now...'" she chose not to mention the FFs with Peter and Elizabeth in the room, "'...see you soon, stay safe.' That's hardly leaving word!" Anna was getting into her lecture mode, and Joe quickly interrupted.

"We've been a little busy, Beauty," he signed. Looking at him again, Anna realized his green eyes were sunken and bloodshot, and his sharp face looked even thinner and sharper, almost emaciated. He looked more exhausted and pinched than she realized the energetic dancer could get.

"That's beside the point. No, that's part of the point," Anna said, refusing to let compassion get her off the subject. "You should have come back to let us help you."

"Well, we were back when it counted, doesn't that matter?" Joe signed, a tight frown forming on his face.

"Of course I'm glad and thankful you were there to rescue Nehi but–" Anna stopped, suddenly noticing her brother's silence. She turned to him, her voice softening. "Nehemiah, what's wrong?"

"It's the panic button, isn't it? What was it?" Peter spoke up. The pain medication sang through his veins, the shock had subsided, and curiosity sparked in his veins. Elizabeth sat still, Peter's head pillowed in her lap, her pretty, round face turning from speaker to speaker as she followed the conversation intently. But her eyes kept stopping at Joe's signs, fascinated by the elegant, swift beauty.

"Panic button?" Joe signed, stiffening like a rod had been driven into his backbone.

"I saw Simmons tonight," Nehemiah answered quietly. Joe's thin hand clamped onto his shoulder, spinning Nehi around to face him, his sharp face tight, his green eyes blazing.

"Did he see you? Knee-High, did he see you?" he signed almost viciously.

"I think he did. But I don't think he saw me, if you know what I mean." Nehemiah rubbed a hand over his grimy forehead, his gaze focused on the baseboards.

"No," said Elizabeth. "Who's Simmons and what do you mean he saw you and didn't see you?" Joe broke in before Nehemiah could answer.

"He didn't recognize you, you're sure?"

"How can I be sure he didn't recognize me, Joe? I don't think he did. I wouldn't be here now if he did, would I?" Nehemiah said, hugging his knees and suddenly seeming very young.

"Is it that sure that if he finds you, you're his?" Anna asked quietly.

"Who's Simmons?" Peter asked.

"Knee-High, you didn't see or hear from him again. No

voice in the street or anything?" Joe signed. Nehemiah shook his head. "Then he didn't recognize you." Joe relaxed a little, but his face stayed tight.

"Who's Simmons?" Peter asked stubbornly, silently wishing he understood those fantastic, beautiful hand motions of the mute. Joe didn't give the twins the chance to answer.

"It's time to leave," he signed, standing up.

"What?!"

"You're leaving again?" the twins burst out, leaping to their feet.

"We all are. It's time to leave," Joe signed. A wide smile spread over Cobeau's simple face, making his thick beard bristle. As usual he had lost the conversation a long time ago. But he understood the twins were joining the Ravens again, and that made him very happy.

"Wait, Joe, you can't just hop up and say we're leaving like that!" Nehemiah spluttered.

"Especially after you disappeared on us for six months!" Anna said.

"Are you still harping on that?" Joe signed.

"Yes I am!" both the twins shouted.

"Who's Simmons?" Elizabeth called up to them. They all paused.

"How come you two are choosing tonight to finally pay attention to something besides each other?" Anna said, her nose wrinkling. The couple snorted back a laugh and even Joe grinned. But Nehi stayed silent and tense. Peter sobered quickly and his good hand moved, tugging on his friend's jacket, demanding an answer.

"Who's Simmons?" he asked again. Nehemiah turned slowly, reluctantly, toward him.

"He's...someone from my life during the disintegration," he said hesitantly. "Not a nice man. He's...the type that shows up in your deepest nightmares and you end up...suddenly awake and can't stop shaking." Peter nodded slowly, quietly linking the inadequate, stumbling words to a number of disturbing quirks he had noticed in his young friend since the twins had shown up in KAM. Screaming in the middle of the night. A phobia of enclosed spaces. A faith more mature and experienced than his years allowed for. His horrible scarring.

"Your panic button tonight," he said simply, with a quiet gentleness that showed he understood. Nehemiah just nodded.

"And he's hunting for you two again," Joe signed, Anna translating it for the couple on the couch. "No, not just again, this time he really means it."

"He didn't mean it last time?" Anna asked, remembering when they had only missed falling into his hands by the gracious workings of Providence. Joe and Nehemiah both shook their heads.

"If Simmons had really been concentrating on finding us, Anna, he would have. And we wouldn't have been able to do anything against him," Nehemiah said. His hands shook and he let one brush against Hope's cool copper side. It was comforting to know he had at least one sure defense with him.

"Don't translate, Beauty," Joe signed, and Anna obeyed reluctantly. "Look, remember that Wolf I mentioned, the one who's in the IDP and at the top of the FFs?"

"Of course I remember, I was going to go hunting with you before you ran off," Nehi snapped. Joe ignored it.

"Wolf wants to finish the business. And part of that means cornering you two, in order to gain whatever information you might have on the treasure–"

"We don't have any information on their stupid treasure!" Anna burst in.

"They think you do," Joe signed firmly, his hand motions cutting through the air. "That's what matters right now. Evil is here on the Wolf's orders to snag you two. It's time to leave.

Every moment you stay in one place, one town, with one group of people, makes Evil's job that much easier."

"And puts the group we're with in serious danger," added Nehemiah. Joe nodded and began to move toward the tunnel entrance. "Are you sure?" Nehi called after him. It wasn't just a simple question. There was a demand behind it, a need to know the answer. The mute paused and looked back. "Are you sure Simmons and this wolf in the flock are looking for us?"

"Yes." Joe's answer was slow and deliberate, his eyes never leaving his tall friend. "There's no other reason Evil would be in town. And they will find you if you stay." Nehemiah nodded, his shoulders slumped.

"But I'm still mad at you!" Anna burst out.

"Don't be." Cobeau's rumble filled the room and the others looked at him, surprise sparking over everyone except Joe. The chimera loomed, big and hairy and powerful. But somehow they had all forgotten he was there. Cobeau naturally slipped into the background, despite his bulk. "Come with me, Miss Beauty, you'll see." The big man enclosed her arm gently in one of his huge fists. Anna and Nehemiah looked at Joe. He only shrugged, his face blank, retreating into his muteness as an escape from the conversation. Anna pursed her lips in exasperation as Cobeau began to lead her gently into the tunnel. But Nehemiah found a smile creeping over his face. It was so like Joe, and so...normal, it suddenly made the rest of this disturbing night seem almost dim. He turned to Peter, took his good hand, and shook it heartily.

"Goodbye old friend. It looks like we're leaving now," he said. "I hope I get a chance to say goodbye to Paul and the rest, but if not, be sure and tell him..." Nehemiah stopped, suddenly realizing he either had to say about a million things, or only one. Cobeau and Anna were out of sight and Joe stood waiting for him at the entrance of the tunnel. He chose one. "Goodbye," he said, and was surprised to find his throat had tightened and didn't want to let the word out. Peter stumbled over his reply, trying to manage an answer through confusion, curiosity, and bone-tiring weariness.

"We'll be praying for you and Anna, Nehi," Elizabeth said earnestly. "You have our information, keep up." Nehemiah nodded, a firm promise in the action, and stepped into the kitchen. He reached into a cupboard, swung two tightly packed bags over his shoulder, and followed Joe toward the tunnel. Peter and Elizabeth stared at the bags; already packed, waiting ready at a moment's notice. This sudden need to run hadn't taken the twins by surprise.

Nehi clicked the heavy door closed behind him, blocking out the light. Closing off another life he and Anna had built up. Nehemiah turned and saw darkness. A thin beam of light popped up and a familiar little 'hurry-up' clicking sounded from the same direction. Nehemiah smiled and began to walk toward Joe and another new start.

The wagon materialized in the night as the twins and the Ravens approached, a black cutout in the midst of the graying skyline. It sat outside of town, where the parkland met the edge of the unpeopled country of KAM. The Wild Lands claimed the right of true wildness. But the unpeopled country still boasted a wildness of their own. The wolf packs ran there. Mostly they preyed on the massive herds of goats, deer, and one horns feeding on the grasslands. But during cold winters, or when disease or fires culled the herds, the wolves turned their eyes to the settlements. People didn't wander unprotected in the unpeopled lands.

A tired grin spread over Nehi's face as he drew closer to the wagon. He lingered, slowing his steps as Anna and Beau slipped inside. Nehi could just make out the details in the paintings splayed over the side as the sun slowly rose over the horizon. The wheels were clicked on, conserving the water reserves for the hoverer coils, making the wagon look quaint and elegant. A shaggy, conical head pushed around the edge of the wagon; a head three and a half feet from the crown of her brown head down to the slope of her nose. Prissy let out a piercing welcome squeal and Nehi laughed in delight. He stood in the cold morning air without anything to his name but the few clothes in his bag and the laser strapped to his leg. But it still just felt right.

It felt like home.

More like home than Paul's basement had felt in the six months he and Anna had claimed it. Nehemiah's eyes darted to his left, to the small blond-headed mute walking beside him. The people made the difference. That's what made this home. Paul was fantastic, but there was something...reserved about him. Something that never quite felt like...family.

The sudden thought sent the faces of his parents and Daniel flying into Nehi's mind. His eyes tightened, his smile leaving. For what felt like the millionth time the nagging, soul-furrowing questions raked through him. Where was Daniel? Was his grumpy, protective, teasing big brother even still alive?

A sharp cawing broke into his thoughts. His eyes flew to the wagon top. A large glossy raven stood silhouetted there, wings half raised, beak open as he cawed at the sky. Nehi felt Joe tighten beside him. He looked at the mute and found himself staring at what seemed a blank rock. Joe's wall had reared up between them. The mute motioned to the wagon door, standing open after Anna and Beau had disappeared inside. Joe leapt for the wagon top, one foot shoving off a wheel as his fingers curled around the short railing, heaving himself smoothly onto the top.

Nehi stood still, watching the wagon top. He saw Joe clucking at the raven, tickling it under the chin, feeding it, and the raven hopping and pecking at the mute as the bird made harsh noises. The light was gray, a mix of night and morning, and the scene came to him in silhouettes. But he thought he saw Joe pull something from the raven's talons, and a glint of white. A paper perhaps? The raven's head ducked and dove, as he dined with relish. The mute sat on his heels, still as stone, his back stiff, his head down staring at something on the wagon top, messy hair splaying over his face like a lion's mane. Nehi took a step toward the wheel to gain the wagon top and see what his friend had found. Then his eye darted to the yellow light spilling from the wagon's interior. He could see Anna through there. She stood mesmerized, staring at something above the little fold out table.

Curiosity pulled him two directions. Nehi chose the light and headed for the day room.

Chapter Six: Ravenized

"And he said, My presence shall go with thee, and I will give thee rest." - Exodus 33:14

"All right Beau," Anna said as she and Cobeau stopped at the back of the Ravens' wagon. She had to swallow a yawn, and blinked hard. She was never good at late nights, and this one had morphed into being practically morning. "I've followed you meekly and let you pull me away without even stopping to say goodbye to Elizabeth, or anyone. But I'm still mad at you and Joe. What did you want to show me?"

"Inside," Cobeau rumbled. Anna rolled her eyes and stepped through the familiar pointed door, painted like two leaning aspen trees crossed over each other. The wagon creaked and shifted with her movement, and she silently relished in it. The room was painted as if it were a mountain meadow flooded with morning sunlight and fringed with trees. Anna's gaze caught the large oak tree in the midst of the meadow. Open mouthed astonishment and delight overtook her annoyance and drowned it. There were the same two ravens she already knew, one large with a beak a little blunted and eyes lifted up to the heavens beyond the tree, with the small green-eyed raven still perched protectively underneath his outspread wings. But Anna had seen these before, and she hardly glanced at them.

Two other ravens perched in the tree. One clutched the branch beside Joe's raven. A handsome bird, strength radiating from him. His head tilted on one side as if he were trying to understand something. His eyes were dark and deep and thoughtful, and as she stared into them she knew it was Nehemiah. Nehi inside, his real self. Only as a raven. His beak stood open, and he seemed to be talking to the other new raven. Anna stared in surprised delight, knowing she was looking at herself. A beautiful, glossy, black bird perched a little above the other ravens. Its wings were a bit outspread as if it simply had too much life to sit still, black eyes bright and merry. Her head (for it certainly was a her though Anna couldn't tell how she knew it) tilted up and her beak stood open, either singing or cawing happily. With all the joy, there was strength in the way the raven perched, and wisdom in her look. Anna wondered in awe if she really was like that strong, joyful, beautiful raven.

Her eye caught the small green-eyed raven and she suddenly noticed a difference from when she had last seen it. The green eyes still shone with the same piercing energy and intelligence, still faced toward the room, and Anna still felt as if he were looking through everyone who entered his domain. But something else gleamed in those eyes, and in the little bird's stance, even in the lines around his beak. Anna felt a thrill run through her as she realized the difference. He had been a somber, solemn bird, wholly focused on watching for trouble entering his territory. Now she saw a hint of happiness, a joy in that raven that hadn't been there before. And the large raven was smiling in pure happiness. How on earth a realistic-looking raven could do that, she didn't know. But he was, and it was Cobeau's smile. And in the way his feathers ruffled, his head turned, the direction of the sparkle in his eye, Anna knew it was the two new ravens that made him smile like that.

"Well, I'll be," Nehemiah breathed over her shoulder. Anna turned to see him staring at his own raven, their skip-out bags hanging from one of his shoulders. His dark eyes studying the picture matched the thoughtful eyes of his raven to perfection. Anna turned farther and saw Joe leaning against the wall, his expression blank. Cobeau squatted beside the mute.

"Joe painted that," the chimera rumbled, a little superfluously. "He wouldn't stop. Repainted you, Miss Beauty, four times before he finally let it stay." Joe prodded him with his toe, and the chimera stopped. But as silence descended on the wagon, he stirred and spoke up again. "You see, Miss Beauty, you were never out of our thoughts. God wouldn't let you be after He put you in our hearts." Joe stirred a little uncomfortably.

"You're a part of us now. We need you. I'm sorry it took us so long to get back," he signed shyly. Anna nodded slowly, understanding it was a very special thing to be ravenized by Joe.

"It's beautiful," Nehemiah admitted. He turned and faced Joe and Cobeau, crossing his arms as a frown crossed his face. "Look, you two, if you've officially added us to your troupe we accept happily. But you're going to have to learn some things. Especially you, Joe." Joe blinked rapidly. Then his expression turned incredulous, uncomprehending. His eyes snapped and his face lit up in elation as he connected with Nehemiah's words.

"Joe," Anna spoke up, unable to hide her grin as the mute did a handspring to the other side of the wagon, giving a silent whoop, "that means you have to change a few things." Joe raised an eyebrow inquisitively at her. Anna found her eyelids were trying to close in sleep, forced them back up again, and went on. "If you really want us as part of you (and I like the idea) you're going to have to act like it."

"Right, and that means no more running away for six months only leaving a short note behind that says nothing much," Nehemiah added. "Instead tell us first, in person. Maybe there's another option than you disappearing, ever thought of that? Sometimes four heads can think of options only one head misses."

"Exactly. And it means telling us if you're in trouble," Anna put in. "This all goes for you too, Beau, are you listening?" Beau nodded, his brow creased in concentration. Anna covered a yawn. It had been a tiring watch waiting for Peter and Nehi to come back tonight, and she was renowned for falling asleep in a moment. "It means you can't just disappear, you have to let us know at least a little of what you're doing. Otherwise how am I going to make dinners on time?"

"And how are we going to know to come after you if you're in trouble?" Nehemiah said.

"Beau, you are going to have to tell us what you're doing too, you understand?" Anna said. The big man grinned happily at her, understanding this was a lecture about sticking together, and liking that.

"In general, Joe," Nehemiah finished up, "being a part of someone else's life means including them in your life. Being there to help when needed, and letting on enough about yourself for others to help you."

"Not as many secrets," Anna said. "We aren't saying you can't have some," she added with a smile at Joe's expression. He had gradually lost his elation. The mute wore a troubled look now. His eyes darted to something white folded on his palm, then back up to stare at Anna.

"So let's try this out," Anna said, a tired twinkle showing in her dark eyes. "What's wrong?"

"I'm leaving again. Glue's taking you up into the mountains..." Joe's hands trailed away.

"See, we're making progress already," Nehemiah said. He slumped into a chair at the table. "Earlier you wouldn't have told us that." Joe smiled, but it didn't quite erase the trouble on his face. Anna's eyes were blinking, trying to keep sleep from taking her over.

"I should have told you earlier about where you're going, I realize that now," Joe signed, quickly. Anna's eyes were closed, or she might have noticed his nervousness. All Nehi saw was that he was out of practice watching Joe sign, he missed several words. "See, I really did listen to you, and I really do understand." A gentle snore sounded from Anna.

"Ok, good," Nehi nodded. "So tell us now. Where are we going, and why haven't you told us about it?"

"There's no time," Joe said, biting his lower lip. "It would take too long, I have to leave now."

"Wait. You're leaving on your own? I thought you meant all of us," Nehi blinked. Joe spun, grabbing his hoverboard from behind the stove, and snatching a black shoulder bag from a corner. "Why on your own?" Joe shook his head, his lips pursed. "Oh come on, will you just explain?" Joe's hand shot up, moving into some sign. He pulled it back almost in the same instant, his shoulders moving in a shrug.

"It's too long of a story for now," he signed, his movements quick. "But I have to do it on my own. I had hoped I wouldn't have to be the one–" He broke off, his face pinched, and even Nehi could see the weariness there. Joe shrugged again, help-lessly, and headed for the door.

"You really aren't good at this whole 'sharing your life' thing," Nehi grimaced. "Joe, whatever you're running toward, remember God goes with you and you've got the VKs rooting for you. Be safe, and don't be such an idiot about Ann and me." Joe paused at the door, shooting him a grin. It held a teasing mysteriousness, a sprite-like impish relish in the knowledge that not knowing the details was driving his tall friend crazy. Nehi just frowned at him. "We can understand you now, and we want to. You told us you trust us. So learn to act like it!"

"If you're still talking to me after you find out on your own, I'll work on that," the mute signed swiftly, and hopped out the door into a shaft of light from the rising sun. Nehi stared at the spot where he had disappeared.

"If?" he muttered to himself. "I hope I saw that wrong." Ne-hemiah sighed and stood up to carry Anna into the night room. He yawned as he scooped her up. Her head lolled onto his shoulder and Nehi found his own eyes heavy with weari-ness. He dropped Anna onto the bottom bunk, then scrambled onto the top bunk. Whatever was going on he was certain of one thing; Joe wasn't going to explain unless he wanted to, chasing after him would just bring frustration to both of them. Nehi decided he would worry about it all after a nap.

Most of that decision came because he refused to admit how mad he was about not knowing what was going on. He refused to prove that impish grin of Joe's right.

Joe hopped out onto the grass and the door clicked closed behind him as he turned. Cobeau stood planted in front of him. The beeches waved gently over his head, greens, browns, and whites melding into a glorious morning as the sunlight grew around them. The big man stood solid, unhappy and un-comfortable.

"Don't like it," he grunted. Joe's hands flew, his signs a blur in the morning light.

"Believe me, neither do I! But your training worked, Meathead brought me the identification of the FF involved in the Geatland heist–" His eyes darted to the little square of white paper folded on his palm and his signs stumbled. He knew the handwriting, even scrawled in blood. And he knew what it meant for a strong man like Wulfgar to be calling for aid. It hadn't just been a heist. Swords against lasers? It had been murder. More death. More mourning and bloodshed. If only he had been there… Joe shook himself and slapped his big friend on the arm. "I know where to go, and I'll get in and out. It's ok. I'm better, Glue, the two weeks rest getting here was enough. It should be about three days."

"Don't like it," Beau growled. Joe rolled his eyes

"I have to get the book back. I need you to take the twins to the cabin, you know that." The mute flipped his hoverboard, making sure it was filled before turning it on. Beau stepped forward and enfolded his little friend in his arms. The mute gave in. He dropped his board and gripped his friend in a bear hug, his feet dangling in the air from the big man's embrace. The mute scrambled free and flipped to the ground.

"Take care of them for me, will you Glue?" Joe signed. Cobeau nodded.

"Miss Beauty and Nehi are good friends," the chimera rumbled. "Real friends. They won't drop you." Joe's hands flew up, signing an animated answer about siblings and vehicles, but stopped with a grimace.

"Thanks for the input, Glue. You can always read me. I'll join you at the cabin by the end of the week. If I don't, give Knee-High my notebook, I left it under the wagon. You understand, Glue?" Cobeau nodded. He caught the little mute to him again, hugging him tightly with all the gentle fervor of his immense, simple love, large tears running down his big face.

"Be careful, Master," he murmured, and for once Joe let the word stand. He laid a hand gently on his glue's cheek, nodded, squirmed out of his grasp, and flipped his board on. The soft hiss of steam broke into the morning air, and a squirrel launched into angry chatter high in a beech tree. Joe hopped onto the board, shifted it left and right in a pre-ride check, and leaned forward, his hands behind his back. The board shot off into the forest, disappearing in seconds, a dissipating trail of steam the only sign. Cobeau gave a little sob and turned back to the wagon. It was hard to let Joe go out on his own. He stopped and looked up past the sky.

"Jesus, watch over him?" he rumbled. The big man stood stock still for a moment, standing with his gaze on the brightening sky. He nodded his hairy head. "Thank you," he rumbled, and crossed to Prissy, already harnessed to the front of the wagon.

The mountains loomed in the distance, a jagged smudge of purple taking up the horizon. Beau stood still for a moment staring at the distant peaks.

A snarl rippled his lips.

Chapter Seven: The Geat's Book

"I laid me down and slept; I awaked; for the LORD sustained me." - Psalm 3:5

The mammoth swayed as she took another step. Her great three toed foot landed with a booming thud, spurting dust and dry pine needles. It left an indention in the red clay. Joe woke up where he lay curled between the monster's shoulder blades. He didn't open his eyes slowly, blinking, and stretching. That sort of activity was a luxury that would have gotten him killed during most of his life. Joe lay perfectly still, nothing to show his state had changed, his breathing unaltered. He registered the morning light and calculated the time and the direction he traveled, smelled the red clay spurting up from the animal's steps and knew what portion of the country he was in. And knew no one but the giant mammoth and the animal's invasive army of bugs moved and breathed near him.

Only then did Joe open his eyes and sit up. He laid his hand on the mammoth's shoulder, willing her to understand his silent thank you. The giant animal probably hadn't even noticed him. She certainly hadn't cared. But she let Joe get three hours of sleep as she moved him steadily the right direction, and offered the protection only two tons of matted fur and stink combined with massive tusks could afford. Joe gripped his hoverboard and slid down the sloped back, his bag tight against his back. He hardly noticed the smell and the bugs skittering in the rust-colored fur as he moved. He tipped over the edge, slipping his board under his feet as he fell. A spurt of white steam pushed into the early morning. It hit the red clay of the dry forest, and the mute shot off.

His muscles complained at him as they fell into the same position they had held so long yesterday. Joe grimaced and shifted uncomfortably. His board shifted with him, and Joe quickly stilled. He didn't have time for a wreck, not now. The note Meathead delivered meant the Geatland heist had worked. Which meant the FFs had completed their work at this outpost and would be picking up and moving. If they left before Joe reached their position, it could take him months to track down the Geatland book.

It had been over a year now, and he still hadn't caught up with the Bible. But that, at least, he prayed and hoped he could find soon. Wolf had dropped clues. If he could just manage this maneuver to keep Geatland and the Prophet's Kingdom from going into disintegration, he could finally start sniffing at the Bible trail. It would have reached Story Land by now. And if they stayed true to their past operations, it wouldn't leave for the People's Kingdom and Freddy's hands until after the dust had cleared from these two heists this week.

And Joe hoped to foil both the FFs' efforts. Which would mean new plans, which always took time, which would mean the Bible should still be in Story Land when he managed to reach the country. Oh Lord, let it be so! If he mistimed it and the book got into Freddy's headquarters, that would in-volve...a lot more trouble.

Joe's heel rammed into the back of his board, cutting off the steam and lifting its nose into the air. The back of the board hit the clay and dug a furrow as it skidded to a stop, Joe still riding it like a bucking horse.

Water. He could hear it, tinkling and splashing, somewhere through the brush and high pines of this country. Water meant a drink (glorious thought!). It meant being able to ditch some of the stink from his night ride, which would be neces-sary if he hoped to slip undetected into the FFs' camp. But it also meant other animals. Every waterhole teemed with life. And finding life in the wild lands usually meant death for something else. Joe flipped his board, clicking it to the holder on his back, and stole through the brush at a quick jog, his sen-

ses on the alert. One horns mooed and munched the dry grass to his left. He could hear the mammoth, steadily thundering her way toward a lower twist of the stream. Something skittered and clicked to the right... Possibly green backs. Joe slowed, veering left automatically. A flash of shiny green feathers glinted nearly a quarter of a mile away and he relaxed a little. That far, he was probably all right. And he did smell like mammoth right now, not like an incomplete.

Human.

He smelled like a human. Joe's lips pursed, his eyes tired as he pushed closer to the stream. A lifetime of being told he was different, having it pounded into him over and over, still surfaced some days. Most days, if he was honest. *"For thou hast made him a little lower than the angels, and hast crowned him with glory and honour[2]."* The verse rang in Joe's mind in Nehi's voice, rolling strong and vibrant as the mute stood alone, tired and sore, and headed for the enemy. Joe drew in a breath, letting himself relish the words again. The truth of his identity carried in that verse. And relishing the friend who had taken the time to speak the words in a moonlit clearing outside of Freedom.

A smile, wide and warm, changed the lines of his scarred face. It felt like a dream to have Nehi and Anna as actual friends; available for joking, laughing, comfort... It was a dream fulfilled, a hope the little mute had clung to through years of stark loneliness. But now... A sigh slid from him, his expression tightening. They would be nearing the cabin now. Tomorrow afternoon, probably around lunch, they would find out. Well, it had been awfully nice while it lasted.

The mute suddenly felt the loneliness around him, felt it pressing in like a well-known monster. One arm stole around his chest as his eyes darted around him, nervousness escalating. But no, he wasn't alone. Never alone now. Joe pulled at the

[2] Psalm 8:5

chain around his neck, drawing out the folk-art pendant of a raven in flight. He pressed the center of the bird's chest. The metal rearranged on his hand, sparkling in the sunlight. The last piece slid into place and Joe held a cross; simple, elegant, a symbol of a love that held him close, that created him special, and for a purpose. His tight shoulders relaxed as he stared at it. Even after he lost the twins' friendship, Jesus would still be with him. He was always near, always holding him fast, granting strength for the jobs He gave. The mute closed his fist on the pendant, feeling the sharp prongs between his fingers, letting himself have the moment of peace.

His shoulders squared again, he pushed the pendant back under his shirt, and trotted on, headed to the tinkling sound drawing him forward. He let it stay shaped as a cross, relishing the feeling of the cool metal against his skin. A risk, to let the shape remain in its true form and not masked by the flying raven. But a risk Joe felt willing to tolerate right now.

Sunlight glinted off water and Joe's eyes lit up, letting everything but a morning drink fall away. He shrugged his bag and jacket off, checked quickly to be sure it wasn't deep enough to harbor some of the more vicious aquatics out here, and slid in without a ripple or splash.

Fifteen minutes later, a small white trail of steam played out behind him as the mute rushed over the clay ground. Thirst satisfied, board refilled, and de-stinked. Well, a little de-stinked. Joe glanced up at the sun as it moved relentlessly across the sky. He leaned forward, increasing his speed to a reckless pace. The wind tore at him, whipping the tail of his mask into a frenzied thing. His muscles complained, some screaming at him as he balanced in the same position, again, and Joe grimaced. The mute squinted through his laser goggles, zooming in on the country ahead, looking for his target. His muscles cringed as he shifted his board and knew he wasn't as well recovered from these past months as he would have liked. He would have to watch himself today.

His goggles rushed over a bubble in the land. Joe's head whipped back to the area; his spine stayed stiff and straight, every other part of him unmoving, keeping the board balanced as he searched. There it was. As if God had been blowing the red clay through a straw one day, and it stuck like that. Joe shifted his board, zooming his goggles out and studying the lay of the land.

It lay in a dip, almost a canyon, the sides of the red walls rising up over the camp. Joe zoomed in again and picked out the two guards placed on the canyon walls. If he avoided those two, approaching by the side should be his best option for remaining unseen. He already had his scramblers running full blast, they should keep him under the digital eye of these people. Joe straightened, leaning back to slow his board. He let it carry him within a mile of the place, then hopped off, clicked it to his back, and started the hike.

Joe didn't plan as he moved. He had no idea what was inside that man-made bubble in the midst of the clay brush land. All he knew was the book needed rescued, or a weird little country would be blood-red with its own dead people. He just prayed Simmons had a job far, far away today.

"What kind of mountains don't even have trees?" Nehemiah grumbled. He dropped another pile of dry bushes beside their campfire and flung himself down beside Anna.

"My, my, still in a grump, are we?" she commented. Her eyes didn't lift from the glowing coals. She picked up a new stick and laboriously turned their dinner, shoving the bird deeper into the red coals.

"Come on," Nehi said, "admit you're mad at him too. Showing up after six months, dragging us away, then rushing off again immediately?"

"You're not mad at him for that," Anna commented absent-ly, rolling a potato out of the fire.

"I'm not? How do you know?" Nehi asked.

"You're mad at him for not taking you along."

An amused snort came from the darkness by the trees. Anna squinted and just managed to make out the head and shoulders of Beau, a darker patch in the midst of the darkness. The chimera was listening.

"Fine!" Nehi admitted, throwing his arms up. "I wish I was along on the adventure, whatever it is."

"New mountains, traveling hundreds of miles a day, and cooking over campfires just aren't enough of an adventure for you," Anna said. "Poor dear."

"He's going after the FFs, and that means information about our Bible," Nehi murmured, softly, almost a whisper. "You know he is. And he isn't taking us for a reason." Anna lifted her eyes from the coals and focused on Nehemiah, holding his gaze.

"All I know for sure, is that Joe said he needed us," she murmured back. "Then he sent us up here. Stop yapping about what we can't fix now, and try and help me figure out how to handle whatever's at the end of this ride." Nehemiah stared at her. He sat back slowly, his expression thoughtful. Anna kept rolling out potatoes. Four more plunked into her boots, steaming and hissing, and warming her toes on this cold night.

"Beau, are you sure we should be eating this bird?" she asked, spinning to the darker patch in the night.

"Not raven," Beau rumbled. She thought she saw his shoulders shrug.

"But somehow crow seems too much like a family member or something. I would hate to feel like I'm insulting Joe's birds."

"Birds eat each other, Ann," Nehi said. He grabbed a potato

then dropped it with a hiss, shaking his fingers. "They're not exactly known for their compassion."

"Butter, if you please," Anna commanded, choosing to change the subject. Nehemiah climbed to his feet and headed toward the wagon for the rest of the meal fixings. Anna began to call other items as she thought of them, slowly working the bird from the coals. Nehemiah shouted back, asking where the tray lived.

A low growl came from the chimera. Anna spun toward Beau, every sense suddenly alert.

"Quiet," he rumbled.

The crackling of the fire took over the night scene. Anna fingered the dirk she kept slung on her belt beside her drawing pad pouch, her eyes darting around the dark fringe of twisted bushes around their campsite. The silence outside their circle of firelight seemed to tingle around her. Everything was so still. No leaves rustling, no birds calling in the night...

"Found it!" Nehi shouted through the open door.

A woosh of huge wings reached for Anna, rushing at her. An enormous, rough caw filled the mountain side, a deep rumble that seemed mixed with a lion's roar. The scent of dead things and huge animal and burnt feathers rolled into her face.

Anna gagged and flung herself toward the fire. One hand jabbed up with her dirk, as the other swung a burning stick toward the sky. She heard a shout lift from Nehi, and felt the rumble in the ground as the chimera rushed toward her. The foul wind beat into her, stirring the fire, churning the flames and sending sparks spurting in every direction.

She saw the wings in the fire's light.

Feathers longer than her arm, speckled black and brown like a rattlesnake's pattern. They stretched around the campfire, easily twenty feet apart on the outward swing. Then they swung back in, and the air filled with smoke and heat and the putrid smell. Anna gagged again. It turned into a cough as black smoke filled her world. The fire snuffed out, the smoke filling her eyes and throat and nose.

Something gripped her waist. A talon punctured her side. Her body left the ground, lifted in that awesome grip. Anna punched her dirk down into the thing clutching her and jabbed upward with the stick. Black smoke poured from it, but the stick's end still glowed red. The stick hit something and she pushed it harder, shoving her strength into it as she jerked her dirk free and plunged it down again. Somewhere outside the whirling putrid wind and smoke, she heard Nehi screaming something and Beau's roar. Burning feathers, burning flesh, it filled her nostrils. The roaring caw rang around her. It rang through her, shaking her insides and rattling her brain as this creature shrieked.

The grip loosened. Anna dropped, banging into the hard dirt. Her neck jolted and the back of her head rammed into the ground. Beau's foot landed by her aching skull, shaking the ground as he rushed at the raptor. Nehi thundered up, dropping to one knee beside her, his goggles on and Hope pointed at the sky. The huge cawing roar filled the world again, echoing off the mountain side to come belting around them, twice, three times. But it trailed off. Lessening as the great raptor soared off in search of easier prey.

"Anna!" Nehi gasped, sweeping his goggles off and snapping them on Hope's holster, "Anna, are you alive? Speak to me, did it eat you?"

"Ok," Anna coughed. She sat up slowly, one hand on the small puncture wound dribbling blood, the other on the back of her head. "Ok, I'm fine with eating bird tonight."

A black-swathed arm stretched from the dark shadows

above the iron girders. The iron fitted together to form a frame, supporting the plastic bubbling into the temporary outpost. Every four feet another slim iron rafter stretched across the hallways, connecting one side to the other and strengthening the whole. Strings of lights stretched between the girders, sustainable bulbs providing a blue-tinted soft glow to light the building.

And providing a perfect habitat for the Black Raider. The shadows above the hanging lights were deep and predictable, ideal for Joe's movements.

His black-clothed arm slid a square screen over the lock on the door, then disappeared again out of sight. Melding with the darkness in the rafters. The screen scrambled codes and options. A series of numbers blinked once. The lock clicked open.

Two guards inside the room swung toward the door. One lifted a laser that hummed and glowed yellow, the other's hand darting toward the alarm button on her belt, both of them wide-eyed and frightened. The hallway stared back at them, starkly empty. Neither guard saw the small black pistol barrel at the top corner of the door. Two soft pops, and a wooden dart sunk into each of their necks. The guards' eyes rolled back in their heads. Their bodies folded forward, softly thumping into the ground. A shadow swung through the door and dropped softly into the room. Blue-tinted light spilled around the Black Raider as he slid to his feet, closing the door gently behind him. The room was small, more of a closet, and as he stepped forward he found he had to stand on one of the guards. But it boasted a meticulously clean atmosphere and perfect climate control for protecting ancient documents.

The book rested on a small table in the center of the room. Joe whipped his bag from his shoulder and had the container open in a moment. As he reached for *Beowulf* and lifted it off the pedestal his movements slowed, becoming gentle and almost reverent. The black book fit perfectly inside his container; Joe knew its dimensions and had prepared for its transport. The paperback crackled and a sliver of yellowed paper tumbled off as he laid it inside. But the silver chain mail of the warrior set against the black background still sparkled in the light. Joe clicked the container closed reverently.

A moment to situate it inside his black bag, and he tightened it onto his back and darted to the door, his eyes on his scanners. Two FFs strode down the hallway, and he could hear their voices, discussing what to dismantle next as they broke camp. Their noise dwindled, then disappeared, and the door opened silently. A black shadow slid out and swung into the darkness of the ceiling. The door clicked closed again and the shadow crept forward. Above the lights, shifting over the rafters through the deep shadows. People rarely thought about keeping a ceiling secure. And they rarely remembered to look up.

The Black Raider stole on, quickly working his way to the edge of the makeshift building. The Raider paused as the sharp ring of metal and the voices of workers reached him from farther up his hall. They were dismantling the frame there. Taking down the tent, readying to leave.

Drat it. That had been his extraction point. Joe gripped his beam, perching like a lemur on the slender metal bar, studying his options. He could just go straight through, puncturing a hole in the top of this place... But they would feel the warm air, the changed lighting, and know he had been here. If they knew he had been here, it would be the work of a moment to track him. Joe did not want a running battle on his hands all the way to the cabin. A sigh blew from him under his mask and he slunk off to explore. Time to find a second way out.

Eight minutes later, Joe was still looking. Another group of agents turned out of a room, moving in an informal march, their bags packed and slung over their backs. Joe ground his teeth in frustration. He had to get out of here fast, before someone went checking on the book!

He froze, his eyes riveted on a doorway opening two yards down the hall.

A familiar form peeked out. Joe could see the man's stomach wobble even from that far away. Freddy's red hair seemed almost purple as the blue-tinted light hit it. The door closed softly behind the FF leader. Joe crouched, staring. Three seconds ticked by. Then he gave up and let himself follow his curiosity. He stole closer, reaching into his bag of tricks as he moved.

He cupped three smoke bombs in his hands, ready and on the alert. Just in case. Only when he felt prepared for anything did he slide his goggles on, adjusting the dials and letting his attention slide into the room down the hall. At first all he saw was a smudge of white and blue. Then it picked through the wall and focused inside the room. Freddy leaned over a table, an intricately embroidered bag open in front of him and a black jewelers cloth splayed over the tabletop. White gloves covered his hands and Joe idly wondered how long it would be before the circulation left his fat fingers.

Precious jewels and intricate goldwork lined the table. The pieces sparkled in the blue light, sending colors darting into corners and off the iron beams. A smoldering rage stirred in Joe's heart. The handsome, brave Wulfgar rose in his memory, along with the hundreds of miners and jewelers who had given their livelihoods to place that fortune safely within their kingdom's barrow. They sacrificed to ensure following generations would have what was needed to protect their history, to keep the kingdom alive. And now here was this cretin, this weakling with blood on his hands, rifling through them like a sack of apples. Joe's hands tightened on the iron beam, his knuckles white.

A blue hologram spurted into life inside that room, projecting from the wall. A dead wolf's head turned slowly. The wolf moved, like a puppet, as a voice barked into the room.

"Getting a head start at dividing the loot, Freddy?"

Freddy jerked, the sapphire he clutched spilling from his hand and tumbling to the floor.

"No!" he gasped. "No, no, of course not. Just admiring them, old thing, only admiring." He reached down and picked up the sapphire. His voice came again, even and steady. "They really are perfect. Fashioned with love, one might say. You ought to be careful, popping out of walls like that, you nearly gave me a heart attack."

"That may not be all I give you if any of those gems are missing," the voice drifted from the wolf's head. Cold, matter-of-fact. "Put them back, Freddy, all of them. And listen, I have orders." Freddy began to carefully repack the gems as the Wolf went on. "The skitterers are in place, and even better than I expected. They'll slip in over the heads of the Prophet's Peace. With your FFs distracting the Black Army with the Geats, that heist should go like a dream. And meanwhile across the world, we've had yet another overthrow in Story Land."

"I have heard rumors," Freddy nodded.

So have I, Joe thought, his mind on his necklace heading for delivery.

"The Hernons are in control now. Unofficially, but whatever, everyone knows they're the real power. I can use them to get at that book."

"Another?" Freddy asked. Joe could only see the back of his head, but he could almost hear the man's eyebrows go up in that question. "So soon after two others, and with the People's Kingdom already in the planning?"

"It's only overreaching if you don't pull it off," the Wolf said. "The Trio and I will handle Story Land, you don't have to worry your pretty red head about a thing. Just make sure you get these two wrapped up. Send Simmons to the cabin tomor-row, tell him to report to the old lady. Oh, and Freddy?"

"Yes?"

"Open the door. I want to see this."

Alarms roared through Joe, fear dropping into the pit of his stomach and twisting it. He jerked his goggles off, his head whipping around the hallway.

Agents stepped out of doorways. Ten, fifteen, no twenty of them. A beam of light hit his rafter, circling him like a deadly net, killing his shadows.

Chapter Eight: Snake Hunters

"Therefore to him that knoweth to do good, and doeth it not, to him it is sin." -James 4:17

Joe leapt off, arching for the next beam down the hall like a monkey. His right hand poured smoke bombs as he moved. A dense cloud of black smoke sprayed into the hallway as the bombs left Joe's hand. Hacking and gasping burst from the FFs. A burly agent grabbed a cryo tube and opened the valve, a roar ripping from him as freezing air sprayed over the bombs. Shouts and curses rose around him as FFs staggered away, hair and skin burned by the cold. But the smoke froze, the bombs turned to solid chunks of ice, and thudded into the ground.

Sunlight sprayed down on the agents and watering, streaming eyes turned up to the ceiling. A ragged hole gaped at them, the arid heat of the dry lands pouring in. A black boot slid out of sight.

"Move!" Freddy roared, his fat face contorted with anger. To come so close and still have the little Raider slip away! And in front of the Wolf...something like that could do more than just tarnish a reputation. It could mark him as a disappointment and bring assassins in the night. Freddy felt sweat gathering under his collar. He stormed into the hall, his strafing laser pulled from where he kept it hidden in his belt, screaming at any agent unfortunate enough to be caught at the back of the flood flowing out to chase down the Black Raider.

Joe scrambled over the bulbous plastic, the ceiling giving under his touch like some kind of evil, half-inflated bounce house. Shouts came from the guards on the hills. Joe dropped to his belly and rolled. White laser bursts lit up around him, melting the plastic. He leapt to his feet and ran, the toes of his soft boots gripping the plastic, zig zagging haphazardly, making for the edge of this place.

All around him, from every direction, came shouts and curses and orders. The whole base had him pinpointed. One against fifty? A hundred?

This was untenable. Unbeatable. And if he died here, the Geats died with him. Joe scanned the area, his mind running through options, looking for anything to help. White laser bursts broke around him, lighting up his world like monstrous, deadly fireflies, drowning out the sunshine.

Sharp cawing broke through the chaos, and Joe's head whipped toward it. A flock of terns. Huge birds, eight feet across, their wings creating a windstorm as they beat the air, just at the edge of the canyon.

A beam shot through his arm and Joe staggered with a silent yell, his feet catching on the plastic. He fell into a roll, calculated to draw him closer to the edge, where this temporary building tumbled off into the dry lands. He was up again in an instant, leaning forward, everything in him focused on the nearest tern. A male, rising slowly. Even with his huge wingspan, it still took time to get his bulk airborne. Joe flew towards him, a black streak in the dry air, abandoning even his zig zags. The screams and curses and whining laser blasts collided with the wind from the birds, their frightened deep-throated squawks. A burning pain sliced through his side, clipping muscles and ribs, drawing ash and smoke and blood. Joe flipped open the flap on the right sleeve of his jacket as he raced. Gadgets and emergency tech lay under it, each item carefully in its own little slot. He snapped up the paracord and pushed the flap down again. Joe's boot shoved off the edge of the building.

For an instant the scene seemed to slow around him. Dry air whipped into his face through the mask, stinging his eyes. Nothing but air around him, the ground ten feet below, white lasers flashing in bursts all around his body. FFs filed out of the building, falling into a loose formation, their lasers' constant whine turning into a hum pulsing in his brain. Joe shot up, legs coiled ready, muscles bunched. Reaching for the only means he had to get out. Reaching for a crazed idea in a crazy, crazy world. Joe's uninjured arm shot out and the paracord snaked forward.

The cord slid over white feathers and dropped back down again. Joe grabbed it, holding both lines as the middle tightened over the bird's neck. A furious, squawk rolled over the land as the tern jerked left, the sudden 97 extra pounds shocking his flight. The jerk was all that saved the bird. Ten lasers hit the spot he had just been, bursting into blinding light. Joe sailed up in a beautiful arch, launching himself past the bird, higher into the air. He let go of one end of the cord. For an instant he went weightless, his arms out, one leg coiled, the surreal feeling of nothing solid around him pressing down on his chest.

Only crazy could save him now. The unexpected, the thing no shooter could predict.

Joe's boot landed solidly on a bird's back. He let himself take a full second to gain his footing, feeling her tremble, feeling her scream in fury and fear.

In that second Joe calculated angles and his own adrenaline-fueled strength. The birds' movement around him, the shooters on the ground. A part of him saw Simmons' sleek hoverer steaming towards them at a furious pace. That would turn all the tables toward the FFs. And if he fell into Simmons hands... He shut it out. Shut out how far away the ground was. Shut out how stupid this was, how impossible.

That no matter how far he ran, the FF would track him now they had him pinpointed.

He couldn't survive this without help. But God had denied him that, leaving him on his own again. He shut it out.

Everything in him focused on the moment. To surviving

another minute.

Joe jumped, arching through empty air. Higher. Farther. Reaching for another living stairstep into heaven.

"Boss, didn't you see the captives executed yesterday?" Taban growled. Atif grimaced inside. He hated it when his men called him "boss" as if he were a gang leader. But he didn't speak his annoyance. Instead, he raised his scanner again and zoomed in on the bulbous building lying below them in the canyon. There was great beauty in this land, without the building. Green bushes and short, flat trees sprinkled among the dry conifers clinging to the red clay. Abundant animal life moved around them, and surprisingly only about a quarter of it deadly. A fox ran past, and Atif followed it with his glasses, the little animal's bones showing up an eerie white beneath the rippling fur. Atif followed it to where the glob of clay-colored, rounded building spilled over the grass like a bulbous slug. He could see into some of the rooms with his glasses. But the interesting things seemed to always happen deeper inside.

"Are you even listening?" Taban asked. "A well placed mine, timed correctly, and the entire complex would fold in on itself."

"I could get you that," Shareef commented brightly, and Atif lost his frown. Those words were becoming a mantra among the little group. Shareef could get anything. He had managed to get them all papers and passes to walk through any border with impunity, as well as a host of equipment. With their new freedom, Naqi's tech knowledge, Shareef's supplies, Taban's weapon skills, and Otar's loyal strength, Atif was feeling decidedly overwhelmed by the possibilities. He wouldn't admit it to his team, but that was the main reason he still had them camped on this red clay, watching, after having found Simmons ten days ago.

"We don't know enough," Atif answered Taban, for once not trying to play coy. "These people are evil, they are dangerous to our brothers and sisters, we have heard the tales and seen the deeds they wreak. But there is more to this. They are playing at something big, planning something larger than an occasional snatching of Christians. We need to know more."

"How much more?" Taban didn't growl. He asked it, needing to understand what they were looking for. The glasses picked through the rooms, eerie white glowing skeletons showing the people. They scurried busily, beginning something. Activity was definitely happening down there.

"This is the belly of the snake," Atif said slowly, his eyes still on the building. "We need the head if we are to kill it."

"The belly has an evil smell," Otar rumbled, his nose wrinkled in distaste. Everyone looked at him. The big man rarely spoke, and even a slight descriptive statement was a new trait they hadn't seen in him. "That man Simmons is evil. Demented with it."

"He is good at what he does though," Taban said. "Which is why we should charge in now, while he is out."

"They are breaking down the building," Naqi commented. Everyone turned their attention back to the busy hum of activity happening at the slug like camp. Quiet settled over the team. Otar stumped over and dropped next to Naqi as the tech man stared at his personal pad, keeping tabs on the enemy. Naqi held up a bag of dried fruit, and it was accepted gladly. Shareef spun toward them and settled on the red clay, munching fruit with his two team members. Taban paced restlessly, like a caged tiger, glowering at the enemy with hunger in his eyes. Atif stood still, his glasses trained on the building.

Somewhere deep inside shouting rose.

"Gear up," Atif ordered sharply. Behind him his team

scrambled, grabbing items and slipping on protective gear. Atif stood stock still, watching.

A circle of the ugly material ripped, flying up like a trap door. Atif's glasses zoomed in on the area, sliding off x-ray in time to watch a black figure dart out into the sunshine. Small, thin, nothing visible but black leather and the hoverboard strapped to his back. The tail of his mask trailed behind him as the small figure gained his feet and ran, his toes digging into the building. Lithe, quick, his darting movements those of an experienced warrior in evasion tactics to avoid enemy fire. Shouts rose from every part of the complex. Somewhere inside someone screamed orders, the anger in the voice making the words almost incomprehensible. White laser blasts flashed into life around the black figure darting along the building.

"Who is that?" Taban asked in some awe, snapping his vest on and slipping his twenty-three weapons into their places.

"Enemy or ally?" Shareef demanded, gathering bags and shoving things in pockets.

"He does not appear on any intel," Naqi reported, "a ghost to the machines. Well, except now we know he's there, and so does the enemy. I am watching all their tracking devices honing in on the black one."

"Do we help this one get out?" Otar growled.

As the figure dropped and rolled (almost certainly hit), Atif's glasses picked up one more thing. A metal cross dangled on a chain around this strange little person's neck. He snapped his glasses onto his belt, his habitual great coat flaring in the dry breeze. Atif didn't need to gear up. He lived in his gear. He spun, his matched healy lasers snapping into his hands, their whine filling the campsite as he faced his team, his voice deadly as he answered them.

"We help."

"Are you sure we're getting close?" Anna asked as she gazed at the gray, rocky heights around her. "This looks close to nowhere." When Joe signed mountains, Anna's thoughts had flown to her own loved mountains in what used to be the Sojourner's Kingdom. Her mountains had carefully tended forests and majestic peaks, covered in waving grasses and sheltering hosts of fat game animals. They inspired feelings of repose, of great peace and ease mixed with majestic adventure.

This marked day three of traveling through the mountains of KAM, and each hour became barer and rockier. Peaks rose up higher and higher into jagged tors that looked as if they were trying to skewer the clouds. They left all vegetation except for a few scrubby pines and bushes that clumped together at the end of valleys. No animals had exposed themselves to view, except for one very skinny weasel, and one large black raven cawing over their heads. Although after the giant raptor incident, Anna couldn't be too sorry about the lack of other living things.

"This place doesn't look inviting," Nehemiah said.

"Where are we going, Beau?" Anna tried again, for the forty-fourth time. (Nehemiah had been keeping count.)

"To a cabin to meet Joe," Cobeau replied again. Nehemiah sighed and Anna grinned at him. No matter how they worded the question that was the only reply they could wheedle from him. It seemed to be the only reply in his large, fuzzy head. Almost certainly that idea had been put there by Joe.

The wagon jerked and jostled over the rough track that made an excuse as a road. Protruding rocks, sudden sinkholes, roots jutting up, there were too many obstructions for a safe hover ride. If the steam jets coiled on the bottom of the wagon pushed off a rock on one side and a pothole on the other, it could cause the wagon to veer and smash into the side of the mountain. Exploding steam tanks are not a pretty thing, and the twins and Beau willingly chose a slower, bumpier ride rather than risk ending up like a steamed bun.

The morning sun beat on the twins' heads as the track tipped suddenly up, winding toward a high, solitary tor scraping the clouds. Prissy leaned into her harness, straining as she pulled the wagon up the steep incline. Anna felt herself tilting backward in her little seat on the roof, and had to quickly adjust. The pig's wheeled shoes began to spin and squeak. Beau pulled the wagon to a stop, slamming the brake down with all his massive strength. One side of the track dropped into shale hillsides, so steep they could almost be called cliffs. On the other side, cracked rock walls jutted straight up. The chimera slid off the bench and his boots scrunched into the rocks, as Nehi slipped off the other side. They quickly slid the pig's wheeled shoes off, checking straps and rubbing her nose, making sure the pig was comfortable in her work. Nehemiah silently thanked heaven he got the side next to the solid wall not the drop off as he handed the shoes to Beau and scrambled back onto the wagon top. Beau settled in his seat, clicked to the pig, and they started up the steep incline again.

For three hours, that interruption remained the most interesting thing in the morning. The wagon rattled and jolted, on and on.

They turned around another bend and the pig suddenly perked up. Prissy's head bobbed rapidly. She let out a piercing squeak, and Anna felt the change in the pull under her as the pig shuffled faster.

"What's she doing?" Nehemiah asked.

"Smells her hay," Cobeau rumbled. They rounded a great mound of rocks and, to the twins' shock, found a vast wooden door set in the side of the mountain. It looked as if a farmer had mislaid his barn door. Prissy stopped, tossing her large head, her piercing squeaks echoing off the mountainside.

"Nehi, open please?" Cobeau asked. Nehemiah climbed off

the wagon, pushed the heavy doors, and his boots dug into the rocky dirt as he shoved it open. The doors swung inward, taking him along as they moved, and he stumbled into a dry cave. It was large, he could sense that, but all he could really see was dense blackness.

A soft, furry head rammed into his side, shoving him to the left. Nehi grinned and moved farther to let Prissy by. The pig slid past, the wagon rumbling behind her. Nehi followed, feeling his way over the uneven floor, glad of the sunlight spilling through the door behind him. The pig snuffled happily and headed to a corner. Cobeau hopped off the wagon, flipped a switch, and flooded the place with light. The twins looked around them in awed delight. The gray uneven sides of the cave sparkled in the light, ornamented with natural crystals. Pearly stalactites hung above them, catching the sheen of the artificial bulbs. On a second glance, they saw it was also a barn. The wagon fit in easily, and Prissy had her own little corner comfortably set up.

Beau hummed, an excited smile on his face, as he filled her trough with fresh water from a spigot set in the wall. Nehemiah wondered what the chimera was excited about as he offered a hand to assist Anna's jump from the wagon and the twins unhooked the pig's harness. Beau pointed at a set of hooks driven into the wall. Nehi and Anna obediently hung the pig's tack from the hooks, noting the perfect length for each piece. Beau nodded once, his silent acknowledgment of a job well done, and headed for a small door on the far side of the cave. He pulled it open and a draft of cold, thin air whistled into the barn from a tunnel. Prissy squeaked, a shrill, obvious request to close the door. The chimera stepped through and began to stride up the winding tunnel. The twins trotted after him, closing the door gently behind them.

The walls of the cave slid down and in, and soon enclosed them in a tight passageway. But air flowed through it, and geodes poked out of every nook, shimmering in what little light hit them, glimmering in a host of different colors. It was enchanting. Beau kept them at a trot, and after two twists another wooden door came in sight. The chimera shoved it open and the twins found themselves blinking and grimacing as bright sunlight and a wailing wind hit them. They stepped out onto a skinny pathway running along a single peak, a shale-filled hill falling steeply beside it. Cold, high mountain air rushed over them as they looked up the rocky path leading over the harsh mountain ground. At its apex a small cabin perched crazily near the top of the jutting tor they had headed for all morning. The peak reached far into the sky, seeming to watch every move made on the mountain below it. Cobeau quickly trotted over the six yards of rocky path, his feet scrunching on the rocks, and threw open the door of the cabin.

"Joe? Are you here?" he called. Such happy expectation rode his bellow, Anna desperately hoped Joe would answer him. Joe didn't answer. But another voice did. A caustic, heckling voice that drawled and grumbled more than it spoke. It sliced through Anna and Nehemiah's chests and seemed to freeze their systems. They stood with one foot on the porch, the other on the step, ears ringing as their hearts began to labor.

It couldn't be.

Chapter Nine: Lost and Found

"Mine enemies would daily swallow me up: for they be many that fight against me, O thou most High. What time I am afraid, I will trust in thee." -Psalm 56:2-3

Atif and his team skimmed over the red clay on their hoverboards, closing the distance to the enemy. They hadn't been noticed yet. A bird's squawk lifted over the shouts and whines. A sharp expletive came from Shareef, and they all looked up again, searching for the black one.

A small, slim figure swung into empty space, a slender cord draped over a big white bird the only thing keeping him from falling into his enemy's grip. The figure let go, the rope snaked off, and the team watched with open mouths as the black one flew higher into the blue sky, arms out, leg tucked. He landed on top a bird. The creature squawked and spun, trying to snap at the thing driving its flight down. The black one sprung off again, lightly, quickly, like a deer through the grass. Only he was twenty feet straight up in the air. He landed on another bird's back and sprang away, one boot pushing off its head as the animal squawked and flapped. The black one spiraled gently like an arrow through empty air. The rope shot from his grip, snaking around a fourth bird. The cord tightened, the bird screamed, and the black one swung at the end and skimmed upward with the skill of a monkey. Going up, always up.

The sound of hissing air and a powerful machine reached Atif and he snapped his attention back to earth.

A gold-colored hoverer shot toward the temporary base. Atif hit the button on his goggles and zoomed in. Simmons watched the scene from that hoverer. His face rippled with an animal fury, and his arm swung up with a make of gun even Atif didn't recognize.

"Now, Otar!" Atif ordered, and hit the button to kill the steam under him. His board slammed into the ground as the team fanned out with perfect efficiency.

A mindless yell loosed from Otar as his finger shoved down on the trigger. The metal tube on his shoulder rocked with the recoil and his feet dug a furrow in the red clay as the force shoved him backward. A mine arched through the air. A black ball, like an old-fashioned cannonball, sailed through the clear blue sky. It landed in the barn-sized doorway of the clay-colored building. A yellow fireball dimmed the sun. The treated plastic that made up the temporary building shriveled, curling on itself like Styrofoam in a campfire.

It bubbled and melted, as the sound of the explosion rolled out and struck Naqi. The young man's ears hummed and his eyes sparked even with the laser goggles dying the world blue around him. But he ignored the noise, the tremors under his feet as more and more mines were launched, and the screams of the wounded. His fingers flew along his slick Peterson Personal, each key recognizing his DNA, the weight and speed of the touch, and responding instantly. The delicate handheld found every electrical circuit and security detail in the building in twelve seconds. Cracking the system was a little harder, and Naqi worked patiently as he ran behind Atif, never more than two feet away from his leader's back.

Atif circled and spun, the plated armored jacket pulling at him with its weight. He felt impact after impact hit him and deflect off, as he moved stolidly closer to the hoverer steaming down toward them. His matched pair of healy laser pistols kicked rhythmically in his fists, again and again as he fired. The enemy at the base swung toward the team. Eight smart ones ran forward and slammed a wide shield in front of the crowd gathered outside. Agents ducked behind it, and laser fire began to brighten the day around Atif and his men.

Simmons stayed focused on the black one, curse the evil

man. The weapon in his hand fired. Silver wires spread out in the sunshine as it sailed straight toward the black one, his left arm reaching higher to heave himself up the rope. The silver webbing hit the black one's outstretched left arm. It wrapped around it, encasing it. Even from his position on the ground, Atif saw the sparks shoot over the wires. The smoke rising from the leather sleeve. The black one contorting, his hold on the rope loosening.

The black one tumbled into a free fall, the wires sparking and smoking as they dug deeper into him. The small form writhed, his body arching with the agony. Simmons veered his hoverer underneath the falling form. Waiting to catch him, to inflict his evil on the one who dared invade the temporary headquarters. Simmons jammed something down his gun's barrel and took aim at the black one again. Atif's face hardened. A yell ripped from his throat, and he spun, his back to the enemies crouching behind the shield. He raced for the hoverer, tucking his healys back into his belt and reaching for a shell. Atif's thumb hit the button on the top of the black egg in his hand. A red light began to blink. He spun on one leg and flung it underhand. The shell rolled underneath the hoverer as the vehicle steamed gently in place.

For an instant in time movement happened faster than Atif could track it.

Simmons dove from the hoverer, dropping the gun and landing in a roll.

The black one flicked his right arm. A white line of smoke and fire shot from the palm of his hand. The force of it kicked him through the air, toward the only cover nearby, and away from the hoverer.

Atif hit the ground, covering his face.

Then the shell exploded.

"So you've finally decided to come back, have you Cobeau? Where's the smelly pig and the little guy?" the voice called from the cabin.

No mistaking it. No one else had that voice. Pictures of growing up swirled in the twins' minds, of countless meals around their simple sweet table, with their mother and father and older brother, the teases and laughter and life. They reeled under the overwhelming intensity of the sorrow and joy that rushed through them. But then a desperate, desperate need to hold the owner of that voice eclipsed everything.

Nehi acted on it first. His legs picked up and he dashed for the door. It couldn't be. But that voice! Nehi's throat felt hot and close and his vision shook as his feet hit the carpet. A part of him registered he was enfolded in well-kept comfort, surrounded by nothing new but everything homey. Checkered blue couches, cozy dining nook, old pictures, faded print curtains. But all he really saw, with laboring heart and a choked sob, was the tall figure who stepped through the paneled door just ahead of them.

Daniel Hillson's jaw dropped. His dark eyes opened so wide they almost hid his eyebrows. Nehi's sob escaped as an explosive, wet laugh. Then he found his feet again and he and Anna pelted into their brother. At that instant, Nehemiah didn't even consider it was more like a six-year-old than his seventeen years. All he wanted, all he needed, was to get his arms around his brother's ribs and squeeze; to feel the breath come and go in his lungs, to hear Daniel say his name. To know he was alive.

"Daniel, Daniel, we've been looking for you so long," Anna murmured in a sort of sob as she held on just as tight below Nehemiah's grip.

"You're alive!" Nehemiah gasped, his voice muffled against Daniel's shoulder.

"And so much has happened!" Anna said, her voice wet.

"You're alive!" Nehemiah laughed.

"Not for much longer if you don't let me breathe," Daniel wheezed. The twins pulled back, laughing and unashamedly rubbing their hands over their eyes. Daniel staggered back against the wall, his arm stealing around his rib cage. But his eyes never left their faces. An explosive laugh, almost identical to the sound Nehi had just made, came from him. Then he lunged forward and caught the twins and pulled them close. There was a tremble in those arms and Nehemiah found he was laughing, and wasn't quite sure over what. But the others joined in. Words began to spill out, running into each other, mixing with the laughter, all of it incoherent. It was Anna who took a deep breath to steady herself, and pulled away to look her older brother over, brushing a hand across her eyes to clear them again.

"You're thin. And pale. And your face! Daniel, what happened to you, are you all right?" Nehemiah stopped talking and stepped back to take his own perusal. Daniel did look worn. He was of the same good build and handsome, dark features as the twins, but now there was a pallor beneath the olive skin. And the left side of his face, from his chin curving up to his scalp, was scarred almost to the point of being unrecognizable.

"I wasn't, Anna, but I'm better now. Or at least, mostly better. The Ravens stashed me here with a sweet old couple, good at healing. I'm almost completely well again thanks to their excellent choice of caregivers. But look at you two! You're a woman now, Anna. And what a woman! And you Nehi, you're taller than me! And..." Dark eyes locked onto dark eyes and the two men studied each other. Daniel nodded and finished his sentence quietly. "A man." Nehemiah gave a little laugh and threw his arm over his brother's shoulders, just blissfully, overwhelmingly, happy to be reunited again. The group moved into the small pine paneled living room and found a wiry old woman with a spoon chasing Cobeau around the coffee table as the chimera sucked on his fingers. Something gray dripped off his hand.

"You stay out of my cooking, you great hulking–" the woman spluttered. She caught sight of Anna and Nehemiah and stopped. She dropped a shocked curtsy, her wrinkled face sharp and her mouth pulled into what looked like a habitual sneer.

"Alma, this is my brother and sister," Daniel introduced with a brilliant grin. His scars twisted the expression, giving it a sardonic, mischievous look, as if he was forever laughing at the crazy things that went on in this world. The old woman dropped another curtsy and moved back through a swinging door, offering a fleeting glance of a white and red kitchen, muttering something about setting dinner for three more. Cobeau dropped onto a worn yellow high-backed chair in the corner, smacking and smiling. Daniel and Anna plopped on the checkered blue couch, Nehemiah perched on an ottoman just in front of them with his scuffed boots scraping the little pleated fringe that ran around the couch. The three looked at each other. So much to say, so much to ask, and such a sudden shock to find themselves together... Where to start, to begin picking up the threads of life after two years apart?

"I heard about the disintegration, and Mom and Dad," Daniel said, dropping his eyes. His smile disappeared, replaced by a sorrow that slid into lines beside his eyes and mouth, lines that marked the mourning as permanent and deep. The mention of their dead parents had the same effect on the twins, the sudden heavy sorrow that had become a part of them. But for Anna and Nehemiah it was strangely comforting to know another soul on this globe still mourned with them. "It was after the fact, too late to do anything about it, and I was buried too deep to go anywhere by the time I did hear. What happened to you two when the crash came? Were you all right? You look good now." Anna and Nehemiah looked at each other. Those four months of despair, of horror and enslavement, stampeded through their minds. Nehi pulled back, his mouth tightening. He didn't want to go into it, not now. Not when he was so happy to have just found Daniel.

"God is good, and we are all right now," Anna answered. Nehemiah nodded, realizing that summation was perfect. It would do for now, anyway. Daniel looked from one to the other, grimaced, and dropped his eyes again. Anna noticed a muscle in his jaw twitching.

"I'm so sorry I wasn't there to help," Daniel burst out. "You shouldn't have had to go through that, through anything like a disintegration, and especially not alone." He looked back up and forced a smile. "But we've found each other now. Together we can conquer the world, and get our own country back too. So don't worry about life, okay, I'll help work it out. Now tell me what you're doing here! How did you meet up with that little scavenger Joe and his big chimera and find me?"

A horrible suspicion suddenly pulled over Nehemiah's happiness like an icy blanket.

"Wait, how long have you known the Ravens?" he asked.

"Oh, I guess it's been close to a year and a half by now."

Bird-scented air swirled around Joe as he scurried up the paracord. The bird wobbled, cried, and fought to stay airborne. It sent his rope gyrating in crazed circles, making climbing extremely difficult, and his muscles jumped and complained in exhaustion. He had nothing to spare to calculate events going on below. But part of him, always on the alert, always afraid, still tracked Simmons. It noticed the man's hand swing up. Noticed the gun fire. Saw it headed for him.

The wires slammed into Joe's wounded arm and wrapped around it, encasing it, and biting deep.

They sparked and burned, digging in. Deeper with each debilitating spark, sending lightning through his spasming muscles and nerves. Joe screamed, his throat raw with the gurgling, wet sound. His mind blacked at the pain. His body relaxed, dropping the rope.

Move! The voice sparked through him, stronger even than the pain. The part of Joe that never slept, always on the alert, always goading him to watch and stay alive. *Move or you die!* Joe's eyes flew open. The world came back in a swirl of colors and incapacitating, burning, eating pain. Air cut into him as he free fell, heading straight toward– Simmons! The terror burned higher than anything. It took over Joe and he moved without thinking, desperate and gasping, as the wires sparked rhythmically through him.

His right arm curled, slipping under his jacket flap, cupping a fire canister in his palm. His thumb jabbed the activator. Flames and smoke roared from the tube and Joe writhed as it burnt through his glove, bubbling on his skin. The force of the shot propelled him up and to the right. Away from Simmons. Joe's hand moved again, fingers clumsy and smoking. He hit the button deploying his glider. A sheet of treated dragon skin from Faeryland flung into the air, attached to his jacket's collar with two slim cords. It caught the air and billowed up.

Joe, sick from the pain pulsing rhythmically into him, eating at his arm, the world a blur of colors and shapes, knew it wasn't enough. The tall green pines were the only place to disappear from sight, and they were too far. His glide wasn't high enough, he would smash into the ground halfway there and be left lying in the open.

He was lost.

Simmons would snatch him up. A breath sucked into his lungs, a gasp of pure horror, everything around him swallowed in the feeling. He shook, his mind swirling off into nightmares as the pain wracked him.

A roar of heat and flames burst into life. It hit him from below and hot air filled his glider. The draft sent him shooting up, faster and higher. Straight toward the tall conifers that offered the only shelter he could reach. Joe gasped as hope invaded him. A little of the pure terror faded, just enough for him to regain some of his mind. He clung to it, dragging more of himself up from the pain and horror, forcing himself to focus and prepare for the crash landing.

He skimmed the top of the first trees, sharp pine needles and bark slamming into him. Joe smashed through it, his glide dropping lower with each second. He tumbled into the next tree. His burned hand gripped a branch and he jerked to a stop, the bark biting into him. The wires sparked and he screamed, everything going dark again. *Get it off. Get it off now or you're done!* The voice deep inside shrieked at him. It wouldn't let him drop and die, not while he could still move. It would never leave him alone.

Joe pulled into a flip, his breath bursting from him in whimpers and gasps. His legs locked around the branch. He let himself drop, swinging upside down as his right arm curled, his fingers scrabbling under his jacket's flap. A loop of rope shot up and tightened over his ankles crossed on the branch, tying them in place. His arm curled again, and this time came away with a small key. He slammed it onto the wires locked over his arm.

White bolts shot through the wires and down his body, almost covering the little mute. His body went rigid, his teeth locked, eyes staring and wild. His mind blanked, dropping him into merciful unconsciousness. Joe's muscles went limp. He unfolded gently and swung, hanging upside down at the top of a huge conifer.

The wires peeled off his smoking arm. They curled on

themselves and slowly dropped away. Ten feet down the tree they tangled in a bloody mass on the dry pine needles of a big branch, and lay still. Joe swung gently in the breeze. All but that restless subconscious unaware of the fight going on back at the base, as mines exploded and lasers dimmed the sunshine.

But he was free from the enemy and living breath filled his lungs. A book lay tucked in the pack strapped to his back. And the cross still pressed against his heart.

Atif's healys whined rhythmically as he kept the enemy pinned behind their shield. Simmons had ducked behind there. He managed to make the dash after the shock of the shell's explosion. Occasionally, between Otar's mines and Taban's furious attacks, Atif could hear the wicked one's bellows as he tried to muster his men into some sort of order. Atif's lasers slammed into the shield one after the other in a constant rhythm, keeping them pinned. If Simmons could be kept immobilized, they might survive this.

"We have a problem," Shareef gasped in Atif's ear. The boss's shot went wild as he jumped, and for a single second Simmons had a clear view. Atif watched as the wicked one's powerful arm stretched over the rim of the shield. He held a long, thin tube. A puff of white smoke spewed from the tube's end, and five feet to his left Taban spun in a neat circle, arched, and toppled backward, hitting the ground. Atif's laser seared over the shield, but Simmons was already back down, out of his sights.

"Get him!" Atif shouted at Shareef. Under his laser helmet, Shareef's mouth curved in a tight frown. But he shot off toward his fallen comrade.

"Almost..." murmured Naqi.

"Not good enough!" Atif almost screamed over the sound of laser bursts and shattering mines. Otar yelled again, that animal bellow that rolled over the clay ground.

The yell was engulfed in a massive, sucking implosion.

An insatiable tugging gripped Atif's body, his hearing pulled into a whine so intense it numbed his mind. He glimpsed people, bushes, even a hoverer, sucked toward the clay-colored building that sizzled into itself, collapsing from the inside. But the blackness was more than the building. It seemed as if there were a hole in the sky, pulling at them, and it was cold, so cold. An instant they felt it, were pulled and dragged toward it, the blackness a monster suddenly blinked to life to snuff out the sun.

Then the tugging shoved outward, in a sickening wave of heat. A yellow ball of flames and smoke rose into the sky. It obliterated the clear blue of the morning, eclipsing it into burning yellow covered by ash and smoke. Atif slammed backward on top of Naqi, heat pressing on him like a giant iron. His head felt exploded, as if his brains shot out his ears. The pressure let up a fraction and Atif gasped and rolled to his knees. He still breathed, alive, even mostly whole.

As he rolled over he saw the miracle.

Steam still spurted from Simmons' golden hoverer. The shell hadn't destroyed the machine, it had just tossed it to the side.

Atif staggered to his feet. He could feel his clothes under the armored vest smoldering and fumbled clumsily for the clip with one hand as he pulled Naqi upright with his other. The gadget man clutched his PP to his chest, red clay clinging to one half of his face, and shock swaying him. Atif kept a hand on his shoulder.

The wicked one's hoverer stood only a few yards away from where the explosion had flung them, oscillating gently as it waited. Atif waved wildly at his men, his skin beginning to burn as his clothes shriveled under the red hot metal of his vest. He dropped Naqi to let the man run on his own and fumbled again at the clip, his lips pressed tight as his feet thudded over the ground. They had only seconds before their enemies collected themselves. The vest thudded into the ground as Atif vaulted into the hoverer. His hand slammed on the primer before he even landed in the seat, pumping madly. Heat coursed through the floor.

Atif slammed the steering stick to the side, the hiss of steam sounded in the sizzling air, and he spun to the left, catching Otar in the belly. The big man tipped headfirst into the hoverer and Atif shot forward. In the back seat Naqi gripped his big friend's vest, trying to jerk him all the way in. A stiff, corpselike Taban landed on Naqi and the breath went out of him in a sharp whoosh. Shareef vaulted into the passenger side. Atif sent the powerful vehicle spinning to face the pines before the supplier's pants touched the seat. A babble of yells rose from his men as tall trees bared down on them. Shareef felt the hoverer shaking, weaving under them as Atif fought for control. He couldn't take his eyes from the thick trunks, visions of being boiled alive by the steam from a crash captivating him. Ten feet, and they would be smashed to nothingness. A cry ripped from Shareef and his hands went over his eyes.

The vehicle spun, shuddered, paused for a moment as if it were gathering itself, and then shot away with a whining hiss. Wind whipped into Shareef, quickening every second till it tore at him. He pulled his hands down with an effort, his eyes closed to slits against the tormenting wind. They rushed over the ground, the forest safely on their left. Shareef fought the wind and pumped the bubble wand. Two halves of a clear shield rose smoothly and clacked together. The wind cut off and relieved gasps filled the little vehicle. Shareef's eyes darted to the speedometer. Eighty, ninety, in fifteen seconds they were coursing over the land at a hundred miles an hour.

"Can't breathe," Naqi wheezed.

"What? Oh, sorry," Otar muttered, shifting off the gadget man. Naqi sucked in air with a cough, doubling over.

"Got it, boss," he croaked.

"Knew you would," Atif grunted, giving one nod of approval. Naqi beamed in the backseat, straightening and getting his breath back.

"Got what?" Shareef asked.

"All the enemy tracking signals are on us, sucked onto this," Naqi said, holding up his Personal Pad. "The black one, if he's still alive, is off free."

"All their tracking equipment is honed in on that?" the supplier demanded.

"Yes, locked on tight," Naqi grinned. "It will stay honed in on this, too." Shareef reached behind him, snatched the handheld, cracked the wind bubble, and flung it out of the hoverer. Naqi's wail filled the interior as the bubble snapped shut again.

"I suppose it will still hold the signals even if it's broken?" Shareef asked.

"Oh now you ask?!" Naqi shouted at him.

"Yes, it will," Atif answered his voice even, as if he was talking about his morning cup of coffee. Quiet filled the hoverer as the steam poured out underneath them. The scanner rushed ahead, dodging the hoverer around major obstacles. Atif veered for the roads created by the massive transports, as Naqi seethed, and Shareef watched the speedometer and the rough ground whizzing by.

Otar bent forward. When he came up again, Taban lay in his arms. The fighter lay stiff and twitching, his teeth clamped in an unnatural grin. His eyes stared vacantly at nothing, so wide his eyelids couldn't be seen. Otar cradled him, trying to still his friend's jerking convulsions. A muffled scream came through Taban's clenched teeth. Naqi looked up at the two men in the front, his dark eyes pleading.

"Here," Shareef said, pulling a small brown bottle from one of his cargo pockets. "Give him four drops of this."

"What is it?" Atif asked quietly, over the sounds of Naqi and Otar trying to pry open Taban's mouth enough to drop it in. The road came in sight at the top of the valley, and Atif veered onto it with a silent, thankful prayer. He felt no strain on the hoverer, even with the rough tracks dug into the clay. Atif pressed it harder feeling the vehicle purring under him.

"Nightwish. It will bring darkness to him, but nothing more healing than that. What did Simmons shoot him with?" Shareef asked, just as quietly. He eyed the speedometer, watching it climb easily to two hundred. They wound up the road, in and out, up and down, the built in scanner zipping them past potholes and fallen rocks, all at a dizzying blurring speed. Yet everything was smooth and easy. He glanced to the side at his boss. It would seem Atif was very, very good at driving. So what had that forest episode been about?

"I don't know," Atif frowned. "Something wicked."

"Who was that flying out of the enemy's camp like an epic warrior from the Tao?"

"All we know is that he was good," Atif answered slowly, his brow furrowed as he thought it over. "Very good, and very unique. I have never seen anything like what he did today. I hope he still lives. His mission must have been important to risk infiltrating the enemy's headquarters when they were breaking camp, with heightened security and everyone out and busy. I wish I knew why he was there... What was that thing in the building that nearly swallowed us in its explosion?"

"I don't know. It was a dangerous looking stick with copper balls, and beginning to swell when I glanced in to try and acquire us a get-away vehicle. That was what I was trying to warn you of. I have seen those type of balls before, on Compton lasers and PUDRE rays."

"A Compton? You don't mean it was some sort of dark matter we exploded in there?" Atif gaped. A cold chill swept over him and he found his knuckles turning white on the steering stick. How close to death had they come?

"Yes. I believe the host of mines Otar and Taban kept launching caused the theoretical happenstance so many have debated about to actually happen," Shareef answered, his voice droll, even amused. "I'm anything but an expert, but I would not call what happened a black hole."

"It was close to one," Atif growled, trying to comprehend what had almost happened. He blew a breath out and concentrated on his driving. It hadn't happened. God was good, and they had not created a black hole that caused a second Collapse, and they were all still alive. For now. Atif was grim as he shot down the road, keenly aware this would be an easily trackable route. Even so, he didn't think they could be caught. This was an incredible vehicle. He sent his mind back to the few times he had seen Simmons in the past two years, quietly closing out all details but the one he looked for. Yes. Each time, Simmons had come in this hoverer.

"Shareef."

"Yes, boss?"

"Atif," the boss corrected absentmindedly. He was thinking again. Good. "We need a D20 tracker, someone to fix Taban, a replacement pad for Naqi, and a place to disappear."

"Kingdom of the Wise. My father knew some people there," Shareef said instantly. A wide smile cut over his freckled face. "Except I can get you a D30 tracker."

Chapter Ten: Brothers and Blackness

"A friend loveth at all times, and a brother is born for adversity." -*Proverbs 17:17*

A year and a half!" It came out a yelp as the truth began to sink in. Daniel went on, oblivious to the shocked glances the twins shot Cobeau.

"Yeah, I know, it's a long time. I was in the Tao when I found them, Joe and Co were in a mess. The traveling company had stumbled across some old acquaintances who didn't think incompletes and chimeras belonged in this world and I was able to help them out of it. They were both annoyingly sweet after that, they wouldn't let me go without doing something in return. You know, I actually told them about the reason I was out, not going so far as to explain our missing book–" Daniel paused. "You two know about the book by now, right?" All the devastation that missing Bible had caused flooded them. Anna and Nehemiah just nodded, they couldn't reply with anything more. "Joe and Co declared they would help me on my mission and appointed themselves my agents for the recovery of the 'lost property,' as I put it. I got the feeling at least Joe understood more than I was telling him. He seems to be a pretty bright character underneath that silent tongue and blank expression. Have you two gotten the same impression? Or have you even met him? I see it's just Co here now with no Joe."

"Oh, we've met him," Nehemiah said. The words snapped, so icy they hung in the air for a second, then dropped to the ground and shattered. Daniel's eyebrows went up. He sat back, eyeing his siblings with interest, waiting to see what happened.

"What next, Daniel," Anna demanded, her face tight and eyes bright. "Why didn't you come home? Did the Ravens slip off again? What happened?"

"So…" Daniel rubbed a hand over his face, embarrassment slipping over his manner. "I don't remember how much you two know about the Tao, but the ruler there can be touchy when it comes to his pride in his people." His voice quickened, the words running into each other in an embarrassed murmur. "I may have been under a lot of stress and done a little insulting and gone too far and ended up in one of their prison camps."

"You did what?" Nehi blinked.

"I lost my temper. I may have called them–" He broke off, glancing at the twins, "yes, well, called them lots of things I shouldn't have when they insulted the Sojourners. It was a calculated attack by someone who's never liked me, I fell for it, and ended up in a prison camp. The Tao snows in for eight months anyway, and I didn't have the chance to break free for almost a year. Even then, the Tao are good at keeping people, and I wouldn't have made it out of their clutches except for the Ravens. They showed up again just as I was steaming out of the pass in this rickety terrible machine I had nabbed for my breakout. I didn't have much of a chance to see what they did, but somehow they blew a whole Tao prison ship. But then that horrible hoverer jammed and I rammed into a boulder."

"What!" the twins chorused, horrified.

"It was this hulking thing, part of a mountain," Daniel ran on, obviously enjoying telling the story to his captive audience. "It loomed up in my sights, and with the stick jammed, I couldn't do anything but watch. Then, 'Blam!' and everything was hissing water and heat and jolting. When I came to, I was here, with Alma and Chester taking care of me, weak, and scarred, and with part of my life gone. I was out for over a month, apparently. Cobeau has shown up twice in the past months with supplies. He told me Joe dragged me out just before the horrible hoverer exploded. It's taken five months to get back on my feet again, and it hasn't been fun. But here I am! Free, and pretty well whole, just with a new smile to show for the adventure."

"I'm glad you're all right," Anna said. "And I think your new smile makes you look...mischievous, and like an interesting person to know. Now Daniel, this is really important to Nehi and I; did Joe know you got caught in the Tao? Did he know where you were?"

"Of course he did," Daniel said, watching his siblings with interest as they both stiffened like the news came as a body blow. "I glimpsed that white-blond hair of his on the top of a building as they dragged me off, he was watching from a distance. Don't fault him too much for it, I doubt he could have done anything to get me out earlier. I know if he intervened at the time it would have just gotten him tossed in with me."

"At the time," Nehi broke in, his words clipped as he chose each one carefully, "you're sure you're talking a year and a half ago? Joe knew you were stuck in a Tao prison a year and a half ago?"

"A little less, but yes, he knew. And since I can guess the next question, it was six months ago when Joe and Co put me up here. So they've known exactly where I am for at least that long. That hover crash did a number on me. Never drive too fast, little brother, it's dangerous," Daniel said, ruffling Nehemiah's hair.

As the hand swiped playfully at his head, a smile spread over Nehemiah, and his heart swelled. He remembered how upset it had made him the last time Daniel did that and he grinned at himself. What a little fool he had been! His smile contorted and he glanced away. His insides roiled and his eyes felt watery as he sat suddenly reunited with his big brother; and suddenly betrayed by one he had nearly claimed as a brother. For an instant rebellion flared, anger lashing out at the One Who should be in control and kept letting devastation overrun his soul. Nehi shoved it down, fumbling for his voice.

"I'll take your advice," Nehemiah managed.

"Are you sure it's been that long? A year and a half?" Anna burst in, unable to wrap her mind around the time frame.

"Of course I'm sure. I may have been unconscious for some of it, and buried in the cold without a watch for most of it, but I'm sure of the time now. What is this, what are you two so shocked about?"

"We've been traveling with the Ravens looking for you for most of that! Well, not the last six months..." Anna answered, and suddenly wondered what Joe and Cobeau had been doing during that half a year.

"We thought we were looking for Daniel and our book," Nehemiah corrected, hot and angry. "Apparently Joe had other ideas of what we were doing. Beau, what do you have to say about this?" Nehemiah barked, spinning on the chimera. The big man beamed at them.

"You're together. Look better that way. More whole," he rumbled.

"Cobeau, you've been keeping Daniel a secret from us deliberately, letting us think you were helping look for him when you really knew where he was!" Nehemiah burst out. Cobeau frowned and his brow wrinkled in concentration.

"You're together now. I brought you here. Now we just wait for Joe." He beamed again as if that answered everything.

"I'm afraid he doesn't really understand time," Anna said, then realized she was apologizing for someone that, at best, had been actively keeping them in the dark ever since they had known him. But she found she didn't want to pull the comment away. Whatever was happening, she knew Beau was convinced he was helping them.

"You're saying you've known the Ravens for a year..." Daniel took up, his voice slow and eyes narrowing, "...they knew who you were, and that you were looking for me... and they didn't tell you they knew where I was?"

"They said, 'Your way is our way,' when our way was trying to find you," Nehemiah growled. "We've asked about you almost every day, and the Ravens never told us anything. They let us assume they didn't know anything about you."

"I don't know what Joe's thinking, but this is a bit much," Anna said.

"Much?!" both her brothers exploded, beginning to grasp the extent of the little mute's knowledge and secrecy.

"I'll tell you one thing," Daniel said, his face tightening as anger began to take him, "as soon as I see that scavenger again, I'm going to take him by the collar and shake him till he tells us why he's been keeping us apart!"

"You should be able to do that soon," a cracked voice spoke up from near the front door. A wizened old man (a very good match for the wiry old Alma, Anna couldn't help thinking) stood by the door looking down the mountain.

"He's coming, Chester?" Daniel asked, standing up slowly, his walk stiff as he moved toward the old man. Cobeau darted ahead of him. The chimera jerked the door open and took the porch steps in one bound. He raced down the steep path toward the little figure in the black jacket and turtleneck sweater. Joe balanced precariously on his hoverboard, tipping and tilting as it zoomed up the path in the evening sunlight.

Anna and Nehemiah joined their brother at the open door, the invigorating mountain breeze twisting around them. The three stood in silence, watching as Beau swept Joe into his big arms and began to swing him around in delight, steam from the board spurting in a cloud around them. They were about to turn away and start fuming again, when Joe moved. He flipped his board off, snapped it to his back, scrambled out of his friend's arms and dropped to the path, all in one swift movement that screamed urgency and danger. The mute began signing things at a furious, almost frantic pace. The distance and speed were too great for them to catch any of it, but

Beau understood. He pelted off toward the entrance to Prissy's stable, rocks kicking up behind him, and disappeared into the depths of the mountain.

Joe started up the path in a stumbling run. Anna noticed he looked worn, more tired than she thought the tough little dancer could get. Nehemiah thought he looked more than tired, but he was too mad at him to try and notice more. Joe's head lifted and his eyes found them through the grimy, sweat-dampened hair hanging over his eyes. His face was drawn and paper white. He locked onto Anna's gaze.

"Run!" he signed as he stumbled forward. Anna's hands went to her hips.

"What do you mean, 'Run'? We're awfully mad at you again and might not listen." Joe grabbed Anna and Daniel by the arms, jerked them off the porch, and pushed them frantically down the steep hill that curved sharply into a sort of stony valley. A stand of scrubby pine trees stood at the bottom of the hill, waving in pathetic dryness and solitude, and Joe's shaking finger pointed to them. Daniel turned and grabbed Joe's collar, his face set in a determined line, his eyes slits. But Anna saw the drawn exhaustion, the fear, and pleading in Joe's face. His eyes met hers and his lips formed one word as clearly as if he spoke it; "Please!"

She grabbed Daniel's arm and jumped. The shale took over, sliding under their feet, drawing them toward the scrubby pines with a sharp, dusty clacking. Joe pointed Nehemiah and Chester in the same direction, shooting up the porch toward them, his right arm rising and falling in a staccato order as he pointed. It would have been shouting, even screaming at them to move if the mute had the ability. The two men moved. Chester stepped off the path, slipped, landed on his backside and slid down the hill.

Nehi didn't jump. He stepped over the edge, leaning sideways, his boots parallel to the hill. And he looked back as the shale started to slip under him.

Joe wasn't there. He hadn't followed. Nehi's hand flattened, diving like a shovel into the midst of the loose rocks to stop his sliding, and his gaze raked the area, searching for the mute. Nehi spotted him leaning against the cabin door post. Joe gasped for breath and swayed, his head bowed like he just didn't have the strength left to keep it up, his left arm rigid against his side, his jacket sleeve torn and grimed. A breath shuddered into him, shaking his whole form. The little musician straightened and darted into the house, his black bag banging and battering his side.

Nehemiah's lips pursed and he clawed his way back up the hill. The shale bit into his palms, and for each step he slid back down half a step. But he moved fast, pulling himself upward and scrambling over the crest on all fours. Nehemiah darted onto the porch and spun into the house. His body froze, his ears buzzing as a part of him said he must be dreaming this whole bizarre day.

Alma had her back to him. She held a Brunhiem laser in her thin arms, its soft whine filling the room. The muzzle pressed against Joe's forehead and pushed him against the opposite wall. Alma's smile was not one of the friendly caregiver Nehemiah had thought her from Daniel's descriptions.

"This uncomfortable position won't last for long," Alma's cracked voice rose over the whine and silence. It was teasing, gleeful. "He'll be here any second now." Hope felt heavy as she jerked into Nehi's hands, and he had to force her not to shake. But his voice showed none of his confusion.

"Put the gun down, and turn around slowly," he ordered. Alma started in surprise. That millisecond of confusion was enough for Joe. He ducked, dropping to a crouch to get out of the rifle's way, and spun in a tight circle with one leg outstretched. Alma crashed to the ground, her head bouncing on the floorboards as she hit. A dart gun appeared in Joe's hand,

and its soft pop filled the room. Alma stilled, all her muscles suddenly going limp. Joe scrambled up and darted to a hallway.

Nehemiah followed, tucking Hope back into her holster. Joe dropped to the ground, and Nehemiah leapt forward, thinking he had collapsed. But Joe's fingers scrabbled around a flagstone on the floor, searching for something. Nehemiah noticed burnt skin and dried blood on his hands. A click sounded. Part of the rough, pine paneled wall fell away. A large black bag lay just inside the dark hole yawning where the panel had been. A musty, cramped smell hit Nehemiah and he fell back half a step, realizing this was more than a hole. A wave of sick fear washed over him at the dense blackness. He didn't like dark.

Joe fumbled the black bag's strap off and stuffed it into the large sack in the recess in the wall. He grabbed the big bag in both hands and pulled. His face twisted, mouth open in a gasping, silent cry. He pulled back, clutching his left arm and stumbling into the opposite wall, sweat pouring from his pallid face. Nehemiah stepped forward and gripped the bag. He hefted it out of the recess in the wall, surprised by its heavy weight. As he swung it over his shoulder, the two boys' eyes met. Joe's were bloodshot and crinkled with exhaustion and pain, but as he stared at Nehemiah an almost uncomprehending gratefulness shone from his expressive face. His right hand lifted, his fingertips touched his chin and tipped out toward Nehi:

"Thank you."

For that second everything was silent. Then a sound broke through, one Nehemiah thought he recognized. Air hissing, almost as if a vacuum were trying to suck air into itself from too small a hole, combined with the sharp whistling of a furious wind. For some reason it reminded him of Lightfoot. Joe's eyes snapped and his mouth twitched with panic. His right arm shot out, pointing into the hole where they had just re-covered the bag, his eyes burning as his expression made it an order. Nehi hung back, his body resisting the musty closeness and dark. And his mind unsure he wanted to follow the little mute blindly into a dark hole, not without at least the begin-ning of an explanation for his lying, dirty–

Joe palm struck Nehemiah in the chest. He stumbled back, his foot caught on the little sill leading into the recess and he fell in, landing with a scrunch on a moldy concrete ground. Joe's knees landed on his chest as the mute scrambled over him, and the air left Nehi's lungs in a whoosh.

A sharp click echoed off stone walls. Musty, complete darkness fell around the two boys as the secret door clicked shut. A polite tapping started on the door to the cottage, Nehi could hear it muffled through the wood paneling. And muffled through the buzzing panic trying to take over his mind. Joe grabbed Nehemiah's arm and tugged. The bigger boy scram-bled to his feet, listening to his breath coming in short pants, rising in pitch till he could hear himself hyperventilating. "Thy word is a lamp unto my feet, and a light unto my path[3]." The verse shot through his mind, and coursed through his body, loosening tight muscles, and evening his breathing. Scattered verses poured through him, jumbled bits of the Lord's prayer, and Psalm 23, rushing headlong into the panic and holding it at bay. In an instant it turned to prayers, and then his prayers turned to begging forgiveness for that moment of anger and doubt at the sovereign hand of God. The Spirit slipped through him, whispering of Love beyond all betrayal and devastations, of God always with him, walking beside him even in the dark. The panic receded. It seethed just under his thoughts, a mass of malicious terror just waiting for his guard to lessen.

Joe tugged again. The mute began to pull him along, some-where deeper into the darkness.

---

[3] Psalm 119:105

Anna slipped and skidded, her plowing shoes making furrows in the shale and dirt. Each step sent a mini rockslide toward the scrubby pines that congregated miserably at the end of the valley. Another rain of the little rocks and dust hit her, loosened by Daniel as he slid behind her. Anna's feet hit solid ground, and she darted toward the trees, calves burning from balancing down the hill. Daniel stumbled behind her, swaying and panting. Six pines leaned into one another, trying to receive comfort from the bitter winds, forming a canopy of dry needles. Anna darted into the stand, her throat caked with dust, pulling Daniel behind her.

"All right, we made it to cover. Now what? And why?" Daniel gasped, leaning against one of the pitiful pines. Anna spun to look for Joe. Her eyes widened, her face hardening. A ruby laser pointed at her stomach, held in Chester's weathered, gnarled hand. A sneer disfigured Chester's thin face as he settled comfortably on the rocks just outside the stunted trees. Anna stared at him, and the emptiness behind him, silently trying to guess what his sudden betrayal and the absence of the boys meant. Sun glinting off copper caught her eye and she looked back at the top of the hill. She spotted Nehemiah disappearing inside the cabin with Hope out in his hands. He moved in the wary, trained way of a soldier ready to spin toward any threat. Anna's mouth tightened and she shot a glance at Daniel. He stood staring open mouthed at the ruby laser pistol, shock so strong it made him forget to breathe. The three people in the thicket just stared at each other.

A dark streak shot over Anna's head, so high up she thought for a moment it might be a black shooting star. It was so fast she hardly had time to glimpse it in her peripheral vision. A sharp hissing sound came from just in front of the cabin. It wasn't steam escaping, it was more like a jet of high wind being sucked into a hole. A deep black ball, nearly ten feet across, appeared on the path just in front of the cabin, a pulsating, whirling mass of lethal dark force. Gravel from the path, shingles from the cabin, grass and shrubs, ripped up and spiraled towards the sucking black ball. For a single second Anna was able to register it all and feel the huge tugging pull from the black ball even from where she stood. A single pounding heartbeat, and the blackness peeled away and disappeared with a wild, desperate hissing wind.

Six men stood on the gravel path where the ball had been. One, a tall, muscular man held a copper stick, about a yard long, with a large copper ball on each end. A smile tugged at the corners of his handsome mouth, but it was a chilling, cruel smile. He hopped on the porch and tapped on the door.

A slight movement in front of her brought Anna's attention back to Chester. He half turned on his rock, his eyes shining, his thin lips parting to call out to the men gathered around the cabin door. Anna had a sudden abhorrence of being noticed by that tall man, so strong it twisted her stomach. Her hand shot out in a jab and smashed into Chester's throat. His shout strangled into a gurgle as he slumped back clutching at his throat and dropping the pistol. Daniel stepped forward, his arm shooting up in a vicious uppercut. The crack of that blow connecting with Chester's chin rang around the trees. Chester's eyes rolled back and he sank to the ground unconscious, rocks splaying out around him as his weight hit.

"Well, I never saw that one coming," Daniel wheezed, shaking his hand, his face strained as he stared at the body. The noise of the men at the cabin hammering on the door nearly drowned it out. He swept up the ruby pistol and clunked the groaning Chester on the head. The old man stopped groaning and dropped limp. "Nice old nurses turning evil and people emerging out of giant black balls... This has been a strange day. Anna, am I actually awake?"

"Yes you are, and Nehemiah's still up there with that man breaking down the door!" Anna answered in a desperate whisper.

"Do you know who that is?" Daniel asked. A deep rumble came from behind them.

"Simmons."

They spun, the rocks underfoot slipping and digging into their feet. Cobeau knelt behind them in the cover of a scrubby bush, his big hands holding his snub-nosed Brunhiem. His simple face was concerned, but not afraid. "Where's Nehi?"

"He followed Joe back up to the cabin," answered Anna. A wide smile broke over the chimera's face. A crash sounded from the top of the hill and Anna's head snapped toward the sound. The comfortable checkered couch lay upside down on the ground, one leg ripped off. She could hear shouting inside, cuss words spewing through the broken window. The loveseat thudded onto the porch, stuffing spilling from knife slashes. More furniture came crashing through windows, and the sounds of dishes breaking and material ripping drifted down the hill.

"Nice folks, don't find people at home and decide to wreck the place," Daniel muttered.

"We need to go," Cobeau rumbled.

"But Nehemiah and Joe!" Anna hissed, keeping her voice down with an effort. "They're in there!" Cobeau shook his head and motioned them to follow him farther down the valley. "No, not with Nehi up there!" Anna growled through clenched teeth, her fingernails digging into her palms. Cobeau looked back and shook his head.

"Joe's too smart to stay with Simmons coming in," Cobeau rumbled.

"We can see the front door, there's no backdoor, and the windows open to sheer cliff-faces! They didn't leave," Daniel hissed.

"Tunnel," Cobeau said. The rock in Anna's stomach stopped twisting, and she felt her lungs expand again. A secret tunnel. It was so like Joe to have a hidden tunnel that even Daniel hadn't found in months of living there, the statement rang true.

"Will Simmons find it?" she asked. Cobeau's head shook back and forth, and he smiled again.

"Joe designed the door. No one finds it but him."

Anna nodded, and drew in a deep breath. Daniel watched as her taut face relaxed and her shoulders slumped in relief. His face crinkled like he was trying to understand. But as Anna followed Beau through the little grove, Daniel turned and walked at her heels.

Anna slid out of the trees and onto a tiny goat track, praying her twin and Joe were safe, whatever they were doing. Beau shifted through the shadows in front of her, silent and large, seeming to naturally slip into the darker patches, the shale hardly even clacking under his large feet. Anna watched, her thoughts surging through her. She knew she should be angry at him. Part of her said she should even be afraid of this big, silent man who told them nothing and kept secrets as large as her own big brother. But somehow, Anna couldn't find the anger or fear in her. Beau paused, his head lifting to sniff the air, and one of his hairy arms stretched back automatically. Toward her. Ready to snatch her to safety if the danger he sensed made it necessary. A raptor's shadow passed by just in front of Beau and soared off over the mountains. He started to move again. Anna kept on his heels, watching his huge muscles rippling under his jacket, and knew what she felt, and that it was right; she never felt safer than when Cobeau stood within arm's reach.

Whatever was going on, whatever secrets lay seething inside the Ravens, she was convinced Beau only knew he was helping his favorite people. Now Joe, this was his doing, and she could definitely feel anger toward him! Anna's feet hit the ground harder than necessary as she stomped up the trail after Beau. Words rushed through her mind as the anger grew, words she wanted to yell in the mute's face the next time she saw him.

Chapter Eleven: Dark Travels

"...I will make darkness light before them, and crooked things straight. These things will I do unto them, and not forsake them." -Isaiah 42:16

Nehemiah followed Joe through the dark, his breathing short and raspy as it bounced off the walls. His boots scuffed the ground, feeling his way over rough-hewn stone. Cold, damp rock brushed his hair and Nehi ducked, cowering, a panicked mewing gasp sliding from him. He hated himself for the noise. The polite tapping on the cabin door became an impatient banging. Nehemiah and Joe inched along the tight passageway, the big bag pressing against Nehi's back and the hoverboard scraping the walls as it lay clipped in its sling behind the mute. A voice drifted from the front door.

"Hey in there, open the door! Sometime in this century!" Simmons yelled. His voice reverberated even through the thick wooden paneling shutting them off from the man. Nehi froze, strangled in the dark. Clammy fingers slid around his hand and squeezed, tugging him gently on. Joe's hand was small, but strong, comforting, and urging him farther away from that hated voice. Nehi mastered himself and the two shuffled ahead in the darkness. A sharp splintering crash drifted to them as the door caved in, but it came muffled by distance.

"Boss, here's one of ours, the woman!" a voice called out. Nehemiah heard Simmons say something in reply, but he didn't catch the words.

Joe jerked forward, his hand snatched from Nehi by the darkness. Nehemiah stumbled forward at the force of it, gasping his friend's name. His boots hit something slippery and flew out from under him. Nehemiah landed hard, flat on his back, on something wet, steep, and slick. The slickness claimed his body, he found himself sliding downward, surrounded by the dark, the damp, and a smell like rotting fishes. His boots scraped uselessly as he picked up speed, unable to stop himself. He felt Joe grab his legs and push them together. Again the touch, knowing a friend was near, stilled his panic and Nehi understood what he needed to do.

He lay back, flipped the black bag in front of him, and kept his legs straight out in front. He started moving faster, and faster still. Cold, damp air whipped his hair into his face, carrying the scent of moldy damp. The path curved, steel slammed into his legs and left side, so hard it bruised to the bone, and Nehi swerved in another direction. Two seconds later, he was banged the opposite direction. Nehemiah screwed his eyes shut and told himself he was back home with Anna on the slide their father had attached to their tree house. It didn't work. A strangled yelp pulled from him as the slope straightened out and disappeared, shooting him through the black air.

Nehi's outstretched legs hit something cold, and the pain of the impact jarred up him to snap his neck. He crashed to a gravelly ground, his heart laboring, his brain aching. The black closed in again in an instant. He clawed blindly along the wet, stinking gravel that made up the floor, the bag dragging behind him with a sharp scrunching sound, looking for his friend.

"Joe?" he begged into the darkness, his voice muted and shaky. A small, trembling hand gripped his searching one and Nehemiah breathed again. He scrambled to his feet, following the tug of the hand he couldn't see. His toe hit the hoverboard. A spurt of hissing air filled the cavern, and Joe's shaking hand rose four inches and let go. Nehi felt clumsily with his feet and stepped onto the board, one hand gripping Joe's shoulder to orient himself in this blackness. The bag almost overbalanced him, and the board shook dangerously under the boys as Nehemiah fought for control. He steadied himself, knowing the machine needed precision. The board straightened. Joe shifted left, and Nehi felt it, joining the movement. The board shifted easily under them.

The mute's hand covered Nehi's for a moment where it lay on his shoulder, and squeezed; the only sign he could give in the dark. But enough. One of comradery, a move that said they were together in this, that the adventure was ready to start.

"Let's go," Nehi nodded. His voice echoed off the rock walls around them.

Joe leaned forward, steam hissed, and they were off. Close, musty air swirled into Nehemiah's face, as his muscles bunched, holding him in a careful balance. He held Joe's shoulder, alert for any movement, any change of direction he needed to follow. The board hissed on, the only noise, carrying them into absolute blackness. Joe shifted right, Nehi following the move carefully. Sometime later he shifted left again, and Nehi copied him, feeling the board picking up speed. The wind cut into them, musty and cold.

On and on they moved, the hoverboard changing directions at what felt like random moments to Nehemiah as he fought to keep control. The dark never changed. The air was stuffy and hard to breathe. It never felt like enough oxygen to Nehi. On and on, for what seemed a century. Muscles tight as he constantly steadied himself against the movement of the board. The pull of the heavy bag made Nehemiah's shoulder throb.

A sharper hiss, a splutter, and the board shivered under them. Nehi's aching knees braced harder as the board bucked. Another splutter and the water supply gave out. The hoverboard slammed into gravel. Joe and Nehi stumbled off, tired legs pumping and fighting to keep them upright. Nehemiah felt Joe's legs give out and tightened his grip on his little friend's shoulder, holding him up as he braced himself against the gra-

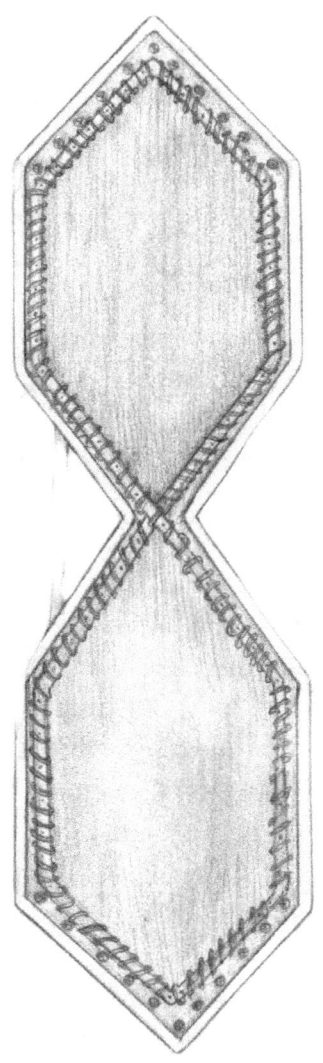 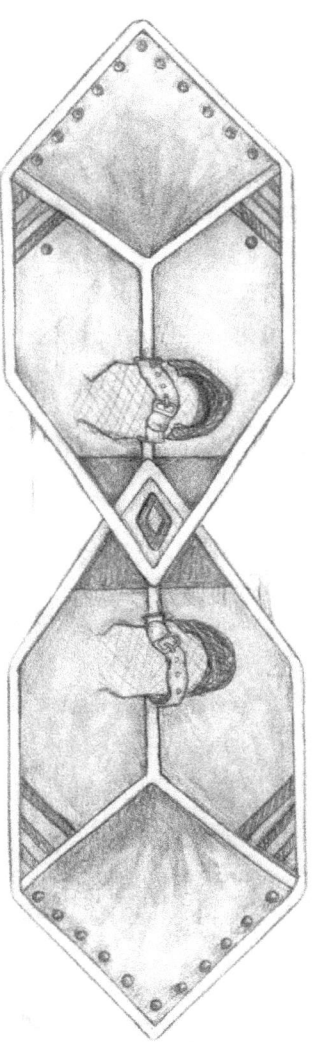

Hoverboard

-vel. A moment of gasping breaths in the close, dark air, and the two stood still. Nehemiah let go of Joe and eased the bag down, trying to look around him. He still couldn't see anything. Oppressive, still silence settled in the blackness. No hint of movement in the stale air. Not a particle of light.

Joe's clammy fingers wrapped around his wrist. Nehi could feel the mute shaking and shivering. He gently folded Nehi's hand around the bag; asking him to keep carrying it. The mute pulled away. A rhythmic scrunch of gravel came in front of Nehi, Joe's boots moving in the darkness. Nehi hefted the bag and followed.

The two boys began to hike through the dark underground world, Nehemiah following the sound of the mute's steps. Gravel crunched under their feet, yielding just enough to make each step tiring. The heavy, damp air never lightened. On and on...scrunching gravel, his own breathing, the bag pulling at him, Joe's noise ahead of him, the still, moldy air. His legs ached and his thighs began to burn at the steady pull of the gravel. On and on...

"Joe, where are we going?" Nehi asked, after what seemed days. His voice came deep and harsh and Nehemiah closed his mouth and swallowed. He hadn't realized how thirsty he was. How long had they been in this blackness? No answer came, no change in the steady rhythm of Joe's boots. Nehemiah suddenly remembered Joe's exhausted gasping against the cabin door frame and wondered how he was still on his feet. He wished he had Cobeau's strength and could carry Joe and the bag.

Then in a flash he remembered Daniel, Joe's silence on something that mattered the world to the twins. Nehemiah pulled away in disgust, pain of betrayal flaming in him. His thoughts began to tumble around and get mixed with his feelings, colliding inside him in a way that made his heartbeat hiccup and thunder. It felt like when he had perched on top of the

Ravens' wagon that night outside of Kallipolis, when who he had thought was a friend had turned out to be a traitor. And yet still a friend. He trudged on in silence, his jaw clamped shut. Anger and confusion and compassion all collided in him, rolling over each other in a horrible kaleidoscope of emotions. Gradually they drifted into an overarching sense of weariness.

On and on, blackness and gravel, on and on, thirst and tired muscles. Nehemiah's legs ached and his shoulders ached more. He stopped and swung the bag to a different shoulder again, relishing in the moment of standing still. But Joe pulled ahead, the gravel crunching even and steady under him. The comforting sense of a fellow human near dissipated as the mute kept marching, eclipsed by the dark. Nehemiah stumbled into a jog until he caught up. He endured the wearying tug of the bag as long as he could before swapping again. Nehemiah swallowed and tried not to think about cold water.

After a few minutes of quiet scrambling, Anna followed Beau's broad back onto a narrow road. A sheer wall of gray rock rose menacingly up on their left, towering over the road as far as the travelers could see. The other side dropped in a steep slope of loose pebbles and dirt, with the view commanding only more desolate gray peaks. The Hillsons found Prissy on the rocky road, harnessed to the Ravens' wagon, her wheeled shoes and leather helmet on. Cobeau climbed up and pulled Daniel and Anna behind him. He clucked to the pig, released the brake, and the wagon rolled swiftly down the track, gathering speed. Prissy's head shot up and a piercing squeal of delight rang from her, vibrating in her huge chest as her shoes rattled over stones.

"Where does Joe's secret tunnel lead?" Anna asked.

"Geatland," said Cobeau, carefully gripping the steering

stick, his eye on the narrow track. "We go there now."

"I've never heard of that kingdom. How far is it?" Daniel demanded.

"End of the mountains," answered Cobeau.

"So not far," Daniel answered his own question. "You know where the tunnel ends, where Nehemiah and Joe will come out?" Beau's big head bobbed. "You are taking us there, right?"

"Taking us to where we'll find Joe," Beau rumbled.

"That's...mostly the right answer I guess," Daniel murmured, still eyeing Beau with suspicion. "But one more thing, we're on a rumbling wagon out in the open, it's not exactly hiding. Won't those angry people back at the cabin spot us?"

"Peaks," Beau said, one hand pointing up at the mountains towering over the wagon. Anna followed the pointing finger and found herself huddling a little closer to Beau and Daniel. The huge rocky edifices made her feel tiny and very crushable. One small wagon on a narrow trail would be difficult to spot. The wagon bumped and skidded, hitting the breeching strap in front of the big pig, and all three tensed. Beau's hand went to the brake, letting it partially down. The wagon slowed, the wheels stopped skidding, and the giant pig rolled on.

"I can't believe I'm going with you again when I have no idea where I'm going or why!" Anna burst out. Cobeau looked at her, his simple face surprised.

"We're going to get Nehi," Daniel put in. "Why did he go back, anyway?"

"I wish I knew! He had his Compton out, something was worrying him," Anna said.

"I wonder if it was Joe," Daniel said quietly.

"Very happy Joe's not alone," Cobeau rumbled, a beaming smile spreading over his face. "Good for Nehi."

"Anna, I want to know all about your relations with these two," Daniel ordered. "Who was that man Simmons? What do you know about the mysterious Joe and Co?"

"They rescue us, rescue us again, get us captured, rescue us out of it, take us everywhere, leave us stranded, and then come back, and never tell us why they do any of it!" Anna burst out.

"What?" Daniel blinked. Anna sighed and began at the beginning, when Joe's raven had found them crouching terrified, broken, and helpless in the woods and Cobeau materialized to spirit them out of their ruined country. It was a long story and the moon shone down on the wagon by the time she finished. A soft bump traveled from the wheels up through the passengers' spines, and the wagon changed from the sharp angle of the mountain pass to suddenly drawing flat.

"We're here," Cobeau said before Daniel could comment on the story. Anna looked up and took it in slowly.

A ring of mountains stretched off into the distance, creating a basin. Smooth, green grass and well-tended dirt roads were Anna's first impression of the country. A carved sign slid past as the wagon rolled onto the road.

Geatland
May the Almighty Father keep you and in His kindness watch over your exploits.
4

The moon glowed full and bright, her silvery beauty sparkling over the grassy land, a river bubbling and dancing through it. A few more revolutions of the wheels, and Anna could make out thatched cottages dotting the landscape.

---

4 *Beowulf*, translation Seamus Heaney, line 316

Cows, sheep, and goats lifted their heads and watched as the wagon rumbled nearer. A rooster crowed, somewhere to their left. A dog barked at the sound, and a cow answered it. Laughter drifted from inside one of the thatched houses. Dancing, yellow firelight spilled into the night from windows, like hundreds of little pricks of candles on a rumpled, giant green table. Anna smiled, relishing the pretty scene.

"Yeah, well, this is nice," Daniel drawled, and Anna looked over at him. His face was strained and he swayed in his seat. "But I haven't been out of that cabin except to step onto the back porch for a really long time. I'm going to catch a quick nap if you two can do without me." A grunt slid from him as he slumped to his side, curling on the wagon top.

"There are beds inside–" Anna started, but Daniel's foot moved, whapping her leg in a teasing kick.

"Stop talking," he grumbled. "The invalid wants rest." She grinned, delight flaring in her at having that grumpy voice back in her life. She leaned forward and laid her hand on Beau's arm.

"Thank you for helping rescue Daniel," she said. Beau's shaggy head bobbed and a grunt came from him. Silence slid over the wagon top as they steamed farther into the country. Anna's head tipped toward the moon, her heart too full to be still. Praise and thanks for the big brother beside her, and prayers for her twin out there somewhere poured from her. But after a few phrases she found it flowing into pleading for Joe. For strength and joy and wisdom for the little mute. Anna let her prayers turn to where the silent voice of the Spirit shifted them, and lifted her little friend to Jesus, wondering why she felt the need to carry him there. But underlying each sentence lay an earnest pleading, a begging request to find out why he had kept Daniel hidden from them for so long!

Vern Tollimé stared at the report on his battered wooden desk. Panicked babblings and screams echoed down the hall. He shuffled another paper on top of the report. The sharp blast of laser fire lit up the hallway outside his office, white light flashing through the cracks of his closed door. Vern slid the papers across his desk and stacked them neatly with another pile, telling himself he didn't recognize the voices. Another blast of laser fire lit up the hall, but it came farther away. The sounds began to drift off to different parts of the building, and on out into the street. Silence crept in.

Oh, how he hated overthrows.

Always a complete overturn, get rid of everyone the past government had in a place of authority. Even the Social Workers, keepers of what peace Story Land could boast, protectors of justice... An interesting word, justice. Vern knew what it meant when he heard someone use it. He knew better what it meant when he used it himself. But justice to whom, and from whom... His thoughts diverted to a surgeon's walled house he knew of in the middle of town and the people who stole inside every Sunday morning. He knew that surgeon could give him a definition of justice. But would he like his answer?

More balls of laser fire blasted the night away outside Vern's tiny, open window. There for an instant, then dying away to let the dark take over again. Vern's ugly face remained expressionless as he drew another report from his drawer and sat it slowly on his desk. He had sent out memos, as soon as he knew for sure. To every desk in the building, every Social Worker out on the streets; Overthrow, get out now. But so few had. So few listened to him, even when he used words he knew they understood no matter their individual stories.

This was the fifth time he had sat through an overthrow. The laser fire sparking outside his office. The pleading and weeping drifting in from the streets. Didn't matter what the weepers said, it always ended the same. As if in illustration, two quick blasts of light flashed through his window, gleamed off the paper on his desk, then disappeared. If there was one overarching truth, Vern had seen it played out by the people around him since he took this job twenty-eight years ago; life is cheap when it isn't yours.

There were so many who lived by that philosophy. He met them everyday in his work. People who created grieving mothers, widows, orphans... Faces of some of the worst he met flew through his mind, and he knew most of them would be down in the streets right now, glorying in the chaos and blood. The Ill Trio would be there. In the background, probably, never out in the full light. But egging on the blood, laughing at the horrors.

Another blast of white light lit up the night like a firework display. The only celebration the new government sanctioned. Always the same. Two more balls of fire blasted into existence for an instant, shining a silhouette of Vern's shaggy gray hair and monkey-like visage on his office wall. A stranger might have thought it was a hallway behind the inspector's desk. The paintwork looked like a hall stretching into the distance, checkered tiles on the wall, light fixtures matching the real ones in Vern's office. New recruits often walked into it, smacking their faces against the paint. Vern never laughed at them. Which somehow made it worse, and most burst into angry complaints about the not-a-hall. And from their reaction, the direction they steered their complaints, Vern could neatly place what sort of person he dealt with.

He would have to go through that all again now. New recruits. The government always kept him. Good old Vern Tollimé, steady rock who knew what's what and kept the peace so the new government could have their fun and ignore most actual governing. It would be new faces all around him, staring blankly when he spoke his randomized words. No one ever got it. If truth is relative, if everything is relative, that meant words are too. If everyone has their own story, you can't have a conversation. If no one holds anything solid in common, words mean something different to each person who hears them, and it doesn't matter which ones you actually speak.

The simple, ordinary face of the surgeon flashed across Vern's mind again, in a scene as clear to him as the report on his desk. Sunshine glinted off the man's ordinary brown hair as he knelt beside the gasping Social Worker, holding the boy's hand. There hadn't been anything even a surgeon could do for that boy. But it made Vern feel better to have the man there, to have a professional say what he already knew. As the boy gasped his last, and Vern spoke the eulogy, the other Social Workers had been angry, or caustic, or just rolling their eyes. "Potatoes are green. Trees never play. We must all choose starfields and collections of spaghetti." But the surgeon...he had stared at Vern with a sober face, one of pity and understanding, and the Inspector knew. That man got it. He understood.

Lights blasted in a scattered glory of white fire, and Vern sighed. Life is cheap when it isn't yours.

He stood up and walked toward the door to head to his living quarters in the basement, ready to get away, where he couldn't see the lights. Couldn't hear the screams and weeping.

A flutter of feathery wings reached him and Inspector Vern spun on one heel, his hand coming up with his strafer laser, his reflexes faster than anyone expected of the stocky man.

A black raven perched on his desk. The bird's head tipped, one dark eye glittering in the light of the streetlamp spilling in from the grimy window. The bird's talons clacked on the desktop as it shifted, hopping to a better position to stare at Vern. A black leather pouch moved on the bird's leg as it shifted.

Well, well, well. Vern had seen a raven like this three years ago, leaving the president's quarters. It left one hour before the overthrow hit; and the president was discovered to be missing. The inspector had left his window open ever since. Patience was one of Vern's strongest features.

Vern slid his laser back into its holster and approached the raven slowly. It watched him, head shifting left and right. But it showed no signs of nervousness.

"Rocker," Vern murmured, his deep gravelly voice as soothing as he could make it. He knew it was the tone that mattered. "Don't bleed or cribbage, eh?" His fingers touched the rough skin of the bird's leg. It didn't startle away, but just fixed Vern with one of its shiny black eyes. The knot tying the pouch to the raven was intricate and would take time. But the pouch itself stood partially open. Vern slid two fingers in and drew it the rest of the way open, peering cautiously inside. A white paper stared back at him. He pulled it out with a soft crinkle.

A flutter of black feathers and beating wings, the thick smell of bird surrounding him, a thump as the raven's feet landed on the windowsill and pushed off, and then the animal was gone. Swallowed by the night, as if it had never been here. Vern turned from the empty window and stared at the small piece of paper folded in his palm. He laid it gently on his desk and unfolded it.

Your book is in danger. Move it, to a place only you know. Trust no one.

The Ill Trio on the move. Going after a necklace of Rachel Jaimen soon. Watch for it, and be there if you want them out of your country. Once they're gone, you can return the book.

Chapter Twelve: The Thain's Hall

"The liberal soul shall be made fat: and he that watereth shall be watered also himself." -Proverbs 11:25

The moon rode high in the night sky, shining on the wagon as it rolled into the midst of a village. They rumbled past thatched houses, empty open stalls, and darkened smithies. Yellow firelight danced in the windows of most of the cottages. A big brown dog leapt to its feet behind a rough wooden fence in front of one of the cottages, flowers cascading over the grass. The dog bounded in a circle, tail freewheeling, bellowing at them. Someone shouted wearily out the window for the animal to hold its peace, and Anna laughed. It turned to a yawn, a big, noisy yawn that she didn't bother to cover. She wished Nehi were there to lean against so she could fall asleep up here.

"Where are we going, Beau?" she asked.

"Local thain's for the night," said Cobeau, and pointed. Anna leaned forward, staring up the dirt road. A large rectangular building loomed at the top of a hill, smaller thatched buildings scattered around it. Something like horns stuck off the top corners. Huge carved doors were flung open to the cool night, and light spewed through them. Even from here she could hear the raucous laughter and dishes clinking.

"Why there, Beau? We always just camp in the wagon, outside of towns."

"Good meat," Beau rumbled, clearly pleased by the idea. He smacked loudly. "And good money from the thain."

"What's a thain?"

"Ruler."

"And this one gives us money because..."

"Music."

"Oh."

Anna looked back at the big building, speculating on the clientele as they drew closer and she could hear things clearer. Not all the voices drifting from that place sounded sober. And all of them sounded male. But then again, no one was shouting obscenities that she could tell. *The night's young,* a part of her whispered as she glanced at the moon. *So are you,* another part of her whispered, and Anna grimaced and chuckled to herself. She wondered if Joe would have come here with her in tow if he were in command. Beau obviously knew the place, she could see it in the way he steered Prissy behind the building to a stable overshadowed by the hall.

Horses nickered and stamped inside the stable. Anna's eyes lit up, her mouth parting at the sound. Horses had been one of her delights before her home disintegrated. Nehi always complained about the mucking up, but to Anna even the chores involving horses seemed delightful. She hadn't seen a single one since disintegration hit. Anna hadn't had the courage to ask Joe what happened to the Judge's stables when the enemy swept in.

The wagon rocked to a stop, and Daniel sat up. Slow and groaning, but his eyes darting around in a way that told Anna he was still whole enough to take in the situation at a glance, already assessing the next step. Her heart lost another weight and soared a little higher.

"I smell meat," Daniel muttered.

"Beau says it's good, and that there's money in music here," Anna said, grinning as she realized the next step for him meant dinner.

"You still sing?" he asked quickly.

"Yes," she laughed, reaching for the handrail to swing herself down.

"Let's hope that meat's as good as it smells," Daniel commented, slowly following her off the wagon. "I've missed creating culinary art with you, Anna."

"Your style is more of culinary perfectionism," she grinned. The shadow beside them shifted and took shape, and Beau stood there, holding out her concert coat. Daniel's boots landed on the hardpacked dirt, he turned, and found himself staring at the silent bulk of the chimera, looming over him and clutching a large blunt instrument. Daniel stumbled back, a little yelp coming from him.

"Good grief, speak or stomp or something!" he complained. "You're going to give me a heart attack one of these days!" The chimera just pushed a guitar at him. Daniel took it warily. The big man spun and started to stride for the building. He shifted to the side, keeping to the shadows automatically instead of stepping into the full glare of the firelight beaming from the windows and open doors. Daniel's eyes narrowed and his face hardened as he watched. Something about the silent, powerful chimera unnerved him.

Anna skipped into the light and spun, staring back at him as she flipped her hair into a loose bun, black curls cascading out of it. The skirt of her long red coat swirled as she spun, her silver IDP necklace (a dove with wings outspread) caught the moonlight, and Daniel's eyebrows rose at her attractiveness.

"Are you just going to stand there sniffing all night?" she demanded.

"You've grown," Daniel grunted. He walked forward, slipping the guitar strap over his shoulder. He slid her arm through his and she fell in step beside him, heading toward the huge doors. "You've become a true beauty, Anna. If any of these people try to get fresh with you, just point them out and I'll break their nose, right?"

"Right. But only after I've had the chance to break it first."

The sound of gravel churning in front of Nehi stopped. Nehemiah stumbled to a standstill, swaying on his feet. Exhaustion climbed through him, from the long fight with a phobia as much as the hike. The small mute shifted in the dark, but didn't walk on. Nehemiah stood in the blackness and forced his mind off the train of thought it tried to divert to (for what felt like the thousandth time) and onto what Joe was doing. He could hear the sound of metal scraping something, a few feet in front of him. A soft click sounded in the darkness. In that disturbing silence it seemed louder than a gunshot. Heavy breathing sounded, a gasp, wet, choking, a sound Nehi knew would have been a scream if the mute had the ability. Silence. Joe's clammy, shaking hand grabbed Nehemiah's wrist. The mute tugged him forward and laid Nehi's hand on something cold and hard. Metal, Nehemiah recognized as he felt it.

A handle!

He dropped the bag and things in it rang and thudded on the hard ground. Nehemiah grabbed the handle with both hands and tugged with all his strength. A stiff crack broke through the sounds of his boots tearing into the wet gravel; a pair of old hinges feeling themselves used again. Nehi planted one foot on the wall and shoved with it, his back muscles straining, his arms screaming, tugging with everything in him. A thick iron door swung open ponderously, squealing in protest. Bright light flooded over Nehemiah. He gasped and threw a stiff arm over his eyes, staggering back a step. The rising sun flooded into the dark passageway. Oh thank God, light! Warm, white, real sunlight! Through eyes streaming from the sudden glare, Nehi looked up, relief flooding into him.

The sudden light, the open outdoors, dissipated the hovering fear; it left him with a weary contented peace. Emotionally and physically drained, but strangely, serenely happy. The dark was gone. He blinked and slowly took in his surroundings.

A green land spread far below him, as he stood gazing out

of the side of a mountain. A vast basin stretched to the horizon, and he could see dots of cattle, strips of road, and clusters of rounded buildings far below and vanishing into the distance. Majestic mountains rose in a rolling, jagged circle around the land, the farthest only smudges in Nehemiah's sight. The sound of flowing water drew Nehemiah's gaze to the right, where only a few yards away a clear river tumbled down into the basin, winding and twisting in the lively static way only a river has. The water drew his eyes and he realized just outside their hideaway lay a beautiful garden, encompassing acres. White statues of stern men in strange outfits with swords at their sides stood sentry between obviously man-made little hills. Beautiful flowers flowed over and around the hills, gathering around the statues' feet, some climbing up the white stone in flowering vines. Nehemiah shielded his eyes from the sun and looked farther down to where the river culminated in a shimmering lake at the base of their mountain. He could see carved wooden structures rising up in a city beside that silver sheen of water.

"Where are we?" he asked, his voice hoarse through his parched throat.

"Right here? The burial mounds," Joe signed slowly, absently. He leaned against the door jamb, his face white, drawn, and expressionless. A pair of goggles dangled from his wrist. Nehi found himself staring at them, wondering what else they could do besides see in the dark.

"That's an ominous name," Nehi said. Joe nodded, a small, exhausted movement.

"But a pretty place." His signs traveled on as he blinked, his face strained and distant. "But nothing of beauty lasts in this dark world." Joe blinked again, long and slow. Then he straightened with an obvious effort and walked out into the sunlight. "Come on, Knee-High, we need to finish this business."

"And find Daniel again," Nehemiah muttered, and his expression darkened. His hand went to his face, running down it in a tired, confused way. "Look, Joe, I don't know what you've been up to for the entire year and a half we've been friends, and I really need to know, but right now... Thanks for saving my older brother."

Joe didn't meet his gaze. But his hands shifted.

"He and Beauty are here, somewhere. Safe." His steps took him around a curve on the path, his back turning to Nehi, hiding any signs. Nehemiah shouldered the bag again and followed into the sunlight.

Daniel and Anna stepped through the massive doors and stopped on a packed wooden floor, dazzled by the blaze and heat and noise. A fireplace roared to their left, taking up almost half the wall. A spit jutted into the fireplace, and a young boy steadily turned the handle making a boar carcass sizzle and sputter on the prongs. Another boy basted the meat and the smell of the cooking marinade filled the hall. Two long wooden tables ran down the center of the huge room, ranged with platters of meat, roasted vegetables, and pitchers and goblets of intricate pottery or metalwork. Men lined the tables, all in raucous mood, loose tunics drawn tight with woven belts, their pants simple wool or linen. Half of them seemed to be in chain mail shirts. The roar of competing stories and anecdotes and laughter filled the hall.

At the back a dais rose, almost as high as the tabletops. Another table stood there, smaller, and intricately carved. The local thain sat behind it in a carved oaken throne. A young man, black hair waving at his shoulders, a crimson cloak draping a black and silver tunic, and massive leather boots. Bright blue eyes, as piercing as a cold winter's day, turned to the newcomers at the doors of the hall. His hand fell to the pommel of his sword. He drew it from its scabbard with a quick, expert movement, the blade catching the firelight with a dazzling glint.

Anna blinked. She had seen swords before, the Ambassador to Faeryland and his entourage carried swords and spears. But the Faeryland swords had a pulse capable of flinging a grown man backward from six feet away. On this weapon she saw no sparks darting, no intricate wiring. This looked like…a stick of sharpened metal. But Daniel's grip still tightened around her arm, and she could feel him tensing, ready to race her out.

A deep bang echoed around the hall as the sword's pommel rammed into the tabletop. The volume of noise dropped a level. The pommel rammed down again, then again, and silence fell. The dark-haired thain rose slowly, impressively, his crimson cloak sweeping behind his shoulders and brushing the ground as he stared at them. Every eye turned to the newcomers.

"My lord," a voice thundered beside Cobeau, and the Hillsons jumped, spinning toward the sound. A tall man with a boar spear and full chain mail stood beside the chimera. "Cobeau Monster-Slayer begs leave to enter your hall. With him come two strangers, tale-weavers, who desire to offer their art for your entertainment."

Silence fell over the hall. An impressive silence, as everyone stared and the great fireplace crackled.

"Greetings, Cobeau Monster-Slayer," the thain spoke. His words echoed through the hall, deep and serious. "Well I remember how you fought beside my father at the border land, protecting my people when the green backs threatened to break through. Ever you are welcome in my hall. Welcome, song-spinners, to the domain of Olofson Bracelet-Giver. I would fain hear your skill this evening, if you are willing to spin your magic under these rafters." The thain's gaze moved to the boy basting the meat. "Boy, fetch your mistress that she and her ladies might partake in the evening's diversion." Then his eyes swept the tabletops, his expression growing sterner. "Shield-bearers and craftsmen of Olofson, your lady approaches. Remember it, and comport your manliness accordingly."

Olofson resumed his seat and reached for his goblet, obviously done with the business. One of the men in chain mail at the end of the bench shifted over a seat. Cobeau slid into the empty place and reached for the platter of meat, as easily as if he did this sort of thing every day. All eyes turned back to the Hillsons, waiting.

"Right then," Daniel murmured just to Anna, softly starting to tune the guitar. "This seems like a place that would appreciate a ballad. You remember that one about David and Jonathan?" Daniel stepped forward and gave a sweeping theatrical bow. He was talking as he came up. Ornately, his words carefully crafted to match the style shown in this country. Anna found herself smiling at how quickly he adapted.

The first chords of the ballad rang around the hall, and Anna hurriedly ran over the words in her mind. Her first note rose clear, stately, and melancholy, lifting to the rafters and filling the huge room. People stilled at the tables, some with meat halfway to their mouths. Daniel quieted his playing and dropped behind his sister. She was obviously more than capable of pleasing this crowd. Anna launched into the tale of doomed friendship, of un-princed Jonathan and reluctant king David. Hardly a sound interrupted her for the entire ten minutes, as she strolled among the eaters, swaying to the music, the firelight playing off her black curls and red coat.

The last note faded slowly, gently, a dying blessing on the friendship that held true through it all. For an instant only the sizzle of the meat filled the huge room. Then the hall erupted.

Goblets overturned as men leapt to their feet, cheering so loud black soot tumbled from the rafters. Anna dipped into a curtsy, smiling at the crowd; but mostly at the young red-haired woman striding in behind the table, a train of eight ladies on her heels. A winsome, twinkling half smile played over the woman's freckled face as she watched the Hillsons. Anna suddenly felt as if a friend had stepped into the room.

An hour later she still felt it, though things had escalated, breaking the austere gravity into wild merriment. She squeaked as two grimy miners grabbed her by the elbows and lifted her onto one of the huge tables running down the length of the hall. Her boots plunked onto the solid wood, and she swirled away from them, her voice laughing as she spun the reel around the warriors and craftsmen. She avoided the cups and dishes on the table that shook and rattled at the volume around them. Men in tunics or vests, ladies in bright-colored dresses, children with dogs at their heels, all of them sang along to the chorus. Even the dogs, howling their enjoyment of the festivities, tails going crazy and stirring the smoke from the fires.

The lady of the hall laid a hand on one of her attendant's arms, her twinkling eyes darting from the girl to a bulky young warrior hovering near the dais. The young lady flashed a smile and bounded down the steps to the warrior. Laughter and loud shouts echoed around them, melding with the reel. The bulky warrior swept the young lady up, dancing her the length of the hall to uproarious calls and laughter. The couple spun around the towering form of Cobeau, and the chimera paused, one foot in the air, carefully balancing two goblets of foaming ale, waiting for them to pass. The dancers swung off, the whole hall clapping and yelling for them as they moved. The chimera sat his foot down and walked on. All eyes followed the dancers, the interesting guitarist, or the stunningly beautiful singer.

No one, not even Anna, thought to wonder who the second goblet might be for.

The hall of Olofson is in most respects a very ordinary hall of a lesser thain, but it stands out from the rest for three reasons that made it ideal for the Ravens. One, the blessed happiness of the marriage between two almost polar opposites, the stark and brooding Olofson and his bright and optimistic Lady Fynaria. Two, their superb meats. And three, the hidden door in the back which leads into a small pine room.

Beau turned, and his shoulder caught the pine board nailed amongst the oak making up the hall. It spun on its hinges and Beau spun with it. The door snapped silently shut behind him.

A crack in the boards let in light and heat from the huge fireplace. The lighting flickered, dim and smokey, but the chimera could see the man at the rough wooden table. A thin man, who sat still, both his hands pointedly on the tabletop, palms downward.

"Is that for me?" he asked. His voice came low, a lisp to it. Beau plunked one of the goblets down in front of the man. The stranger looked up, his rank brown hair hanging in long greasy strands around his face. He let his disappointment show. Beau plunked the second cup down and pushed it toward him. The man's face lit up. "I knew I could trust you and your little black master," the man fairly oozed as his hands wrapped around one goblet. "I am here when the Raven's note told me to come. You are punctual, to the minute. What is this 'task' for which I will be 'paid well?'"

Beau reached into his coat and pulled out a bulky envelope. He dropped it on the table and it made a soft "clunk." Joe's bad handwriting scrawled across the front. The man picked it up cautiously, as if afraid it might bite his dirt-smeared hand. He read the words, glanced up at the towering chimera standing still and silent, and read them again.

"Story Land? It is a long distance," he ventured. Beau just stared at him. The man drummed the tabletop, his broken fingernails making a strange staccato sound. "Half now the little Raven says?" Beau reached into his pocket and pulled out a black pouch. It clinked as he moved it and even in the dim lighting the man's eyes shone as he stared at it. But he glanced back at the words scrawled across the envelope.

"We will find you if it isn't delivered," Cobeau rumbled. His words were quiet, for him, but the growl filled the little room. The man's Adam's apple bobbed on his thin throat. Silence fell between them as the muted sound of Anna's merry reel, the stamping and clapping, drifted in from the main room. The man nodded, quickly, a little nervously. He downed one of the goblets, stuffed the envelope under his ratty tunic, and reached for the other drink. One hand stretched out toward the chimera.

"I will deliver it. Give me the fee."

Anna still stood on the tabletop as the chimera slipped back into the main room, the reel spinning around the rafters. The shadows were strong in the corner with the pine board, and no one noticed his reappearance. He held two empty goblets and strode for the table to plunk them down amidst the rest of the dirty crockery.

Anna caught Daniel's eye as he leaned against the wall across the room, the reel flying from his guitar. He nodded to her and Anna slowed the song. The couple whizzed by again, their steps slowing with the notes, people shouting and clapping rhythmically in their fervor. Anna let the last three notes slow farther, then drew it to a stop. Cheers shook the smoke-blackened rafters, and Anna laughed, the sound drowned in the cacophony. The noise subsided marginally and Daniel slid skillfully into its place.

"What will it be, my lord?" he called up to the dais. "Another new song never yet heard in your green land? Or perhaps a tale of places far from here? Though I hesitate to offer it..." He paused for emphasis, his eyes sparkling as his lips curled in a smile, the scarred half of his face giving it a crooked, interesting look. "I do not think I could rival the stories I've heard flitting through this hall. Perhaps we, poor strangers to this wonderous place, might learn more of your own history as we renew our strength?"

"Stop and eat, song-spinner," the lady of the hall answered, her voice laughing. "You have earned your meal and much more besides." Olofson sat silent and still. But his hand lay in his lady's white one as she directed her women to refresh the tables.

Anna's gaze stayed on her big brother as she hopped off the table onto the dirty floor. He stood in a small crowd, talking and laughing and accepting a large horn filled with something that bubbled and foamed. He slid into the midst of these people, listened enough to find out what they liked, how they spoke, the sorts of things they valued, and easily tailored their performance to it. In a way, he reminded her of Joe. Smart and adaptive, always watching, always analyzing, making his decisions by what he saw around him. But there the similarities ended, she thought with a smile as she watched Daniel guffawing at something someone in his crowd had said, slapping a huge smith on the back so hard the man's nose dipped into his drink. A tall man in an intricate tunic turned from where he stood beside the fireplace, his eyes flitting between the dark thain and Daniel.

"My lord, the boar still requires time before it is ripe for the eating. Mayhaps a tale, stranger?" Others around the man snatched at the idea, starting to chant for a story. More took it up, and soon the word rang through the hot, smoky room. Daniel held up a hand in acknowledgment, nodding at the request, and a roar went through the hall. He downed the rest of the contents of his horn, slapped it on the table and spun to face the people.

"The night lay dark around him, the third time he almost died." Silence fell, as everyone waited to hear the next words. The crackling of the fire took over the stillness. "His name isn't important. Let us call him Happy. For he was most days, as he worked his land and carried his livelihood home. Until the swarm of slavers broke through the defense's walls." A few little "oohs" and "ahs" went around the room. "They took his wife, his sweetheart, his one true love. Happy came home to find his door broken and his heart gone. He didn't wait any longer than it took to gain his weapons before he set out on their trail." Daniel's voice stretched through the room, fascinating his hearers as he went on, weaving a story of true love and close shaves with death.

Anna had heard it before, in various forms, and she only half paid attention as she wound around the chairs to the large form in the shadows at the back of the room. Daniel used to come into the twins' bedroom when they were small and tell them bedtime stories. Their father had done it first, until Nehi blurted out one evening that Daniel's stories were better. Dad had laughed and let their older brother take over the chore. She knew Happy regained his wife, settled somewhere with fat cows and good cheese, and she was glad of it.

The wooden chair squeaked as she settled beside Cobeau. He handed her a slice of meat skewered on a dagger. She took it, tucked her feet up on the chair next to her, leaned comfortably against his side, and began to munch.

It was good meat.

Chapter Thirteen: Watcher of the Hill

"A man shall be commended according to his wisdom: but he that is of a perverse heart shall be despised." -Proverbs 12:8

Morning sunshine touched the shutters, spilling through the cracks onto the packed earth floor. Anna sat up, the mattress crinkling under her. A groan escaped her and she rolled her aching neck. She clambered up and into her dress and pulled the door open. Bright sunlight flooded into the tiny little building set apart for her use, and birdsong and smith's hammers melded with the glorious smell of sausages, eggs, and tea. Anna practically skipped out onto the dirt path.

Today she got to return to the wagon again (much better than that straw-filled, poky mattress), and find Nehi and Joe. A song from last night hummed from her as she spun into the great hall. It looked very different from yesterday. A few soggy patches on the floor showed where drinks had spilled and sunk deep into the earth. The tables sat empty and cleaned, chairs tipped leaning against them, waiting to be occupied. The huge fireplace stood empty and cold. But sunlight streamed through the open shutters, and the busy hum of work came from the servants moving in and out with breakfast things.

Beau sat at the top of one of the tables, a plate heaped with sausage and steaming potatoes in front of him. He paused in his breakfast to wave his fork at Anna. She smiled and waved back.

"Daniel?" she asked. Beau shrugged and Anna rolled her eyes. "Go roust him out, Beau, I'll make sure your breakfast stays here," she ordered. The chimera got up reluctantly and trotted toward the door to obey.

Half an hour later they were zipping along at a good pace, the wind bubble up, the steam blowing strong, and Daniel still complaining.

"It's too bright and too early!" he grumbled. "And sausages are way too heavy for breakfast, my stomach feels like it's sagging."

Anna ignored him with practiced ease. She watched the people instead, enjoying the sights of busy farms and artisans as the country began to move this morning. Green fields rolled off on either side of them, broken by forests creeping down from the mountains that surrounded this basin.

They traveled on, deeper into the country. Anna caught glimpses of men out tending their fields, or herding their animals. People sending sparks flying in their blacksmith stalls, or hawking their wares. Some of the old men just sat in the sun, leaning on nicked swords, discussing past glories. Women in long dresses chased happily screaming children, chatted over their rose bushes, scrubbed laundry at the riverside, and helped their men folk in the fields.

Bands of warriors scattered over the landscape, almost as numerous as the flocks of sheep. As they turned one corner on the white dirt road, twelve mounted warriors thundered past, a shout lifting from their throats, swords drawn. Anna and Daniel sat up a little straighter, straining to see what they rushed toward. It looked as if they thundered down a green field on a clump of tall green plants. They had thick straight stalks (the smallest six feet tall), the only leaves four small root-like protuberances flaring where their stalks met the grass. On top the stalk was a green bulb, almost like a tulip before it blooms. They weren't particularly pretty plants. But surely clearing even such big weeds was the job of the farmers, not warriors geared for battle.

An exclamation came from Daniel as the first of the warriors reached the plants. The bulb nearest to the soldier unfurled with furious speed; it was a sickly pink inside, wet and membranous, with white teeth lining the outside of each of the five petals. The stalk shot forward, and the plant tried to furl closed on the warrior's arm. The Geat's horse sidestepped neatly, as the warrior's sword slashed out. The blade severed the bulb from the stalk. It fell to the ground, furling and un-furling like something in the death throes. All across the field similar battles raged. Anna saw a pack of the plants retreating, their four leaf-like roots digging in and out of the ground till they blurred, as they pulled the plants toward the forest at a shocking speed. The wagon turned around another curve and the noise of the battle drifted off behind them. Anna and Dan-iel looked at each other. They turned slowly to the chimera, as he hummed his tuneless hum, his eyes on the road ahead.

"So..." Daniel drawled. "Are there lots of those things here?" Beau shrugged, his eyes still on the horizon. "Uh huh. What are they?"

"Teeth tulips," Beau rumbled. Silence fell around the com-pany.

"Really?" Anna asked. Beau's big head bobbed.

"We're planning on avoiding them, right?" Daniel demand-ed. "I mean, while that was interesting and all, I'm too tired this morning to fight a giant plant with teeth." Anna suddenly remembered Daniel should be resting. She shoved him in the shoulder.

"Bed, brother," she ordered.

"You're not in command. Not since you bargained our ser-vices so cheap last night, I don't trust you in command now," he grumped. "Olofson would have given us a whole chest full of precious metalwork, gold and silver and goods. But no, you just had to say, 'The joy of bringing our work to you is its own reward.'" He snorted and Anna giggled at his high-pitched sing-song imitation of her

"Oh stop, you old goat," Anna grinned at him, "he still gave us more than we can spend in months, and you caught his la-dy's expression as easily as I did. We couldn't take more than he could afford, his people need something. And I knew you agreed, you shut up right at that point and let me take the lead just so you could grump about the decision today."

Daniel's mouth shut into a tight line as he blinked at nothing for a moment. Then he launched smoothly into complaining about the sausages again. But after a few sentences his words slurred and another yawn took it over, his head hanging. Anna shoved him in the shoulder again and pointed at the skylight leading into the day room. Daniel turned and shuffled wearily towards it.

Anna quickly got her older brother into the wagon, tucked Daniel in the bottom bunk, and paused as she turned to go. Daniel's soft snores slid into the night room, as sleep took him hard, healing his body. Anna looked up at the stars on the ceiling, shining faintly with their glowing paint, and wondered where Nehemiah and Joe were. She prayed they were all right and headed for the skylight and the wagon top again.

As she heaved herself back into the sunlight, she found the wind bubble up and the landscape a blur. She scuttled forward and settled in her little rounded seat above the driver's bench. Beau looked up at her, his hairy face breaking into a huge smile. Anna smiled back and let the silence linger. After about half an hour, a blur of brown appeared in front of them. It grew quickly larger. Beau leaned forward and cut their speed. As they slowed Anna could see the details of the area. A city spread across the green land. Wooden houses, trading posts, smithies, goldsmiths, stables, a conglomeration of human activity and usefulness. People hummed and buzzed around them, busy with a thousand things. Anna noticed almost all the men had swords at their waists, many with spears and chain mail added to their armaments. Mounted warriors milled amongst the crowd, with intricate helmets, cheek guards hinged and fashioned to look like a wild boar with tusks bared.

The buildings clustered around one huge edifice. A rectangular building stood at the top of a large green hill, the first of a series rising to form the foothills to the eastern mountains. In the distance behind the hill Anna glimpsed flowers and statues, and a river cascading down into the basin. But the building overshadowed it all. A huge, sprawling edifice of carven wood painted in blood reds and twisting blues. Seeing it in the morning sunlight, Anna suddenly felt as if Olofson's hall was a tiny plaything, a child's imitation of this real grown-up hall. She shook off the thought quickly, feeling vaguely guilty and very glad their hosts from last night couldn't read her mind.

The roads grew crowded with people as they drew closer to the enormous hall. All a little stiff and serious as they stared curiously at the strangers rolling by. Anna smiled as a group of children ran past to gawk at them, breaking into laughter and yells. She slid onto the bench beside Beau and pumped the wind bubble down. The hum of the city filled the air, voices yelling and calling to each other, horses whinnying, the rumble of wheels and ringing smithies. Spices and rich earth, humanity and horses, the smells wafted into Anna's senses.

As they started up the hill, she noticed some of the buildings had reliefs carved into them; bold scripts she couldn't read, figures acting out scenes of a history she didn't know. She watched another crowd of children race down the street yelling something and found she was laughing at their game. There was something strange, yet nice in this place. The wagon pulled up to the massive stables behind the hall and settled onto the ground as Cobeau shut the steam off. Stable workers strolled closer, eyeing the giant pig with interest, a little wary of her steam-powered shoes.

The thunder of horse hooves on packed earth rolled up to them, and Anna spun in her seat. A contingent of warriors, boar-helmets glinting in the bright morning sun, swept up to their wagon. The leader pushed forward, a tall man with a brown mustache curving into a neatly trimmed beard, face stern and manner stiff. Gold wove inside the silver of his helmet, twisting into a magnificent gleaming boar. He urged his horse closer till the animal touched the wood, prancing and flinging his head. Anna couldn't resist. Her hand went out, laying gently against the horse's neck, feeling his scratchy hair, his warmth, his muscles twitching, relishing even in the horsey smell lifting from him. The horse ducked his head, and his nose shoved into her, a proud demand for attention. Anna stifled a delighted laugh and rubbed the heel of her hand over his face. His owner pretended not to notice.

"Welcome, Cobeau Monster-Slayer," his voice rolled over the company, deep and authoritative. "To me and my liege, your presence is most welcome in this unsettling time. Where is Ravenswing Ashe-Maker? His note reached us, albeit too late."

"Joe will be here soon," Beau rumbled, hopping off the wagon and striding toward Prissy. Anna scrambled down to the pig's other side and started to help remove her tracings.

"Do you bring news?" the man asked, his eyes focused on Beau. Anna looked up at him. She might have imagined it, but it seemed as if the words had changed, dropping lower, urgent, almost desperate for an answer.

"Joe will be here soon," Beau rumbled again. The man sat back on his horse, his face stiff and expressionless. The backdoor of the wagon flew open with a bang, and five boar spears dropped, pointing at the doorway.

"Whoa," Daniel commented. The leader's horse pranced backward till the man could see the newcomer.

"I am Wiglaf, Shield-Bearer to King Hrothgar the Seventh, and Watch-Keeper on this hill," the leader's voice rolled over Daniel. "You come with Cobeau, a warrior of renown amongst us, and so I do not press you for your allegiances. But I still desire to know your name, and what you do in these lands."

"Daniel Hillson, a traveler," Daniel answered, his voice ringing with an authority of his own, almost a challenge to this stranger. "My sister and I don't plan on posing any danger to your king, or your people."

"It is well. I would fain hear more of you, but I must bear news of Cobeau's coming to my king. Come." Wiglaf's boots thudded into the dirt as he dropped from his horse, flicking the reins to one of his company. He began to stride for the hall without even glancing behind him to see if Daniel obeyed. Daniel looked over at Anna and raised one eyebrow, a comment on the leader's abruptness. Beau shoved Prissy's tack into its spot inside the wagon bench, waved the stable workers at the big pig, and trotted to catch up to Wiglaf. Anna fell in step beside him, catching Daniel's arm in hers. As Wiglaf strode past, boar-helmed warriors stationed around the hall stood suddenly taller, spears shooting straighter. Wiglaf took no notice. He led the way quickly to the great doors of the hall, where a huge man stood sentry.

As they walked up, a green stalk dropped off the roof. Anna caught an instant's glimpse of a bulb unfurling, white teeth and pink membrane aimed straight for the sentry's head. A stench like rotted meat and dead things swept over her.

Then Wiglaf's hand shot out.

He caught the plant at the stalk just under the bulb and jerked it away from the sentry. His muscles strained and he ripped the bulb from the plant's body. Green juice spurted from both ends as the bulb furled and unfurled, like a snapping animal. Wiglaf's fist smashed into the center of the bulb with a wet squelching sound. The plant gave a strange sort of gurgling squeak and its petals went limp. The warrior flung it on the ground behind him.

"It is becoming an infestation," Wiglaf murmured, and strode forward into the hall. Daniel steered his sister far around the plant, glaring at the bulb as if he suspected it might suddenly grow green wings and fly at them. The smell of the thing was horrible.

As she stepped inside, Anna found her steps slow to a stop. She stared at the massive doors, her mouth hanging open in admiration. They stood twenty-four feet over her head, figures carved into scenes all over the hard wood. Battles between single opponents or hulking monsters seemed to be the most prominent. Some were excessively bloody even as wood carvings. All of them were fascinating, dealing with a history Anna longed to know more about.

Daniel's arm tugged at hers and Anna walked reluctantly away from the doors into the hall. But as she looked around her, Anna's sense of awe and delight rose higher. Thick pillars rose in two lines down the length of the immense hall, each one carved with more of the intricate scenes of a history Anna didn't know. The pillars supported rafters arching two stories over her head, each one a carefully crafted figure of a massive warrior, boar helmets meeting at the apex of the ceiling. With each step the painted eyes of the giant warriors watched her progress. At the back of the great edifice stood two thrones of beaten, intricately worked gold. A huge man sat in the largest of the thrones. His black beard (peppered with gray) flowed down his gold-linked chain mail to his waist, blue eyes bright and clear. Anna couldn't help thinking he looked like Olofson's grandfather.

"Cobeau has entered our lands," Wiglaf boomed. It echoed around the hall. Anna suddenly realized the echo effect must be a design of the builders; a people who took delight in the majestic and dramatic, it seemed. "We still await Ravenswing. The Great-Chested says only to await the small one." Anna glanced from Wiglaf to Beau, stifling a laugh at the name tacked to the chimera. Somehow it fit though. "I know little of the strangers."

Daniel and Anna suddenly found about forty pairs of eyes focused on them from those gathered in the hall. Worried eyes. Anna suddenly felt the tension in the room. It didn't come from a fear of the newcomers, there was something else afoot here.

"Greetings, Cobeau, warrior from over the mountains," King Hrothgar rumbled. His voice filled the entire hall. "You are welcome to me this day. Though some there might be who speak ill of any travelers from outside our land at this time, I know your honor and loyalty to our house to be firm. Who travels with you to these great lands we claim as home?"

"Anna and Daniel," Beau rumbled. His mouth closed and he stood still staring at the gathered company. Daniel rolled his eyes, took a step forward, and lifted his voice to accommodate the echoing hall.

"I am Daniel Hillson, son of Titus Hillson and this is my sister, Anna. We too seek, uh, Ravenswing, as you called him. Our brother travels with him." Daniel's voice dropped to a mutter that only Anna and Beau could hear. "'Travels,' right. We hope that's the correct word anyway, and 'victim' doesn't fit better."

"What do you–" Hrothgar began, but stopped suddenly as a cold wind rushed into the hall. The sky outside darkened, suddenly and sharply, as if a black blanket obscured the sun. Hissing, whining wind hit the walls and bounced into echoes. Hrothgar's eyes grew wide as he stared over the crowds' heads at something outside the great open doors. Anna turned just in time to catch a glimpse of the sight that turned his face pale.

A great black bubble enveloped the plain just outside of town. Jagged white lines shot over it as it undulated, a hurricane-force wind rushing around it. No, sucking into it.

An instant she saw it there, a glimpse, as whole swaths of soil and grass ripped from the plain and hurtled toward the blackness. Then the wind changed to a frantic hissing wail, the blackness peeled back, like an ocean tide on a frantic high speed. One second to see it all, then the blackness, the freezing wind, the whining hiss, it all disappeared.

Five hundred coal black warriors stood marshalled on the plain.

Silence crackled in the great hall. The Geats' faces were ashen and drawn as they stared at the army just outside their city. The king rose from his throne, slowly, deliberately, his expression hardening into one of a seasoned warrior looking on a new battle. A battle he knows he cannot win.

Daniel leaned close to Cobeau.

"Still got that impressive weapon stock in your wagon? I think we're going to need it."

Chapter Fourteen: A God of Liberty

"And where the Spirit of the Lord is, there is liberty."

-2 Corinthians 3:15b

Nehemiah gave a little groan as he hefted the bag again, swinging it up from the smooth grass beside the river.

"I hope this thing is important after I've lugged it this far," he grunted. Joe glanced over his shoulder, setting the hoverboard down after refilling the tanks.

"It's important," he signed. The mute slid his cupped hand into the river dancing beside their path and splashed the cold water on his face. Nehemiah took the opportunity to clip Hope's goggles on and zoom in on this new country. He focused on a sprawling city at the edge of these gardens, a huge rectangular building watching over it all. He could make out soldiers with silver helmets around that hall. He scanned farther and could see a wide plain stretched out before the city, with farms and thatched houses dotted here and there. Nehi turned his eyes back to the city. It teemed with life, and he could see more of the silver-helmed warriors scattered throughout the crowds. Were they wearing...swords? Nehemiah looked up at the statue towering over the two boys beside the river. It was a slim handsome man with a long flowing blanket hanging from his shoulders, a sword drawn in his right hand. Nehemiah looked at the solemn face of the young man and thought it looked like David, about to order his men not to kill Saul. Although he wasn't sure about the blanket.

"Joe, what's with the blanket?" Nehemiah asked as his friend stood up, his legs shaking so hard at the effort Nehi could see it. Joe looked up at the statue, his grimy hair dripping water down his pale face and leaving streaks of dirt. And... was that dried blood coming off his hair?

"Not a blanket, it's a c-l-o-a-k. A sort of coat here." A smile shot across his tired face, and a glint of humor showed in his reddened eyes as he shoved the hoverboard around to face the plain. "You'll like this country, Knee-High. It's bizarre and a little violent sometimes, but they're honorable, brave, and a good people. Usually."

"So you think Anna and Daniel are safe here somewhere?" Nehemiah asked as he stepped up on the board, positioning the bag again with a grimace at the pull on his tired muscles.

"As safe as anywhere in this nasty world," Joe answered, his signs small, depressed and defeated.

Joe's head shot up and he suddenly went rigid, staring down to the valley. Nehemiah tensed, looking for the reason. A sharp whistling wind, the same he had heard outside the cabin, drifted to them faintly. Nehemiah strained to see closer, a hunger to know what this strange sound meant pulsing inside him. The source blinked into view and his jaw dropped.

A huge black bubble enveloped the grassy plain, fluctuating and pulsing like a live thing, hissing with wild wind. It ripped up everything within a quarter mile of it, pulling objects into itself. Like the force of a tornado, grass, animals, thatched huts, rolled and broke and sucked into the roiling bubble. Nehi caught a glimpse of the awesome, terrifying object, there for an instant. Then the debris collapsed on the plain. The sharp hiss rose to a frantic pitch, the blackness peeled away, mushrooming into the air and disappearing in a second. If Nehi had blinked he would have missed it. The black bubble left behind five hundred well-equipped soldiers in coal black uniforms. Nehemiah gaped, his jaw on his chest. One minute the plain had been empty and now it was filled with soldiers from the Kingdom of the Prophet's Peace!

Joe leapt onto the board with a mad energy, his toe kicking the power to high as he moved. In one second his feet slid into the slots, he balanced, leaned forward, and the board shot ahead at the command. But the mute's muscles spasmed. His body folded over, slowly, as if it just gave out. The board wobbled and tipped, shooting left. Nehemiah's arm darted around Joe's chest, pulling him close, balancing for both of them. The board evened out. It shifted lazily forward, as Nehi felt Joe's chest heaving in sharp gasps. The mute reached up, his hand gripping Nehi's arm. Joe pulled forward, and Nehemiah took the hint. He increased their speed, gently, making certain he could control the board with Joe and the bulky bag.

The wind began to tear into their hair, whipping blond and black till it wound in and out with each other. The board wooshed over the smooth dirt paths of the garden, always downhill. Nehemiah watched the plain drawing closer quickly, almost as if it rose up to meet them, growing a little larger in his vision every moment. Joe sagged against him. Nehi felt the mute's weight change, his head lolling. He risked a glance down. Joe lay asleep, propped against his tall friend.

Nehemiah watched the path ahead of him, carefully avoiding rocks and pot-holes as they rushed downhill. He could only spare the occasional glance to see what was happening on the plain below. A group of soldiers in silver helmets formed in front of the Black Army. But the silver ones seemed a very small number. They filed out quickly and skillfully, dropping into ranks of footmen, with horsemen behind. Nehemiah got a confused idea of two groups of pieces set up on a grassy green board, both waiting for the other to make a move. The move came from the black pieces. A contingent of the black clad soldiers marched toward the rows of silver soldiers, every piece of equipment in place, every step perfectly attuned to its neighbor; a creature of one entity, one purpose, drilled for just one thing in life. The Black Army lived and died committed to their work.

The board hit level ground and Nehi carefully straightened, rebalancing with his burdens. Soft green grass covered the plain, good stuff for the hoverboard. Nehi leaned right and sent them dashing toward the rear of the silver soldiers. It was an educated guess, knowing just a little of Joe's history with the Prophet's Peace, and how desperate the little mute had been to reach this green country. The wind cut into Nehi's face as the hoverboard rushed over the grass with its soft swish, and the line of silver-helmed soldiers drew closer.

Dust rose on the path leading from the city and a man in a crown and long fur-lined cloak swept up, surrounded by an escort of spear bearers. The party thundered past the silver-helmed soldiers into the center of the plain and the crowned one reined in sharply. His horse plowed a furrow of good black earth, and Nehi almost felt he could hear the thump of the man's boots hitting the ground as he leapt off. The man began to march for the black soldiers, his escort falling into place neatly behind him. Another tall man strode beside him, his helmet flashing gold amidst the silver of the filigree forming the boar shape. But one man towered over all the rest as they moved across the plain. Nehemiah spotted Cobeau walking in the midst of the escort, just behind the one with a crown.

A glint of sunlight on glossy black hair caught his eye. He turned so suddenly he almost overbalanced the board, looking for it. Anna and Daniel stood on the hill at the top of the city, watching the proceedings. Nehi blinked, zooming his goggles in to look closer. Anna's arm shot out, pointing toward the rushing hoverboard and the two boys. Daniel's shot out almost as fast, pulling hers back. Nehi could almost hear him hissing in her ear, "Don't point them out!" He was right of course. It's a dangerous thing to be noticed by armed people, and there were about eight hundred of them out here on the grass. Daniel disappeared behind the enormous hall and Nehi paid attention to his board again, facing back toward the silver soldiers.

He found the tall gold-helmed stranger looking their direction. Nehi glimpsed bright eyes in a grim face staring straight at him. Then Nehemiah reached the rear of the line and he leaned back, kicking the board up and staggering onto the grass. Joe stiffened, his eyes shooting open. He broke away, disappearing into the line of silver soldiers, his hand on Nehi's arm, drawing him along.

The warriors glanced at the boys, but didn't move from their ranks as the two wove in and out of their lines. Joe walked swiftly, steady and competent, his face a stony blank. He held his left arm stiff at his side, but otherwise he seemed at ease striding into the middle of two armies faced off for war. Nehemiah kept behind him, wondering if he looked half as competent and doubting it, the big bag pulling at his sore shoulder. They drew closer to the front line of the silver soldiers, and Nehi could see the two groups talking in the middle of the plain. Nehemiah paused in mid-step as he caught sight of a familiar face in the midst of the black clad contingent.

"Simmons is here again," Nehemiah muttered to Joe's back. The mute just nodded.

The stern figure with the golden boar and bright eyes suddenly stood in front of them, so suddenly Nehemiah stepped back and blinked. He swept his goggles off and clipped them to his holster, waiting to see what happened next.

"Ravenswing, we have been watching for you," the man said, his blue eyes fixed on Joe. "Did you find it?" It was a desperate whisper; Nehi felt a world of roiling emotions in those four words. Joe motioned for Nehemiah to let down the black bag. The mute dropped to his knees, pulled out the smaller shoulder bag, and handed it up to the man. The stranger's face shone with relief, wonder, and joy as he focused on Joe again, his mouth moving wordlessly. The mute motioned him toward the group in the middle of the plain, and the stranger melted away.

Joe stayed kneeling, head bent, staring at the grass. Nehemiah watched a breath shudder in and out of his little friend.

"I don't know what you're up to, Joe. I'm in the dark here," Nehi said. His knees hurt as he dropped to kneel in front of the mute. Joe's head lifted slowly, achingly, staring up at Nehi through bleary eyes. "But we are holding the Light. I can tell these people need you. Keep the vision burning, let that light of His hope shine through you, and take strength from it; God's right here with us and waiting at the end to say, 'Well done, faithful servant.' Come on, let's drive the dark back a little more."

Nehemiah climbed to his feet and held out a hand. The mute took it, shaking as he used his friend's strength to gain his feet. He looked up at him again, bloodshot green eyes meeting deep dark ones. Joe gave him a nod, his jaw squaring, and moved toward the leaders grouped in the middle of the plain.

Rachel Jaimen stared at the dirty, bulky packet. Her maid carried it in by a corner, her nose wrinkled, and laid it on the vanity in front of her mistress. Something inside it went, "clunk."

"Out," Rachel ordered, waving a hand toward the door. The maid swept out, her heels clicking against the floor as she nearly ran. She had no wish to have another jeweled mirror flung at her for being too slow to exit. Her scar still stood livid on her forehead from the last time.

The door clicked closed, and Rachel stared at the packaging. It smelled of ale and filth. She turned it delicately, her perfectly manicured fingers barely touching it. The writing was in a surprisingly good hand. Only her name and address. But she had just moved into these new quarters after the overthrow, barely a week ago. Rachel's red lips moved up into a smile and she reached for her penknife, relishing the moment.

She did love a present.

She tipped the envelope carefully. Something wrapped in a black jeweler's cloth clunked onto her vanity. A card tumbled out on top of it. Rachel picked up the card. It was a gift certificate, for a specific weekend at a local total makeover salon; plastic surgery, hair implants, even changing the skin tone to a certain degree. Well, of all the gall! Who thought she needed changed? Rachel looked at herself in the mirror, turning her perfect head, her red lips pursed. Her high cheekbones, smooth features, willowy frame, all of it perfect. A vision of beauty. Still... She studied the card. Her lips moved in a smile that marred the beauty. A look of spite, of a vicious humor playing through her. It might be fun, just to tease dear old Mark. Her fiancé was a pitiful excuse of a man, a weakling in almost every area. But a Hernon, the ruling class now. Rachel studied the card again. She didn't want anything that would jeopardize her position, at least until the wedding was finalized. But wouldn't he fly into a tizzy if she went and changed...what? Everything?

A laugh flew around the dressing room. Outside the door her maid shot a look at the butler, setting a vase of perfect flowers on the bedroom's nightstand. Worry shone from both their faces; that sound meant no good. Still chuckling, Rachel flipped the black jeweler's cloth open.

A necklace of fantastic worth twinkled in the dressing room lights. Rachel's mouth fell open slowly, her dark eyes widening in wonder and delight. Her finger ran along the certificate, feeling its smooth sides. A vision of Jill popped into Rachel's mind, and it decided her. Jill, the fair-weathered friend. Well, friend may not be the right word. Work associate? They had run together before Jill found her Bill and became one of the Trio. Rachel's eyes rolled, her pretty face changing to one of disgust and hatred. But then that smile

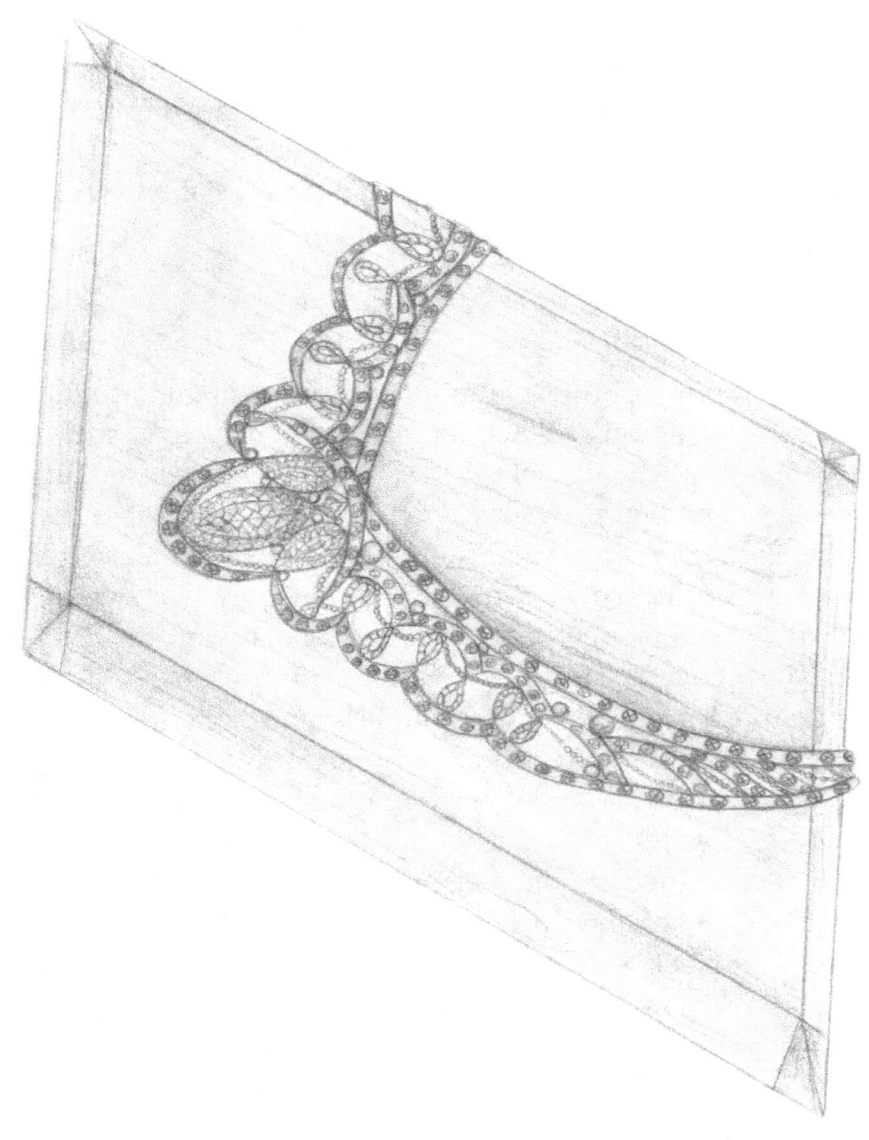

Necklace

came back. Wouldn't it be fun to get a new look, then go to Jill with this lovely on. Rachel picked up the necklace, gently, reverently, turning it so the jewels sparkled and danced on her ceiling. That would show her.

Rachel drew a quick circle around the weekend next month, marking it as taken. She would do it.

They kept moving, till Nehi found himself slipping into the midst of the group talking between the two armies, past the spear-bearing bodyguards in the rear. The bodyguards looked at the boys. Their gaze fastened on Joe, and none of them moved to stop them. Nehemiah slowed as they drew nearer to the big man in the crown, wondering what they were doing here. A finger jabbed him in the back. He spun toward the jabber and he found his brother smiling at him. Daniel's dark arms wrapped around Nehi's shoulders and squeezed in a bear hug, and Nehemiah's tired, dirty face broke into a grin. He let the bag drop as Daniel stepped up next to him, and the two brothers waited for what would happen next. The man with the crown stood two men ahead of them, livid as he faced a tall black clad soldier. Each party kept a careful, respectful distance. The black one moved with a swagger, a white sash around his waist, swaying as if he had too much energy to stand still, speaking with a visible sneer. Simmons stood near the swaggering one. His gaze wandered around the grassy plain, as if he were bored with it all.

Joe slipped away from Nehi, back into the line of silver soldiers. But he took care his friend saw him go, making two quick signs as he moved; "Watch me."

"Ahmed of the Prophet's Peace, you are a coward!" the king's angry voice rang over the plain.

"For refusing to settle this in single combat?" the dark soldier sneered. "I think not. I do not doubt I could defeat you, Hrothgar, Seventh though you be. But I know your people stand helpless before my army. Swords against lasers? There is no contest here."

"Then we make it one!" the king thundered. "I will lay my sword aside, let it be grappling. Any champion you send against me, by might of naught but my arms and the will of the Father I will defeat him! You have no right to be here on our lands. We have done you no ill. But fight me if you must, and I will prove the better man!"

"And I tell you, King Hrothgar," the soldier answered, cruel amusement in the words, "show us your book and we will agree with you and leave without a fight." A shadow fell over Hrothgar's face. There for an instant before he overcame it and stirred, his shoulders squaring as he moved to answer. A hand gripped his shoulder and the one with the golden boar helmet stood beside him. Joe's black bag hung limp from one shoulder, almost empty, and a white hard shell box lay in his hand.

"Wiglaf, Shield-Bearer to the king," he introduced himself, sweeping Ahmed and his officers with his proud gaze. He clicked open the white box and reached in. "You say we have not our book, and thus you invade our lands without warning or provocation. But I have proof you are wrong." His hand lifted high, so that everyone on the plain could see what he held.

An elegant black book lay in his palm. The cover was warped and mildewed. The pages were yellow and even from a distance they could see the ancient paper crackling as he turned the book gently. But every breath caught, every eye opened wide as they stared at the collection of brittle pages within the tattered cover. Wiglaf lowered it, laying the book on his other hand and gently, oh, so gently, shifted through the pages in front of Ahmed and his cohorts. Proving it held the history they claimed, not just a set of empty yellowed pages.

Nehemiah stood close enough he could see some of the words and he craned his neck, trying to see more, his eyes shining. Wiglaf took a step back, replaced the book in the case, clicked it closed, slid it reverently into the shoulder bag, and handed it behind him to a young man, almost a boy. The young one turned and made for the city at a quick trot, heading toward the fortified hall with his precious cargo.

Nehemiah swallowed hard. It took him a moment to find his voice.

"I've been banging that bag around all night. Joe didn't tell me what was in it!" he hissed.

"Joe doesn't tell anyone anything remember, Nehi?" Daniel muttered back. Nehi looked at the little mute, not bothering to hide the daggers in his eyes. Joe stared at Ahmed and Simmons and didn't seem to be paying attention to Nehi. Nehemiah followed his gaze. A vein stood out on Ahmed's neck and fury flared in his face.

"But you can't have that, we were told–" Ahmed began to splutter. His mouth snapped closed and his gaze darted to his ally. Simmons' expression stayed the same easy sneer habitual with him. But a hint of interest glinted in his eyes as they moved over Wiglaf. His gaze suddenly shifted and locked onto Nehemiah standing in the back of the group, he and Daniel towering over most of the silver-helmed soldiers. Nehi forced himself not to recoil, his heartbeat thudding. He met the look, shoulders squared, begging God for strength. A calm bravery swept over him that he knew wasn't just from himself. He recognized the feeling from sitting on a rooftop in the Prophet's Peace, broiling under the sun and waiting for Joe to move; peace from the hand of God. Anna standing watch on the hill flashed across his mind and a smile shifted the corners of his mouth. She must be praying again, he thought.

"Things can always go wrong, Ahmed," Simmons drawled, his gaze shifting away, squinting between the soldiers at the small black and blond smudge of Joe. "But I don't see what dif-ference it makes if they have that wad of paper or not. They're still not agreeing to convert to your Prophet, are they?" Ah-med's eyes snapped back to King Hrothgar. There was a thoughtful look on his hard face that Nehi didn't like.

"You swore just now that you would take your men and go if we could prove our book still in our midst," Hrothgar thun-dered. The voice was deep and dangerous. But not hopeful. He knew too much to expect this black clad soldier to give up the field on such a flimsy thing as a promise. "Prove your honor and abide by your word." Joe's eyes shot to his friend, locking onto Nehemiah's dark gaze.

"Get up there and translate," he signed, the movements forceful and urgent. Nehemiah stepped up next to Wiglaf and Hrothgar, a part of him wondering what on earth he thought he was doing. He kept his head faced to the Black Army, but his eyes stayed mostly on Joe as the mute stood buried in the silver-helmed warriors, out of obvious sight of the soldiers of the Prophet's Peace.

"It is true. We will overwhelm your small army and take your book with ease. You do not even have the most ancient of firearms," Ahmed said, his sneer coming back. "I ask you now, King Hrothgar, will you and your people convert to Islam and the peace of the Prophet's ways, or will you force us to take our own measures?" Hrothgar straightened, his head high. His eyes met Ahmed's and there was fire there.

"We are men of Geat," Hrothgar rumbled. "You would have us bow under your yoke, turning us into slaves and taking our lands and freedom. We will not convert!" Nehemiah's heart swelled as he heard those words come from this stranger be-side him, the same words he had said so often to his old mas-ter.

"You are not thinking what you are saying, Ahmed Q-a-r-e-e-b," Joe signed, his hands a subtle blur as he kept them low.

"You would be starting a war that would bring war on your own country." Nehemiah translated it to the black clothed soldier, his words firm. But even to him it sounded faked, like he was reciting something.

"I do not know who you are, boy," Ahmed spat out at Nehemiah. "But I can see you are not from this country. What does any of this have to do with you?" *Good question,* Nehemiah thought, and he gave Joe a sidelong glance. Joe just shrugged, telling his friend to answer it in his own words. Some help he was. Those days of torment under a member of this people flooded his memory again, and Nehemiah glanced at the two brave warriors standing beside him. He knew his answer.

"I am a Sojourner of the Way, and my country no longer exists. But I am of the same mind, at least in this," he said. "My God is a God of liberty and peace, of joy and freedom, and you would destroy all of it. You would force your own law on those who don't follow your despairing, false religion. You say Allah brings peace, but I know the truth. When you follow Allah's ways to the end, he is a prophet of blood and cruelty. I follow a God of love, strength, and liberty, the liberty these men are protecting in their country." Joe began to sign again, sliding his words onto Nehi's little speech. Nehemiah's voice rang as he translated, allowing the men gathered around him to think it was his words.

"I stand with these men, and I promise you this, Ahmed Qareeb; if you attack this country without cause, your country will pay. Prophet's Peace will be humiliated and overrun. It will be forced to let go of not only this country, but the others you have wrongfully overthrown." How on earth was Joe going to make good a threat like that? Nehemiah glanced at the bag by his feet and thought he probably had ways of making it good. "This Simmons who you count as a valuable ally will be one of the chief actors to overthrow your own country. Are you listening, Ahmed? Even as we stand here, the theft of your own book is being enacted by these people you now call allies! Skitterers, spider drones armed with sarin gas, are setting up right now to enter your vault. And the streets around the house are empty of soldiers. You know I speak the truth; today is the one day they can get in."

Murmurs, little cries of dismay and fury flew through the Muslim contingent. The black clad soldiers pulled back, staring at Simmons, till he stood alone on the grass. His greatcoat billowed out in a breeze, flaring like broken bat wings, and a copper wand glinted in his belt. Simmons' eyes narrowed to slits as he stared at Nehemiah.

"Who are you, boy?" he spat. Nehi felt his skin crawling, his muscles spasming at the old terror. His fist clenched and he waited for what might come.

Chapter Fifteen: Blood and Ash

"For the LORD your God is he that goeth with you, to fight for you against your enemies, to save you." -Deuteronomy 20:4

I don't know you, boy." Simmons face rippled with evil, his voice ringing with such cruelty, even Hrothgar and his bodyguard stepped back. Wiglaf's face tightened, his mouth a hard line, and his hand dropped to his sword hilt. Simmons took a step nearer, his lips twitching into a smile. Nehi stood his ground. "Oh, I know more about you than anyone here. What makes you turn a scream to a shriek, what happened in Abid's closet, your deepest scars." His sneer was sultry, bantering, a man who knew he twisted an emotional thumbscrew tighter with each syllable, and delighted in it. "But I don't know you. Looking men in the eye like you're one of us. Saying things you can't know anything about."

"I'm Nehemiah, saint loved by God," Nehi answered, a little smile spreading over him. His words came quietly, but filled with a steady confidence. The love he spoke of warmed his tone, giving him such a steady peace it almost radiated from his manner. Around him heads tipped, faces curious and a little confused.

"And who is this?" Simmons hissed suddenly, turning on Joe with a ferocious predatory speed. Only Nehi noticed the spin took the man another full step closer to him. The silver soldiers pulled back, automatically, hardly realizing they moved, till Joe stood exposed in view. Ahmed and his men fell back farther, their fair faces white as they watched their ally transform into something evil. A snarl flickered over Simmons' face, his head tilting to one side and his eyes brightening unnaturally. His voice was a low, menacing hiss that carried over the plain. "What's wrong with that arm, little one? A bit sore?"

Joe dove into a roll, his back thudding into the grass and propelling him forward, his laser goggles popping over his eyes as he moved. Grass tufts and dirt erupted around the mute, as Simmons' laser whined. Laughter billowed from him, crazed, harsh laughter that said he was toying with his prey, rejoicing in the palpitating fear he knew he was causing. Nehemiah let a shout rip through his tight throat as his hand dropped for Hope. Simmons' heavy Krackmen crashed into his kidney, with all the ferocious speed Nehi would never forget. Pain sizzled through him, his body folding on itself. The Krackmen filled his vision as Simmons dashed it up toward his face. Nehi managed to jerk his arm up. The heavy laser cracked into his forearm, absorbing some of the force of the blow before it glanced off and smashed into his face, sending him crashing into the dirt.

"Not now, boy, I'll be back for you after I've dealt with this one," Nehemiah heard Simmons hiss. Nehi's vision sparked as he curled into himself. Part of him heard the black soldiers moving, the officers spinning toward their men. Readying the ranks to fire on the enemy.

Simmons' laser rose, his smile twitching as he spun toward Joe. The mute flung himself to the side, skittering over it like a broken crab, left arm stiff, his face a strained white mask. Simmons leapt forward, his eyes bright as the laughter came. It melded with the growing clamor of a battlefield, whining lasers priming, swords clashing into shields, officers yelling orders. For Nehi the world spun in fuzzy images, as he slowly pulled himself to a kneeling position. He thought he recognized the chimera's footsteps thundering into the earth in a run.

Yellowing teeth glinted behind Simmons' smile as he darted over the grass, devouring the ground separating him from Joe. Two shadows fell across him and the smile became a snarl as he spun. Simmons turned and saw the last two things he ever saw in life; Cobeau's raised Brunhiem and Wiglaf's falling sword.

A whine and a flash of light, a crunch and sunshine glinting on steel; what was left of Simmons folded over gently on itself and collapsed in a smoking, wet pile.

Cobeau dropped the muzzle of his short laser toward the grass. A trail of white steam drifted from it as it recharged. Nehemiah focused enough to see copper glinting in the chimera's hands. Beau charged down the plain, spinning his upper half to point his hands back toward the king as he ran. Half a double-Kerr shield twinkled in the sunlight as it lay strapped to his palms, two copper discs made up of honeycomb shapes.

"Fire!" Ahmed screamed, his face suffused with a wild fury, a vein still pulsing on his neck. As Nehi focused more he could see Ahmed's officers behind the man, a worried clump staring wide-eyed at their leader. Lasers leapt up in the arms of the Black Army's front rank.

"For honor and the Geats!" Hrothgar and Wiglaf's voices melded in a great roar, lifting over the drawn out scream of Ahmed's anger, carrying back up to the hill and out over the plain. Every warrior in the silver ranks echoed it, shields and spears lifting, feet beginning to slam into the earth as they charged toward the enemy. Among the ranks white lasers began to hit, flashing into the sunlight, dropping Geats in their mad charge, leaving smoking bodies and screaming men. Their king led on, his huge feet pounding into the earth, his blue eyes focused on Ahmed, his face aflame with a thirst for the man's blood.

Daniel whipped in front of the king, palms pointed toward Cobeau, copper Kerr shield glinting in the bright morning sunshine. A wall of red honeycombs shimmered into the air between the Geats and the Black Army. White balls of laser fire slammed into it, lighting up the morning with an unearthly glow. Hrothgar's heels plowed a furrow in the soft ground as he slid to a shocked stop, his sword tip hovering just above the red. His head turned slowly, and he glared at the stranger. Daniel stood with feet planted against the force rocking into the shield, blue-tinted goggles pulled over his eyes, his body carefully behind the red wall.

"This is not your fight, Sojourner!" Ahmed screamed over the constant whine of laser fire, and the softer, deeper pulse of the atmospheric shield absorbing the blows.

"My bile rises for it, but I agree with the enemy," Hrothgar growled, the thirst of battle still working on his scarred face.

"Lasers against swords, your highness?" Daniel said, shaking his head. "That's not bravery, that's suicide." His voice lifted into a shout, his cynical tone carrying over the grass to the Black Army. "Yeah, well I happen to be behind this shield too you'll notice, you blood-thirsty idiot! I think that makes it my fight!"

"You cannot reshape that shield forever!" Ahmed shouted back, his voice hoarse with the fury behind it. Daniel's lips pursed, and Hrothgar's eyes narrowed as he saw the expression. He didn't understand much about this sort of warfare. But he understood outflanking. Wiglaf stepped up beside Daniel, his face stern and blue eyes blazing.

"What do you need, warrior from over the mountains?" he demanded.

"Someone with a good knowledge of lasers to take out that madman!" Daniel answered, as the laser fire slammed into a constant white blur against the red. He could see the Black Army reforming, the back ranks beginning to flow out as the front kept them pinned, readying to close on the Geat's left flank.

"I've got it," Nehemiah answered, stepping up beside his brother. Hope glinted as he steadied her with both hands, his goggles turning the world a dyed blue. In one beautiful, fluid moment, Nehemiah swung around the Kerr shield, sending a flurry of shots into the enemy ranks. The Compton fired gamma rays, invisible to the human eye, and it worked in silence. But as Nehi swung back behind the shield his work was evident.

Ahmed's mouth snapped closed and he dropped to the ground, his face draining, both hands clamping onto his leg; a gaping hole smoked in the center of his thigh, ash flecking off it. The officer in the midst of the ranks, reforming them, acting out his commander's will, fell out of sight. But his screams of agony carried clearly to the Geats. Four more among Ahmed's officers collapsed, ominously silent, whisps of smoke trailing off their still forms. Nehi took a breath, his back close to his brother's, forcing his tight muscles to relax. Then he swung back out, his finger clamped on the trigger. Fourteen men in the front rank fell in a line, collapsing on the ground, their legs useless, their cries and screams raised to join the clamor. Their mates beside them cowered. But the second rank filled the hole in an instant, as those on the edge swung their lasers toward this deadly shooter beside the king.

Nehi didn't give them the chance to focus their aim. He swung forward again, Hope firing constantly. In two seconds ten more dropped on the edge, and he pivoted back behind the shield, his back ramming into Daniel's.

"Wait," Daniel ordered before Nehi could take a fourth shot. "They've gotten your position now." His voice rose into a shout. "Hey, new commander! Aren't you forgetting something?" A thickset, middle-aged man turned his head from his wounded, focusing past the shield on Daniel. "I know what the security is like for your book. I trained under my father, Titus Hillson, I toured your House of the Book once. Is this the sixth-month mark for airing the building?"

"I am Mufasa al Abdul, and I do not answer the enemy," the man rumbled. "You will be dead in–"

"Is this the day the vents open?" Daniel shouted. The man's

lips pursed and even from their distance they could see the worry tensing his body.

"Yes."

"Then my brother told you the truth. This whole takeover is a distraction, a way to get the army out of the capital. This contingent came from the capital, didn't it?" No movement answered him. Which was in itself an answer. "You know your security is down today, on the one day it shouldn't be, because this Simmons showed up with his gadget to zap you all over here. Get home now or your book is gone."

"Christian!" the man spat. "You speak in lies and riddles!" But his eyes darted away as he said it, his fist balling and loosening rhythmically, showing his fear. A sharp whistle came from down the ranks. Nehemiah spun, focusing on the crumpled little dot of black in the midst of the green grass. A white hand rose, pointing at the towering form of Beau, standing alone on the plain. His feet stood planted firm, holding the atmospheric shield steady, keeping the Geats from devastation by laser fire.

"Keep him talking," Nehemiah ordered Daniel, and broke into a run. He found Wiglaf racing beside him. He didn't question it, just leaned into the run, adrenaline masking the way his tired, bruised muscles complained. Behind him he heard his brother keep shouting. A part of him registered the way Daniel skillfully wove facts into fear, plucking small things from the past, weaving them into a knowledge that was crystal clear and deadly. The suddenness of the enemy's presence in the Sojourner's kingdom; the work of Simmons and his black bubble. The perfect timing today; the draining of the Prophet's army in the capital just at the hour it was needed most. The certain knowledge of even the means of the theft; skitterers could fit through a vent, and carry off a book.

Nehi and Wiglaf reached the huge chimera, sword and laser drawn, watching for some sign of what to do next. Beau slid the straps from his hands, only his fingertips keeping the shield up. The red wall shimmered dangerously, the white laser blasts still slamming into it. Wiglaf leapt forward, his legs matching the chimera's stance, arms reaching up for the straps. Beau slid them smoothly onto the Geat's hands. The shield shook, but held firm. The chimera darted away without a glance back. Nehi's heart began to thunder and he felt his mouth go dry as he looked past the tall Geat. The Black Army's rear advanced, swinging slowly, ponderously. They were almost within aiming distance of Wiglaf's back.

Nehi jerked Hope up, his finger pounding down on her trigger again and again, evening the odds as best as he could. The advance wavered, shaking under his sudden deadly assault. But the Black Army did not stop because of their dead. A sure home in Allah's eternity waited for the dead in battle, and their training held true in even the scrawniest of soldiers. Nehemiah risked lifting his finger off Hope's trigger, turning to look desperately behind him, searching for Beau. The chimera had better have an idea...

Beau darted up next to Joe, where the mute knelt over the dead form of Simmons, a black smudge in the middle of the green grass and pooling crimson. Joe pulled the black coat away and reached for a copper wand strapped to the dead man's waist. His face contorted in a gasp as he pulled it free, his lithe fingers programming something on a small box in the center of the thing. Beau's huge hand closed over it and Joe sagged. Cobeau shot upright, his hand lifting over his head. A copper wand caught the sunlight in his big hairy hand, held high over the laser fire, over the red shield, over every head on the battlefield. Two large copper balls stood on the ends of the wand. Wiglaf's eyes darted from it to Hope's two Z shielding balls, held close together in their wood and copper casing.

"What manner of device is this?" he asked, a grudging wonder in his words.

"I don't know. But it had better be good," Nehemiah growled, and spun back to the enemy, Hope leveling again.

A shout came from Mufasa. The ranks of the Black Army froze. Nehi risked a glance behind them again, his goggles zooming in on the enemy leader. He stood over the prostrate Ahmed, as a medic knelt next to the gray-faced wounded man, trying to stop the hemorrhaging from the sheered bone and muscle. Mufasa's hand was against his jaw, and Nehi knew he was relaying his order to each soldier through their bone plants. His eyes were focused on the copper wand in the chimera's hand.

Silence filled the plain, a tense stillness as everyone waited. The Geats rocked on their heels, swords up, mounts shifting uneasily, all of them out of their element, trying to fathom their role in the midst of this magic flashing about their plain.

The chimera flipped the copper wand toward Mufasa's head. It spun lazily as it flew true, sunlight flashing off its metal. Mufasa's hand shot up, catching the wand. He staggered back at the weight, his arm dropping heavily.

"Go." Cobeau's deep voice rumbled over the crowd and reached even to the soldiers in the back lines. The leader's hand shot to his jaw again, giving an order. The Black Army's ranks closed in. Black uniformed arms lifted, going onto their fellow's shoulders, all of it merging into a single black mass. A lieutenant dropped his hand on Mufasa's shoulder, adding him to the mass of black-clothed humanity spilling over the torn up plain. Mufasa smashed his hand down on something in the center of the wand.

The strange hissing wind curled around Nehemiah, freezing, breath-catching. A dense darkness blocked out the sun. He felt himself jerked forward, tugged remorselessly by a horrible, icy force that pulled each sinew a different direction. Wiglaf roared beside him, fighting back against the pull. And then suddenly it let them loose. The sky cleared, the wind disappeared into the bright stillness of the morning. Nehi stumbled, his head whirling and his body shaking uncontrollably from the cold.

Steady arms caught him, and Nehemiah blinked Wiglaf's stern face into focus. He blinked farther down the plain and saw Daniel trotting his way, the shield down. And the Black Army gone. All of them. Even the dead and wounded. Beau stepped beside them, Joe cradled in his arms. The mute's face was waxen and strained, his body soaked with a clammy sweat, his right hand clutching his left arm again. Nehemiah controlled his shaking body and straightened, staring at the torn up field around them.

The only sign of the near overthrow of this little country was the ripped-up grass and a darkened patch of dirt around Simmons' dead body.

Chapter Sixteen: Heorot Hall

"My people are destroyed for lack of knowledge." -Hosea 4:6a

The door closed behind the queen and her retinue, leaving the strangers in their own small building, set near the great hall. Anna blew a curl out of her face and straightened, her hands leaving the carved scene of a bear hunt running along the windowsill. She took two more seconds to stand in the sunshine, staring at the view of the country. She could see everything from here on the hill. The far blue mountains she and Beau and Daniel had come from last night. The dots of livestock and cottages. The quarter mile of bare, ripped up earth where the Black Army had stood less than an hour ago. Anna turned and strode toward the couch, ignoring the way her stomach tightened and bile rose at the task ahead of her. She plucked a vial out of the wagon's doctor kit and held it out to the chimera. "Beau, is Joe allergic to this?"

"Doesn't take pain meds," the chimera rumbled. Joe curled tense beside him, his breathing shallow, his eyes partially open but unfocused, as if he wasn't really there.

"That's not what I asked," Anna said, her words sharp, an order behind them. The chimera glanced down at the vial, hesitating. "Is Joe allergic to this?"

"Addicted to it once," Beau rumbled, with a hint of surliness at being ignored and overridden. Anna picked up a syringe and began to fill it from the vial.

"Yes, so he told us. But that was before, and he has us near now too. We can help you keep him straight if he needs it." She flipped the mute's left arm up, found a vein, and got it started in his system. Her months in the cellars helping the doctor, and out in the wild lands with no doctor but their own abilities, had turned her into a skillful nurse. Today she found herself thanking the Lord again for the hidden blessing of being made to learn the art. She spun to the mantelpiece and chose a dagger from amongst the array of neatly arranged weaponry hanging on the wall. "Nehi, do you have any suggestions?"

"Be quick," he said, his voice tired and his eyes closed. He sat limp in a carved chair, long legs splayed out in front of him, his head leaning against a magnificent silvan's fur. "Don't bother it more than you have to." Anna nodded as she gently pressed the tip of the dagger to Joe's right jacket sleeve and began to slit the seam. The mute's eyelids fluttered open as she worked, and he looked up at her, green eyes bloodshot and still crinkled with the lines of pain. But awake and a little easier as the drug pumped through his system. Anna gave him a smile, as gentle and reassuring as she could make it.

"Don't ruin jacket?" Joe signed, his movements small. Anna snorted back a laugh, tight and short. Daniel started in his chair at the unexpected sound, sitting up and blinking at the world.

"That's not exactly what I'm worried about Joe," she said. "But ok, fine, I'll be careful so it can be repaired." She gently peeled the sleeve back, dreading what she would find. A bloody mass of deep swollen bruises and oozing welts greeted her, crisscrossed with wire thin cuts. Two long slashes ran the length of it, thin, but deep enough Anna glimpsed white bone from one. Daniel grimaced and turned his eyes away. Cobeau wrapped an arm around his friend, large tears spilling down his face.

"It heals," Joe signed, his green eyes still focused on Anna.

"The wounds themselves aren't that bad," Nehi put in from his chair. "But the method of putting them there…" Nehi's eyes shot open, focusing on something far away from the wooden room.

"Why do you know about this kind of…wound?" Daniel asked.

"How long did he have you this time, Joe?" Nehi said, ignoring his brother.

"'This time?'" Daniel and Anna chorused.

"He didn't really," Joe signed, his face deathly white and blank as Anna finished peeling the slashed sleeve away. "Fired it at me remotely, the setting on high. But I always carry the key with me, and so got it off. Something else was there though, someone..." His strained face crinkled, trying to sort out a confusing memory. "They should have traced me. Should have caught me easily before I made it near the cabin..." He shook his head, blinking. "I got it off, I got out."

A soft knock on the door interrupted, and Daniel shouted for them to come in. The door to their private building opened and Wiglaf and two servants walked in, carrying platters of steaming food. The men in the room brightened, sitting up and straining to see what created the smells. Anna swept a clay mug of steaming potato soup from one of the platters as Wiglaf walked by and handed it to Joe as she turned back to her kit. She reached for the needles as Joe drank gratefully, leaning against Beau's thick side.

The door closed softly behind the servants and Anna spun back to the couch as her brothers headed for the round table with the steaming dishes. She found the practical part of her brain (the one that took over when the rest of her would rather run from the room and cry somewhere) was glad of the blanket laid over the delicate embroidery work of the couch. It only took a few tense, painful minutes to clean, stitch up what needed it, and wrap the bandages neatly. As she finished Joe lay partly conscious against Cobeau, his breathing shallow and sobbing out of him. Anna pushed his dirty blond hair gently out of his eyes.

"It's all right, Joe. You're all right now," she murmured. The simple kindness made Joe's breathing easier and brought him back to them. Though she wished it sent him the other way, into blank unconsciousness. Silence fell around the little group, the only noise the clinking of the earthenware bowls and the doctor's kit as Anna cleaned up.

"You didn't answer my question, Nehi," Daniel said. "How do you know about this?" Nehemiah pushed his sleeve up. Two long, skinny scars ran down the length of his arm.

"The marks stay," he said. Daniel's face turned ashen, then suffused with anger. He rose to his feet, trembling with rage.

"Simmons never should have been," he muttered through clenched teeth. Anna and Nehemiah watched him in surprise, Nehi with one hand on the jug of fresh milk. The brother filled with just anger was new to them. Daniel saw their expressions and sat back down, his anger quickly turning to embarrassment, a deep sorrow scoring it. "I never should have left you two at home, I should have taken you when I went book hunting. Simmons never should have had the chance–" He broke off and averted his eyes from Nehemiah's thoughtful gaze. Nehi turned his attention back to filling his mug.

"It was this man Simmons, that Cobeau and I dealt with?" Wiglaf's serious voice came from a dark corner. The Ravens and Hillsons jumped to an undignified height. Milk pooled over Nehi's plate and he snatched his bacon out of it with a growled complaint. Wiglaf stood so still and quiet none of them realized he had stayed.

"Yes, that's him," Nehemiah answered through a mouthful of bacon. He swallowed and went on. "No, that was him. Thank you for that, Wiglaf, for stepping in on the instant."

"I was not needed. Cobeau would have dealt with him well without me," answered Wiglaf with a shrug. "It was he who had our book?" Everyone looked at Joe. The mute huddled against Beau's thick side, his eyes bloodshot and his face still pale and strained. *He looks ageless again,* Anna thought, and turned quickly back to cleaning up the doctoring things, hiding her sniffles behind the work.

"Yes, he had the book," Joe signed, his movements small.

"Well, really his boss, the Wolf."

"Pardon my ignorance, Ravenswing Ashe-Maker, I do not understand your language from over the whale-roads. I am but a man and not touched by the hand of He who unravels the water-ropes."

"Water-ropes?" Anna asked.

"What's a whale-road?" Daniel said with a raised eyebrow.

"Who's 'he'?" Nehemiah asked, his head tipping in curiosity. A laugh changed the lines on Joe's sharp face, a slow, long, and merry laugh, traveling deep inside him and starting to heal where Anna's antiseptics couldn't reach. He began to look a little more like the cheerful young man the twins knew.

"You three sound so much alike," he signed with a smile. "I told you it's a weird place. It's a poetic country here, all about –."

"I don't know that sign," Nehemiah said, his brow creased as he tried to puzzle it out.

"Never mind," Joe signed, his eyes twinkling.

"I do not understand your words, Ravenswing," Wiglaf interrupted, "but I know you understand mine. Thank you." Joe looked at him in surprise. Anna had noticed that was his usual response when someone thanked him; most people must not bother. "There was no reason for you to step in and save our land, and yet you chose to face even this man Simmons for a people that are not yours. Other warriors before you have chosen to travel far to lend their aid. But even the mighty Beowulf came to Heorot because of old love between his father and the Shieldings. You chose to aid us for no other allegiance than your own honor and love of good things. You have earned for yourself a place in my mind as high as any warrior."

"I'm not a traveling warrior," Joe signed, the twinkle getting stronger in his tired eyes. "Not your kind, anyway."

"What?" asked Wiglaf. Cobeau opened his mouth to translate, and Joe quickly put other words in it.

"You do me more honor than I deserve Wiglaf, Watch-Keeper of the hill," Joe said through his big friend. "I am only a servant carrying out orders as best as I can."

"Whom do you serve, Ravenswing, and why is he concerned for our little land?" Wiglaf asked with interest.

"The same great God as Knee-High, the One Who retained your liberty today. Remember, we talked of Him before," Joe signed.

"Who is this God?" Wiglaf almost demanded. Anna interrupted.

"Joe, when did you last sleep?"

"I got a nap on the way down from the garden with Knee-High," Joe signed, his smile turning facetious. Anna just stared at him. Joe rolled his eyes and then let them close, his head limp against his big friend. "I don't know how you and Glue do it, Beauty, but you always know. Thursday morning. For a few hours."

"That was about fifty hours ago!" Nehemiah blinked.

"I wouldn't have been in time to get you out of the cabin if I had stopped, or to get here," answered Joe with a one shoulder shrug. His eyes opened again, staring at the wall, his twinkle gone. Nehemiah didn't need him to sign the rest of the statement. After Simmons, alone, with the arm, it wouldn't have been hard to stay awake.

"Joe, go to sleep," Anna ordered, waving at Beau to move. She caught her friend as the chimera obeyed and Joe tumbled awkwardly, too exhausted and weak to even try and stop himself. She bunched the blanket under his head, laying him down gently as Beau happily headed for the food. Anna caught his eye and he smiled up at her, a shy thankful look. "Joe, thank you for rescuing Daniel," she said, her words quiet and intense. The mute's eyes dropped, suddenly turning away. Anna went back to her efficient bossiness. "Now, you're not alone anymore, and I can tell the pain has eased a little." She knelt, looking him in the eye. "One of us will stay right here with you, promise. Sleep." Anna pulled the silvan fur off the carved chair and draped it over him, ignoring the grime gathering on the priceless pelt. It was harder to ignore the smell. She plucked a curly rust colored hair (as long as her arm and nearly as thick as her pinky) off Joe's jacket and her nose wrinkled. "And when you wake up, head straight to the bath. You've been cavorting with a very smelly, large animal."

"I hear and obey, my lady," signed Joe half seriously and half in fun. His hands tumbled to the couch, his eyes fluttered closed. His breath steadied, slowed, and evened out in sleep. Wiglaf broke the silence, his voice soft.

"I am sent from the king to learn when best to begin the celebratory feasting." He nodded toward Nehemiah and Daniel, both beginning to nod at the table, their eating slowing as their eyes blinked hard, almost asleep. "I will deal with you on the matter." He hesitated a moment, and his steady confidence wavered, a hint of embarrassment creeping over him. Anna clicked the kit closed and turned to the tall man in the corner, lifting her chin in an order to spit it out. He did. "I would also apologize beforehand for the ways of my people. Some there are who do not see the worth in a woman's wit. Others, like unto myself, have found more wisdom from a woman than the most seasoned of warriors, and learned to cherish it and seek it out. But there are many who think it ill for a woman to be more than a child-raiser or pretty form. Do not be too harsh on ideas allowed from our book." He rushed on, nodding again at the table; Daniel's head lolled on the wood, his limp hand still holding his fork. "It would seem all of your company needs rest. Shall we feast tomorrow morning, perhaps, at sunrise?"

"Tomorrow is Sunday," Anna said. "Allow us a few hours in the morning, if you will."

"May I inquire what is particular about that day?" Wiglaf asked. He spoke hesitantly, but a bright spark in his face spoke of a hunger, a deep desire to learn more.

"Do you know anything of the Sojourners?"

"We have kept mostly to ourselves, lady. The mountains close us in, and it is well that way. Outside influences come mainly in the form of ravenous beasts intent upon our blood, or like unto those we faced in the fields this morn."

"Oh. Well, Sunday is the day we set aside to worship God."

"The same God Ravenswing spoke of just now?" The words came quickly, that hungry hope for knowledge strong in his manner. "May I... It is a great affront to even ask of the heroes of the hour, I well know. But could I beseech you to take your worship in the Heorot Hall, that those who wish to know more of this may learn?" Anna hesitated for just a moment, her thoughts on how nice it would be to spend the morning with her brothers in these pleasant little rooms.

"Of course, we would be honored," she smiled. "After breakfast perhaps?" Wiglaf's face lit up, his movements pleased as he nodded and headed towards the door. It closed behind him and Nehi slumped forward, pillowing his head on his arms with a little groan.

"Great, now we get to take a nap and then perform a service none of us are qualified for in front of a whole group of eager rubberneckers," Daniel drawled, half his face still pressed against the table.

"What did you want me to do, tell him God is reserved just for these 'warriors from over the mountains' they keep mentioning? We'll just treat it like Nehi and I have done while traveling with the Ravens. A few passage quotations and we're done." Anna said. She prodded Nehi in the ribs till he jerked up with a sharp complaint. "Come on, to the bath, you smell like you've been hanging out with Joe. Go. Beau, leave some food for me, if you please."

"Don't I get bossed?" Daniel pouted.

"Only if you can't take care of yourself like the rest of these men," Anna snapped as she herded a complaining Nehi out of the room. Daniel laughed and stood up slowly to head toward one of the bedrooms.

A soft scratching marked the movement of the skitterer drone. Its fourteen legs moved rapidly across the script carved over the House of the Book. Rapid but soft, each leg touching the stone for an instant, then off again. It crouched, emitted a soft whirring sound, and a round disc planted itself from the drone's belly onto the side of the building. A single line of green numbers ran over the front of the disc, scrambling all outside communication. Usually the area around the House of the Book was populated by a whole contingent of the Black Army, five hundred pairs of eyes constantly glancing up to check the building. Someone would have noticed the movement on a usual day.

But today the streets were oddly empty. Devoid of all coal black uniforms.

The skitterer scuttled across the building's front toward the single small vent. Its legs flattened, its footlong body fitting easily between the open slats of the grill. Usually the heavy metal grill lay closed, all security locked down so that even a gnat would be hard pressed to find an entrance. But once every six months, the House of the Book acquired an airing; experts reported it helped keep the precious holy book from crumbling to dust.

The skitterer slid down the vent, using it like a slide. A soft white glow showed the end of the ride, light spilling in from the hallway. Two of its legs lifted, crooking like a tarantula warning off a predator. The hooks created on the two legs caught the edge of the vent with a tiny metal, "clang." The sound was soft, hardly more than the natural movement of air through the vent. The skitterer moved forward quickly, slipping out to latch onto the hallway's roof.

The sound was small. But the guards' helmets recognized it as foreign.

An alert flew onto four military helmets on four guards, the ones left behind when the Black Army darted off to overthrow a new country. The red light flashed in their visors at a furious pace. Four hands in four different sections hit the alarm connected directly to the Wazir's council chambers, as four guards spun cautiously toward the threat.

None of them knew their alerts stopped at a small black disc attached to the top of the building.

Their movements were swift, almost silent, shuffling toward the threat. Guards Two and Four saw each other first. Slipping into the hallway, helmets scanning, searching for the foreign object. Guards Three and One stepped in from their own sections, and the helmets located it. A small metal object in the far corner of the hall emitted a signal recognized as a high threat. Four Brunhiems whined and flashed, and one old fashioned projectile pistol barked for good measure. The bullet hit the object just after the lasers, and a wad of molten metal spun with a whine, a hole through the center. Four guards began to straighten their stance, relaxing with the threat taken care of.

Above their heads the skitterer's belly opened. It didn't send another metal disc designed to draw out the guards. Now it lowered a plastic tube filled with a clear liquid. The tube traveled into an aerosol gun. The skitterer pressed the nozzle.

Sarin gas spewed into the hallway.

Four guards, bodies losing control. Breath stopping. Four thuds, convulsing on the hallway floor. Their movements stopped. The skitterer moved, quickly, headed toward the inner room with the soft scratching of its fourteen jointed legs. The door stood closed, even on this day. The lock took fourteen different codes, and ten different DNA scans to open. Even when unlocked, the vault in the center of the House of the Book took two grown men to heave open. But the vent above the door stood cracked today. Only a crack, a half a foot in diameter. But to a skitterer, it would be enough. The soft clinking of metal filled the hallway as the drone rearranged itself. Changing from a foot wide body to thin enough to fit inside the grill.

Eight of its legs shifted quickly to one end. They flattened, only the end joint crooking. Reaching toward the vent. Ready to pull itself inside, to drop over the book, encase it in its metal body, and slip back out again into the sunshine. In three minutes the skitterer would be gone, away with its prize. The legs drew it forward, scraping against the vent.

A flash of white light filled the hall.

Two sharp clangs rang as the skitterer hit the ground, in two pieces. A hole through the belly of the drone glowed red, still curling on itself as it melted from the laser's heat.

Mufasa lowered his rifle. His breath came stinted and tight through his mask as it filtered the air. But a sniffle still slid from him as he stirred the smoking remains of the gadget.

His son lay lifeless behind him, a guard's helmet still blinking a red warning in the visor.

But their book, their *Holy Karan*, was still safe on its pedestal beyond the door.

The Prophet's Peace would live another day.

"'And as Moses lifted up the serpent in the wilderness, even so must the Son of man be lifted up: That whosoever believeth in him should not perish, but have eternal life[5],'" Daniel continued, his voice ringing through the great hall, strong and full. The acoustics caught it and bore it past the oak pillars standing in two lines under the rafters carved into giant warriors, weaving the verses through the crowd. King Hrothgar and his pretty queen sat straight and tall in their thrones, faces alert as they listened.

Daniel looked at his brother. Nehemiah stood beside him, matching height for height, his bruised face the mark of a hero here amongst this company. His voice came softer than Daniel's, less thundering and theatrical. But more real, to Anna as she listened. The voice of someone in love with the words he spoke. Feeling them deep inside his soul, grateful once again for the truth as it rang through him.

"'For God so loved the world, that he gave his only begotten Son, that whosoever believeth in him should not perish, but have everlasting life. For God sent not his Son into the world to condemn the world; but that the world through him might be saved. He that believeth on him is not condemned: but he that believeth not is condemned already, because he hath not believed in the name of the only begotten Son of God. And this is the condemnation, that light is come into the world, and men loved darkness rather than light, because their deeds were evil[6].'" Visions of Abid and Simmons, of the musty darkness he and Joe had hiked through, of the clammy terror of the dark itself, flowed through Nehi. His face was sober as he ended, his mind on the little mute curled asleep beside his big hairy friend a building away.

Anna stirred beside him, with a soft rustling of the cream-colored dress a queen's lady had provided. It flowed around her, black curls rippling over her shoulders. Her voice rang through the hall, her smile and flashing eyes lending it a joy

---

[5] John 3:14-15
[6] John 3:16-19

deeper than the words themselves.

"'The night is far spent, the day is at hand: let us therefore cast off the works of darkness, and let us put on the armour of light[7].'" Anna's eyes went to Daniel.

"These are the words of holy Scripture, God-breathed, and forever true," Daniel's voice rolled out. "Go and live them. Amen!" Three voices intertwined in a doxology, spun towards heaven's throne. The twins sang it with hearts overflowing, fighting back the choking tears as their brother's voice mixed with theirs. It brought back every Sunday morning at their church, every family worship after dinner, so many memories bound up in the simple, beautiful words. To have Daniel singing it with them again brought the memories to the surface with a clarity that stung.

It stung especially with the two missing voices, their father's bass and mother's soaring soprano. It seemed a hole in the world, an empty black strand that intertwined with their notes.

The last word died into silence and the siblings looked at each other. How did they exit the scene? Anna's eyes moved left automatically, and the brothers knew she wanted to check on the invalid. The king stood, a smile fastened on his face, and the siblings slipped off the dais as he began his speech.

"Warriors of Heorot Hall, yesterday the threat to our kingdom loomed large in the morning sky. But the Lord of Life did not leave us without aid. We stand indebted to the Sons of Titus, Cobeau, and Ravenswing Ashe-Maker. They will find my gift giving liberal indeed." A roar ran through the crowd, and Anna's eyes swept the hall. Mostly men, only a few scattered servant girls moving amongst them. All of them stern and eyeing the tables sagging with food and drink, obviously hoping this boring talk would be done soon. "I will not keep you now, for it is thirsty work to overtax the ears. But as we feast, let

---

[7] Romans 13:12

Gribald spin his song!" Another cheer went up, this one more enthusiastic than the first, and the general drift of the crowd headed toward the tables.

A man in a crimson tunic, a harp in his hands, and brown hair flowing down his shoulders, leapt onto the dais. He struck a chord that rang through the hall, mixing with the low murmur of conversations.

"I sing of deeds daring, of honor bright shining
"Of warriors of might and deeds of great light
"Of Daniel Fox-Tongued, Cobeau Monster-Slayer,
"Nehemiah Truth-Teller, and the small book-taker
"Ravenswing he who walks in shadows and runs in blood."

"Is that a good thing?" Nehemiah murmured in Daniel's ear.

"Here, you bet it is. The more blood the better, have you listened to some of these conversations?" Daniel muttered back, his sardonic smile breaking over his face. The harpist sang on, painting lurid details of a great many feats none on the field had actually seen happen. According to him, at one point Cobeau speared three men on one spear, then charged a fourth, the three bodies flopping around on his weapon as he ran. Hrothgar faced off against fifteen giant warriors, and came off the winner, though his sword snapped cleaving the skull of the last one.

Anna slipped out the side door before she could be caught by curious bystanders, headed to check on Joe. Daniel and Nehi weren't quick enough to join her. Bustling humanity swarmed around them, and names and questions bombarded the brothers. Daniel took the questions, answering most, brushing off others with easy rudeness that no one seemed to resent. He moved as he talked, steadily shifting toward the tables sagging with food and drinks. A noisy half hour spun past

Nehi before he managed to slide out the main door of the hall and slip to the side, just out of sight. A breeze blew into his hot face as the hum of the crowd dropped behind him. The country stretched out below, green and beautiful. He blew out a sigh, his stiff shoulders relaxing as he plopped to sit on the edge of one of the wide steps.

"It is a tiring thing to be hero of the hour," Wiglaf said, amusement playing under his voice. Nehemiah turned and saw the warrior leaning against the side of the hall, a tattered green cloak fluttering around his ankles, his helmet in his hand, and a smile on his face. He held out a wooden bowl, filled with cheese and dark cherries. Nehi took a square of cheese and smiled back.

"It's a lot better out here," he said honestly. "Too crowded and hot inside with everyone."

"I know you would be alone," the warrior commented. "But I would beg a boon before I lead you back to your rooms by the back ways."

"There are back ways?"

"There are always back ways, the trick comes in knowing where they lie." Wiglaf dropped to sit on the step just below Nehemiah's perch. The Geat stared out at the spreading fields and hedgerows marking out his country. "I know not where to begin, I find so many questions racing in my heart!"

"Try one," Nehi offered.

"The verse your brother spoke last, it mentioned 'being lifted up as the serpent in the wilderness...' I think there is a world of stories contained within that one phrase?"

"You're right," Nehi nodded. "But for the moment, I'll jump to what the verse is actually talking about. You get the main idea, right? We're all sinners, we've all done things that God says we aren't supposed to do, and so we're all condemned by Him. And we have to be perfect to be saved. So we can't save ourselves."

"I did understand that," Wiglaf nodded, but his brow creased. "Our history speaks of the Life Giver, the Lord Who creates and sustains, it is not a new idea to me. But to have the fact of sin explained is new, and then it... it clashes with the joy I see in your sister, the steady strength you and your brother bear."

"That's because it's just the beginning. So we're all fallen, and can't save ourselves. God solved that problem when Jesus, the Son of the godhead (don't ask yet, wait till I finish), came down to earth and became a human. He lived a perfect life, and chose to offer himself as a sacrifice for us, in order to bring us back into God's favor."

Nehi reached into his collar, pinched the chain hanging around his throat, and drew out his IDP sign. Wiglaf leaned closer, his eager hunger strong. The first thing he noticed was the scars crisscrossing the young man's olive skin, like a mole's raised furrows across a smooth field. But he looked past them and saw a pendant of an open book lying on Nehi's palm, made up of intricate wheels and cogs and stamped copper. Nehi pushed the end of the bookmark lying over the open page. The musical tinkling of metal rearranging drifted through the air, and Wiglaf's eyes widened as he watched the book rearrange, turning into the shape of a cross. Nehi held it up. The copper sparkled in the light as it turned gently on his chain.

"Ravenswing once showed me like unto this," Wiglaf said eagerly, "when we spoke in the great hall, he and I and my bro–" The warrior broke off suddenly, pain shooting over his face. His eyes darted away, and Nehi saw him focus on a forested area a few miles to the east of them. Wiglaf spun back to Nehemiah, his manner even again. "I did not understand then. Perhaps you can tell me now?"

"Jesus was lifted up on one of these made of wood," Nehi obliged. "In the old world (the very old world) people were executed on crosses like this. Jesus, Who is both God and a perfect unfallen man, let Himself be nailed to the cross. He died in our place. All we have to do is look on Him and believe that He died for us. That He took our sin, and His goodness is enough to get us to heaven and make peace for us with God. That's it." Nehemiah slid the cross back under his jacket and reached for a piece of cheese.

"How blessed you are to be one of His people, you from over the mountains," Wiglaf said, longing clear. Nehemiah nearly choked on his cheese as a laugh broke from him.

"No, Wiglaf, you idiot, it's not just for 'my people,' when I say 'we' I mean..." His hand moved back and forth between he and Wiglaf. "We, we two sitting out here in the sun eating cheese and cherries. All men are called to believe on Jesus, the One lifted up for us."

"I don't understand, I thought this holy book has been gifted to you, that the Sons of Titus stand as protectors for the words of your God," Wiglaf frowned. Nehemiah lost his smile.

"We did. But then the same ones that tried to take your book took ours."

"This Wolf Ravenswing spoke of?" Wiglaf asked, his face hardening.

"Yes. We lost our country because of it, and... so many people were lost with it." Nehemiah turned to stare at the pretty, green land stretching out below him. But he didn't see it. In his mind he saw the packed road he and Anna stumbled across that first night of the disintegration, saw the faces of friends lit by the burning town, running, screaming, the invaders behind them with firing lasers...

Yesterday they had saved two countries from that same fate. The fact flashed across his mind with the sudden brilliance of a laser's flash. It tingled through him as everything around him brightened and the beauty sharpened in his focus. Two countries, saved from disintegration. Because of their work.

"It is lost for always?" Wiglaf asked. Nehi blinked, coming out of his own realization with difficulty.

"Not for always. We're going to get it back. I'm pretty sure Ravenswing has a good idea of where to start, too."

"I owe much to the Sons of Titus, and especially Ravenswing and the great Cobeau. I would pay it back if I might." Steel jingled beside him and Nehi glanced idly over at the warrior. He found Wiglaf on his feet, stern blue eyes staring at him, his sword drawn. "Nehemiah Truth-Teller, I pledge my sword and my body to this adventure. I would see your book returned."

Chapter Seventeen: Handing a Rope

"My little children, let us not love in word, neither in tongue;
but in deed and in truth." -1 John 3:18

Bright morning sunlight lit up the dew drops scattered over the honeysuckle, making the white flowers glisten and shine. As they warmed in the sun, the flowers began to emit their luscious, sweet scent, bathing the air with a delicious beauty. Anna breathed deep and kicked her feet, her pencil scratching over the paper laid on the hard white drawing pad. She sat on a bench in the garden surrounding the burial mounds, under a honeysuckle arbor. It was a fine morning three days after the battle between the Geats and the Prophet's Peace. Four new burial mounds scarred the spreading green. The Geat dead from the battle lay piled inside. Well, their ashes lay inside, after they had been burned on a pyre. These people were definitely weird. But there was a solemn beauty to the ceremony honoring their dead, and the scene taking shape on Anna's paper spoke of firelight on grim faces, the mounds in the background.

She idly watched the tan dirt of the path spurt up with her kicking. Her cloak fluttered in the breeze, and she drew it closer, enjoying the comfort. It might be bulky, but it was decidedly comfortable. A soft hum invaded the flower-perfumed air and Anna glanced to her left. Nehemiah lounged on the bench beside her, one leg on the seat the other splayed on the road. His head leaned back against the trellis, his eyes half closed, and a dreamy smile on his face as he hummed a hymn.

Anna found her heart swelling with unspeakable gratitude. Seeing him now, like that...it was like the picture in her notebook, the one from before the disintegration that Joe had picked out, of Nehi daydreaming. The scene she had never thought to see again. Her brother was more than just at peace this morning, he was relaxed and happy, dreaming of something hopeful. His scars snaked out from under his three-quarter sleeve jacket, harsh reminders of all things wrong and evil. But they were scars now; the wounds were healed. Anna turned away before he noticed her staring and swallowed a sniffle. God was very good. And in His own timing, He answered prayers.

Anna's head jerked back as something tugged her braid, and a squeak of surprise slid from her as she fought for balance on the bench. A whoosh of air went over her and she saw Joe flipping over her head. The mute landed on the dirt path, and dropped to sit, hugging his knees and grinning at them on the step below their feet. His hair hung wet and clean from a bath, and he wore a loose white cotton tunic and green breeches, waiting as a tailor worked on his jacket.

"Ouch!" Anna said, and Nehi chuckled at how obvious an afterthought it was. Joe immediately looked remorseful, and Anna's expression morphed into one of imperiousness. "I forgive your impertinence, peasant, committed upon my fine tresses." She dropped the teasing manner and studied him with her nurse's eye. "I'm glad to see you finally woke up, I was beginning to wonder if you would. You look better." She took in his happy, thin face and his arm resting fairly easy on his knees and nodded. "Much better."

"I am better," Joe signed, his grin coming back. "Slept for three days, ate lots, got a bath, and now found you two."

"What did you do with the bandages on your burnt hand? The salve should still be marinating, you had some bad injuries there."

"Couldn't sign with it, didn't like it, left it off on purpose," Joe signed quickly. "I'll be fine, it already feels better. Where's D?"

"Who?" Anna blinked, and then remembered their brother hadn't earned a sign name yet. Nehemiah uncurled himself from the bench and pivoted to face the mute. He had lost the happy peace.

"Before I answer any questions, I want an answer from you," Nehemiah demanded. Joe's face fell. Anna could watch him pulling back as he looked warily at Nehi. "We're not marching through the dark, or desperately trying to save a kingdom, and you're finally awake and looking normal. Now…" Nehemiah's head went up, his shoulders squaring as if he were entering a fight. "Why did you lead us on all these months, letting us think you were helping us look for Daniel while you really knew where he was?"

"Why didn't you just tell us? I started giving up hope he was still alive! You even had him up in your cabin for six months, three short days away from where you dumped Nehi and I, and you didn't tell us! We should have been able to help him when he needed us, Joe," Anna added, her tone hurt and reproachful. Surprise shot through the twins as Joe winced and turned his gaze away.

"I should have told you earlier," he signed, his movements quick and smooth. *As if he had already planned what to say,* Nehi thought. "I recognize that and am asking for your forgiveness for it. Why I didn't?" Joe's right shoulder rose in a shrug, his eyes darting up to the twins. "Most of it was just time, honest. I have a hard time trusting people with anything, even information, because…because lots of reasons, and remember you two had just proved you were who I hoped you were and then you went running with the KAM IDP. We were never alone to tell you about it before Glue and I had to rush off to reach the Tao pass in what I hoped would be in time."

"Why did you rush off?" Nehi demanded. Inside he mentally found himself adding, *To rescue my own brother without telling me, and leaving me out of it completely.* Anger flared and he carefully pushed it down.

"I told you in the note–"

"This note," Anna broke in, her voice sharpening as she pulled the crumpled, dirty scrap from her leather pouch, "says practically nothing and you were gone for six months!"

"Wait," Joe signed quickly, alarm clear on his face. "I did tell you why; Evil was on your trail, headed to find the Ravens' wagon to get at you two. If we were to keep traveling together, we had to throw him off the scent, make him believe you weren't traveling with us. That worked, and it took one month."

"Then, instead of coming back to tell us you had an injured Daniel stashed away, you..." Anna prodded, her lips still pursed as she waited to hear more.

"Then Evil got smart. Wolf wanted the Black Raider." Nehi and Anna stiffened. "Evil started grabbing Christians, and made sure I knew, waiting for me to come rescue them."

"And you did," Anna said. A statement, soft, but as firm as Nehi's earlier demand. Joe shrugged, his eyes darting off and his shoulders slumping with a little of his earlier heavy weariness.

"I had to. I meant to just rescue the first one and then step back and think of a way out but...there's always the next. And Evil shoved enough at me that I didn't have the chance to step back and think, even when I knew I was walking into a trap. I almost died." A little smile flitted over his face, softening his troubled expression. "But God's gifted me Glue. He pulled me out. Basically held me down and said 'no' and got me back to you two. Then I spent the night helping Knee-High and P get back home, and when we got to the wagon that morning, Meathead waited for me with news of this weird little country's stolen book. I had to run off right away to find it."

His hands clasped in his lap, waiting for a response. The seconds ticked on as the twins watched him, hoping he would sign more.

"Joe," Anna broke the silence, her words hesitant. "That's

not all of it. It can't be. Why didn't you tell us before? There's no reason I know of to keep you from telling us where Daniel was immediately after rescuing us, that first day. You knew, and told us nothing even when you heard us begging for news from random strangers! Why keep it silent for a year? And surely you could have sent us a note by raven, or something, after you rescued him six months ago! I should have been able to take care of him when he needed it, Joe!"

"She's right, and you know it. Are you going to tell us?" Nehi demanded.

Joe's bottom lip went between his teeth and he stared at the ground. A silent half a minute ticked by. He looked up and met their eyes.

"You remember how I told you I trusted you back in KAM?" he began to sign slowly, his green eyes tight. "But that I couldn't tell you everything?"

"Because you were worried about our giving ourselves away to someone dangerous," Nehemiah nodded, "I remember. What's that got to do with anything? It had better not be what I think it is."

"It is," Joe signed back. The mute hunched, gnawing his lower lip, his sharp face lined and afraid. Anna and Nehemiah weren't used to his dropping his mask so completely. It was disturbing to see his usual easy humor so firmly squelched. "My reason for keeping D a secret is wrapped up in the stuff I can't tell you. Not yet. I should have told you earlier than I did, I see that now, I hurt the Hillson family and I'm sorry, and I'm asking your forgiveness for that. Am I forgiven? Or maybe on a probation period?"

"That's not good enough. I can't forgive you till you tell me what I need to forgive you for," Nehemiah almost snapped. Why couldn't he just talk to them? It was what friends did, explain things when asked. Joe looked at his lap as the breeze blew the honeysuckle scent around them. His shaggy blond hair hung down and covered his expression so only the tip of his sharp nose and his tight frown could be seen. The mute began to sign again, not changing his position.

"I can't. I won't. You have the right to know, Knee-High, and I respect your insistence. I respect it, but I won't answer it." He suddenly looked up at them, his whole being rigid with a vibrant earnestness, but his eyes snapping, mouth parted and twitching with fear and pleading. "It's for your own sakes. Honest, please, please believe that! If I tell you what you want to know, right now instead of when the time's right, you die!"

"Stop freaking out and just talk to us," Nehemiah said, irritation clear. "All I want is an answer to why you hurt us by keeping this a secret. And speaking of secrets, what about that scribbled note, 'Watch out for the Judge,' the one you squirmed out of explaining. Will you explain that?" Joe looked wholly wretched but he met Nehemiah's glare and shook his head.

"No. It's part of the same thing. I can't tell you now."

"You mean won't tell us. Whatever this 'thing' is, it's about us, and it's important. That little bit I know. You admit we have the right to know, but you still refuse us an answer. Joe, this isn't an isolated incident, you keep doing things like this, and even suddenly turning us over to enemies–"

"And getting us out again," Anna murmured, but her brother ran on.

"You're really not giving us a reason to trust the secretive silence you keep rubbing in our faces!" Anna laid a hand on Nehemiah's arm to tell him to stop, but it was too late. The words were out. Joe turned his face to the side as if it had been slapped there. For a moment he stayed that way, his breathing labored, and his head bowed with something. Nehemiah thought it was shame and glared at the blond head. But Anna knew it was sorrow and really wished she could hug him and tell him it would all be all right. If this lasted for much longer, she would.

"I don't care," Joe signed, his hands cutting through the air with vicious movements, his face still turned away. Both twins got the feeling it was more to himself than to them, as if he was fighting this fight with himself as much as with Nehi. "This is about a lot more than just keeping you safe, if I give in...I can't. I won't answer. This one secret I'm keeping. Knee-High, you can say what you want, and you can do what you want. You're a free man. I've been alone before, and I can still win this fight without you. But I don't want to!" His head snapped up and he faced them again, his words pouring out in a torrent that was hard for the twins to follow, and the intense pleading back on his features, speaking volumes while his words only explained the titles. "It's your choice, Knee-High, and whatever you decide I won't stand in your way. I will go on with this fight without you, but I want you with me, I really want you with me, because I like your friendship, and I need you. I can't tell you why I'm keeping so much back, but if you could just, please, please, not drop me, don't throw me away, I–" He stopped signing and looked back at his lap, suddenly blank and stiff. All his pulsating emotions were so firmly tucked out of sight it was like he turned a valve to stop the flow. "I'm truly sorry, but I will not answer your questions. It's for a really good reason. I would still very much like to keep your friendship, if I can. It's your choice."

Silence came on the little group, and it was far from an amiable one. It stretched on and on. Anna held her hands in her lap, knuckles white as she gripped her fingers to keep from slapping Nehemiah and telling him to pick Joe up off the ground. That wouldn't solve anything at this point, confound it. If Nehemiah forgave Joe now without an answer it would be handing him a rope. If Joe was true and who he said he was, it would be used to bind them gently together as friends for life. But if Joe was a traitor, a madman, or anything other than the faithful brother he seemed to be, he would certainly hang them all by that single rope. It came down to who Joe actually was, what he did when he disappeared, and he wasn't telling all of it. The minutes stretched on, adding up. Joe sat still and blank, staring at his hands. Nehemiah watched him silently.

Anna fidgeted and watched Nehemiah watching Joe. He had always been better at knowing people. It would have to be his decision. And she decided she would abide by it. Though whether they stayed with him or cast him off, Anna was determined to let Joe know she still counted him as a dear friend. Come to think of it, the fact that both boys had ignored her since the outset of this argument meant they knew where she stood. Oh well, she would say it anyway if she had to. The minutes kept climbing until they had reached half an hour. Anna gave up on her fine resolves. Her fist came up and slammed into Nehi's shoulder.

"Ow, what was that for!" Nehi yelped, nearly tumbling off the bench. A husky note was in his voice; it told Anna he wasn't making this decision lightly. The debate raging inside was costing him.

"You've thought long enough," she snapped, and motioned to Joe impatiently. A deep sigh came from Nehemiah and Joe turned a wretched face to him, haunted and scored by sorrow and care, all his white scars breaking into the natural lines and standing out in sharp relief. His green eyes had a hint of bloodshot stress in them again.

"You really can't give us anything but a refusal to give us anything?" Nehemiah asked quietly. Joe shook his head and bit his lip. Nehemiah grimaced and met Joe's begging eyes. "I don't know what this is about, and it frightens me. But you don't frighten me. Even when you pull rotten stunts like hiding our own brother from us and then refusing to tell us why. I don't think I could feel safe and happy around you if you really were something as awful as I was thinking you might be. Feelings aren't the best measuring tools, but I know God gave them to us for a reason. I'm going to trust mine over my head now, Joe. I forgive your lying skullduggery, and don't you dare betray my trust and prove my head right!"

The mute's stiffness fell off him like a weight. He sagged, left hand splaying out on the dirt road for support, relief almost radiating from him. He sucked in air, and seemingly began to breathe again after thirty minutes of holding it.

"Thank you," Joe signed simply. Anna blew out a relieved sigh.

"Well, I'm glad that's over," she said, and quickly offered a change of subject. "What did you do with Hadring, the grand sword Hrothgar apparently gifted you a couple years ago?"

"Oh, yeah, look at this, Joe!" Nehi burst in, his face brightening as his hand dropped to his side. He drew a short sword from a plain leather scabbard, and held it out toward Joe. Blue steel glinted in the bright morning sunlight, an inscription running down the fuller of the fat, beautiful blade; *Nehi Truth-Teller won me upon the Ashefilled Plain.* Joe's shoulders rolled as he eased stiff muscles. A lingering nervousness tightened his face, but Anna could see his normal self stealing slowly back as he leaned forward to look.

"Ooh," Joe mouthed, and touched the edge. He pulled his hand back quickly, exaggeratedly shaking it. "Sharp, too!"

"Well, yes, when you stick your finger on it," Nehi snorted with a laugh. "So what happened to yours?"

"It's inside a green back somewhere, running around in the Eastern Forest," Joe signed carelessly, and tapped the hyphenated title engraved on the blade. "I like it. It fits."

"It's better than Anna's," Nehi grinned, and his sister rolled her eyes.

"I like these people fine, but they don't really know what to do with women," Anna commented. "Most seem to have a vague idea they should be a pretty face in the background.

Wiglaf's better about it. He seems more sensible than the majority here."

"So what did they call you?" Joe asked.

"'Warrior's-Comfort,'" Anna answered before Nehi could butt in with a teasing comment. "Not that I'm complaining, mind you. I'm fine with being the comfort in the background while you menfolk go off with your shiny blades and lasers and whack each other. But when you're all killed or come limping home wounded, it's the ladies that hold things together and keep the world running as we look out for our families."

"True enough," Joe laughed. "And I wouldn't want anyone better to accomplish it."

"So who gave you that name, Ravenswing?" Anna asked. Joe looked a little embarrassed, but a merry twinkle sprang into his green eyes.

"Actually I gave myself that name when I was stranded here for a couple of months. 'Joe' positively ruined the atmosphere in this weird little country." The twins laughed, they had been here long enough to understand at least that much. An affable silence came on the company as the sun smiled and the honeysuckle kissed the air. Nehemiah went back to leaning against the arbor, one leg tucked comfortably on the bench, staring at the sky. Joe began to pluck honeysuckles off, pinch the end, and suck the sweet nectar, studying the flowers with an artist's eye as he enjoyed them. Anna started her sketch again, hummed, thought, and enjoyed watching the two boys relaxed and untroubled. It had been so long since they had been together and peaceful.

"You know what I think?" Anna broke the quiet. "I think this country isn't that much stranger than KAM or the Kingdom of Gaia. They're set up on false ideas too."

"I guess that's true," Nehemiah said thoughtfully. "This country is more obviously strange, but the others are as false to reality as this one. And the souls are just as real here as they are there. Although I'm not sure 'false to reality' is the right phrase, more like mired in an older reality. Joe, they have an ancient language in their book! Wiglaf showed me some of the lines carved around the pillars in Heorot, and it's fascinating! Even some of the letters are different, but when he read it for me, some of the words are almost recognizable as our language. And when he read the words, it was like...rolling thunder and horses hooves in a gallop and–"

"Please make him stop!" Anna groaned, and Joe laughed. "He's become infatuated, he even asked Hrothgar if he could read the book."

"What did the king say?" Joe asked.

"'No,' of course," Nehi frowned. "He was long-winded and polite about it, but it was a definite no."

"Too bad, it's a pretty good read."

"Wait, they let you read it? Why?" Nehi demanded.

"Nobody let me, I just did," Joe signed, his twinkle strong. "I was bored and I like to read."

"Read a book? Just because you were bored?" Anna said in sharp surprise.

"You have all the fun," Nehi sighed, and drifted onto another topic. "I got into a conversation with Wiglaf the other day," he said. "He pledged his sword to our adventure, he wants to come along and help find the Bible."

"What!?" the mute signed, coming to his feet with an easy leap that made Anna smile. It meant the little dancer's vitality was coming back to him. "We can't take W with us, he's convinced he's a – !"

"I don't know that sign," Anna said, "but I suspect 'Geat' just from the violent way it looks. What's that have to do with anything?"

"It means he's never even crossed the mountains. It means his idea of a good time is to go find a one claw and rip it apart with his bare hands!" Joe spluttered, his signs running into each other and getting mixed. His hands trailed off and his face went blank. His bright, expressive eyes dimmed to show nothing of what he was thinking, and he plopped down again in front of the bower.

"What are you plotting?" Nehemiah asked.

"It also means W would learn about the world," Joe signed slowly. "And have a chance at the fund of knowledge you Hillsons hold on the Bible, the only real reality. It means he could come back here with it. With all of it. That might be the best protection we can give this funny little country. And the best protection we can give a lot of other people."

"What people?" asked Nehemiah.

"Why does it need protection?" asked Anna. Joe grinned at them.

"When will you learn to state your questions one at a time?" he signed. "What's going to happen to the J-o-n-e-s? Where do they have to go now that they've been tagged?" Anna and Nehemiah blinked and looked at each other. Joe nodded. "Exactly. Without the Sojourners, the choices for free countries to send people are limited. This is one of the few that allows strangers into their borders, allows people to make a living on their land, and doesn't oppress people for being members of the Way, chimeras, or even incompletes. They think Glue and I are exalted personages, after all!" Joe said, laughing.

"Well, you are here," Anna said. "You've gained the honor they give you by being a brave friend when they needed one most."

"And don't call yourself incomplete, and Cobeau being a chimera doesn't make him any less of a man," Nehemiah said, his voice sharp.

"All right, all right," Joe signed, giving the twins a grateful, surprised look. "Anyway, this country isn't going to stay free without help. The FFs didn't get the book, but the Prophet's Peace know Geatland is here now, nestled on the very edge of their black borders. They'll be back. Maybe not with the SOLTD, I expect that's back in FF hands by now, but they won't need it if they come with any force."

"Hold on, the what?" Nehi broke in quickly, swiveling to face Joe, his laziness morphing into a tense curiosity. "That's the black bubble thing, right, the thing that dropped five hundred soldiers on the plain?"

"What is it?" Anna asked.

"Why haven't we heard about this amazing thing?" Nehi asked, eyes bright and begging.

"Is it really a bubble?" Anna grinned.

"The freezing, the wind, the dark, it seems almost like a partial black hole effect–"

"But that can't be right!" Anna finished Nehi's thought. Joe's hands came up over his face as he gave a dramatic, silent cry.

"You are relentless!" he signed, but there was laughter behind it.

"Come on give, please," Nehemiah begged, "the SOLDT, you called it? What does that stand for, or is it just its name?"

"Speed Of Light Transportation Device," Joe signed. "It's not on the market, the FFs have been using prototypes, improving it as they go. As far as I know, theirs are the only working SOLTDs on earth."

"It transports people?" Anna asked in fascination. Joe just nodded.

"Speed of light, how?" Nehi asked quickly. "That's impossible, isn't it?"

"It uses the same technology as my Dark Ray," Joe signed, "and your Hope, Knee-High. But while the Compton works hard to keep the dark matter and dark energy from mixing, the SOLTD lets them mingle. It mixes dark energy and dark

Wiglaf and Meathead

matter, creating a black hole"

"What?" the twins burst out in disbelief, and a smile curved over Joe's face at their identical reaction.

"But it controls its effects, and uses the energy," the mute just kept signing. "The inventor of the SOLTD found out that if you're the one creating the black hole, you end up in a calm center within it, a sort of eye-of-the-hurricane effect. And he used it as a space-warp bubble. It feels out a person's bioelectricity, using it to sense where the traveler is, and grabs the patch of ground and air and matter you're standing on. It transports all that where you program it to go, allowing you to survive the speed of light."

"Program it, how, how do you make it go where you want?" Nehemiah prodded, fascinated.

"Two smaller bits of dark matter and dark energy," Joe signed. "You send them on ahead to wherever you want to go. Then you open the bigger balls to let the real mass of dark energy and dark matter mix to get you bubbled in the blackness, and it zips you away, drawn to the two bits of itself waiting."

"But how do you get the little ones there?" Nehi demanded.

"The magnetism of the earth draws it, and can be used to calculate the position, now stop!" Joe laughed. "I don't know how it works in – though I'm hoping to find out eventually. Maybe even soon, I want to go hunt down the inventor of the SOLTD and get him to teach me."

"What's this?" Anna asked, doing her best to replicate the sign they didn't know.

"M-i-n-u-t-i-a," Joe fingerspelled. "Anyway, back to what we were talking about before you derailed it with your everlasting curiosity. Prophet's Peace knows Geatland is here now. They will try to swallow it, like they have so many. The king understands the oppression that will come if Islam takes over.

But all he has to hold back a well-equipped army is swords and spears, and not many of those. Not much good. If we take

W with us we can train him in regular warfare and help him understand the threat Geatland faces, and the sanctuary his country is."

"Do you really think Hrothgar will welcome a large group of strangers?" Nehemiah asked doubtfully. "They seem a little wary, with their 'Watchers on the hill' and all."

"They're careful, but actually ok with newcomers, something about how the hero's ancestor was a waif set adrift in a boat," Joe answered and swept on before Nehi could ask about it. "And especially after W explains to him it's just until we can get Sojourners back in working order–"

"And if we explain to those we send here to be polite to the country's strange ideas," Anna put in.

"I think it would work," Joe finished. "But it's going to take a lot of patience on our part, and a remarkable Geat hero to make it happen."

"I've heard that phrase a lot around here. What's it take to be one of these coveted Geat heroes?" Nehemiah asked.

"Lots of blood," Joe grinned. It turned into a thoughtful look. "Honor. Crazy bravery. Loyalty. It helps if you're a part of the royal bloodline, too. Most of the t-h-a-i-n-s here are related. W is only distantly related."

"Are there any more like Wiglaf? They seem like good men to have around," Nehemiah commented. A shadow darkened Joe's face.

"There were. Three, two brothers and a cousin that was like a brother. Now, after the FF swept in, there's just W."

"Well, that's sobering," Anna commented.

"What sad things is the little scavenger telling you?" Daniel spoke up from their left, and the three looked over to see him laboring up the path. They shifted to face him, letting his intrusion change their little group, and stiffening to hear what business brought him all the way up here.

Chapter Eighteen: Wolves and Suspicions

"Beware of false prophets, which come to you in sheep's clothing, but inwardly they are ravening wolves." -Matthew 7:15

D on't dwell on the sad things," Daniel commented. "It's a peaceful morning,"

"Yes, and no more Simmons!" Nehemiah smiled. Some of that blissful peacefulness slipped back into his manner at the words, and Anna suddenly realized why her twin seemed more like his old self.

"No more Evil!" Joe signed back with a brilliant grin.

"Did you get the directions for fermenting the spiced ale like you wanted?" Anna asked Daniel.

"You want to make ale?" Joe signed, a smile twitching his lips as he looked up at Daniel.

"Oh I got that fine, it just took a little wheedling," Daniel said. "Did you know it takes two years to make a decent batch, and up to ten for a really good one?"

"Maybe you can use some as a toast at my wedding then," Anna said. "Come on, now I'm thirsty. For water though, I can't stand your spiced stuff. Blech!"

"I hear and obey," Daniel said, with a flourishing bow. He slipped Anna's arm through his as he came up, and began to walk back toward town. Anna smiled at him, and tugged, trying to make him walk faster. Nehemiah rose lazily and strolled off to follow his siblings, Joe falling in beside him.

"Did I give you enough time to talk to the scavenger?" Daniel asked over his shoulder. Joe broke into a laugh. Daniel ignored him. "Did Joe fess up about this past year or is he still a blank wall?"

"Timing," Nehi said promptly, stepping up beside his brother. Anna twirled ahead of them, humming a song as she moved. Joe loped up to her, his whistle harmonizing with her hummed hymn. He held out his hands, Anna slid hers into his, and he spun her in a circle. It turned to a furious, dust-raising dance, moving quickly down toward the city, Anna's laughter and Joe's whistled song setting it off. "Anna and I only just made it into the Ravens trust, then Joe and Co had to run off and do rescue work for six months. He didn't have time to tell us till we had already found you."

"Uh-huh," Daniel said, his natural sarcasm strong. He stared at his brother as they strolled, and Nehi attempted a blank face. "You look really guilty, I'm guessing that means you know there's more to it. There has to be. Why didn't he tell you where I was before that, the whole time you were traveling with them?" Nehemiah's shoulders slumped.

"Joe wouldn't tell me anything. He says it's a secret he's going to keep, because it would be dangerous for us to know it."

"Dangerous how?" Daniel asked, his voice sharp.

"Joe says Anna and I can't act, and the minute we come up against this Wolf in the FF and IDP, whoever it is, we would give ourselves away and get slaughtered. I don't know, maybe he's right, Dan."

"Don't call me 'Dan,'" Daniel growled, his eyes narrowing as he stared up the path at the mute. Joe's black boots were a blur as he swung Anna in and out, spun her back and forth, her navy blue dress furling and unfurling like a flower on steroids. Her laughter still drifted back to them. "You realize he could be hiding anything. What if he's the one who leaked out the news about our missing book? The one that brought disintegration on us?"

"Daniel, I trust him," Nehemiah said, suddenly stopping and facing his brother. "I can't give you a concrete reason why, but I trust him, I like him and Beau, and I'm incredibly thankful we fell into their arms. I want to help him as he hunts down this Wolf."

"I don't trust him," Daniel stated. His voice rose to a shout and he turned to make sure Joe heard him. "I don't trust that little mute! And it's going to take a lot to change my mind!" The dancers swirled to a stop, Anna bright-eyed and glowing, Joe looking back at the brothers with his normal easy smile. He shrugged and grinned at Daniel.

"I do trust him, though none of you seem to bother with my opinion," Anna called back, tossing her braid over her shoulder and stomping toward them. "I'm beginning to think you've all been in this country a little too long."

"Of course we care what you think," Nehemiah grinned.

"We just know you're a soft pushover who trusts every-body, and you already like the Ravens," Daniel drawled. "Well, if you two gave in that quick, I'll just have to be the one to watch our backs. How do we know the Ravens are even look-ing for our Bible? They made you think they were looking for me. And Joe hasn't told you two anything about this Wolf in the flock yet." Daniel spun to the mute, his chin lifting in a challenge. "How about it, Joe? Knowledge is power, if you're really trying to help us we should know something, right?"

"Knowledge is dangerous," Joe signed, his signs quick and contained, as if every muscle just became harnessed for battle. His humor and peace disappeared, swallowed into serious hard lines. "We try not to even mention the Wolf out loud. There are contacts everywhere, Wolf has whiskers feeling out everything that happens in this world, noticing when people take an interest. And you don't want Wolf noticing you. The monster claims lives. Not just killing them, though I've seen fields of the dead piled high in massacres, and long slow deaths even the Battle Kingdom would shudder at, all person-ally brought about by Wolf. But it's worse if you're kept alive. A pawn, a plaything in a monster's world. Don't talk about the Wolf. It might be noticed." Nehi's translation dropped away, and the bright sunshine felt colder around the little company.

"So is that what you are?" Daniel demanded. "A pawn and

plaything of this Wolf?" Joe's green eyes flew up to Daniel's, holding them as he signed.

"No. I've managed to keep out of Wolf's jaws so far, by the grace of God. I'm going to bring the Wolf down. But it will take time, Wolf's too powerful to just sweep in at random."

"If this Wolf is so powerful, how come I haven't seen much evidence of him yet?" Daniel asked. "I mean, besides what I've heard from you about what this 'monster' does."

"Wolf brought disintegration to the Sojourners," Joe signed. Nehi's translation stumbled as he said the words, his heart twisting as the memories flooded him again. Joe just kept signing. "Wolf is obsessed with the 'treasure' the Sojourner Judges supposedly hold, and rushed in with the intention of finding it, or at least information about it. That failed."

"An obsession is a weakness. We can use that," Daniel said, his voice clipped. Joe nodded. "But that still leaves almost a year and a half since the Sojourners. If this Wolf is so powerful, why haven't we seen more from him?"

"Joe's never said it is a 'him,'" Nehi put in, and Daniel glanced at his brother, surprised Nehi had caught such a simple, important fact when he had missed it. Nehi just started translating again as the mute's hands moved in the sunlight.

"I've never signed I know who it is, either. You're all just assuming my hunting means I know the name, but you can know a great deal about what a person does without knowing their identity. Anyway, a jilted lover has Wolf in their sights. They're pretty evil sights too, and almost as intelligent as Wolf, and it's driven the monster's head down for a time. I'm in contact with the lover, we've attained a pact to see if we can take out Wolf. If I know where Wolf is, one quick word from me to the lover at the right time could bring the monster down. I know where the lover is too, and I think I'm one of the few who holds that knowledge."

"It seems like jilted lovers always throw cogs in the wheels of these masterminds," Anna commented. "One would think if the mastermind is so smart they wouldn't be so quick to go around doing the jilting."

"When your own desires become your obsession and your gods, common sense no longer has much of a hold," Joe signed.

"Joe, I don't like suspecting people, and you've left the door wide open," Anna said, her pretty nose wrinkling. "You've left us suspecting everyone–"

"–and suspecting everyone is not healthy," Nehemiah added. Joe's green eyes started twinkling as he signed his answer.

"Do you suspect Paul of being the Wolf?"

"Paul? Of course not!" Nehemiah said indignantly.

"How about Peter?" Joe signed.

"What a nasty thought, of course it's not Peter!" Anna said. Joe went on listing names, and at each one the twins became more adamant the traitor in their midst couldn't be them. Joe suddenly started laughing.

"See how much I've corrupted you two, you suspect everyone!" Joe signed, Anna translating it, smiling despite herself. "And stop assuming I know who this Wolf is."

"All right you win, but I'm going to win the race back to your wagon," she said, reverting to her favorite pastime of running. Nehemiah took her up on it, and the two dashed off, drawing a line of dust behind their flying feet. Joe leaned forward, ready to race after them, but Daniel's hand shot out. He latched onto Joe's shoulder and jerked the mute to a stop. Joe's boots shot out from under him, then scrabbled on the dusty path as he regained his stance.

"I want to talk to you," Daniel said, ignoring the indignant look the mute shot up at him. "First off, thanks. I would have died on the plain outside the Tao if you hadn't stepped in, and I am grateful. I owe you one, bigtime. Now, Anna and Nehi told me you don't lie. (Apparently they don't count hiding the truth for over a year as actual lying, but whatever, I get it.) I have a question, and I want an honest answer, and no running away or dodging it. You told the twins you rescued them from the disintegration as a favor for our father. Is that the only reason?" Joe shook his head, stuck two fingers to his eyes and moved them smoothly to point at the twins, then drew them across his throat and stuck his tongue out, his green eyes rolling back into his head expressively.

"Okay, you didn't want to see them die," Daniel said, forcing himself not to smile at the incorrigible mute. "But I think there was another reason you haven't told any of us. Was there another reason?" Joe's head shifted to the side, looking away. Daniel stuck a hand under his chin and pulled his face sharply around again, keeping the mute staring up at him. "I happen to like those two young people very much, and I'm going to see they're safe. Is there another reason you've kept my brother and sister near you, Joe?" The green eyes were dim and unexpressive as they met Daniel's. For a moment both stood still. Joe was as blank as Daniel had ever seen him, and he gave no answer. Daniel let go of him in disgust, almost as if it stung his hands to touch the mute.

"Are you two ever going to get here?" Nehemiah's voice floated playfully back down the path. Joe sped off to catch up with them. Daniel followed slowly, his face troubled and his eyes never leaving Joe as the mute raced past Nehi, punching him in the arm with a neat side spin and shooting off again before Nehi could grab him. It turned into a violent game of tag, as the three people jabbed and spun and dashed in spurts into the city. As Daniel plodded on, the threesome plopped on a hitching post outside of Heorot, waiting for him. The mute's hands began to move in elegant shapes and figures in his own language, saying something. As he neared the group, Daniel realized they were carrying on the same conversation, with Joe supplying names of the possible spy amidst the sheep, and laughing as Anna and Nehemiah adamantly rejected all of them.

"I notice you've ignored two names," Daniel commented as he moved into the group. "What about the Ravens?" Anna laughed, and Nehemiah turned to Joe with a grin.

"Ravenswing Ashe-Maker," he said theatrically, "are you and Cobeau secretly helping a nefarious and dastardly evil group intent on destroying members of the Way?"

"I want to go find Glue," Joe signed, and began to move off. Daniel's eyes narrowed, and the twins gaped at the mute.

"Joe, that's not funny!" Anna called as she hopped up and began to follow him. Joe twisted around, a mischievous smile on his face and his green eyes bright with enjoyment.

"I thought it was pretty funny the way you and Knee-High dropped your jaws," he signed as he danced backward into the stable yards. The head groom gaped at him and the sandwich he held plopped to the ground as he stared after their illustrious guest. Cobeau heard them coming. He pulled open the postern door to the great hall and enfolded his little friend in his big arms. Joe yelled in mock, silent surprise and scrambled onto Cobeau's shoulders. He kicked him playfully and pointed forward. Cobeau grinned and jogged into the empty, cool, dimness of the great hall, in and out of the carved pillars, with Joe perched on his shoulders.

Anna and Nehemiah only glanced at the two, knowing how the Ravens acted when they finally caught up on sleep and were actually feeling fed, well, and safe. They turned to packing up the things the Geats had showered on the heroes of Ashedown. The Geats seemed to pride themselves on generosity, it had taken a great deal of diplomacy to avoid taking a houseful of goods. Anna still secretly regretted having to turn down the horses Hrothgar paraded before them. She put it out of her mind as she flipped through the pile of lovely dresses Queen Arnea had supplied, and admired the boot dagger again.

"I'm glad she gave you more," Daniel commented, and Anna looked up to see him leaning against one of the carved pillars, watching her. "You look ravishing in the long, elegant dresses they make here."

"Well thank you," she smiled, bobbing a little curtsy at him. Cobeau thundered past with a roar, and Daniel started to the side, an exclamation slipping from him. Joe balanced on the chimera's shoulders, laughing his silent laugh, swiping at the ceiling beams.

"Joe!" Anna called up to him. "What do you want done with this black bag of yours?" Joe caught a ceiling beam, spun off Cobeau's shoulders and dropped onto the floor on his fingers and toes, his left arm held protectively against his chest.

"Be careful with that, please, it's slightly fragile," Joe signed as he moved over to her. "Goes back in its place in the wagon, I'll take it."

"Before you do that, can I look inside? I'm curious what I was lugging all over," Nehemiah asked. Joe paused for a second. Then his head bobbed a yes. A loud cawing drifted through the small door, and Joe gave a grin.

"Jewel," he signed, recognizing the call of his raven. He darted toward the door to find his bird but twisted around as he moved. The comfortable dimness of the hall mixed with the bright sunbeams shining through the open door, shifting as people moved outside, intercepting the sunbeams and changing their slant. It made him a changing mix of shadows and light. They played over him like a mottled blanket, till his solid form seemed to lose its solidity, to melt and reform, as changeable as the light. Anna suddenly had a distinct picture of her little friend dancing into the darkest parts of the world, carrying those who could not carry themselves out into the light of Christ's truth. In and out, till he was shadow and light himself. Living in a world of secrets and danger, but with the light steadily pulsating in his deepest parts.

"Check out the notebook, you'll like that," Joe signed as he moved. The sunbeams caught him, the light won, and he raced on out of sight.

Joe spun to the left as the dirt paths diverged, and headed to a small hut situated just beyond the stables of Heorot Hall. A wince crinkled his eyes as his arm pushed against the heavy door and swung it open, but no trace of it showed on his face as he stepped inside. The little man in the center of the room looked up from his scissors and threads. A smile flitted over the man's face and he held up Joe's black jacket. The left sleeve looked whole again, black as ever and ready for wear. But the mute's head tipped as he noticed the material was different than the rest of the jacket. It looked thicker, and bumpy.

"We of the Geats have a rare talent," the tailor said, his eyes twinkling. He picked up a dagger from off his bench, spun it till he held it underhand, then slashed down hard at the left sleeve. The dagger glanced off. Joe stepped forward, quick and interested, running a finger over the place the dagger hit. "You won't find any damage. Your sleeve is repaired with the leather from a stumpy tail lizard." Joe's head shot up to stare at him, astonished delight clear on his features. The tailor beamed and held out the jacket as if it were a delicate jewel. "This, Shadow-Walker and Book-Taker, is our most coveted secret. No one speaks of it to those who come from over the mountains. But you have earned the honor. It is wealth too, great wealth for a whole sleeve to be made of it, for the leather takes long, long hours to cure and work before it is ready to form. Generations go into the making of one coat of stumpy dragon armor. We know you will use it well."

Joe took the jacket reverently, his burnt fingers running down the bumpy new leather. He looked up at the tailor and bowed, deep and humbly. He understood the honor he held.

Cobeau followed Joe out of the hall, and the three siblings were left alone with the black bag. Nehemiah pulled it open, and Anna and Daniel leaned over his shoulder to see what mysteries it contained. A lot of bits of wires and metal and plastic that didn't seem to go anywhere or fit into anything were its chief occupants. Then Nehemiah's hand closed on something round and cold, and he pulled out a copper ball, almost identical to the two balls contained in Hope. Almost but not quite. This copper ball was three times the size of those in his Compton.

"Is that what I think it is?" Anna almost whispered. Nehemiah nodded, too awed and horrified that he had been bouncing this thing around on his back.

"It's a dark energy ball," Daniel murmured, and his hand slid over his brother's shoulder to pull out three more, grunting at the effort. "There's more in here. What is Joe doing with these?"

"Don't even bother wondering, we all know he won't tell you," Anna commented. She poked Nehemiah's shoulder impatiently. "Find the notebook he mentioned!" Nehemiah slid the copper ball carefully back in and pulled out a glossy black folder. It looked thin and uninteresting. But he doubted the contents would prove so mundane as he opened it carefully. The three siblings gazed in surprise at ten thin papers, encased in protective plastic. Yellowed with age, faded blue lines ran across them, each with three holes in their left side. They were so old the pages were brittle to the touch. Daniel's eyebrows rose till they almost met his hairline.

"Those are..." he whispered, paused, swallowed and went on his voice still awed. "I've seen pages this age before. Whatever they are, these are relics from the past world. Don't take them out of their plastic sleeves, Nehi, they could crumble to dust. I can't read the words in this light, what does it say?"

"It's a journal," Nehemiah murmured. He began to shift

through the pages with gentle reverence, telling bits and pieces of what he found. "Most of it has to do with a son, Lu. The writer seems to think a lot of him, and is excited about something. It skips around a lot, and some of it is so faded I can't read it. The writer's excited about something they just gained, and is giving it to Lu when he's old enough to appreciate it." He shifted a few pages. A gasp broke from Nehemiah, echoing in the empty hall. His siblings jumped. "Lu's last name is Hillson!"

"Wait...something important passed on to a Hillson generations ago... Could these be about whatever treasure it is we Hillsons are supposed to have?" Anna asked, touching one of the plastic sleeves gently, awe on her face. Was there really a treasure? What was this thing that had killed their country and was trying to kill them!

"Does it say anything about what it's supposed to be, Nehi?" Daniel asked quickly, eagerly. Nehemiah shook his head, fascinated by what he was holding in his hands.

"Who wrote this? What do those faded lines mean? Why the holes, is it some sort of mark from the last world, to show the papers were important or something?" Nehi muttered. Daniel slapped his shoulder, impatient for a better answer. "No, it says nothing but a few phrases about whatever the thing is. The rest is all just daily happenings and how cute Lu is."

"How old is this? This is...amazing. How did Joe get these?" Anna asked.

"He wouldn't tell us if we asked," Daniel snorted. "And there's no way to know if he has more of these hidden in that wagon of his, or somewhere else. Anna, Nehi, I don't trust that little Joe. Or his big, powerful friend who does whatever his master tells him." The twins looked up at their older brother, not sure what to respond. A huge shadow engulfed the light and Cobeau suddenly loomed over the group.

"Time to go," he rumbled. One big hairy hand reached down, snapped the notebook closed, slid it in the bag, and tossed the bag over his shoulder. He strode out into the sunlight, and silence filled the hall. Nehi stared at his empty hand, still in midair as if the notebook was there.

"Do we follow, or do we go our own way?" Daniel asked quietly.

"Do you know the next step to restore the Sojourners?" Nehemiah shot out. "Do you have any idea at all where the FFs are or where they might have our book?"

"How would we go, is slightly more to the point," Anna said, Joe's desperate pleading for their friendship playing in her mind. He needed them. "We don't have any means of traveling except horseback without Joe and his music. I don't want to face the wild lands with a few lasers and horses!"

"Joe has all three of us tied to his apron strings," Daniel growled. Anna giggled. Her big brother looked at her irritably.

"Sorry, the thought of Joe in an apron is funny," she shrugged. Nehemiah grinned and Daniel rolled his eyes at her.

"Look you two, I'm watching out for you now. I know you're sort of grown, but I'd really appreciate it if you let me help with the big decisions like, Nehi, suddenly disappearing inside a dark tunnel with a guy whose trustworthiness is dubious, to say the least. Got it?"

"Ok, Danny," Nehi grinned at his protective brother.

"Right. And don't call me Danny, you know it drives me crazy." Cobeau stuck his hairy head through the door again.

"Time to go," he rumbled. The three siblings moved silently out the door to join the Ravens, ignoring all the stares that hit them when they walked out onto the open hill. The sturdy Ravens shack was already hovering, hissing gently as it stood higher than usual, pushed up a foot above the ground by the jets of steam whoosing out of the copper coils. The picture of the sunlit forest plastered over the side of the wagon, with ravens soaring and cawing, seemed to come to life with the undulations. But Joe was nowhere to be seen. Nehemiah stopped beside the wagon, scanning the crowd for the little mute. A shout ripped from him and he jerked back as something gripped his ankle. Joe crawled out from under the hovering wagon, back to his usual black slacks and jacket, wet with warm steam. Laughter creased his face.

"Sorry, Knee-High, couldn't resist when you were right there," he signed, and paused to wipe his muddy hands on his wet pants. "Glue tells me he told you to come. Actually, I asked him to come and was going to ask you about it."

"About what?" Daniel said suspiciously, as Nehemiah translated. Joe glanced at him appraisingly and turned back to the twins.

"I'm going to Story Land for a day or two, to clear up some trouble," he signed, waving up at his raven perched on top the wagon, as if the bird's appearance explained it all.

"Story Land, I've always liked that name," Anna said parenthetically. "It sounds so peaceful and pretty." Joe gave her an odd look but Nehemiah spoke up before he could sign anything.

"What trouble?"

"There's a group of thieves - - there and the IDP are getting blamed for it," Joe signed.

"What's –" Anna asked, doing her best to copy the two signs she didn't know. Joe laughed and Anna smiled good-naturedly and stopped trying.

"Wreaking havoc," Beau said.

"What?" Daniel asked feeling extremely confused and a little left out.

"The signs, wreaking havoc," answered the big man.

"Back to the point..." Joe signed, and gave his little whistle asking Beau to translate for Daniel. "After that situation in Story Land is fixed, I'm coming back here to pick up our Geat warrior, and am off to the People's Kingdom to look for that inventor I mentioned. I've already set it up with the king and W. So, do you come now, wait here and go later, or wait here as the first of the refugees?"

"Go now, I say," Nehemiah said immediately.

"Yes, after all, we are in your oak tree," Anna responded, and Joe beamed at them. He looked at Daniel with respectful inquiry and waited. Daniel looked back at him with undisguised mistrust.

"Go," the oldest Hillson finally answered. "I'm beginning to think I'd rather have you in sight, where I can at least guess what you're doing." Joe's expression grew a little colder, but he just nodded and motioned them onto the wagon. The Hillsons clambered up and chose their favorite spots, and Beau clicked to Prissy. With a piercing squeak from the pig, the company rolled out of the city and on their way.

"I have one more question," Joe signed suddenly, spinning to face the Hillsons on the wagon top. His manner changed, growing shy, a little nervous. His eyes sought Anna, and she felt herself tensing, unsure she wanted to hear this question.

"What?" she asked.

"Will you make more of those brownies for us?" Joe asked timidly. Anna's laughter rolled around the little group and she nodded. The mute gave a brilliant grin and swept up his whistle, tucking his feet underneath him and leaning comfortably against his big hairy friend.

The sound of Joe's whistles soared around the wagon top, accompanied by the twins singing, and much laughter. They were rested and replenished, and Joe felt he was leaving behind the darkest parts of his life as the wagon rolled forward. And if they could recover the Bible in Story Land... A host of possibilities danced through his mind, each ending with the Sojourners restored, a Hillson back as Judge. Maybe even a home. His eyes turned to the horizon, willing it to turn to the wet, steamy country around Story Land. Just let the Bible be there waiting for them, and all might be repaired!

Rachel Jaimen stared at the set of frames splayed over the wall. The necklace around her amber throat felt heavy, constricting. She could see her face reflected in the glass covering the precious pages. Except it wasn't her face, not really. Not the one she recognized. Rachel didn't take comfort in her exotic beauty, not right now. Not when faced with these.

So old, the pages were so old. Yellowed and brittle, faded blue lines running across them, the three holes in one side an odd break to the symmetry. The scrawled ink running over the pages was faded, in some places too faded to read. Jill's face appeared in the reflection beside Rachel's. Jill of the Ill Trio smiled, watching Rachel through the reflection. A chill ran down Rachel's spine.

"From the last world?" she asked. She tried to make it sound flippant. But even to her ears it came out small, awed, a little frightened.

"Yes, sweety," Jill smiled. Rachel could feel Bill pacing restlessly behind them. Tall, handsome, cruel as a winter's night.

"What do you do with them? It would take a real collector to buy these, and that kind of fence–"

"Oh, we're not selling them," Jill laughed. It had a condescending tone, like a grownup explaining something to a child. "We've been entrusted with them by a... Friend."

"Someone more powerful than your Hernons," Bill put in from behind them, amusement in the words.

"Someone more powerful than anyone in this country. Anyone in a single country, our friend manages to get into all of them. And we are 'in' on all the big capers. I know you hoped you could come flaunting that necklace and walk back out with it, proving what a pretty, bigshot you are in this regime. But sweety..." Jill motioned up at the pages. Relics of a last world. Priceless antiquities, precious treasures, symbols of money and power beyond anything that Rachel had ever dreamed.

"If you had come yesterday," Bill spoke up, stepping up to Rachel's other side, "we could have shown you something really impressive." His voice dropped, till it came in a whisper hissed in her ear. "We had a book here."

Rachel pulled back, staring at him, disbelief clear on her astonished face.

"Yes," Bill grinned, his voice still a whisper, "a book, big, thick, old leather cracking with age...it was beautiful. We just sent it off with Will. He's taking it over the transport lines to its more permanent home."

"We're involved in so much more than you know, sweety," Jill said, in what someone who didn't know her would have called a gentle voice. "Come on now. Hand it over."

Rachel unclasped the necklace with clammy, cold fingers. She let it drop into Jill's outstretched hand.

Continue the Sojourner epic in

Ravens Refuge

Appendices

903

March 234: *Born in KAM, marked as GI, "adopted" by the In-complete Keepers of the People's Kingdom.*

April 238: *Successfully ran from the IK Station.*

August 238: *Picked up by Geego Thomle's slaver caravan.*

January 239: *Sold to Bart Meilson as a pet for his ninth birth-day present.*

"You must form the 'b' very particularly, Master Bar-tholomew," James Yolden droned. The nine-year old Bart sat with his head on the desk, gouging holes in the wood with his pencil. He showed absolutely no interest in the re-medial writing tutorship his parents insisted on his taking. Yolden kept droning, doing his best not to show the loath-ing bubbling in him for this horrible boy.

In the back corner of the room, two bright green eyes gleamed, staring at the shimmering board with a fascinat-ed hunger. Those eyes tracked every movement the young tutor made as he formed the letters of the alphabet. Again. The incomplete sat on his haunches, perfectly still in the orange one-piece suit purchased at the local pet store. Its long sleeves covered the bite marks from the other pet liv-ing in the house; a large rottweiler consigned to the out-doors in all weathers, left alone and angry. The sound of Bart's pencil jabbing into the wood filled the room. The in-complete sat eerily still, except those bright green eyes. He lived in the background, a forgotten entity by now. Four months had gone by since his purchase as a birthday pre-sent, much too long for anything to retain Bart Meilson's interest.

A sharp crack rang through the room as the pencil fi-nally snapped under the rough treatment. The tutor closed his eyes, the left one twitching.

"Go fetch another one," he ordered. Bart was out of his seat like a bullet, darting into the hallway. Yolden watched him go with a sense of guilty relief. He knew the boy would-n't come back.

Bright green, blending with white-blond hair, caught

his eye and he focused on the hunched form in the back of the room. The pet ducked behind a shelf, out of sight except for a sliver of orange. Yolden, bored out of his wits in this house of selfish idiots, let a sudden whim take over.

"It's all right. If you're curious, why don't you come try it yourself?" he said. He spoke mainly to himself, knowing the beast wouldn't understand the words. Two green eyes peeked out from behind the shelf. A prickle of interest crept into Yolden. "Yes you, come on," the tutor said. He held out the stylus. The tiny, thin form slid out into the sunlight streaming through the window. He shuffled silently, hesitantly toward the young tutor. Yolden didn't move, finding himself holding his breath, trying not to startle this little thing away. The incomplete stole closer. He glanced up briefly, and for an instant the tutor fancied he saw wonder and fear playing over the sharp face.

Then the incomplete snatched the stylus. He bounded onto the tutor's chair by the board and drew the tip through the green lines. A wobbly 'A' formed in the blue sensory lines of the board. Yolden's face paled. More letters, each one a little better as the beast grew in confidence, flew over the board. Twenty-six letters took shape in a child's scrawl, in less than thirty seconds. But the stylus moved on. "Cat," "pen," "dog," words flew from the thin fingers onto the board. Yolden staggered back a step, his mouth open and his whole world crashing around him. This wasn't possible. It couldn't be possible, this was a beast, a wild animal! The stylus moved, quickly, easily.

My name is Joe.

The incomplete spun, two green eyes looked up at Yolden, meeting the tutor's shock. A smile shone like the rising sun on the face of the incomplete. The face of Joe.

A choked gurgle slid from James Yolden. He turned and darted from the room, overturning Bart's desk as he dashed out.

Joe's brightness faded. But a smile still stood on his thin face as he turned back to the board. A picture of a kind-eyed, sharp nosed tutor began to take shape in the lines of the sensory board. The little fingers formed two words under it with painstaking care, laid the stylus down, and stole out of the room before anyone found out and beat him for his impertinence in touching things he wasn't made for.

James Yolden never came back to see the heartfelt "thank you" scrawled in a child's hand under his kind-eyed portrait.

February 240: *Acquired by the Advancers of KAM for testing.*

Test Case 289 shuddered, his arms hugging his thin knees as he stared at the back of the white sign. He couldn't see the words on the notice strapped to his kennel door. They had put it up two days ago, and he knew his time in these endless white rooms had ended. A sign meant one of two things. Someone had claimed you. Or else the white workers came with the needle. None of the other kennels were occupied this week, no one to tell Case 289 what his sign said. The others had all been taken long ago. Or else the needle, the twitching, the sudden rigid stillness.

Which was it for him?

Even the rigid stillness meant an end of the white rooms. For that he could be grateful.

Voices in the hall. Case 289 strained to hear them, stiffening. The voices came closer. They stopped at the door. It swung open, quickly, efficiently, and more bright light flooded the white room. Two white workers strode in and Case 289 shrunk back, his arms tightening around himself. The clang of the kennel door opening vibrated inside him. He stared out through lowered lids, trying to see what the workers held without accidentally meeting their eyes.

Meeting a complete's gaze never turned out well for the incomplete. Something snapped inside them, something that recognized...what? That he was really like them? A flutter of hope, never fully dead inside the boy, stirred again.

He saw straps and a stick. No needle.

The workers reached in and grabbed him, pulling him from the cage. They kept talking, over him, ignoring him as if he were a rock or a stuffed bear. Something about a doctor's birthday party and too much wine. Case 289 felt too agitated to understand it as they crossed his arms over his chest and began to strap the harness on. Tight, always so tight. The stick clicked on, pushed, and he moved. No choice behind it, he had to go where the stick pushed him.

His ears sang. They shoved him down the hallways, into elevators, toward the lowest level. He was getting out.

Out! Was there still a sun? Still a breeze, air that didn't taste like cleaner and dread?

Who had claimed him? Maybe it was...no, he would die before he went back there. But maybe... The hope fluttered a little higher, a little more alive, beating inside him like something reborn struggling to take a breath.

Maybe someone good had claimed him. Maybe someone who would notice him. Who's notice wouldn't turn to sticks and whips. Maybe someone who didn't even own a whip!

The elevator doors pulled back and sunlight hit him in the face.

Case 289 didn't remember the steps he took. The faces or conversations around him. All he knew was the sun, the air as the stick pushed him through the glass doors into the outside. The breeze caressed his pale face like the touch of a long-lost friend.

The stick pushed, lifted, his feet dangled. The sun cut off into darkness. Case 289 stumbled to his knees as the workers shoved him into a small kennel in what seemed like a tin room. The kennel swung closed, pushing uncomfortably on the stick. His heart leapt to his mouth, horrified it would press the correction button on the end. A metal door slammed closed. Darkness, deep, black, and complete, closed around him. An engine started somewhere on the other side of this metal room. A rumble, movement, and his kennel began to jump and vibrate as the white workers took him somewhere.

Still, that hope fluttered inside him. It stayed alive through the hours of growing stiffness, silence and darkness.

They were hours he looked back on with longing during the following days; hours when the hope still lived.

March 241: Bought by Jarl Furt, the Music Maker, traveling musician and cat burglar.

April 243: *Upon the death of Furt, able to slip off into the street of Hurn in the Kingdom of the Wise.*

June 244: *Captured by Gretta Netters, Purveyor of Inferior Peoples.*

September 244: *Sold to Valus, pawn shop owner in Kallipolis, for odd-jobbing, renting out, and venting anger.*

February 245: *Freedom purchased and home established by Joshua Noble.*

October 246: *Rescued the chimera Cobeau in the People's Kingdom.*

November 248: *Joshua Noble betrayed and slaughtered in the arena of the Battle Kingdom.*

December 250: *Met Nehemiah and Anna Hillson.*

Chimeras

Report: Chimera Handler Carl Savenberg, Camp 24

You requested information on the Gaurdog team, Shadow Fangs, operating from within our camp.

The team is run by two chimeras from batch 244-269, DNA 720 *Rottweiler* and human embryo 1301. They are littermates and have been allowed to keep the names assigned by their dam, Calla and Cobeau. We have allowed them to hunt together due to their skills complementing each other. They work best together.

The Shadow Fangs formed when Calla and Cobeau had reached the fifteenth year. Even young, they proved a promising team, Calla being a natural leader and Cobeau keeping the team in line with a centralized goal. Very abnormally for a guardog pack, in twenty-six missions they have only lost one packmate, and that unavoidably due to enemy fire. Cobeau carried the corpse of their packmate the entire six day trip back to camp in an astonishing show of efficiency at leaving no trace behind of their presence (though the team barked about 'loyalty' to a fallen pack member).

The Shadow Fangs are a strangely tight-knit and devoted company for a pack, and I do not recommend trying to rearrange the team, or harm one of the members unless the others are properly contained first. We lost two trainers to unofficial corrective measures Calla and Cobeau deemed too violent against their pack. Of course severe punishments were enacted, and it is unclear if they would dare to once again commit violence against a trainer. But I report it as a matter of full disclosure. It is camp policy to make a three day public execution of any chimera who seriously harms a trainer. But we made exception with the Shadow Fangs, cutting off the punishment before debilitation or death because of their extreme usefulness to the state.

The Shadow Fangs have been allowed this and a few other "loosening of the leash" because they have proved to be strong allies for the state. It was their team who infiltrated the Northern Kingdom of the Wise's treasury and redistributed the gold within our own state. It was also their team which went in first in a stealth operation when the Battle Kingdom pressed on our borders last season; the Shadow Fangs permeated deep within the enemy lines and decimated hundreds. It is my firm belief the pack instigated the withdrawal of the Battle Kingdom troops.

In conclusion, yes, it is my belief that the Shadow Fangs would be a viable option for the retrial of the Dark Horse operation. I could recommend no better pack for the job.

-Carl Savenburg

Cobeau watched as his big brother stood taller still, his muscles rippling along his thick shoulders as his chest seemed to expand. The female, Ydara, gave a little smile as she loped past with her pack. Cobeau watched, squatting on the ground beside the fence in a rare off duty moment. His eyes kept flicking back and forth between Ydara and Calla. His brother stopped expanding as the female passed. But as he turned back toward Cobeau, Calla's face held the goofy grin his brother had come to dread.

Calla slumped against the fence, and his elbow shoved into Cobeau's thick side in the usual friendly way. But butterflies flitted through Cobeau's stomach as he copied the move, shoving at his brother with a grunt.

Ydara meant change.

Change meant trouble.

And trouble usually led to painful death.

Cobeau looked at his brother's face; thick brown hair curling in its long beard, his eyes closed as he leaned back in the sun, relishing the moment of stillness, of quiet. The butterflies flew into a storm, ramming around in Cobeau's insides. All he wanted was peace. This right here, with sunshine and quiet and Calla beside him. Cobeau's eyes flew to Ydara's pack, running the perimeter checks, and he knew.

His days alone with Calla were limited.

Lasers and Gadgets

In the early days of research, the main problems with using lasers as a weapon were the source of energy and the heat emitted by the process. It takes so much power to create a weaponized laser, the apparatus used to excite the atoms was too heavy for even a tank to carry, and handheld weapons were out of the question. Also, most of a laser's energy burns off as heat, before the laser light becomes strong enough to be useful. One more problem with the practicality of lasers was atmospheric interference. A high concentration of dust or water in the air might tamper with a laser's accuracy, bending the beam, or causing it to reflect off the atmospheric conditions.

The first two problems were finally solved by the Pylum battery. A man named Ralph Pylum, in the year 20 of the Book Base Age, discovered a battery powered by heat. It is the perfect solution for a laser weapon energy source. The Pylum battery requires an initial charge, which it uses to start the lasing process in a weapon. The laser passes through its chosen medium and begins to bounce between a complicated series of mirrors, increasing the atoms' excitement and thus the power of the laser. This is called priming. Some take more time than others to reach a weaponized level of energy, it depends on many factors including the size of the battery and the medium chosen. But as it primes, the laser is giving off wave after wave of heat. The Pylum battery absorbs it and uses the energy. This creates a weapon which basically powers itself. If allowed to sit unused for some time the battery loses its charge and needs a "jump start" of external heat to start the lasing process. But if kept in proper order, a Pylum battery laser will provide its own energy indefinitely.

Atmospheric conditions are still an issue with some lasers, throwing off the accuracy. The lens of a laser (what the beam is finally sent through, after the energy has climbed to useful levels) as well as the lasing medium affect the accuracy. It is possible for the beams to be reflected back, or even scattered. This kind of reflection would be too weak to cause much damage, unless they landed in a person's fragile eyes. Because of this danger lasers are never to be fired without safety-dyed goggles.

Brunhiem

The laser of choice for the Judge's Guards, the Brunhiem is a compact liquid fiber laser. The lasing medium is optical fibers, coiled to pack more power into a weapon that is smaller, lighter, and more easily maneuverable than almost all its contemporaries. The Brunhiem employs three separate packets of carefully coiled optical fibers. The packets each have access to the Pylum battery, a relatively small affair for a laser. Because of the smaller size, the Pylum does not consume all the heat created by the lasing process, and so is surround-ed by a liquid coolant, running through tubes wrapped around the battery. The separate beams from the three packets combine in the reflective chamber as the weapon primes.

Priming: 3 seconds
Health Length Without Charging: 2 weeks
Weight: 9.27 pounds
Accuracy: Excellent

Toaster

A large optic laser employing several stages of photon conversions for optimum interaction with the target. The Toaster starts in the first chamber as infrared beams, travels through special optics to become green light, then converts to ultraviolet in a third chamber. By the time it releases from the third chamber, the Toaster beam is one of the more powerful laser weapons employed. The three different phases of the photons however make it too large for a handheld weapon, and most used in the field are from KAM's design of a truck-mounted version.

Priming: 15 seconds
Health Length Without Charging: 10 days
Weight: 208.6 pounds
Accuracy: Tolerable
Strength: Decimating

Ruby

A mass market weapon, the Ruby is a solid-state laser found in most kingdoms during the Book Base Age. It employs a synthetic ruby rod as a medium and is prized for its small size. Because of the single-handed size, the battery is necessarily smaller, making the power less effective. It creates a lethal laser shot, but only at a range of up to six feet. A popular choice for personal defense, but not optimal as an army weapon.

Priming: 4 seconds
Health Length Without Charging: 5 days
Weight: 6.3 pounds
Accuracy: Average

Strafer

Setup very like a Ruby laser, this is a close range weapon used for personal defense. It is small enough even for concealment upon a person, a rare thing with a weaponized laser. The strafer varies from the Ruby in the makeup of its lenses. The strafer has a combination of five lenses, carefully overlaid with one another, capable of being aligned into one stronger beam, or shifted to create up to eight different beams. In a close quarters fight it can be used to take down multiple enemies, making it ideal for self defense.

Priming: 4 seconds
Health Length Without Charging: 5 days
Weight: 6.5 pounds
Accuracy: Average

Krackmen

The Krackmen is a prepossessing weapon with its intricately crafted red carbon stock. It is a dye laser utilizing rhodamine, and the accuracy is legendary, though the priming time is a serious drawback to the weapon.

Priming: 7 seconds
Health Length Without Charging: 1 week
Weight: 15.9 pounds
Accuracy: Exceptional

Healy

Termed by some a variation of a Brunhiem, the Healy laser is a liquid fiber laser, with the battery wrapped in liquid coolant, as the heat from the lasing process is not fully consumed by the Pylum. It contains four chambers of optical fibers. With the smaller size, and the four chambers placed directly against the Pylum battery, the priming time is excessively short, and the energy impressive especially with being emitted almost immediately.

Priming: 1.5 seconds
Health Length Without Charging: 2 weeks
Weight: 9.47 pounds
Accuracy: Excellent

Blaster

A large, bulky laser of intertwined carbon stock and diamond glass, employing a ruby medium, the blaster is an expensive and heavy weapon. But it is excessively powerful for a personal laser, capable of taking out three men from a distance of sixty yards. The blaster became renowned when employed by the KAM special forces, and proved its worth in the battle of 189BB when the kingdom was invaded by Lord Greydown VI of the DarkWind (a short lived but violent country, as the magic sword that the rebels hoped would defeat the first Lord Greydown and reset the kingdom's goodness, turned out not to be magic after all; the Greydowns were not pleasant rulers, and remained the rulers). KAM decimated the invaders, and the world thinks twice before attacking the kingdom now.

Priming: 4 seconds
Health Length Without Charging: 4 weeks
Weight: 31.27 pounds
Accuracy: Excellent

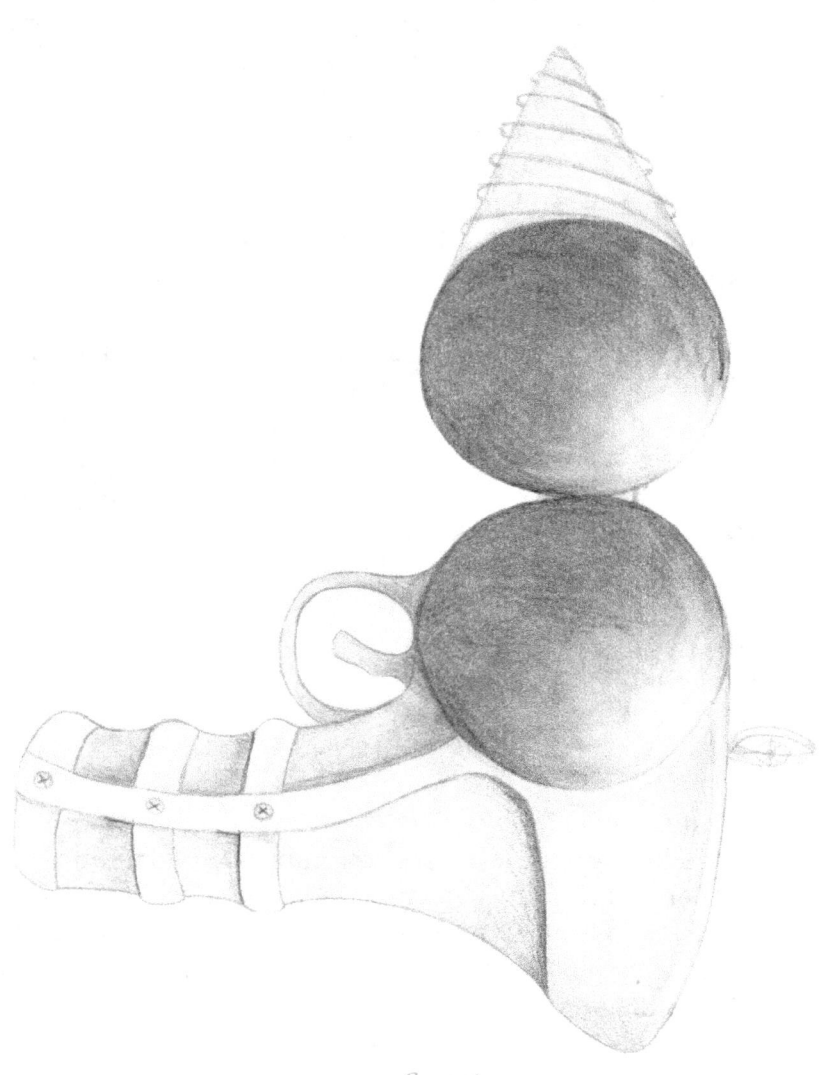

Compton

Compton

A revolutionary weapon, the Compton laser is the first to utilize dark energy and matter as an energy source. Two balls of carefully fashioned Z shielding are bound next to each other in a copper fitting. Inside one is a ball of dark matter, inside the other dark energy; they are small enough as to be almost trace amounts. But when activated, a "window" is cracked between the two. Dark matter and dark energy excite each other when combined, and create what science currently sees as an inexhaustible source of energy. The gun then utilizes Compton scattering between the two balls to harvest gamma rays. The rays are fired through a crystal lens fashioned after the Krackmens' excellent design. Gamma rays are invisible to the human eye, and so most Compton guns are sold with specially dyed goggles to allow the shoot-er to see where his rays land. Currently thought inexhaustible, nearly unbreakable, and as small as a Ruby laser (though considerably heavier), a Compton is viewed as the best weapons breakthrough since the Pylum battery.

Priming: 0 seconds
Health Length Without Charging: Unknown
Weight: 9.4 pounds
Accuracy: Very Exceptional

Kerr Atmospheric Shield

The Kerr shield employs lasers to temporarily ionize the atmosphere, thereby creating a refractive sheet to deflect enemy fire. It can alter small parts of the earth's natural occurring atmosphere, creating lens formations that magnify and change the path of electromagnetic waves. It utilizes the Kerr Effect, a change in the refractive index produced by electric fields, a change in proportion to the square of the electric field's strength.

In other words, it transforms a select part of the atmosphere, creating a honeycomb-shaped shield that refracts laser light. It also has a magnification quality, making it useful for reconnaissance. There are personal Kerr shields, and double shields that can be used by up to four people to create an enclosing square. The ones most often seen during the Book Base age were the double-handed personal Kerrs.

PUDRE Dark Ray

The Pulsating Ultrasonic Dark Ray Emitter, or PUDRE, came on the market ten years after the invention of the first Compton laser pistol. Observing the interaction between the dark matter and dark energy, the inventor of the PUDRE foresaw a different use than the laser; through careful experimentation he discovered how to form a localized, directed black hole effect. The ray beams a concentrated black hole, sucking anything it hits into the devastating dark force. It is capable of twisting steel and titanium, breaking diamond glass, generally wrecking anything it hits. The distance and concentration of the beam can be adjusted, its range being between six yards to twelve yards.

Speed of Light Transportation Device - SOLTD

A foray into new technology during the mid-200s of the Book Age, the SOLTD utilizes dark matter and dark energy to form what the inventor, Quintus Leeman, terms a space-warp bubble. Originally he was searching for a method of time travel, and speculated on the possibility of creating a time-warp bubble by the use of the black hole. Through careful experimentation he discovered there is a calm at the center of the massive force caused by mixing dark matter and energy, and it is possible to be enclosed safely in the midst of the swirling mass of a black hole by intentionally causing it. The bioelectricity of living beings is "felt out" by the black hole as it forms, and it molds itself around it. The SOLTD makes it possible to move large amounts of living things at the speed of light, if there is no break in the chain of bioelectricity within the center of the hole.

The inventor admits it was an accident that set him in history as the first SOLTD traveler. During an experiment his assistant entered, opening the specially-reinforced door. The black hole currently formed in his lab sensed a small source of other dark matter and energy and the inventor found himself displaced, suddenly in the Kingdom of the Wise quite literally crashing in on the inventor of the PUDRE, as Hyram Grange completed his work on that gadget. Leeman did not travel through time as he had originally hoped, instead he found he had moved kingdoms with almost no time involved. He was quick to see the possibilities of the SOLTD as a transportation device.

The method of programming the direction of travel took him two years to perfect, and to this day only those specially licensed to build the SOLTDs are allowed to know the intricacies of the method involved. We do know it employs small bits of dark matter and dark energy, attracted to particular places through the peculiarities of the earth's magnetism. The smaller pieces are carefully introduced to the larger pieces contained in each individual SOLTD's Z shielding balls. Through this they come to "know" each other, thus eliminating the possibility of multiple SOLTDs detecting the same pieces of matter and energy and intersecting.

The SOLTD changed the course of the Book Age, allowing those kingdoms and peoples who first attained proficiency in the gadget to gain a solid foothold over those slower to acknowledge the incredible usefulness of being able to "zap" people anywhere on the planet. To this day it marks a turning point in the technologies of mankind.

Kingdoms Worldviews

The Kingdom of Autonomous Man (KAM)

Book Base
Humanist Manifestos, I, II, and III
Copywrite by the American Humanist Association.

Government Structure

Humanists are concerned for the well being of all, are committed to diversity, and respect those of differing yet humane views. We work to uphold the equal enjoyment of human rights and civil liberties in an open, secular society and maintain it is a civic duty to participate in the democratic process and a planetary duty to protect nature's integrity, diversity, and beauty in a secure, sustainable manner. [Manifesto III]

The here and now is all that is. We, as the highest race, have the ability and responsibility to help each other and the world around us. Science and socialized government can achieve these goals.

These are at the core of how KAM functions.

The Kingdom of Autonomous Man exists as a haven of free thought and open hands. Provided newcomers do not strive to propagate a religion based on deities that cannot be proved scientifically. Or attempt to hoard or monopolize their commercial business. Or knowingly cause harm to other citizens. If these (and a few other reasonable limitations) are adhered to, there is little that is outlawed within the kingdom. Free expression is applauded.

The government consists of a body of two-hundred officials, elected by the citizenry of the kingdom. General elections are held every five years. After the general elections, a minutia election is held; four double officials are elected from within the body of the two-hundred. These four become overseers of the affairs of state. Out of those four, one is selected to be the highest official, affectionately (and unofficially) termed "the chairman."

It is the duty of the chairman to be the tie breaker among the four double officials, and the chair is usually seen as the true leader of KAM.

The freedom for people to do what they like, the natural resources and industries, as well as the inclination to accent hard work and individual accountability, have compiled to make KAM a prosperous kingdom. The government requires heavy taxation from its people and distributes the accumulated funds to those people and institutions it deems necessary.

Religious humanism maintains that all associations and institutions exist for the fulfillment of human life. The intelligent evaluation, transformation, control, and direction of such associations and institutions with a view to the enhancement of human life is the purpose and program of humanism... A socialized and cooperative economic order must be established to the end that the equitable distribution of the means of life be possible. [Manifesto I]

Some have expostulated this has resulted in a large number of people who do not embrace the need to pour their work into the society to benefit the general mankind. In a word, panhandlers, who care only for a free handout and not for their neighbors. It is a verifiable fact that the outskirts of the larger cities have become rundown areas where rent is not charged and people who do not earn paychecks emerge to beg from those who do earn.

Others have noted (in political criticisms or letters of complaint to KAM's government) that the over taxation of the wealthier citizens causes migrations to other kingdoms. It is again, a verifiable fact that almost every person within the higher wealth bracket immigrate to some other large advanced kingdom.

Incompletes and Chimeras

FIRST: Religious humanists regard the universe as self-existing and not created. SECOND: Humanism believes that man is a part of nature and that he has emerged as a result of a continuous process... [Manifesto I]

Humanists find that science is the best method for determining this knowledge as well as for solving problems and developing beneficial technologies... Humanists ground values in human welfare shaped by human circumstances, interests, and concerns and extended to the global ecosystem and beyond. We are committed to treating each person as having inherent worth and dignity, and to making informed choices in a context of freedom consonant with responsibility. [Manifesto III]

KAM upholds the theory of evolutionary science. That mankind is evolving continuously to a higher state. The state funds a great many scientific institutes and research labs, including the prestigious Institute of Science and Advancement located in the center of its capital. Individuals within the kingdom look forward to their children becoming a part of the higher races that will develop as chance, nature, and scientific man mold them.

Those born without all the natural abilities are not fully formed humans, in KAM's judgment. Those without fully developed intelligence, or without the power of speech or hearing, those who are born genetically imperfect, are considered lower down on the evolutionary tract. They have somehow missed a step on the ladder, and are therefore not fully human; like an ape, one of our long-time ancestors. They are Genetic Incompletes.

It is unacceptable for a GI to remain in KAM. The citizenry have been known to be sentimental over the subject, and it is also possible a slipup might cause a whole strand of incompletes to infect the human line. The citizens are not allowed to keep GIs, they are only allowed for exportation to other kingdoms.

[Warning: Mildly Graphic Topic] The Advancers have instituted very similar policies about GIs as they use with stray animals taken in KAM. When a GI reaches an age that their bodies develop from juvenile into a more mature adult (typically between 12 or 13), they are carefully sterilized to guard against polluting the human race. Most GIs dealt with by the Advancers are newborns from KAM's hospitals, and are not yet eligible for sterilization. But occasionally stray GIs are taken within the kingdom, or those who return again for reasons unknown. If a GI returns for the fourth time, after the usual tests have been processed (typically a period of twenty-four hours), the GI is marked as an "uncooperative troublemaker" and administered a lethal dose of pento-

barbital. In such cases, it is considered an unnecessary expenditure to also apply the sterilization.

Sometimes, in the quest for knowledge and further medical advancement a GI is acquired for testing purposes. But KAM is very careful to provide good care and has a policy of never keeping a single test subject for over eighteen months. They make a point of being a humanitarian kingdom.

Chimeras are several rungs lower down the evolutionary ladder than GIs. They are interesting animals, and if properly kept in check, are allowed to be owned as workers inside the kingdom. The state has instituted a restriction on the numbers, however, and closely monitors the chimeras within KAM. There is a moratorium within the kingdom against creating more chimeras. As one prestigious KAM professor put it, "We know now no higher race will come from a mix of animal and human genes. It is a step backward on the evolutionary track, not forward."

Art and Music

Humanists find that science is the best method for determining this knowledge as well as for solving problems and developing beneficial technologies. We also recognize the value of new departures in thought, the arts, and inner experience—each subject to analysis by critical intelligence. [Manifesto III]

This is a continuation of the same quote used in the discussion of incompletes and chimeras. In order to gain a full understanding of KAM's books, it should be recognized that while science is held in high importance, the benefit of mankind is held even higher. Art and music fall under the category of bringing value to humanity, and so are prized. Free expression and individuality are carefully husbanded by the state and citizenry of KAM. That, and a fairly high immigration rate and general prosperity, makes the arts within KAM a virile and eclectic community.

Science and Advancements

Science has sometimes brought evil as well as good... Using technology wisely, we can control our environment, conquer poverty, markedly reduce disease, extend our life-

span, significantly modify our behavior, alter the course of human evolution and cultural development, unlock vast new powers, and provide humankind with unparalleled opportunity for achieving an abundant and meaningful life. [Manifesto II]

Science is the trump card and the hope of KAM. With time and the proper breakthroughs, man should be able to conquer all problems through scientific advancements. The state funds numerous scientific studies and labs across the kingdom. Most national holidays are based on some portion of science.

Army

Humanists long for and strive toward a world of mutual care and concern, free of cruelty and its consequences, where differences are resolved cooperatively without resorting to violence. The joining of individuality with interdependence enriches our lives, encourages us to enrich the lives of others, and inspires hope of attaining peace, justice, and opportunity for all. [Manifesto III]

KAM is not a warlike kingdom. They do not strive to expand their territory at the expense of other kingdoms, or to exact vengeance on rivals. However, they are a practical people. Other kingdoms are warlike, and envy KAM's natural resources and prosperity. KAM found it necessary to have a standing army for defense.

KAM's army is outfitted with modern kit, and well trained. The other kingdoms tend to view it as a well-fed tiger resting in its lair. Nothing to worry about unless you tread on their toes; but when roused, beware, they are very capable of finishing what you start.

Social Structure

Ethical values are derived from human need and interest as tested by experience...

Life's fulfillment emerges from individual participation in the service of humane ideals...

Working to benefit society maximizes individual happiness. Progressive cultures have worked to free humanity from the brutalities of mere survival and to reduce suffering, improve society, and develop global community. We seek to minimize the inequities of circumstance and ability, and we support a just distribution of nature's resources and the fruits of human effort so that as many as possible can enjoy a good life. [Manifesto III]

The here and now is all that is. We, as the highest race, have the ability and responsibility to help each other and the world around us. Science and socialization of the Kingdom's wealth can achieve both goals.

How do these play out in reality in the kingdom? Mostly in education, taxation, and hard work. Everyone has a job. Most see their worth through how well they can help society through what they do, and how good a paycheck they achieve. Social status (how big my house, how fancy my vehicle) is a large factor inside KAM, as it is very difficult to measure *"inherent worth and dignity" (Manifesto III)* without anything to go on except hopefully being evolved enough to be part of the higher race. How much you earn is one measuring tool. It would be quite inaccurate to say it is the only one, however. Many find their worth in training the next generation, or creating beneficial scientific breakthroughs, counseling the needy, any number of things to help their fellow man.

The new generation is the hope of the kingdom, and they are treated as such. Parents receive substantial stipends from the government for each child. Large families (more than four children in a home) are frowned on, however, as it poses a greater possibility of poor conditioning during the formative years, and also risks overpopulating the world. Enrollment in the government schools is required, and teachers are kept strictly to curriculum developed to form proper adherents to KAM's philosophy.

Anyone is welcomed within the borders of KAM. If someone holds ideas different from theirs, they are mostly shrugged off and tolerated. However, if someone insists that ideas different from the Manifestos are the *only* correct ones, and insists that KAM's philosophy is false, that begins to pose a problem. Young people might listen to the agitators, and it could cause unrest in the social system. If an agitator continues to hold onto their own subversive ideas, they will find themselves arrested, and sent to a center in the mountains. The Center is run by the Advancers, and it employs a great number of phycologists and brain specialists, as well as a few philosophers and experimental doctors. It is believed that such cases are victims of their upbringing or an inherent lack within themselves. Those interned in the Center are treated more as insane and sick then as law-breakers.

If, after a period of two years, no progress has been made on an agitator and they still insist on holding to their subversive ideas, they are deported to other kingdoms. If they are deemed "cooperative" they are allowed back in KAM, but surveillance is required to be certain they do not relapse into former thinking.

Geatland

Book Base
Beowulf, translation by Seamus Heaney

Government Structure
"I took what came,
cared for and stood by things in my keeping,
never fomented quarrels, never
swore to a lie. All this consoles me,
doomed as I am and sickening for death;
because of my right ways, the Ruler of mankind
need never blame me when the breath leaves my body
for murder of kinsman."
[Lines 2736-2743]

Their book base is an epic poem dealing with the life of Beowulf, a Geatish warrior prince. The lines quoted above are from a moment when an elderly Beowulf reflects upon how he acquitted himself as king of the Geats. It is a strict monarchal society. Geatland is ruled by a king, with lesser thanes in charge of individual warriors, all of them fiercely loyal as a matter of pride and honor. However, their book has a good deal to say about what makes a good king and a bad king. The kings of Geatland strive to be brave warriors, generous, protectors of their people, and filled with wisdom, and it tends to fall into that order of importance.

"*It would be his throne-room and there he would dispense*
his God-given goods to young and old -
but not the common land or people's lives."
[Lines 71-73]

At first glance, the Geats seem like bloodthirsty warlords. They are, but there are several important checks to their waring. The book has many stories of battles and feuding between the Shyflings, Geats, Danes, and Swedes. Battles abound in the book, and bloody deeds on the battlefield are praised and honored. But we also find passages (like the first quoted in this section) in which not seeking out or creating quarrels is praised. On the whole, the heroes of the story are the defenders not the instigators.

"*I have suffered extremes*
and avenged the Geats (their enemies brought it
upon themselves, I devastated them)."
[Lines 423-424]

A warrior's strength, prowess, pride, and bravery are coveted in Geatland. The only thing coveted more is honor. It is a very specific honor shown by only the best of heroes, and because of that we have a certain breed of warriors. The best Geats have a tempered strength.

"*Thus Beowulf bore himself with valour;*
he was formidable in battle yet behaved with honour
and took no advantage; never cut down
a comrade who was drunk, kept his temper
and, warrior that he was, watched and controlled
his God-sent strength and his outstanding
natural powers."
[Lines 2177-2183]

In Geatland, just because you feel like a fight, and want to go beat someone up, isn't enough reason to do it. But if someone instigates a fight, you should be able and ready to rip their arms off with your bare hands.

Historically, Geatland was setup when the most renowned warrior, Hrunting Wyrm-Slitter, was crowned as undisputed king. His line has continued throughout the history of the kingdom, occasionally jutting off to a nephew or cousin when a direct heir is not forthcoming. Two queens have ruled absolutely (Grithold the Fair and two generations later, her granddaughter Frehough Word-Wise) until sharing their rule after marrying suitable warriors among their thanes.

To the surprise of the country's few outside historians, every ruler has truly striven to govern Geatland according to the advice summarized in the last lines of their book:

"So the Geat people, his hearth companions,
sorrowed for their lord who had been laid low.
They said that of all the kings upon the earth
he was the man most gracious and fair-minded,
kindest to his people and keenest to win fame."
[Lines 3178-3182]

Incompletes and Chimeras

"What God judged right would rule what happened
to every man, as it does to this day."
[Lines 2858-2859]

There is no formal explanation of the Almighty God spoken of in Beowulf. But it is very clear He is in charge of all things, including the creation of life.

"...and the clear song of a skilled poet
telling with mastery of man's beginnings,
how the Almighty had made the earth
a gleaming plain girdled with waters;
in His splendour He set the sun and the moon
to be earth's lamplight, lanterns for men,
and filled the broad lap of the world
with branches and leaves; and quickened life
in every other thing that moved."
[Lines 90-98]

Nothing is said directly to the subject of incompletes and chimeras, but it is inferred any defect in a man is what "God judged right" [Line 2858]. Historically, the incompletes are treated merely as other humanity within the kingdom. What they do dictates how they are treated; if they are people of honor and bravery, they are respected as much as any other within Geatland. Chimeras are rarely found in Geatland. It is a remote, small kingdom that until the arrival of Ravenswing Ash-Maker in the year 247 had very little contact with anyone else in the book age. However there are songs of a Venroot the Massive who appears to be a chimera revered for his great strength and vicious fighting prowess. The songs about Venroot go back as far as 156 BB and speak of his "being birthed by the mountains." It is likely he found the tunnel passage Ravenswing and Nehemiah Truth-Teller use in the famous lay about the battle of the Ashefilled Plain.

Art and Music
"Sad lays were sung about the beset king,
the vicious raids and ravages of Grendel
his long and unrelenting feud,
nothing but war; how he would never
parlay or make peace with any Dane
nor stop his death-dealing nor pay the death-price."
[Lines 151-156]

Song, poetry, sweet harp music, many such things are mentioned in their book. In fact the book itself is a poem. Any deed of renown is sung about for generations among the Geats. A poet can be revered within the kingdom. Another thing very often mentioned is cunning artisan pieces. Beautiful metalwork, wood carving, smith work, etc. The book opens with a description of a hall built with architectural grandeur. Beautiful things made by skilled hands are valued by the Geats.

Science and Advancements
Nothing is mentioned within the book about this subject. It is so very silent on the matter, it could be construed as being ambivalent, or even against technology. Historically within Geatland, there is no objection to technology, but also no craving to create their own. A man's own strength, or artisan pieces of great value, are what is coveted and not a scientific finding that has no real solidity.

However, once the world-shaking technology of firearms and lasers entered their lands from outsiders, the Geats were quick to see the advantages of the weapons. It took time to change the cultural aspect of hand-to-hand combat and sword-smithing to a kingdom of modern weapon-bearing warriors. But the Geats are not fools, despite what an outsider might think at a first glance, and modern warfare technology quickly took hold in Geatland after the demonstration of a laser's usefulness.

Army

"Yet the prince of the rings was too proud
to line up with a large army
against the sky-plague."
[Lines 2345-2347]
"The lord of the Geats took eleven comrades
and went in a rage to reconnoiter."
[Lines 2401-2402]

The army inside Geatland consists of every man who can wield a blade. Which is every man born inside the kingdom. It is not an organized army, however. If the king finds need of warriors, he sends out a call and his thanes gather their fighters from where they might be farming their land or working their forges, and come to his aid. There is a hierarchy of greater and lesser thanes within Geatland (mostly founded on birthright, though an exceptional warrior can find themselves very quickly placed among the greatest thanes). This hierarchy works out practically as ranks within the army.

In the history of Geatland it is rare for more than perhaps fourteen or twenty warriors to be called at a time. There is a patrol along the borders fighting the wild beasts year-round, and each thane takes a turn with their warriors at the duty. But occasionally something larger looms. Such as in the year 89 BB when King Othew died suddenly without an heir, and two factions arose. Most supported Othew's nephew, Hrothgar the Second, but a small few preferred Othfrea, a distant cousin. The kingdom was mobilized by both sides, thanes chose where their loyalty lay, and Hrothgar and his troops quickly slaughtered the opposition. (There are lovely lays honoring the final stand of Othfrea and his guard, even though he was the enemy.) Another instance came in the winter of 145 BB, when the great grey wolves overran the border guards and flooded into the kingdom.

Social Structure

"Beowulf, son of Ecgtheow, spoke:
'Wise sir do not grieve. It is always better
to avenge dear ones than to indulge in mourning.
For every one of us, living in this world
means waiting for our end. Let whoever can
win glory before death. When a warrior is gone,
that will be his best and only bulwark.'"
Lines 1383-1389

Honor is the pivot on which the society of Geatland turns. If you were to define what the word honor means to a Geat, the majority of it would be a spewing of stories about warriors' great feats, bathed in blood, proud heads lifted high above every other warrior on the battlefield. That is definitely the main idea behind their definition of honor. But, there is more to it. A warrior might be the best in the business, but if he is a liar, a backstabber, and a bully, his honor will be greatly tarnished. A careful reading of their book brings in the ideas that a real hero doesn't instigate war, doesn't take other people's lives lightly, always abides by an oath, and even tries not to be goaded into a fight that isn't necessary.

Obviously, with the main idea being to gain glory through feats of arms, most Geats don't take peace-making very seriously. But it is true that those who do, and yet when the fight does come to them still prove their skill in battle, are respected more than those who go about breaking chairs over unsuspecting people's heads to try and get a brawl going.

Under the king, the lesser thains have their sections allotted to them throughout the kingdom, rearranged occasionally by marriages or allotments to cousins and such. Historically, some thains have risen and tried to grasp at neighboring land-holds, but for the most part the thains and their warriors are content to gain their honors and sate their bloodlust with the packs of animals ranging around their fertile basin. Because of the bare mountains surrounding them, and the fertile nature of their basin, there are always plenty of hungry large beasts to go around. Under the thanes, are the common people; the warriors, farmers, artisans, and women.

The only female fighter in *Beowulf* is the hell-spawn Grendel's mother, not exactly an example to be followed. The women in *Beowulf* are spoken of in conjunction with marriage. They are mourners for the fallen, or stately queens carrying the mead cups to the warriors in the hall to honor the victors of the fight. Within the book, women are mentioned as a combination of bridges between peoples (by daughters of one royal house marrying into another royal house), or queens viewed with respect, and maybe even a little awe. After Beowulf defeats the monsters and frees Heorot, we are given a scene with the queen advising the king, in lines 1167-1186. After listening to her advice, the king seems to act on it, showing he values her wisdom. Later in the book, we are given a picture of absolute power by a woman, even over strong warriors. It is a passing account of a viciously jealous queen, in which the poet concludes:

"A queen should weave peace, not punish the innocent
with loss of life for imagined insults."
[Lines 1942-1943]

Most in Geatland hold to the philosophy a woman should be a background character, taking care of the food and children. But there are others who take the interaction between Hrothgar and his queen more seriously, and hold that a woman should also have ideas, and her wisdom should be listened to.

The Geats are a proud people. Proud of their ancestry, their kingdom, their book, their artisan skill, etc. Insulting their way of life might bring about several challenges to decide the matter through a fight. They prefer single combat, especially without weapons. But along with all the fighting and bloodlust used to gain honor and renown, the Geats are also a helpful people. They see how Beowulf came to the aid of Hrothgar, and others in the poem who rose up to protect those who needed it, and are quick to do the same. Generosity is the second most praised thing in the poem, just after a hero's fame.

If one avoids insulting their culture, and doesn't mind an excessive amount of boasting by everyone, it is a pleasant place to visit.

Recipe

Triple Chocolate Fudge Brownies

1 cup butter
¾ cups semi-sweet chocolate chips
2 cups sugar
4 eggs
2 teaspoons vanilla
1 ¼ cup flour
½ cup coco powder
½ cup semi-sweet chocolate chips

Place the ¾ cup chocolate chips in a microwave safe bowl with the butter. Heat for sixty seconds, remove, stir, and see if the chocolate has melted smooth. If needed place back in the microwave for another twenty second, then stir again.

When the chocolate and butter are smooth, scrape into a mixing bowl with the sugar, and mix till combined. Add the eggs and vanilla. Add the flour and coco powder, and stir just enough to combine. Add in the ½ cup chocolate chips, and give it one more stir.

Scrape into a greased 9x13 baking pan and bake at 375 for 25 minutes, or until you just begin to see that lovely cracking you get on the top of brownies.

Sign Language Alphabet

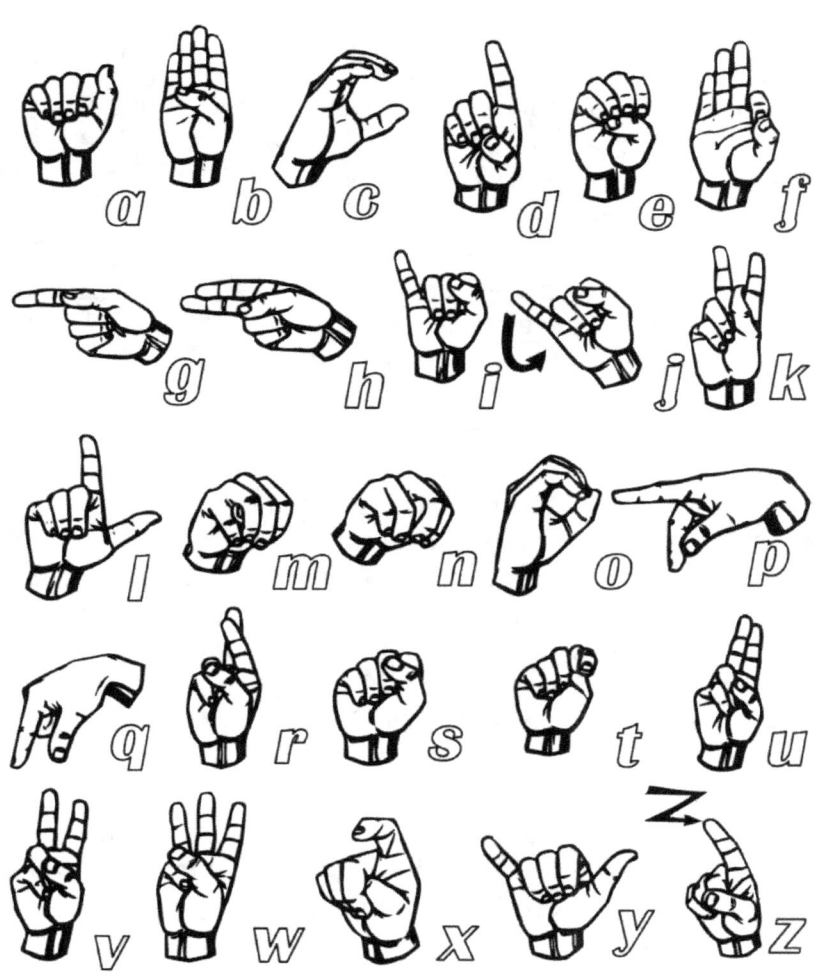

Author Bio

Catherine Gruben Smith lives in the middle of Texas, which she begrudgingly admits is probably better than a magical tower. She grew up mostly in a dusty town in the southern New Mexican desert and will always carry the quirks. (Yes, New Mexico is a part of the United States, and no, she was not a missionary, and yes, you can drink the water.) It is her delight and privilege to be a housewife, mother, and an Earl Gray con-

noisseur. Another of her constant activities is trying to keep her dogs from terrorizing the house and neighborhood with their determination to be always underfoot and hungry. (The work of a dog lover is never done.) She has always been fascinated by the written word, philosophical reasoning, and good stories of bravery and honor. When not writing, reading, chasing children or dogs, Catherine can be found board-gaming, baking, hiking, or possibly broad sword fighting with her older brother. If you want a fuller explanation of Catherine, go and read Psalm 30. The heart and purpose of her life can be found there, especially in the last two verses.

Catherine prays reading her books will help her readers find the urge to get up off the couch and serve. The Lord of all life calls us to the battlefield, to mop up the enemy after He has won the war. Don't sit on the side-lines. We have the tools to fix this broken world.

Where to find more information, or contact Catherine:
catherinegrubensmith.com
catherinegrubensmith@gmail.com
postetenebrasluxbooks.com

Books by Catherine Gruben Smith

Sojourners:
Ravens Ruins
Ravens Rescue
Ravens Return
Ravens Refuge
Ravens Raid
Ravens Rebirth

Dreaded King Saga:
A Son Rises
Reign Falls
Knight Duty
Heir Raising
Splitting Heirs

Knight Jobs Series:
Wail of the Wyrm

Parabaloni:
The Parabaloni
The Slingshot Effect
As the Eagle Flies
Solitaire
Adele Angst
Blind Leader
Gathering Shadows
Black Out

Faerytales of Deweot:
How to Unmake a Dragon
Faery Wings and Pirate Things

www.ingramcontent.com/pod-product-compliance
Lightning Source LLC
Chambersburg PA
CBHW070557260626
47161CB00002B/632